I0615148

Stacey Gatrost

A *Second* REFLECTION

1st Edition

Gatrost, Stacey
    A Second Reflection / Stacey Gatrost – 1st Edition

    ISBN: 978-1-7323535-3-4

    Library of Congress Control Number: 2018905866

Book design by Kristyn McQuiggan (Drop Dead Designs)

Dedicated to my parents, Douglas and Marie, with much love to you both.

CONTENTS

I have come to drag you out of yourself, and take you in my heart. I have come to bring out the beauty you never knew you had and lift you like a prayer to the sky.

—Rumi

Chapter One

Keeping Secrets

There was a subtle quietness of the night when he entered the space of the darkened upstairs bedroom. The curtains fanned slightly, as if to acknowledge his arriving presence. The ethereal energy that emanated from him gave off a soft white radiance that, like him, was indiscernible to the human eye. The grandfather clock on the floor below chimed eleven times, not disturbing the occupants of the house. His attention rested upon Hannah. It was not unusual that he had come. Someone always comes at such a time as this. His form hovered within three feet above the floor near where she lay undisturbed on the right side of the bed she shared with her husband. The moonlight flickered across her skin, as the shadows from the branches of the palm tree swayed outside the window. The quickening rhythm of her heartbeat and breathing were perceptible as his energy enclosed upon hers.

She stirred only slightly before her eyes danced rapidly under their lids. His intense and narrowed gaze did not deviate from her soft blue aura. She stirred slightly as the images he imparted to her subconscious mind began to fill her dreams that she would vaguely remember only bits and pieces of later. He willed her to remember what she had forgotten to remind her of the infinity of the soul and of its vast experiences over lifetimes. He could see her energy heightened as he shared his memories with her, resulting in an increased glow of her aura. He came to remind her who she is and would always be. Her movements increased until her husband stirred but drifted back to sleep. His aura was rich yellow and soft green. She startled and bolted upright out of sleep with short, labored breaths, her eyes wide and glassy, filled with confusion as she shifted her eyes around the room, not looking for or expecting anyone, only reassuring herself she was where she thought she was. The dream was lucid and had felt real. Calm relief washed over her as her navy eyes focused on her familiar surroundings. She lowered herself back onto the bed. "It was only a dream," she whispered to herself, pulling the warm blanket over her shoulders, welcoming the security of it and the warmth of her husband's body next to her. The moonlight shifted slowly, replaced by the dawn's sunlight. The dreams continued but did not awaken her again.

At six o'clock, a rooster crowed increasingly louder. The aroma of coffee that had been preset to brew a half hour before had wafted through the house and filled Jesse's nostrils, prompting him to take in a deep nasal breath as the cellphone alarm bolted him out of sleep. He fumbled to shut it off. Hannah's form snuggled against him, one of her legs intertwined with his own. The slight shift in his position made it easier for him to face her. Her breath was warm on his face. His lips brushed against her forehead affectionately without arousing her. Jesse was unaware of the presence in the room as he propped himself up on one arm to gaze at her. It had been another restless night. He sucked in a deep breath, not ready to face the dawn, wishing he could sleep a little longer. He breathed a deep sign of resignation to another long, tired day ahead of him. He touched the back of his fingers to her skin. He feathered his fingers to her ear and pulled the hair from across her face. Adoring her was easy. He tried to ignore the uneasiness that chipped away at him.

There was something troubling her. He knew that. Fear gripped him like a vise at times, as he felt her distancing herself from him. He had never given her any reason not to trust him or be afraid to confide in him? She could tell him anything. Lately, she was evasive. That was what was troubling him. Thinking back to when they had first started dating, he considered himself lucky she chose him, despite all the football players who had vied for her attention, and who she gently and respectfully, while trying to preserve their dignity, had turned down each one of them. He remembered his frustration that half the team had asked her for a date, knowing she was dating him. Maybe they thought it wouldn't last and they would get their chance, each having his own hope he would be the one she'd hang on to. Her soft skin covering her ribs and lower back met the large palm of his hand as he softly caressed her. Her scent was like clean linens in the breeze that was uniquely hers. When he had mentioned to her a couple times how much he loved her scent, making a poetic effort to describe it to her, she had thought he was imagining it or making it up to entertain her. His wounded pride was forgotten with her contagious laughter. "Only dogs or animals can recognize someone's scent," she had mused, but despite his argument that every person has their own scent, and he could identify hers in any lineup while blindfolded, he finally said, "It's just hard to describe," and did not pursue the matter again. That had been almost two years ago.

Lately, her gradual distancing and self-isolation left him feeling disconcerted and helpless, despite efforts on his part to get her to let him in, share the burden, and confide in him. Fear was not a feeling he was accustomed to feeling, not in the way he felt it now, not with her. Their relationship had always been solid and happy. Even now, she denied being unhappy, assuring him nothing was wrong, but the gulf between them left him feeling an anxious dread that swallowed him at times. Whatever it was, it felt bigger than him and perhaps even bigger than her. He felt helpless to resolve it. Then, as always, the fear that had held him in its grip released him, as if an unseen someone or some-thing had rendered it powerless.

Ethan was their only child and the light of both their lives. Despite attempts to get pregnant and produce a second child the last couple of years, all efforts had been unsuccessful. He often wondered if that was what occupied her thoughts, that she might not get pregnant again. Each day, he told himself he was doing his sincere best and was in fact a good, if not wonderful, husband. Today, like all the others, he felt grateful she was with him, still.

"Hey, sleepyhead," he whispered in her ear. Her brief stir gave him pause to smile. The slits of her eyes were barely parted while her long hair covered half her face.

"Coffee!" she exclaimed weakly in a raspy voice, not fully conscious. His kiss barely brushed her lips.

"One cup of coffee coming right up, Babe," he said tiredly. His feet pressed into the plush carpet as he stood, slid into his boxers, and left the bedroom. He always paused at Ethan's room. His little body looked so comfortable lying in his twin bed, bundled up under his Avengers comforter wearing his Captain

America pajamas he had gotten for his fifth birthday. A smile lit Jesse's face as he quietly closed the door.

He placed two full cups on the coasters she kept on her nightstand. "Hannah?" She stirred again.

"Let me sleep five more minutes, please."

Jesse sighed. He hated waking her and was tempted to let her sleep in, but if he did, he feared it may not play out in his favor later. The sleepless nights she had been having was taking its toll on both of them. Sleep was deluding him, too, as she thrashed in the bed keeping him awake at night, a lot of nights lately.

"It's Friday, Saturday Eve, Babe," he reminded her. "Maybe you can catch up on some rest this weekend, or you could tell Miranda you need your Zzzs today." Hannah's sleepy, smiling eyes were inviting, as she reached her arms around his neck. The spark he saw in her eye made him want to believe everything was okay, and that he had been overanalyzing.

"Okay, I can do this!" she mumbled, pulling herself up, fluffing the pillow she propped against the headboard. She was really sexy, he noted, wearing one of his T-shirts she occasionally slept in. She propped the coffee cup on her knees that were drawn to her chest and struggled to keep her eyes open. A moment of lazy silence passed while they sipped the caffeine. She couldn't seem to stop yawning.

"Now you have me started," he complained, yawning back.

"I know, I can't seem to stop," she replied lazily and then smiled. Her eyes were starting to water from it.

"Didn't sleep well, again?" he asked. He knew she hadn't.

"Not really." Her mind didn't seem focused, and her voice was slightly raspy. She took a long swig of the rest of her coffee and set the cup down.

"I hear melatonin is really good for sleep," he added nonchalantly.

"So, I've heard," she commented dismissively. "You ready to take a shower?" she asked, without waiting for his response, oblivious to the well-concealed anxiety he was feeling. Insecurity with his wife was the last thing he wanted to deliver. The shirt fell halfway off just as the door closed behind her. He closed his eyes as a faint smile crossed his lips, followed by the release of a long breath he hadn't even realized he was holding.

Her hair was already cropped on top her head in sudsy shampoo. He began to wash it for her and massaged her scalp. He loved pampering her. Her hands fell to her side and she tilted her head back as she let him take over. After she rinsed it, she turned and faced him, putting her arms around him and pressed her cheek to his chest, holding him without saying anything.

"Hey, you okay, Babe?" he asked. The look in her eyes told him she was unsure how to answer the question, maybe had been dreading him asking it. She paused before she released him but held his gaze for another half minute, as if she was looking into his soul, then smiled.

"I'm alright," and leaned into him again, holding him even tighter. "I love you, Jess," she finally said, his anxiety and concern now palpable to her. He pressed her tight against him, cupping her head into his hand.

"I love you too, always have and always will," kissing her nose. "At the risk of sounding like a broken record, if you want to talk about what's keeping you awake at night, you can tell me anything, you know that, right?"

"Of course, I do, Jess," she said. It almost seemed as if she were about to confide whatever it was but instead, "I'm fine, just tired. I'm just having insomnia. It'll pass. Always does. No need to worry," she said, trying to sound assuring.

Everything inside told him her withdrawal had more to do with the dreams rather than mere insomnia. He hoped the dreams weren't caused by anything in the shadows of their marriage. Fighting an internal battle was tough enough without inflaming the situation and creating conflict where none exists. His dad certainly had his share after returning from war. His mother had always emphasized to him that his father would talk about what happened to him when he was ready, and until then, pushing was something she would not advise. It could result in reactions one would regret.

The last visit to the OB/GYN had left Hannah distraught that the chances of her getting pregnant again after so many times of trying did not look good. He wondered if not being able to have another baby was leading to a meltdown? He was completely fertile, so the problem had not been with his inability to get her pregnant. The pregnancy with Ethan had been difficult. She had close calls and had to be on bedrest for most of the third trimester. It was more typical of her to blame herself than to blame him. Her nature was not of someone that assigned blame where it was not deserved. Fairness and open-mindedness always defined her. It was no one's fault. It was a situation they both faced, not one she faced alone. Not once had he ever felt disappointed in her or given her a reason to ever feel that from him. He had always respected her feelings and tried to be sensitive to them, and he always offered her reassurance they would be okay either way. Sometimes he silently questioned if she agreed with him about that. She was an adoring and loving mother. Ethan made her shine every time she looked at him. They had both wanted him to have siblings to grow up with. Adoption was not out of the question.

Through the mirror, he watched her dry off with a towel and apply white linen body lotion to her olive skin. He was boyishly handsome with black hair that had a hint of wave, brown eyes, and athletic build. The shaving cream was cool across his face. With razor in hand, an icebreaker was needed.

"Maybe I'll grow a goatee," he said out loud, intently observing his reflection with a Marlon Brando frown, turning his profile from side to side as he stared at his reflection. Hannah stood behind him and laid her chin on his shoulder playfully.

"I'd have to start wearing red lipstick then," she said teasingly as she watched him shave. He towel-dried his face and resumed his Brando frown, moving only his eyes to look down at her, then back into the mirror, deciding he was going to take the bait.

"Red, huh?" She grinned mischievously. His eyes were not lost on her as Hannah turned and dropped her towel. In that moment, they both seemed to let go of whatever tension was hanging in the balance, and he took her in his arms and for the next uncounted minutes, all their energy was spent on each other.

She blow-dried her hair and put on a very slight amount of makeup. Her beauty was exquisitely natural. Her hair had begun to turn silvery gray at the age of 22, but she had embraced it rather than tried to change it. It hung down over her shoulders and halfway down her back like flowing strands of silk. Her olive complexion accentuated her navy eyes, naturally dark lashes, and arched dark brown eyebrows, which were the color that her hair had been before it had turned silver. Her six-foot stature, just four inches less than Jesse's, gave her the elegance of royalty. She was strikingly beautiful and sexy no matter what she was doing and regardless of what she was wearing.

She put on her lipstick and her eyes danced at him. "Should I buy the red?" she asked teasingly, still holding the pale lipstick she had just put on. There it was, the smile that had defined her the very moment he fell in love with her. Her squared jaw with her hair flowing around it that hung almost to her elbows. In fact, she didn't own any red lipstick. Her lips were a nude-mauve color that accented her perfectly straight, white teeth. She had the most captivating smile, as she stood there having put on her knee-length cotton pink robe revealing her athletic, tan legs and bare feet, decorated in pastel pink nail polish. There was nothing flashy about her. She was just who she was, a natural beauty by every definition.

They had met 12 years before, when they were both 16. He had been the new guy in high school, having moved from San Diego, and from the first day of their junior year, the moment he laid eyes on her, Jesse *knew* he was going to marry her. Three years later, at the end of the college freshman year, their wedding had been grand, no expense spared, and most of their high school classmates attended, as well as some college friends who made their appearances too! Her white gown had flowed 10 feet behind her as she walked down the aisle with her, then, ash brown hair pulled back and tied up in interlocking French braids. The memory of that moment flooded him. When he kissed her after saying, "I do," he believed himself to be the most fortunate man on the planet. He just hoped his fortune would last. Another set of thoughts followed suit, "I've got to snap out of this! Maybe I need to go talk to someone," he wondered, though he had never been in a therapist's office in his life. Right now, he didn't want her to sense his worry. He knew he had to stop torturing himself lest he incite a self-fulfilling prophesy he would never wish on anyone. A moment later, the worry had again vanished. It was like his emotions rolled in like a wave and then receded into the sea again, and that also puzzled him. He kept feeling like there was some unseen force that calmed him when the anxiety exceeded a certain threshold.

He emerged wearing gray pants and a button-up light blue shirt that fit his form nicely. Any woman would find it hard not to take a second look. Dressed and ready for work, he went to Ethan's room while Hannah continued getting ready. "Hey, Little Man, time to wake up." Ethan's eyes opened staring into his father's eyes. The smile that spontaneously appeared on his sweet face revealed he still had all his baby teeth.

"Daddy, can I have pancakes?"

"Sausage or bacon?" Jesse asked.

"I want sausage with syrup on them," he exclaimed.

"You got it, kiddo. Now, out of bed!" Jess twirled him around his shoulders and carried him toward the kitchen as the child squealed and giggled. He sat him on the bar stool, and told him, "Watch Daddy do his magic," and walked to the cabinet, reached for all the makings of pancake mix from scratch and began heating two skillets while whistling quietly, "Don't Worry, Be Happy." Ten minutes later, "Voila," Jess said proudly as he set Ethan's breakfast in front of him and gave him a glass of chocolate milk.

Cooking was another passion Jesse had inherited. His dad had also enjoyed it, saying, "Cooking is an art, and any man would do well to master it." Jesse intended to do just that and made plans to attend school to become a high-class chef, but he pursued computer engineering instead. He didn't want Hannah to *have* to work, and his job had sometimes allowed him to work from home, which was always nice. He knew Hannah loved working part-time as a photographer, and for her, it wasn't about money. She had a passion for beauty and for capturing it.

"As always, the kitchen smells delicious!" Hannah said as she walked in and sat next to Ethan. She reached down and gave Ethan a kiss on the forehead, "You arc going to be so big and strong when you grow up, thanks to Daddy's cooking!"

Ethan grinned, "I know it," widening his smile, filling his mouth with a bite of sausage.

Jesse smiled blushingly as he poured Hannah another cup of coffee and poured her creamer in and stirred it and set the spoon down and gazed at her. She looked back at him and thought silently to herself, "He is so good to me." She stood there leaning against the bar counter and admired the man she had married. He and Ethan were her life, and it had been a happy life. She thought about all the people in the world who struggled with relationships, who suffered misery and unhappiness being with the wrong person, women who suffered domestic violence, the men who committed it, and vice versa, but she counted her blessings that she had a husband that loved her, who she fully trusted to be loyal to her.

The first two years after they married, she had been unable to get pregnant and had finally gone to a reproductive medicine specialist, as nothing seemed to be working. Finally, she conceived and from the moment she knew she was pregnant, she had prayed every day that nothing would go wrong and that she would not miscarry and have to start all over. Months went by and trimesters, though the last trimester had been difficult, finally she gave birth to this tiny miracle who now sat next to her. It had been the most joyous day of both their lives. She became momentarily lost in her thoughts, wondering if she would ever be able to conceive again. She hoped so.

"He is such a wonderful father to Ethan," she thought. Ethan looked more like Jesse than he did her, which did not disappoint her in the least. Jesse was tall, standing six feet four inches. Most of the time he wore Khaki shorts or jeans and a T-shirt that revealed his muscular build. He had thick, dark brown hair that was short but long enough to run her fingers through it and have it curl around them, but she could swim in his dark brown eyes. He was the mirror of kindness and tenderness.

Lately, she had been having unusual dreams, that had cost her sleep. They weren't *bad* dreams, just puzzling and vivid, that sometimes woke her up at night. Other mornings, she knew she had been dreaming but couldn't remember the details. The lack of sleep was catching up with her because she found herself being preoccupied much more than usual, often going to bed early from mere exhaustion. Jesse had shown nothing but compassion and was aware she was not sleeping well, so he hadn't pushed for sex. The dreams were troubling her though, because they were persistent, and she had begun to wonder if there was some underlying meaning or message being shown her that she was not understanding or reading into them.

Jesse sat down next to her, "How about we get my sister to watch Ethan tonight, and you and I go out for dinner and then to the Grand Theater and take in whatever play is showing and come back home and hit the replay on our honeymoon?" as he pulled her close and held her in his embrace. "We can sleep until noon tomorrow," he told her, with a suggestively smirked grin, feeling hopeful, trying to make things normal again, adding, "Rachel's been after me anyway to let Ethan come spend the night." When she returned the smile, he knew it was a date. "I'll call Rachel on my way to work and make the arrangements."

After breakfast, Jess told Ethan, "Go brush your teeth, Little Man." With another moment alone, Jesse held Hannah in his arms, put his forehead against hers, and with their lips nearly touching, he told her, "I love you." He tilted her chin and kissed her, first teasingly, then with every ounce of love he felt for her. Hannah pulled away, smiling up at him.

"I'm going to go help Ethan get ready for school." She was feeling suddenly preoccupied with her dreams as if something were taking her back to them. Realizing her abrupt withdrawal, she smiled back playfully, revealing her very distinct dimples, as she left the kitchen.

She laid Ethan's clothes out and helped him get dressed, gave him a kiss on the cheek.

"I love you to pieces," squeezing him playfully.

"I love you, too, Mommy," he smiled back at her.

"Mommy has to go get dressed," she told him. She kissed him one more time.

Twenty minutes later, she emerged wearing jeans with designer tears in the knees, brown ankle boots, a white buttoned blouse with sleeves to the elbows and a tan sleeveless cardigan that hung halfway to her knees. She had been a photographer for a travel magazine when she was in college that was based in San Francisco, where she had met Miranda, who was three years older than her. The two of them had become close friends, and later they both decided they would work freelance and make their own hours. It was basically Miranda's business though. Hannah worked with her because she enjoyed photography, but family was more important to her than a career; therefore, she didn't go into partnership. Miranda had come from a wealthy family, not to mention she had received a substantial divorce settlement later, but Miranda had always been resourceful, earning her own money and had never felt the need to be on someone else's payroll. She had tried to persuade Hannah to be a model, herself, and though she could have even been a supermodel, Hannah didn't want the stress of pursuing it. She didn't want the attention nor to be in the spotlight. She preferred working from behind the scenes. Photography had been her passion, though she did get a paycheck. She enjoyed photographing anything from wildlife, city structures, houses, and landscapes and had decorated their home with many of the pictures she had taken. She saw beauty and awe in so many things in life. She saw art wherever she went, and she was happy with the income she earned for something that was not at all work but from a passion she derived so much pleasure from. Besides, a lot of the photos she took were for her portfolio she wanted to pass down to Ethan, and hopefully, his siblings, if they were able to give him any.

As Hannah was finishing her coffee, Jesse walked in the kitchen carrying Ethan on his shoulders.

"All groomed and teeth brushed!" Jesse said enthusiastically.

Ethan grinned big to show his teeth, and informed Hannah, "I even used mouthwash!"

"You did! No kissing the girls in kindergarten, young man!"

"You're funny, Mommy," he told her blushingly, covering his face with his two little hands, giggling.

"I'm going to get this little guy to school, and then off to work for me," Jesse crooned as he leaned over to kiss Hannah, then stooped down so she could kiss Ethan, who was still perched on his shoulders, before they each went their separate ways. "Don't forget, we have a date tonight, he reminded her," with his lips touching hers. He looked at her longingly, wishing they could both just skip work, talk about *everything*, but a moment later he was backing out of the driveway. Ethan sat in his child seat in the backseat, and Hannah was standing in the driveway, waving goodbye to both of them before getting into her own car. She had realized she didn't have her keys in her hand and had started fumbling in her purse but waved at them one last time before going back in the house to search for them.

Ethan had been waving to his mommy and watching her wave back to them as they were backing out the driveway, swinging his hand happily at her, but started waving more slowly, as he saw a stranger seemingly materialize next to his mother as she waved back, smiling at them. The stranger was looking toward them, as they were leaving, and Ethan could see he had a kind face. He smiled at the stranger, who in turn smiled back and held up his hand, waving with two of his fingers. When they pulled out onto the street, Ethan turned looking over his shoulder towards their house. He saw his mommy disappear into the garage to go back inside the house, but the stranger stood nearly statuesque as he watched Jesse and Ethan drive away.

Inside, Hannah found both her keys and her sunglasses on the counter but realized she also did not have her cellphone so walked back upstairs and retrieved it from the nightstand. A few minutes later, she was out of Presidio and on the 101 going north. She had an off-site photo shoot on the west side of Tiburon this morning at the park overlooking the bay. She turned on her radio, as she neared the Golden Gate Bridge and changed the channel until she heard Sia singing, "Breathe Me." She drove on toward Mill Valley/Tiburon exit thinking how much she appreciated that the haze had cleared, and the sky was amazingly blue, true to the weather forecast the last three days, making it a perfect day for the bay and the Golden Gate in the backdrop. She always enjoyed off-site photo shoots because she enjoyed the outdoors. She thought about the fact that she and Jesse still occasionally enjoyed date nights and was looking forward to this evening. It had been months since they had gone to the Grand Theater, but it was where Jesse had taken her on their first date. He had really wanted to impress her, he had admitted a few years later, and she smiled thinking he really knew how to make a girl feel special, and throughout the years, he seemed to only get better at it.

She got off the exit and turned east, wondering what was playing tonight. The last time they had gone, Pyramus and Thisbe had been playing. She thought about the selfless love they had for each other, and though the story was sad, she imagined a happy ending as they walked off into the afterlife with her hand in his. He would take her to dinner first. It was going to be a lovely evening, "I can hardly wait," she mused, feeling sexy to be dining with her sexy husband in a darkened room full of candlelight and waiters in tuxedos. She knew she had been giving him less attention the last couple of months, and she was determined to make things right again. She sincerely wanted this night to be special. She couldn't think of anything that had triggered the dreams. She reminded herself that she knew she could never have imagined a happier life. "I've got to get a grip on this," she decided. Maybe she would confide in Miranda what had been going on and get some feedback. Yeah, that is what she would do, she decided.

"Hey, Ethan, how would you like to go to Aunt Rachel's tonight, while Daddy takes Mommy on a date? Kyle got a new puppy last week, and I bet you would love to play with him."

"He got a puppy!" he exclaimed getting louder with each syllable, and his little heart-shaped face lit up. Jesse watched him through the rear-view mirror, thinking he should get Ethan his own puppy. Seeing his reaction to hearing about Kyle's puppy inspired him that it would be a nice addition to the family. As he considered that thought, Ethan asked him, "Daddy, who was that man in our driveway standing by Mommy?"

Jesse glanced back at Ethan, query, "What are you talking about, "Little Man?"

"You know, that man that was standing next to Mommy, when we were leaving?" he exclaimed as a matter of fact, sounding frustrated. Jesse pondered this. He knew kids had imaginary friends, but Ethan had never indicated he had one before and never seemed prone to making up an imaginary person. Jesse thought about how to respond to this.

"Well Bud, I must've been so busy looking at your mommy that I didn't see him. You know how daddy loves looking at mommy, don't ya Pal?"

"Come on Dad, how could you not see him! I mean, he was right next to her!" sounding exasperated.

"Maybe you can help me remember. What did he look like?" Jesse asked cautiously.

"He was tall, like you but he was dressed different."

"Oh yeah? Dressed different how?" Jesse was becoming concerned, as he realized Ethan believed what he was saying.

"I dunno, just different."

"O-o-o-kay…did he look like a nice man standing next to Mommy? Was he scary looking or friendly looking?"

"Friendly," he told his dad decidedly, which Jesse somehow felt a relief. At least his son's imagination hadn't produced any monsters that he could tell. Imaginary playmates are one thing but this seemed a little eerie.

After puzzling over this surprising conversation that he was having with his son, Jesse tried to dismiss it for the time being, so he called Rachel, his sister, to make sure she could watch Ethan that evening. She answered on the third ring.

"Rach, hey Sis, just wondering if you could keep Ethan tonight. I wanted to take Hannah out. A marriage needs date nights, you know," he said smiling, thinking his marriage was in desperate need of one at this moment. "Please say, yes." He loved his sister, and they were close. Kyle was her only child, and she always knew how excited Kyle was to see Ethan."

"Sure, absolutely!" she replied genuinely happy to have her favorite nephew come visit. Rachel loved children, and was an elementary school teacher, who was in the teachers' lounge putting her lunch in the frig when Jesse had called.

"Thanks, Rachel, I love ya! What would I do without you?"

"Probably have fewer dates with your wife, I would imagine," she said cheerfully and began to laugh.

"Okay, I'll see you tonight, Sis. Thanks bunches!" as he ended the call.

He looked back at Ethan, "You don't think I have to worry about this guy, do ya? You don't think he was a secret boyfriend or anything like that, right?" deciding to play along with Ethan while trying to learn more about what he might be imagining.

"Da-a-ad!"

"What?"

"Not her boyfriend, silly!" Ethan giggled.

Jesse grunted under his breath, "I hope not," so that Ethan could not hear him but then said, "Oh, I know that!" and scrunched his face, as if to say, "Give me a break."

They were six blocks from the Montessori preschool, which Jesse had to drive further across town for, but they thought putting Ethan in a Montessori education was worth it. He looked at the clock on the dashboard. The clock said 7:52. It seemed he was hitting every light this morning. The sun was hitting him right in the eyes. Jesse squinted, trying to see the traffic light. It was a couple more blocks, and they had come into a clearing where the buildings were no longer blocking the sun coming up in the east directly ahead of him. He leaned over to reach in the glove box for his sunglasses. He retrieved them quickly and was fumbling to put them on as the light turned green. He didn't notice the garbage truck that was barreling down the hill headed north and straight towards them. The impact was instant, causing the car to collapse from side to side as it was thrust into the median where there was a concrete encasement a block long containing Palm trees and shrubs separating the divided lanes. The median had not been enough to halt the collision, and the truck proceeded to roll over top of the small red Prius, further collapsing the car from top to bottom. The truck continued over the top of median, taking a palm tree down and crashed into a parked car on the opposite side of the street, knocking it into the adjacent building before it came to a halt. Metal and glass debris had flown everywhere. As if in slow motion, people were getting out of their stopped cars and bystanders were running toward the scene. The momentary silence of the aftermath was deafening.

Chapter Two

Date Night

When Hannah pulled into the park where she was to meet Miranda and the models for the photo shoot, she noticed they were all waiting for her. She parked along the shoulder of the road and stepped out of her pearl white Honda Accord, and saw Miranda waving. Hannah returned the gesture and reached back into the car for her camera and then began walking towards Miranda. She saw Miranda's RV parked not far from where she had parked. The models would use it to change into the various outfits they would be modeling. Miranda had a very captivating personality. She was always smiling when she greeted someone. She loved people and no one was a stranger to her. People naturally were drawn to her, just as Hannah had been when she first met her. She had an uncanny ability to put people at ease. Miranda was beautiful inside and cute on the outside with her curly black hair that hung to her shoulders, eyes that looked like sapphires bordered with naturally long lashes, and dimples that reflected inner joy on her countenance more times than not. She was not as conservative as Hannah and enjoyed the darker lip colors that Hannah did not tend to wear. She had a 5-feet 4-inch frame that was not skinny but not overweight either. There were six models gathered around Miranda. Hannah figured she was getting to know them, offering them reassurance, helping them feel relaxed while they waited for her to arrive. When they saw Hannah, one would think they were meeting Miss Universe, they thought her to be so beautiful.

Miranda said, "Ladies, meet your photographer," looking at them with an anticipatory smile. Just as she expected, their jaws dropped and eyes widened as if they were synchronized on cue to do so.

"I thought you were another model!" one said.

"That's what I thought!" another said.

"Have you done modeling," another asked.

Hannah smiled warmly and negated their assumptions in a manner of humility, and Miranda added, "Ladies, I've been trying to get her to model for years! There's no convincing her. She's far more comfortable on the other side of the camera," looking at Hannah teasingly. She, too, had always wondered why Hannah had no interest in a modeling career of her own. Each to their own.

Miranda looked up at the clear sky, "We have the perfect day for this," spreading her arm span to the sky. Hannah agreed. The breeze was soft and a little static, which would add a nice effect with the models' hair blowing gently in the wind. Sailboats were spread out on the bay, and a cruise ship was just passing under the Golden Gate Bridge, which made it even more perfect. Hannah raised her camera and the girls took their places as Hannah snapped pictures. An occasional jogger and a few walkers were out and glanced their way when they passed by. Hannah continued taking pictures. She guessed the girls were barely out of high school, and Miranda was getting them boosted into their careers and helping them build their own portfolios.

She took pictures of them engaging in their camaraderie on their breaks, even when the girls didn't realize they were being photographed. Their moment-by-moment poses were so fluid that they made modeling seem easier than it really is. They had actually needed very little coaching, which made the morning go by quickly and smoothly. They had used the RV to change their outfits, some of which Hannah wouldn't mind adding to her own wardrobe.

At 11:30, Miranda suggested to wrap it up and call it a day. The girls had each had their own transportation and were already in their cars. "How about lunch?" she asked Hannah.

"Sure, let's just take my car and eat here, and I'll drop you off on the way back. There's a restaurant right up the road that serves pretty much anything you want, so let's just go there."

"I really want some scallops. It seems like forever since I've enjoyed a succulent dish of scallops," Miranda said dreamily with a sigh, her voice trailing, as if it were a tragedy that needed to be rectified. She was already tasting them in her mouth.

"I'm pretty sure they have scallops," Hannah told her, humored by her friend, enjoying her theatrics.

A few minutes later, they were being seated at the restaurant. "I have a date tonight," Miranda told Hannah proudly.

"Really! It is about time Mir!" which is what Hannah often called her. "Who's the lucky guy?" she asked excitedly.

"He's an underwear model," Miranda put out there, knowing Hannah would find that a tad bit amusing.

"Come on! Seriously! You! An underwear model? Are you recruiting him?" Hannah giggled helplessly.

"Not yet, I haven't, but maybe I will," Miranda said smugly, and took a sip of her water.

Hannah studied her. When she decided Miranda was having fun with this, she almost choked on her own water laughing, and then together they just enjoyed the humor and laughed together.

"Seriously, tell me about this guy," Hannah prodded.

"Well, actually, he just moonlights as a model on the side, but not for underwear. I was just liking the idea, ya know! I mean, I wouldn't be offended if he wanted to model underwear for me," rolling her eyes while enjoying the thought. "I have to say, the idea is pretty enticing," a little more seriously, then thought better of pursuing that idea any further, at least for the moment, laughing under her breath and expressing a devious grin.

"So, seriously, pray tell, what does he really do when he's not *moonlighting*?" appreciating Miranda's sense of humor, but growing more curious.

"Fit modeling for fitness magazines," Miranda lit up, as if to say, "Ta da! I have pulled a man of steel out of my hat!"

"I see!" Hannah's eyes widened, smiling.

Miranda said, "He's actually a physical therapist, but I needed a moment of girl time entertainment," lightheartedly.

"Did you meet online?"

45

"No, we didn't," she said seriously, sitting up straight. We met at the veterinarian's office yesterday. I had to take Aristotle to get his vaccinations, and he was there with his dog, this beautiful border collie, Tilly. It was kind of magical, just when you least expect to meet someone, ya know? Anyway, he's taking me to dinner tonight, and I have to say, I'm a little excited."

"It's been a while since you've had a date with anyone, so you have a right to be excited. I'm really happy you met someone. This is good news, Mir!"

"Yeah, I kind of think so, too, I mean, it feels good!" She gyrated in her chair like she was struttin' her stuff.

"It's okay to move on, and I think this will be good for you, but you have to be open to good things coming your way," Hannah reminded her.

"I know, and I think I am now, moving on, that is."

"Moving on is a process, and it takes the will to do it. This is a big step for you, but it's a step in the right direction," Hannah told her.

"I think so. I mean, I feel good about it, so it has to be a good thing, right?"

"Try not to think too much. Just let it unfold and ride it like a wave," Hannah suggested.

Miranda looked up at the ceiling in brief thought, then proclaimed, "I like that analogy!"

She agreed with Hannah, she really did need to allow herself to have fun and be open to possibilities of love again. It had been almost a year since she and Mark had divorced. They had been married four years, and Miranda had no idea anything was wrong, until he took her out to dinner and quietly told her he wanted a divorce. He had assured her it was nothing she did wrong, that it was not her fault, but he had just never had closure with a woman who had written him a Dear John letter while he was in Afghanistan. He had intended to move on. Then he met Miranda and had married her. Afterwards, he again ran into the old flame, and they had begun talking, and now that he was home and had not reenlisted, they both realized they still had feelings for each other. It wouldn't have been fair to either Miranda or him if the two of them stayed together, and he had always wondered what could have been. It was over just like that. Miranda's world just fell apart in one sweep, and her confidence in the right guy coming along had been shattered. Hannah had been the only person she had truly opened up to about how devastated it had left her feeling inside. Miranda had always told herself that someone even worthier of her would come along when the time was right, and so for her to feel excitement that she actually wanted this date, that she had allowed herself to be vulnerable, when she had turned down so many, she decided was progress for her. She still had her guard up, which may be why she disclosed this upcoming breakthrough to Hannah in a teasing manner. If it didn't work out, she had already made light of it by joking that he was an underwear model with the no-big-deal attitude, which admittedly was all in fun. She had enjoyed watching the look on her face. Also, if it didn't work out, it would be easier to say it didn't work out with an underwear model than to say it didn't work out with the physical therapist, she reasoned.

"His name is Alex," Miranda said more seriously now. "I've been bracing myself, but I'm trying not to be so damn *tense!*" drawing the word out for emphasis.

"Stop, don't brace for anything, just be yourself and trust that you've met him for a reason, and allow yourself to have fun and don't look for pain where none has presented itself. You can't leave the door open for the past to color your future, not when you're talking about painful memories and a series of disappointment. That kind of history does not have to repeat itself. Look at me, Miranda," Hannah ordered.

Miranda looked up from her glass of water she had been twirling the straw in and appreciated what her friend was telling her. "You're right," she said, forcing a smile.

"If you are going to be ambivalent, let the excitement of this date win out and kick your reservations to the curb. You deserve to be happy, so BE happy! It's a choice, you know."

"I don't think I could have a better friend than you. Thanks."

She observed the quiet sincerity as Miranda processed the admonition. "There's nothing to thank me for," Hannah told her. "I care about you, and I'm not telling you anything that's not true."

"You know what? I'm going to do this, I'm just going ride the wave," she said decidedly. She held her arms out just a little like she was doing a balancing act on a surf board.

Hannah smiled at her as she sipped her water, "Enjoy it! It's a new chance for some romantic adventure. I'd embrace it if I were you." Miranda started to say something, but Hannah raised her hand to silence her, "No excuses!" Miranda thought she sounded almost like a sophomore teacher she once had and said as much. She appreciated Hannah's good fortune and the fact that she was so level-headed and always seemed to give good advice. Hannah, in a sense, was Miranda's role model on love, someone she wanted to emulate. She didn't envy her that she was still with her high school sweetheart and still happily in love. She saw her as a teacher, someone that could help her to grow and bounce back from the darkness she had felt, as if she had been sucked into Devil's Triangle, and if it had not been for Hannah, Miranda often trembled at the thought of what direction her life would have taken. She had not handled the divorce well at all. She had been second fiddle to another woman, and to finally learn that had left such vacancy in her very being. It had been Hannah that had finally got through to her that she had to find happiness and wholeness from within, first and foremost, before she could truly appreciate the joy of her physical senses and what others brought to the table of life. Miranda believed, as she reflected, she had come a long way. Though she came from wealth, she was never as close to her parents as she would have liked. Her mother was not close to her mother, and from what she knew, her grandmother had not been close to her great-grandmother, either. Miranda seemed to have had the misfortune of this inheritance. She had grown up alone, without a brother or a sister. Hannah had nurtured her more than her parents had, especially after her world had turned upside down.

Hannah, on the other hand didn't come from wealth, but she had very nurturing parents, and a husband who gave her anything she wanted or needed, and Hannah didn't require much to be happy. Happiness just naturally came to her. It was part of her essence, and she had always been confident in her abilities and her direction in life. In fact, life seemed to be gentle on her, as if she possessed an entitlement to all things good. Even so, she was so humble. Miranda had never witnessed Hannah be rude to anyone. She never thought she was better than anyone else. Even in college, Hannah did not belong to clicks. She stopped for strangers and homeless people that needed food or money. If she didn't have cash, she had sometimes hurried to Carl Jr.'s or McDonalds and came back with a combo meal for them. She was just like that, and so Miranda had always had more admiration for Hannah than jealousy.

Just then the waiter came, and Miranda ordered the scallops with French fries with a side salad and Hannah ordered a grilled chicken salad. After the waiter took their order, Hannah casually said, "I have a date with my husband tonight."

"O-o-h-h, where are you two lovebirds going?"

"He's taking me to the Grand Theater. That's where he took me on our first date," Hannah thoughtfully remembered. "He's such a romanticist. I love that about him."

"I hope I have what you have someday," Miranda told her longingly.

"You will! Don't ever doubt that. You're redefining yourself. You are not going to lose someone who is meant to be in your life. Use that self-fulfilling prophesy in your favor instead of sabotaging yourself," she chided.

"I've been working on that, I promise," Miranda assured her.

"I know you are," Hannah said, as she leaned over and run her fingertips back and forth through Miranda's hair in a sisterly way. "He's a lucky guy if he gets you," she reassured her. Hannah and Miranda had been friends since college, and Miranda had always had laughter in her life, but after Mark left her, she felt like Miranda had sometimes hidden behind her sense of humor, but Hannah enjoyed the laughter they shared, even though she knew it had also become Miranda's coping mechanism. Miranda had buried herself in work, often working more than Hannah did, so oftentimes Hannah would invite her for some girl time just to try to help her reestablish balance and let her talk. This time, it was Hannah who needed to talk.

Hannah thought about her words before she spoke. "Mir, something has been happening with me lately, and I haven't even told Jess."

Miranda decided to hold off on taking another sip of water. Just as she had the glass to her lips, she slowly set it down. "What is it, Hannah? You know you can tell me anything," she said softly, hoping it wasn't cancer or some life-threatening disease, already feeling a slight alarm.

"I've been having unusual dreams, and sometimes I just feel like someone is watching me or like something is about to happen that is out of my control or something *is* happening. I don't know," she said sadly.

"What kind of dreams?"

"I barely remember any details at all when I wake up, but I keep dreaming about someone…people, and it's like I'm in a different lifetime, a completely different era of time," she said, still trying to find the words to describe them. "I know everyone in my dream, while I'm dreaming it, and it is all so vivid and real, and I feel such strong feelings about the people and everything that's happening in them, but when I wake up, it's all so vague, and I can't recall a single face or…it's like most of the frames are missing from a movie and the dream doesn't even make sense. It's enough to puzzle me if it were just one solitary dream, but I've been having them almost every night, and they wake me up, and I want to go back and finish the dream, pick up where I left off, find out who everyone is and what it all means." She hesitated while she tried to recall details. "There's a man, a man in the dreams, a man that it feels like I'm in love with, in the dream I mean, but I have no idea who he is. I wake up and I either can't go back to sleep or I do and don't dream about it again the rest of the night, so I don't ever find out," she drifted off. "Mir, it feels so real." She gave pause before she spoke again. "It all sounds so utterly ridiculous listening to myself talk about it," she conceded.

"I believe I know what you're talking about. I mean, I've had a few dreams like that over the years, but not so many, but I remember feeling dumbfounded when I woke up because it was like it wasn't a dream at all, yet I knew it had to be," Miranda considered as she recalled her own dreams she had

had, which were only a handful at best. "Just like you, everything was vague, like my memory was wiped after I woke up."

"That's the perfect way of putting it," Hannah agreed. "It's affected my life at home. I'm distracted, exhausted from lack of sleep, and then I'll sleep 10 hours and be fine, without dreaming anything! I haven't been myself, and as much as I know that I haven't, I just haven't shared what is happening to me with Jesse. He probably thinks I'm just being hormonal," she said smiling weakly, concern etched on her face.

Miranda took a breath and said, "Listen, Hannah, Jesse is no flake. He would understand if you confided in him about this. He is an open-minded guy, and he loves you and would be supportive. You don't doubt that about him, do you?"

Hannah shook her head, "No, but he may not understand why I'm dreaming about another guy that I'm in love with that I know is clearly not him."

"Okay, I understand where you're coming from. You're right, I would probably be afraid of including that part, I mean, you really don't know who it is or even when it is, or if it is or ever was, so I totally get that." Miranda observed Hannah, who finally looked up from the table.

"I wish I knew where it was all coming from," Hannah said. "I know dreams are often unfinished business and sometimes the subconscious mind's way of dealing with life, but *this* life, right? Right here in the present? It doesn't feel like that is what these dreams are. They seem completely unrelated to anything I have going on in this life. They aren't *bad* dreams," she continued as an afterthought. "They seem so real that they are confusing me. Sometimes I wonder who I am, and I've never felt that way before. I've never wondered *who I am!"* I've always just felt, I'm me, you know? But in the dreams, I feel I'm me, but *me* is someone else," she explained, not really knowing any other way to describe the overwhelming confusion and feeling she had been experiencing.

Miranda asked, "Did you have another dream last night?"

"Yes, I did." I tried going back to sleep but I think it took a while. It seemed I had no more fallen back to sleep when Jesse woke me up. I've been seeing concern in his eyes. He knows something is going on, but I just haven't told him."

"Because of the other guy, you're in love with in the dream," Miranda clarified.

Hannah nodded in agreement, "Yes."

"You haven't done anything wrong, nothing to cause him to lose trust in you. Remember that, okay?"

"Why do I feel so guilty when I wake up?" she questioned helplessly.

"This is what I think. I believe it's because of the *emotions* connected to the dreams and how they are still attached to you when you wake up, and it's those emotions that are causing you to feel guilty, but you're not guilty, Hannah. Sweetie, you're not guilty of anything," she said soothingly.

"You're right, I haven't *done* anything wrong." Nevertheless, she still felt unfaithful to her husband. "It's just I don't understand having such strong feelings for someone I don't know! That I've never even met! Someone who may not even exists!" Hannah's thoughts continued, "But in the dream, I *know* him. What I can't figure out, Mir, is that I love this man in a way I never loved Jesse. More than I can even imagine loving anyone, while I'm *in* the dream that is."

Miranda searched her friend's eyes and knew Hannah deeply felt and believed in what she was saying, and she picked up Hannah's hand, "We are going to figure this out, whatever it takes." As Hannah gazed back into Miranda's eyes, she trusted her completely with what she had just shared with her.

Their lunch arrived and Hannah quickly changed the subject, "Maybe you should bring Alex over one evening for dinner. We could play Pictionary or something."

"That could be interesting!" Miranda mused.

"It would be fun. We should do it," Hannah insisted.

"Okay, well let me make it past the first date first, okay!" Miranda begged with a throaty laugh.

"Deal." Hannah agreed.

Hannah took Miranda back to her RV and before she got out, "Call me tomorrow and let me know how your date went with Alex. Don't keep me waiting," she insisted, grinning broadly.

"I promise your phone will be buzzing," Miranda assured her. "Wish me luck! Oh, and enjoy your date night!" Before she closed the car door, Miranda turned back, "And Hannah, don't hesitate to call me anytime, night or day when you need to talk. I'm here for you no matter what."

Miranda walked towards the RV, and Hannah headed back towards the 101 going south. She remembered she needed to stop at the drycleaners to pick up the white down comforter she had dropped off nearly a week before. After that, she wanted to stop and pick up some wine and brandy to restock the bar. She thought about Miranda taking Aristotle to the vet and remembered her own furry friend. He had been gone for two years now. Moses had developed diabetes and quickly deteriorated despite all efforts to save him. He was so beautiful, black and white tuxedo Maine Coon that had the personality of an old dog. Other times, he behaved as if he had a human soul. He had lost half his body weight, going from 19 pounds to a mere 10 pounds. She had given him insulin shots twice a day and made many trips to the vet, but in the end, she mercifully had him put to sleep. She had not missed the cat hair around the house and on the bed, but she missed *him*, and sometimes thought she may like to adopt another pet. She had not decided if should wanted to get a cat or a dog though. All she knew was that having a pet gave fulfilment to her life that her husband and son did not. Pets are like a missing link to happiness, she thought. She had always had a pet growing up, and to her it seemed unnatural not to have one, but she had wanted some time to adjust to missing her friend before she got another. She would put it on the back burner for now. A few minutes later, she pulled in front of the drycleaners.

As she walked in the drycleaners, a bell rang as the door opened and a woman appeared at the counter wearing a nametag identifying her as Robin. "Hi Robin, I'm here to pick up my down blanket," handing her the item number.

Robin looked at it and said, "I'll be right back, Mrs. Barstow," and disappeared from the counter. Just then, another customer walked in, who looked like she was in her eighties, whose hair was an unnatural blueish gray, who reminded Hannah of a third-grade teacher she once had whose name was Mrs. Belle, although she was nicknamed Mrs. Bluebell by some of the students. She saw Hannah standing there and began to vent.

"I just got out of a nightmare of traffic. There must be an awfully bad accident that has roads closed and traffic backed up everywhere. I thought I was never going to get here," she said exasperated. "Bus just about ran me into another car pulling out in front of me. Everyone was blowing their horns. What do they expect me to do when there's nowhere to go but to just sit there! I think I should've stayed home today."

Her voice was old with misery. Hannah thought to herself that driving in San Francisco traffic had to be quite challenging for some, and she sympathized with the woman.

"My husband is not around to do the driving anymore. It might be time for me to move somewhere less congested," she continued. Then she seemed to notice Hannah more clearly after she finished venting.

"You have the most beautiful hair. My hair used to be long like yours if you can imagine that!"

Hannah was almost ashamed of herself for imagining her with long blue-gray hair, although she felt sure it would have been a different color when she was younger. She smiled at the woman and said, "You still do have lovely hair."

The woman smiled, "Thank you," touching her hand to her hair. Hannah thought, that one compliment seemed to make her day.

Just then, Robin came back with her down blanket and said, "Here it is," and laid it on the counter while she rang up her ticket. Hannah paid her and swooped up the blanket and thanked her. As she started to walk out, she turned to the woman.

"I hope you have a better rest of the day." The woman thanked her.

"I hope so, too, dear," and smiled exhaustedly, as she turned to Robin and fumbled for her ticket.

Hannah made her way to the grocery store and picked up wine and brandy, and then decided she would add a bottle of bourbon to the list. She and Jesse were not heavy drinkers by any means, but sometimes at night or on weekends they enjoyed a nightcap together, and she considered the possibility Miranda might bring Alex over for introductions. While she was there, she picked up some cheeses, guacamole, and a large container of mixed nuts. After making her purchase, she walked back to the car and put the bags in the trunk. She looked at the time and saw it was 2:10.

She decided to go ahead and pick up Ethan. He would be in daycare now. She got a few blocks away and realized the traffic must be what the woman in the drycleaners was talking about. Traffic was being detoured so it would take her a little longer to get there, but the daycare was open until six. She turned on Pandora radio to the Coldplay station and listened to Paradise. Finally, traffic let up and it took her another ten minutes to get there. The daycare was secure, and one had to sign in and produce proper identification at the front desk before the girl behind the desk would unlock the doors to allow anyone to enter. She signed her name on the sign-in sheet and wrote down the secret code. If you didn't know the code, you didn't get in. The daycare staff were familiar with most of the parents, but every parent still had to show an official ID. Hannah and Jesse had appreciated the security, as any parent would. Handing the girl her ID, she checked her registry.

"I don't show Ethan was checked in today, Mrs. Barstow. You think your husband may have picked him up right after school let out?"

Alarmed, Hannah said, "Surely Jesse would have called me if he were going to do that," feeling confused. Sometimes Jesse did pick Ethan up from kindergarten, when he got off work early, but it had always been communicated who would be picking him up. She immediately pulled out her iPhone and dialed Jesse's number, but it went to voicemail. "Hey Jesse, I'm here at the daycare to pick up Ethan, and they are saying he isn't on the registry today. Did you pick him up after school? Call me back ASAP, love you."

After putting her phone back in her purse, she asked, "Is Ms. Pido still here? She's his teacher. She might be able to tell me if Jesse picked him up."

The girl searched the computer screen and said, "It looks like she left right after class today but let me call her number." Thirty seconds later, "I'm sorry, she's not answering her phone; it went to voicemail. Let me call Mrs. Babcock. She might know if Ms. Pido has left or not."

Mrs. Babcock apparently answered as the girl spoke to her briefly and then hung up. The girl relayed, "Mrs. Babcock said that Ms. Pido left at noon due to an emergency, I'm sorry, Mrs. Barstow. Would you like me to contact the Director? Ms. Pido always updates her class attendance but she didn't today."

Hannah thought for a moment and decided, "No, I'm sure Jesse picked him up like he has other times. He may have taken him to the new Disney Movie he's been wanting to see. He wouldn't have his ringer turned on if they were in the theater. I'm sure I just forgot," Hannah told her with obvious concern, trying to forge a smile.

Hannah drove home trying to remain rational. "I just don't remember him telling me he was picking Ethan up today," she thought to herself. With so much lost sleep and the exhaustion, she probably just didn't remember. She tried calling Jesse again and still got his voicemail. This time, she did not leave a message but hung up instead. Finally, she rationalized she was overreacting and it wasn't like her to overreact to anything. Then she decided they may be swimming in the pool and didn't hear the phone. "They're probably just having some father-son time and I'm being silly," she told herself.

The drive home seemed to take a lot longer than usual, but she finally pulled in the garage. Jesse's car wasn't there. She let out a deep breath and told herself he must've taken Ethan to the theater, thinking I would be home later than sooner. After all, she usually got home around four, but today, it seemed Miranda was eager to get ready for her date and was not really in the mood to work, reflecting back. She got out of the car and retrieved her bags and down blanket and entered the house through the kitchen door leading out of the garage and pressed the remote to close the garage door.

She sat the bottles down on the kitchen counter and carried the down blanket to the bedroom and laid it on the bed. Then she walked to the walk-in closet and browsed what she might wear tonight. She had been looking forward to their date night. Jesse always knew how make her feel special and pamper her. He deserved his own pampering. She held out her powder pink dress and let it dangle in her hand for a moment, biting her lip, thinking it had been a while since she had worn it, so she took it off the hanger and laid it on the bed. She walked back to the closet and found her matching shoes that were two-tone navy/pink heels. She laid them next to the bed and thought she would pour herself a glass of wine and get ready to run a bath and add some lavender oils to the water, but first, she went back downstairs and began taking the bottles from the bag and was stocking the bar. She then opened a bottle of wine for herself and poured a glass of 1992 pinot noir to sip while she soaked in the tub. Just as she was about to take the glass and walk back upstairs to run the bath water, the doorbell rang.

"Probably Girl Scouts," she thought, but then reconsidered it was a little too early in the day for them. She sat her glass on the kitchen table and walked into the living room. Just before she made it to the door, the doorbell rang again. When she opened it, two police officers stood there, each removing his hat.

Chapter Three

Shock

Hannah stood there stoically speechless. The officers had been very tactful, sensitive, and not just blurted it out. They summarily told her it had taken over six hours and using the Jaws of Life to free her husband and son from the wreckage. The driver of the dump truck who hit them had suffered a heart attack, and they believed him to be deceased before impact. The truck had pinned the Prius to a center wall in the median. One officer said he hoped it would be of some comfort for her to know that they most likely had not known what hit them or seriously doubted they even felt anything. They did not suffer. Death had been instant. When the truck hit a couple of parked cars across the street, it had also ripped into the building and came to a halt inside a music shop that would not have opened until ten. No one had been inside. They were profusely apologetic and asked if they could do anything for her or call anyone to come be with her. Hannah declined and stoically thanked them. She did not envy them for that part of their job, and she didn't want to make it any more difficult than it already was by breaking down in front of them. This did not feel real! The shock swallowed her like a wave crashing in on her. She dismissed them quietly and closed the door.

Her back pressed against the door as she leaned backwards against it. Her head began to pound and her hands became clammy and cold. There was a surge of nausea that started to form in her stomach. She ran to the bathroom and heaved until she lost the contents of her lunch. Her skin formed beads of sweat on her forehead. She doused handfuls of cold water to cool her face and dried off with the hand towel. She wretched once more and threw up again. The room seemed to spin. She steadied herself on the sink and reached for the doorframe. For a moment, everything seemed to go black, but she was conscious, still standing. A minute passed and her eyes came into focus again. She went to the kitchen to pour a glass of water and held the glass to her lips, taking big gulps of lukewarm tap water but felt more nausea, which she staved off the urge to vomit by pausing for smaller sips. She felt her heart pounding and could hear her heartbeat in her ears. Her phone was in her purse on the kitchen table. She reached in and found it and dialed her parents. Her father answered on the third ring.

"Daddy, I need you and Mom to come be with me," her throat dry and her voice suddenly hoarse.

"Hannah? What's happened?" He tried to keep his voice as calm as possible but it held a thread of fear that had tied its knot in his words.

"Jesse and Ethan were in an accident. They're gone. I need to you and Mom to come be with me." There was profound numbness in her words that her father had never heard before. He forced himself to remain calm for her sake.

"I'll get your mother, and we'll take the first flight out." Then he asked, "Hannah, honey, is anyone with you that can stay with you until we get there?"

"I'll call Miranda. She'll come over." Her throat began to hurt from what felt like stricture. Her tongue and mouth were like cotton and her voice grew more raspy.

"Alright, Hannah, call her so you're not alone. I'm going to call the airport and get your mother. We'll let family know, honey. We're on our way," he assured her.

"Thanks, Daddy. I'll see you when you get here," she said mechanically.

"Hey, we'll get a rental car, so don't worry about meeting us at the airport," he added. "You don't need to be driving, okay."

"Just hurry," she answered.

She called Rachel, Jesse's sister, and told her. The phone call to her seemed to have reinforced the surreality she felt. Then she called Miranda. It went to voicemail. Then, she remembered Miranda was on a date tonight. She had completely forgotten. She picked up the glass of wine and drank all of it and then threw the glass and heard it shatter against the fireplace.

As if in slow motion, she sank to the floor and curled her knees to her chest. She cried inconsolably until she could barely breathe. Everything the officers had told her replayed in her mind, one word at a time, the words randomly reciting themselves in her mind. A semi-invisible veil of surreality engulfed her, taking her breath away. Air felt absent as she gasped. It felt to her as if there had been a separation of her body and soul, and she could see her physical self in photographic frames wailing and writhing inconsolably, while her soul sought solace that seemed not to exist. It was the first time she felt there were more parts of her than what she saw in the mirror. Had she, too, suffered a death? Was her soul now separated from her body? Disorientation now consumed her. She was no longer certain if her reality was of a physical or nonphysical dimension. She didn't know if she had fallen asleep, if she was dreaming the most lucid dream she had ever experienced and would wake up from the horror of it, but it felt to her she had been sucked into a vacuum and was floating without gravity, looking out over the universe, seeing all the stars, and then, the vacuum released her. She could feel the floor under her. She opened her eyes that were now swollen and felt salt that had dried on her face from crying.

She pulled herself up and realized she had collapsed and lost consciousness. She slowly staggered to the kitchen, not sure if she were floating or if here legs were actually carrying her. She retrieved a glass from the cabinet and went to the refrigerator and poured a glass of water. Her whole body was shaking. It felt like her insides were violently quivering. She gulped the water emptying the glass. The clock on the microwave said it was 7:45. She looked out the kitchen window and could see the sun was lower in the sky. It was evening. All she could feel was a gulf of surreality. She felt no sense of time. It seemed like five minutes ago, her life had spiraled into oblivion, but it also seemed like infinity. She sat down on the couch staring at nothing. She could not bring herself to go upstairs where the bedrooms were. She couldn't, knew she couldn't face Jesse and Ethan not being there, never being there again. She took slow deep breaths and closed her eyes as if closing her eyes would make the horror disappear. The shaking seemed to subside. She stared blankly ahead looking at nothing but thought something moved in the periphery of her vision, a flash of white light. When she turned, she saw nothing. She refocused her eyes and searched the room, still seeing nothing. Tears streamed down her face again. She couldn't stop the tightening spasms of her lungs rendering her almost unable to breathe.

Tears poured hot down her face and she could taste the salt on her lips. Everything inside her was screaming, "Why? Why have you taken them? Why didn't you take me? Why?" she begged for an answer. The question resounded over and over in her mind. The house was now dark, but she didn't bother to turn on the lights. Her mind played a reel of how the day had started with laughter at breakfast, that he had brought her coffee to her this morning, and then she had watched them leave in the car, waving to her. The rerun played over and over again in her mind, one flashback after another. In the blink of an eye, her life had been changed. It felt like the lights went out inside.

There was a slow awareness, an instinct, someone had been listening to every plea of her soul and had been witnessing the torrent of tears that would not stop. Someone was with her, watching her. She looked around the room again but saw no one. She raised herself off the floor and laid down on the couch and drew her legs in a fetal position and pulled the throw over her head. The tears came again and she felt them streaming across her nose and soaking her pillow. She had fallen silent with an occasional hitch of her breath until she sedately fell quiet.

In the corner of the room stood a stranger, watching her intently and soberly. He was tall, muscular, and had shoulder-length golden, straight, light brown hair, rounded, brown eyes, and a squared jaw. He was wearing a singularly colored outfit of dark brown silky appearing shirt and brown appearing trousers. Over the shirt, he wore an open vest of leathery rustic texture, pointed cut in the front exposing a brass buckled belt that that looked similar to a chainmail with shields, over the top of the buckle and along the bottom of the buckle, bordered by solid brass. Over the vest, he wore a long, mid-calf length coat with a parched, rustic design, heavier leather texture than the vest and bore a V-shaped collar. It had a wide lapel, and there were brass buttons that lined each side of the outer edge of the lapels, which went down just above the waist. There were double cuff-linked brass matching buttons on each sleeve.

He wore brown leather boots that came to below his knee that had a double strap, each secured by a brass buckle. He had come to comfort her but he would not reveal himself until the time was right. Until it was, he would remain hidden from her.

The sound of her phone felt like a dream, but she uncovered her head and saw the light from it and answered.

"Mir?"

"Hey, I missed your call. Alex and I went to a movie, so I had the ringer off. How's the date night going with your hubby?" she asked cheerfully.

"Mir, there was no date night. Jesse and Ethan are gone," barely able to say the words.

"What do you mean they're gone?" Miranda asked, as fear gripped her like a vise, and she felt her throat tighten.

"They were killed in a car accident today. Mir, I need you," her voice raspier than before.

"Oh, my God, Hannah, I'm there sweetie, on my way right now!" I promise I will be there in less than

20," and then she heard silence and saw that the call was disconnected.

Hannah covered her head again. It seemed like only seconds that Miranda was beside her. When she pulled the cover back from Hannah's head, Hannah turned her eyes away from the light that had been turned on. She could see a male figure standing behind Miranda, who was now knelt down beside her, caressing her face and saying something to her. Everything seemed garbled.

"Miranda, she's in shock, and we don't know if she's ingested something or not. I'm calling EMS," Alex told her rapidly.

Miranda sat Hannah up forcefully, and sat beside her, holding her in her arms. "Hannah, have you taken any pills? Talk to me!"

"No," Hannah barely whispered. "They're gone, Mir, they're gone."

"I know sweetie, I know. We are going to get through this together. You are not alone, you hear me, Hannah, you are not alone. I'm with you every step of the way, I'm with you," Miranda began to sob.

Hannah could hear an unfamiliar male voice, muffled as hearing it from another end of a tunnel, "She's in shock. Her husband and son were in an accident today and didn't survive," lowering his voice so Hannah would not hear. We're not sure if she's taken any medications or not. Please get here as soon as you can. Thanks," he responded gratefully to the voice on the other end of the call.

Alex told Miranda, "EMS is on their way."

"Thanks, Alex," Miranda told him as he knelt down in front of the couch and pulled Miranda close to him and touched his forehead against hers. "We'll take care of you, Hannah," he said empathetically, putting his hand on hers.

"She's my best friend, Alex," she mouthed, her voice cracking as she was trying to whisper to keep Hannah from knowing she was falling apart. She knew she had to be strong for her. She kept Hannah in her arms.

"I know, babe, I know," he told her. Miranda barely noticed that he called her "Babe."

Alex softly touched his lips to Miranda's as drainage ran down her nose across her lips and chin, and he pulled out a handkerchief and wiped her nose and all the mascara running down her face. He thought to himself that is the most touching first kiss he had ever had, filled with more energy and emotion than the typical normal kiss, but it was bonding. Miranda seemed stronger for the reassurance of his gesture and composed herself and turned her attention immediately back to Hannah who had her knees pulled to her chest and had one cheek leaned against her knee. Her eyes were closed and she was mouth breathing and sniffling. Alex went to find some Kleenexes for her and returned quickly with a nearly full box. Miranda pulled out some and started to wipe Hannah's face. She could tell that snot had dried and caked around her nose and even smeared on her face. She wiped it off and told her to blow, and Hannah took the Kleenex and blew her nose. Alex went to the kitchen to get her a glass of water and brought it back and tipped it to Hannah's lips. She tilted the glass and held it and began sipping it. Then she leaned her head into Miranda's shoulder and cried. Alex knelt down in front of both of them and took both women's hands in his. While waiting for EMS, Hannah's phone rang, but Miranda answered for her. It was Rachel. She had let the family know. Miranda informed her they were transporting Hannah to the hospital due to shock and wanting to make sure she had not overmedicated on sedatives. She promised to call back as soon as she had been evaluated, and she was able to tell them how she was doing.

Ten minutes later, EMS was knocking at the door.

The trip to the hospital had been a blur for Hannah. Miranda had told Alex she would ride in the ambulance if he wanted to leave and go home, because she was not leaving Hannah's side, but he insisted on staying with them, so she rode with Alex who kept up with the ambulance. Once there, blood tests were ordered stat to check for any overdose or alcohol level, in case she had mixed the two, but had come back negative. She was given intravenous fluids and Ativan to calm her and help her sleep. The ER physician admitted her for observation overnight while nurses kept a close eye on her just as a precautionary suicidal watch while Hannah slept.

Miranda called Hannah's parents, who had already arrived in San Francisco and were in the process of getting a rental car. She updated them and was relieved to know Hannah had already called them, that she had had the clarity of mind to call them. They thanked her for her call for letting them know where she was.

There were two recliners in the hospital room, and she and Alex sat in them. The nurses provided each one of them with a blanket but neither could sleep. Alex nodded off a couple of times, as he had gotten up at 4:00 a.m. and put in a full day's work at the hospital, but Miranda sat there watching her friend, imagining herself in her position, thinking back of moments here and there, glimpses of memories she had witnessed between Hannah, Jesse, and Ethan, admiring what a beautiful family they were, how happy they had been, even less than 24 hours ago, and now two of them were suddenly gone. She felt tears etch down her face, as she reflected how life was so hard, but even the kindest, most wonderful people in the world experience grief, but how much greater the pain when the ones who pass are so young in life. The pain is even less bearable when we don't know what happens to them, what comes after, or if we will ever see them again. To be in that mindset, to not know or have any confidence whatsoever they are still near, would be devastating beyond imagination. It's not about being deserving or not deserving. It's not about punishment. We all are here living a temporary life with temporary bodies, and none of us knows how long we are here for. But everyone's life is with purpose and no one ever leaves without having affected the lives of others, for good or for worse, every life is in itself a lesson for both the one who lived it and the ones who were touched by them. No one's life is ever without meaning or value. How sad for those who don't see *they* have value, that their *life* has value. How little they see. How blind they must be to believe they are worthless. Everyone's life is priceless to *someone*.

Her thoughts went on and on, as one's thoughts often do when life is called into examination, and we assess our friendships and relationships with others. How are some people so much more aware of their capability of love, while others feel they have nothing to offer anyone else? Why do so many people avoid love and relationships while others embrace them?

Miranda was certain the answers to who we are or why we make the choices we make are not all buried and hidden in the memories of one solitary lifetime. The soul remembers and recognizes *everything* and *everyone*. Miranda had always believed this. She was not afraid of death because she didn't see it as death. What grieved Miranda was watching someone she loves hurt and grieve so deeply. But in her mind, it's better to experience that and have loved than to be so cold and indifferent. That is what is the saddest of all, she thought. As her mind wandered, Alex woke up from a short nap and saw Miranda was sitting there awake.

"Hey, Babe, sorry I dozed off," he told her profusely apologetic.

"Oh, you should sleep. I'm fine. I was just thinking I would go get some coffee."

"I can do it. You don't have to get up, just sit there and rest, okay?" pressing his palm to the side of her face affectionately. "I'll be back in a minute," bending down to press his lips to hers for a lingering kiss.

Miranda smiled appreciatively as she watched him leave the room, aware of how close she felt to him already. She pondered a little longer.

Hannah was still. She hadn't moved since they sedated her. The room was a private room, a dim light that was used for a nightlight offered a candlelight glow to the room. Machines were monitoring her vital signs. The head of the bed was semi elevated, and the nurse had left an extra blanket folded at the foot of the bed in case it was needed.

Miranda stood up and walked to the side of the bed and very softly caressed Hannah's hair. She looked peaceful as she slept. She hoped she would be the kind of friend Hannah needed, as this was going to be a long road for her. She reached for her hand and held it in hers.

Moments later, Alex was back with two cups of coffee. He handed one to her in a to-go cup. He placed an arm around her as they both observed her vital signs on the monitors, but with nothing else to be done, they sat back down.

Alex began, "I lost my brother to a car accident eight years ago."

"Oh Alex, I am so-o-o sorry."

"It's okay, now. It was a difficult time, but I grew a lot from it. It really helped me put life into perspective, you know?"

Miranda listened, and before the night was up, they had felt an unexpected bond that can occur when people are real with one another from the heart and not hiding behind facades or being plastic about who they are.

Miranda nodded, understanding. "Was he like your best friend?" curious to know.

"No, he and I had differences. We were nothing alike, and neither one of us could relate to the other. He was older but he had trouble coping with life, it seemed. His high school sweetheart left him for another guy, and it just seemed to go downhill from there for him. He was angry. I don't think he ever got over it. I never understood why or how he gave one person so much power over his life, but he did, and he just couldn't see that or take back his own power to be happy. He was lonely, and he didn't have to be. Sad, you know, and what's worse, I felt powerless to change that for him. We all did, Mom, Dad, my sister. It was like watching him self-destruct and not a damn thing we could do."

"People get angry when they're scared," Miranda replied. "They say things they wish they hadn't said and respond in ways they wish they hadn't. It doesn't make us bad people. It's part of being human. We do it because we love, and we can't berate ourselves over what we can't take back or change. You just have to move forward and trust that somewhere out there he knows you love him and you wanted the best for him."

"I believe he does. It took a while to believe that, but I do, now. And, I believe he's okay now, and that he's looking back on his life with a clearer perspective," his expression resolute in the belief. "I don't believe he's beating himself up anymore where he's at now," punctuating with a "humph" in his breath. A faint smile crossed his face.

Chapter Four

Rubik's Cube and Rabbits

The room seemed to spin, as grief consumed her, but Hannah pulled herself up, walked slowly, trying to collect her balance and when she did, she ran upstairs, feeling everything in slow motion, soundless, her heart beating against her eardrums – *ba-dump, ba-dump, ba-dump!* She ran to Ethan's room, and there he was, playing with his Rubik's cube.

He looked up and saw his mother and said, "Hey Mommy, look! I did it! I finally figured it out!" She stopped, panting, feeling relieved, thinking this was another dream she had had, only a really bad one, a nightmare, and she walked up to him and leaned over and picked him up, hugging him, and smiling with tears streaming down her face. He told her, "It was easy, Mommy! It was so easy!"

"You're a smart boy," she told him. "Daddy and I knew you would finally figure it out."

"My friend showed me how, and after that it was so easy," he said excitedly.

Hannah puzzled asking, "Who is your friend, sweetheart? Someone at school?"

"Nah, he's your friend too! He was standing next to you this morning when Daddy was taking me to school. He's really nice."

"Honey, there was no one standing next to me this morning when you and Daddy left."

"Yeah there was. Daddy didn't see him either, but he was standing real close to you. How could you and Daddy not see him?"

"I don't know, honey."

"Mommy, are you sad?"

"Sad about what, sweetheart?" smiling a laughter of relief that this had all been a bad dream.

"About me going away?" he told her.

Suddenly, she felt she was in a lucid dream, and wanted desperately to keep from waking up. "You don't have to go away, Ethan, honey. You can stay right here with Mommy and Daddy," as tears started to stream down her face again.

"I think Daddy is going to stay because he isn't ready to go yet, but I want to go," he said excitedly, smiling and showing his baby teeth.

"Where you're going, honey?"

Ethan reached up and took Hannah's hand, "Come on, Mommy, I'll show you!" Hannah took Ethan's hand and the wall opened up to them like a veil parting, and they were in another dimension where there were hills and hills of lavender, blue, and red flowers and a stream of aqua blue water, lined with trees of gold and shrubs the color of magenta. Rabbits ranged in color from gray, white, and black in color, and bicolor, which was Ethan's favorite animal. They hopped right up to him. There were beautiful colors of tropical fish swimming in the stream that looked like the fish in Ethan's fish tank, only larger and far more colorful. She could see humming birds and baby bears playing but no mother bear. Ethan had always had a fascination with bears, she thought. As they walked toward the bears, they stopped for a moment and Ethan said, I can understand them, Mommy. They can talk, but they talk without talking with their mouth, and I can understand them and they can understand me! Even the rabbits can! It's so neat!"

Hannah smiled, tears still streaming down her face, and she said, "That's so neat, sweetheart" and laughed to keep from breaking down crying.

"Don't cry, Mommy," and he reached around her legs and hugged her. She picked him up and told him she loved him too. Ethan then told her, "There's my friend! Come meet him!" and he took her hand and begin running, and in the distance, there was a large tree with expansive branches that branched out like a mushroom and had deep red leaves, and stepping out from the tree was a figure, dressed in solid dark brown attire with an overcoat, who had long, light brown hair flowing to his shoulders. As they drew closer, Hannah immediately recognized him and quickly sucked in her breath and stopped, her legs feeling limp. His smile was very kind and compassionate. He seemed to study her features intently. Every ounce of her being was overjoyed to see him.

All she could whisper was, "It *is* you." She felt her mind whirling. Then she heard muffled voices outside herself, and then she drifted again. Then there was nothing.

Her parents arrived at the hospital shortly after 2:30 a.m. Hannah was sleeping soundly. Miranda told them they had given her a sedative, and they each thanked her and Alex for being there and taking care of their daughter. Knowing the weekend was going to be long, preparing for the funerals and attending the memorials, they suggested Miranda and Alex go home and try to rest to save their strength, because Hannah was going to need the strength of others to get through this. Miranda was reluctant but knew her parents were right.

She admired the stoic strength they were displaying, and realized where Hannah had inherited her strength, but knew with their sensitive nature, they would break down when Hannah wouldn't see them cry. She could see their eyes were red and puffy from crying before their arrival. It was going to be so difficult for them to see Hannah the way she had already witnessed seeing her tonight. She was their daughter, and they would hurt and suffer with her, trying to bear her burden. She could see where Hannah got her looks, too. Her dad had dark brownish-gray hair and a mustache, with dark blue eyes that could stop a woman in her tracks. He was well over six feet tall and still had a nice physique. Her mother was tall, slender, and had naturally gray hair that hung to her shoulders with a natural hint of low-lights, although Miranda did not believe she colored her hair, as Hannah had told her once that her mother's choice to be natural had inspired her to stay natural, herself, even though her hair had turned at such early age. Hannah needed her to be strong, so after each of her parents hugged her, Miranda let Alex take her home.

The services were beautiful, but because of the extent of the injuries, both Jesse and Ethan had closed caskets. The funeral home was packed, and the funeral home staff had to set up an overflow area for those who had come to pay their respects. Many of Jesse's coworkers had come and some had shared beautiful and touching stories about working with Jesse. Some shared what he knew of Jesse's love and devotion to Hannah and to Ethan. It was a celebration of their lives that Hannah and Jesse's family truly appreciated. The sun was bright in the sky and though many tears were shed, the love and support that brought everyone together was indescribable and so comforting. After the memorial services, Miranda had arranged catering at Hannah's home knowing they would clean up everything once it was over and Hannah would not be left with a mess to clean up or people lingering to do the cleanup that she didn't want there. She knew Hannah would be emotionally exhausted and only want the people there that she felt closest too. She had not known how much food to have catered so she ordered more than less, knowing that if there was too much left over, she would donate it to the homeless or youth shelters.

Two months past, and her parents never left her. It was now August. They took turns checking in on her of a night. Her dad would sit on the couch with her, after they had coaxed her to come out of her room for a while. He would put his arm around her and just sit with her while she sobbed into his neck.

"I know, baby. Get it out. Let it all out," he told her. Her mother had even helped bathe her and wash her hair. Miranda and Alex would come over and offer to relieve them so they could get some fresh air. Sometimes, they accepted just so they could mourn without Hannah seeing them crying. Sometimes they came back with a few things from the grocery.

One morning after breakfast, which Hannah barely touched, they all sat at the kitchen table sipping coffee.

"Hannah, sweetheart, your father and I have been talking," her mother treaded carefully, "We're concerned about you staying here by yourself," looking to Hannah's father for backup, "and we wondered if you would feel better coming to stay with us for a while, as long as you like." Her expression was cautious how her daughter would perceive her suggestion.

"What do you feel like you need right now? What can we do to help?" her father asked.

Hannah had been listless for the first month, so withdrawn, occasionally speaking and responding in short responses to their efforts to comfort her, mixed with both crying and an effort to laugh at the same time when they reminisced about the time they had all come to visit them in Arizona and Ethan had just marched in, only two years-old and asked where his play drawer was in the kitchen. "It was so cute. You always had a play drawer when you were little," her mother reflected. "I'd be cooking and working in the kitchen, and you had your own drawer that I had put all kinds of things in to entertain you, second from the bottom so you could see in it." She was lost in the memory, which made her smile. "You would just stand there and keep yourself entertained for the longest time," she started to laugh and cry simultaneously. I was able to cook and wash dishes and keep an eye on you all at the same time." Her mother smiled as she recounted the memory. "I knew exactly what he was talking about when he asked where his play drawer was," she laughed but tears fell down her cheeks. Her father folded his hands over his face like one would in prayer, resting his elbows on the table, to try and hide his tear-filled eyes, his lips quivering in a sad smile. They had reflected on happy memories and tried to be strong, speaking of Jesse and Ethan in a manner that was a celebration of their lives, remembering things that made them laugh, as they always did as a way of honoring someone that passed. It had always been their approach to death. They grieved but as best they could, they tried to focus on happy memories. It was how they found comfort and processed their grief.

"I appreciate the offer, both of you, but I'm not ready to leave here," staring at the table, then looked up at her dad, then to her mom, hoping they understood. She rubbed her temples, that ached from the strain of crying so much. Her face hurt from swollen sinuses. Her eyes were puffy and bloodshot. She took another sip of coffee. Her mother's deep sigh made her look up at her to see her concern.

"I have to process this and I can't do that if I leave and go stay with you," she told them blankly. As much as I know you want to help, I'm not ready to put that kind of distance between the home I shared with them by going to Arizona. I need to feel close to the place we made memories, which is here, at least for now. When I'm ready, I will come stay with you guys a while," trying to sound amenable to their suggestion without flatly turning them down. She couldn't leave. She just couldn't, not yet. She couldn't think that far ahead. Not now.

Both parents looked at one another, and her dad was the first to respond, "Okay, honey, we understand. It's alright. If that's what you need right now, then we support you, and if and when you need to come back home, you know we'd love to have you there, for as long as you like or need," offering acceptance. He reached over and rubbed Hannah's arm like a father would, more than just a light caress. He wanted her to feel the depth of his love in that touch. She reached up with her other hand and cupped his appreciatively.

Her parents had never felt so helpless. Later that night, as they prepared for bed, Kathleen spoke.

"Nate, how can we just leave? I'm scared for her. I don't think she needs to be alone. It hurts so much to see her going through this. I wish I could bring them back, make this all go away, take all this pain from her," tears filling her eyes, as she looked up to her husband for answers. Her grief for Ethan and Jesse had been overwhelming, but she knew, rationally, there was nothing they could do to change how much they would miss them or make it easier to get through their own grief. Right now, Hannah was their immediate concern. As much as they loved their only grandchild and son-in-law, and as hard as it had hit them and tore their hearts out, they needed to be strong for their daughter. They knew her pain had to be so much more than their own. She was with them every day, and her world was ripped out from under her. "What do we do?" searching her husband's eyes for his wisdom and the right answer, if there was a right answer.

He placed both hands on her shoulders and looked her in the eye, "We need to let her process this. There's nothing we can do that is going to change and take away what she has to go through, and I know how you feel. I feel it too. We are going through this as a family. We are only a phone call away, and she's knows she has our support and love. I think what she needs and wants now is her time with Him," pointing upwards. We need to let her have that, because we can only do so much, Kathleen." He kissed her forehead and held her tightly. His tears fell.

Chapter Five

The Dime Fell

One moment Jesse was driving and having an unexpectedly interesting conversation with his son on the way to preschool and the next second, he was walking with Ethan in a magical place where wild animals were not afraid of humans, and he could understand all of them as they greeted them. It was the most beautiful place he had ever seen, and Ethan was instantly joyous to be there. The rabbits were flopping right up to him, faster than he could pick each one of them up. Blue birds were landing on his shoulders and humming birds were hovering in front of him and they were chirping, welcoming him. Understanding these creatures' communication had been incredible. Blue flowers blanketed the ground and adorned the trees for as far as the eye could see, which was far. Brilliant colored tropical fish swam in the bluest brook he had ever seen. Then Ethan saw some bear cubs and started running toward them growling playfully at them.

"Ethan, wait! No!" but it was too late, he was already in a pile with them. Jesse ran frantically to stop any harm to Ethan, but when he got closer, he could hear him laughing and giggling, and Jesse realized the bear cubs were having as much fun as Ethan was. The cubs recognized him! Jesse looked wildly around expecting the mother to come charging towards Ethan, rubbing his hands through his hair with increasing panic, but the cubs seemed to be alone, unattended. "What is this place?" Jesse wondered in complete amazement, feeling drunk with awe. "This place is breathtaking," everywhere he turned, vibrant with color and absolute beauty.

In the far distance, he saw a girl coming over a hill where an aqua-colored stream ran through, outlined by magenta foliage, crystal rocks, and trees of gold. Her cream-colored dress came just below her knees and flowed like that of a dancer, freely and loosely like silk. She was moving towards them with fluidity and gracefulness. Her steps were deliberate, and with each one step she took, she moved forward fifty feet, yet remained graceful and emanated both power and softness. A huge female lion walked beside her that stood as tall as a horse, instantly alarming him. She was still some ways off, but he noted he could see details much more clearly than he ever had been able to before, and he had always had perfect vision. The distance rapidly closed between them, and he saw that she had long golden blonde hair with loose curls flowing halfway down her back. Her hair seemed to have a reflection of the sun beaming off it. Her skin was creamy and smooth. Her form was petite. Her rich blue eyes glittered with specks of gold, and her lips were pale pink, very natural looking, with a pinch of color to her cheeks. She was unearthly in appearance and had on what appeared to be ballerina slippers that matched her dress, which he noted showed a slimming waistline that pointed down in the front into a V-shape. The dress was meticulously tailored, and the fabric appeared to be a very fine-looking micro fabric. She wore a string of the most exquisite pearls he had ever seen around her head, each pearl bridged to the next with white gold bridging that resembled two perpendicular shapes of a human eye with a hollow middle, that fit her head like a crown. She wore an eloquent, long silk, soft pink scarf tied loosely around her neck and hung narrowly almost to her waist. She had a subtle blue, green, and yellow aura all around her that was pulsating. He was surprised he could notice such details when he was staring into the eyes of an enormous, giant lion whose eyes came face-to-face with his own before it had lain down merely six feet away, fully facing him.

He continued to stare at the lion who seemed unperturbed. He turned slowly and looked towards Ethan and saw that he was getting up to rush over toward them.

Jesse yelled at him, "No, Ethan, don't move, Buddy, stay right where you are!" but it was too late. Ethan continued running eagerly toward them. Jesse would have to have superhuman strength to tackle this lion if it attacked his son, but he wasn't going to back down, and braced himself in the fight mode if the lion even looked like it was going to attack Ethan, who was now only a few feet from it.

"I'm Erianthé. Do not be afraid, Jesse. Ariel, pointing to the lion that rested beside her, will not harm Ethan or you. You can relax," she chuckled, then held her smile as she admired the creature beside her.

"Where are we and how did we get here, and how do you know our names?" Jesse asked her, painfully confused. Her voice was calming, and he could sense his own anxiety diminishing.

"You are in a place Ethan has created with his imagination," she answered him.

"You're saying my son created this, this … place?" he stammered doubtfully, nevertheless in awe, taking in a 360 view that seemed to flow for scores of miles and miles, not sure if he could find that to be a credible answer. "Did he create her too?" pointing at the lion and feeling completely baffled but still guarded.

"No, Ariel is far older than I am. She existed before all of us."

"Oh, that explains everything!" Jess said mockingly, not sure how to wrap his head around this experience.

Ethan was petting Ariel, who rolled over on her back to have her belly patted and rubbed. The child was so amazed and looked up and proclaimed, "Look Daddy! Ariel likes me!" giggling and laughing. "You like me, don't you?" cooing while he laid his head on her chest, as Ariel gently put her paw on his head to hug him back. He was so tiny next to the creature. Then she began licking Ethan's face, and he squealed with laughter and excitement.

"Erianthé, uh, I really need some answers. What is going on? How can any of this be possible?" scoping the scenery with his hand, waiting for an explanation. "I'm dreaming, right?" It seemed like a dream but yet he knew it was more real than anything he ever remembered in all his twenty-eight years. All those years now seemed like some kind of drama that had been played out, and this, this seemed even more real than anything he had experienced since as far back as he could remember, his first memory being when he was three!

"This is the way Ethan envisions Heaven, and because in the spirit world, we create what we desire and what we believe in, this is what he created," Erianthé explained to Jesse.

"I want to stay here, Daddy!" as he commanded Ariel to let him ride on her back so they could go play with the rabbits, and Jesse stared in disbelief as Ariel trotted off with his son. The rabbits did not shy away or seem afraid of the giant beast, nor did she hurt them, but nudged them with her nose, while the rabbits gathered around Ariel who laid down and began bathing each one of them.

"Absolutely amazing," Jesse whispered to himself, dropping his jaw. He was trying desperately to think.

"The last thing I remembered was taking Ethan to school," Jesse drifted off staring at nothing now. The reality of what was happening flooded him. He looked up, searching her eyes, not wanting it to be true. "Tell me this is all a dream."

"Jesse, your experience with your earthly life is fulfilled, as is Ethan's."

The memory seeped back to his consciousness, "We were in an accident…I remember a sudden jolt and ...." It hit him, "No! I can't leave Hannah! Our time can't be over, it can't! I have to be able to go back to her," he pleaded. He could not imagine what she must be feeling, and suddenly he felt anguish build inside him. "I need to see her again. She needs me! I have to go back!" He looked at Erianthé with intense anguish, not for himself but for Hannah.

"You have the free will to do what you want to do Jesse. No one is stopping you, but if you go back, you will be an earthbound spirit, without a physical body. Do you realize that? You will not have the physical body to continue to enjoy earth life or to experience it the same way you once did. It's possible Hannah won't realize you're there."

"You mean to tell me I can't reenter my body, that Ethan and I can't go back and be who we are, uh were?" he asked, feeling his heart sink. "That we can't be revived? Resuscitated?"

"Jesse, the injuries to your bodies were far too severe, for both of you. I'm sorry," she told him compassionately, allowing him to process the information. Erianthé knew it was natural for many who passed over suddenly to want to stay, while most of the time souls were eager to move on. Earth life was challenging and sometimes harsh, so most did not want to linger, except those who didn't get a chance to say goodbye to loved ones, who felt loose ends they needed closure to, and oftentimes did not realize they had even separated from mortal life, unless they had seen it coming, but many *don't* see it coming. Jesse and Ethan had not seen it coming, but Ethan was not old enough to really be attached to the earth's dimension yet, so he wanted to stay in the world he had created with his imagination, what he now perceived as heaven, and did not want to go back. Erianthé instinctively knew Ethan would choose to enter his mother's dreams and say his goodbye to her and comfort her in his own way.

"Then I choose to go back to be with my wife," he told her, looking over sadly at Ethan, seeing how happy he seemed to remain here. He knew Hannah would be overwhelmed with grief, and also that he was forced to choose between his son and his wife. He could see clearly Ethan was completely happy and seemed carefree, accepting of the sudden and very unexpected turn of events. "The faith of a child,"

Jesse said to himself quietly. "He seems to have naturally adjusted," watching him with amazement.

Erianthé sensed what Jesse was thinking, "You don't have to worry about him. He will be fine. I am his guardian, and I will take good care of him," she reassured Jesse. "When you're ready, Jesse, you can cross over anytime. Just as you choose to stay and comfort Hannah, you may also choose to return when you feel ready."

"I can? And how does that work if I don't come with you now?"

"You will know when that time comes. And it will not be me that you will be coming with. I am Ethan's guardian, not yours."

"Where's mine? Do I have one?"

"Everyone has one, Jesse. Of course, you do," she said, laughing now. Her soothing laughter infused him to the very core with a peace that calmed him and gave dissolution to the shock and disorientation he had been feeling. It was the light in her eyes, so full of love and calm, as if she could heal someone just by gazing into their own. "When you decide to cross over, your guardian will know and be waiting for you. You are being allowed to see Ethan is in a good place where he will be happy and safe from harm. That is why you are here with him," extending her hand, "in this place, before he proceeds to an even more glorious dimension. When you are ready to cross over, your experience will be all and more than you imagined. We each experience crossing back into the spiritual realm according to our expectations and beliefs."

Jesse sighed and looked longingly at Ethan, still playing with Ariel and the rabbits. "I need talk to my son." The feeling of acceptance and peace had washed over him. He leaned over the lion and picked up the child who had been kissing a rabbit on the top of its head and was holding it out for Ariel to kiss it, too. Ariel had gently touched her gigantic nose to the rabbit's tiny one while the rabbit displayed no fear of this predatory creature. Jesse marveled at this interaction between the lion and rabbit.

"You have to leave for a while, don't you, Daddy?"

"Yes, Little Man, I need to go check on Mommy, but I will see you again soon, I promise."

"I know, and when you and Mommy both come back, we'll all be together again," he said, smiling.

"That's right, son, we will be together, one day, all of us, soon. So, are you okay to stay with Erianthé until I come back?"

"Yeah, I am," he told Jesse resolutely with a carefree smile.

"I love you, Ethan, and Mommy loves you, and don't you forget that."

"I won't, Daddy, I promise. I love you and Mommy too!"

Jesse gave Ethan one longer hug and set him down. Looking around, he accepted they both were in the afterlife, or at least some version of it, a gateway perhaps. He was not having a dream. He instinctively knew they were in no danger and never would be. Part of him did feel a deep, permeated sense of joy and only the love that surrounded them here. Every fiber of his being was very much alive, as was Ethan's, that there was no death in physical dying, and as he had always believed, it had been an instant transition of quickening and life even greater, more wondrous; nevertheless, he was also deeply concerned for Hannah, and knew he had to return to her, knowing things would not be the same since he was minus a body now.

"Bye Daddy," Ethan shouted as he ran off with Ariel to go play with the bears, his feet not even touching the ground. Jesse could hear him laughing as he ran.

He focused on Hannah and was transported in the direction he wanted to go. He felt himself moving faster than the speed of light and was instantly in the bedroom of the house he and Hannah had shared, and she was laying a pink dress across the bed and setting out a pair of shoes. He followed her as she walked back downstairs, calling her name, but she didn't see him or acknowledge his presence. She began taking bottles of wine from a paper bag and stocking the bar and then opened a bottle and poured a glass. She seemed happy. "She must not know what's happened yet. I have to get her to listen to me!" he thought to himself. It seemed like only seconds since he was driving Ethan to school. She was still wearing what she had on that morning. Now that he was back in earth's dimension, he felt more anxious and tried to summon the peace he had felt just an instant before.

"Hannah! Please, Baby, I'm here, I need you to hear me and know that I'm here!" He could hear her softly humming, but she was totally oblivious to his presence.

Just then, the doorbell rang. Jesse transported himself to the other side of the door and saw it was two police officers and knew what they were here to tell her. He heard one of the officers tell the other one, "I hate this. It's the worst part of this job." The other one nodded solemnly. Jesse was immediately back at Hannah's side.

"No! No!! No!!! Hannah, don't open it, please don't open it," he begged, but she set her glass of wine on the coffee table and walked over and opened the door, and there they were, two police officers, removing their caps like they were getting ready to salute the flag. Jesse listened as they explained what had happened. He couldn't believe what he was hearing. He didn't remember any of it, and certainly

Ethan gave no indication of remembering any of it. He kept his eyes focused on Hannah's as she listened to the words that would turn her entire world on a spinning dime. The gleam and sparkle he always saw when he looked into her eyes was dimming, and then the dime fell, and her eyes seemed void and blank.

No wonder, knowing their thoughts and seeing in their minds what they had witnessed at the scene of the accident, Erianthé had told him the injuries were too serious, that they couldn't return. Thankfully, the officers had not gone into the details of the injuries with Hannah, but they had described the accident, which only inferred the extent of the injuries. Jesse stood behind her, had tried squeezing her arms and pressing against her trying to make her feel him there with her. When she closed the door, she seemed drained and he saw a lifelessness in her soul as if her soul itself had been anesthetized. She had run to the bathroom to vomit, and he could see the muscles in her ribcage heaving painfully. He listened as she made the necessary phone calls. Rachel! He would have to go to her. He had to go to his parents. He had to let them know he was okay! After Hannah had hung up, a glass shattered against the fireplace. He watched her sink to the floor, as her knees gave out on her. He sat down beside her and put his arms around her and tried to tell her he was alright and that Ethan was alright. He kept telling her he loved her but she was oblivious.

The wall across the room disappeared and a powerful energy with an encompassing glow flowed into the room. His eyes were penetrable. Hannah showed no signs of acknowledgment. Jesse didn't want to leave Hannah's side, but he slowly rose, and walked over to the being who had entered, thinking this was his own guardian that Erianthé had told him about. "His blue and green aura was highlighted with a hint of purple, similar to Erianthé's. "Have you come for me, because if you have, I can't leave my wife, not yet. I'm staying until I know she's okay! I haven't even been able to get her to hear me so I can say goodbye to her, so I can tell her I love her! I'm not going!"

"I'm not here for you, Jesse, he said with kindness. I'm here for Hannah," not taking his eyes off Hannah as he spoke.

"Hannah?" Jesse repeated. "Is her life over too?" he demanded.

"No, it's not over."

"Then why are you here for her, I don't understand. Is something going to happen to her?" Jesse felt panic return.

"No," he reassured him as he turned to look at Jesse. His presence was powerful and consuming. He was as tall as Jesse, but much more muscular. His stature resonated strength and his eyes were piercing and intimidating, yet Jesse saw no darkness in them. "I'm here to offer her strength through the grief she now bears."

Jesse turned and looked at his wife, who was inconsolable, barely able to breathe for the congestion that was building up from crying.

"Can you help her then?" Jesse asked desperately. "Look at her! She can't hear me! She can't see me! I feel helpless to help her!" Jesse felt anger rising because he *did* feel so helpless. He was still feeling disoriented from the transition. He felt more concerned for his wife, who was left behind to endure losing her family than he was of what awaited him. His concern for Ethan had vanished. He was happy and very much alive. If only Hannah could know that! He knew and had witnessed it firsthand. He had never seen her cry like this, and to see her in heaves and trying to catch her breath was more than he could bear.

The stranger watched Hannah intently and then slowly walked toward her. Once he was beside her, he held the palm of his right hand outstretched toward her. The heaving immediately stopped, and she laid down on the floor and closed her eyes. Her breathing quieted. She fell instantly asleep, just barely hitching her breaths.

"How did you do that?" Jesse whispered, in awe, now beside him.

"Jesse, remember who you are," he told him. When you are mortal, remembering seems an impossible task, but now that you have left your physical body, once you are reoriented to the spirit world, you will remember who you've always been. You will remember not only this mortal life, the memories of which will not be taken from you, but your infinite existence and all those memories of who you are as an eternal being will return to you. Who you are and what you can do have never been altered, not even in mortality. As a mortal, one simply does not remember anything before they were born into mortal life, but that does not and has never changed who you *are*. It's what you are able to remember that is altered when you come to earth, my friend, and what you are unable to remember about yourself, you are also unable to perceive about yourself. It will come to you," he said smiling compassionately. "Focus within. It will come to you," he reiterated. Then, he was gone.

Chapter Six

The Silhouette

September came. Hannah lie sleeping, as the sun had already come up and began to project rays of light through her bedroom window. There was total stillness, total peace as she slept. With an instant, she woke up and opened her eyes as she laid with her face towards the window. In the sunlight, there was the silhouette of a man, just standing there, watching her. She could see his outline. He had long hair and was tall and brawny, and the clothing seemed to be that of a cape or long coat hanging from his shoulders, but the sunlight behind him prevented her from seeing his face or the details of his attire. She felt totally peaceful and unafraid. She felt no threat at all, no danger posed by this Being. After a minute, her eyes reflexively blinked but she allowed them to close and stay closed a moment longer, feeling as if she could go back to sleep and somehow feeling protected by whoever this was, an angel perhaps? She opened her eyes again, and all she saw was the sunlight coming through the window. She looked around the room but saw no one.

It was the same presence she had felt the day of the accident when she felt someone was with her, watching her, after she had found out about Jesse and Ethan and had gone into shock. She vaguely remembered feeling she was not alone. Was she imagining this? It felt too real, and she knew she was not dreaming just now. She was clearly awake and had just seen someone standing in her room. Whoever it was did not frighten her but had a very high-energy presence in that his presence was unmistakable, even without seeing him. He possessed a calming presence. In that waking moment, Hannah was sure she was not alone and had not been alone since she lost her husband and son. An acute sobering of her psyche brought her into full focus.

She sat up in bed and stared toward the window where she had seen him. Why had he disappeared, she wondered? Even if she was losing her sanity, becoming psychotic, or hallucinating, she knew one thing, she felt comforted by whatever the explanation was, ... whoever. She felt she was hanging on by a thread, and she wondered if he was here to help her survive.

She remembered that Miranda told her she had set the coffee pot to have her coffee ready at eight this morning. She checked her iPhone and it said 8:35, so she decided to get out of bed and go get some coffee. She was wearing one of Jesse's long-sleeve, gray dress shirts to sleep in that hung midthigh of her legs. Her hair was mussy and all the swelling had finally gone down in her eyes after her doctor had put her on something for anxiety to help calm her. The coffee pot was half full, and she took some creamer from the frig. She sat down at the kitchen table and looked out the bay window.

There was a bird perched on the privacy fence and a humming bird flying around the bird feeder. Immediately she remembered the dream where Ethan took her to a place where there were humming birds. She reflected upon the dream, feeling it was real and that her son was in a good place, and he was happy with the things he had loved in life and was fascinated by. She sipped her coffee and watched the humming bird, believing her son was also enjoying hummingbirds. Maybe he could be watching the same hummingbird from a different dimension, she thought. It was comforting to imagine it was possible.

Then she remembered, in the dream, Ethan told her that Daddy wasn't ready to leave yet. What did that mean? She took in a deep breath and slowly exhaled. The deep breaths seemed to help, as her diaphragm felt like it had been squeezing and suffocating her in spasms. She tried to clear her mind and let answers come to her slowly.

Too much thinking had put her mind in overload, and she had been unable to function. She had finally collected herself enough to convince her parents to return home without her. They had done so reluctantly but at last gave in to her wishes. She felt she was surrounded by love, and whatever the source of it was, she wanted to be alone with it. She questioned, did it come from within or was it separate from her? Whatever it was, it was real. She hadn't told anyone she felt someone was with her, watching her, since the accident. Anyone would most certainly think she was delusional, and she wasn't sure she wasn't, but if she was, she didn't want to broadcast it.

Every microsecond of her existence felt inexplicably and unceasingly surreal. The only person she felt she could truly talk to about what she was experiencing was Miranda. She poured more coffee and walked to the living room and sat down on the couch and pulled her legs to her chest. The tears began to quietly flow, just like every other morning since they were taken from her.

She made an effort. "I know you're here. I feel you." After a long pause, her voice broken, "Am I losing my mind? How do I know if I'm not? If you're here, and I believe you are, prove to me I'm not going crazy." Immediately, the Smart TV turned on and Good Morning America filled the screen. Hannah stared at the television, and then scanned the room for the remote. It lay three feet away on the coffee table. Nothing had touched it.

"Okay," she spoke more cautiously, "I didn't turn the TV on, so that means you did," she spoke softly. "Jesse, is it you? She paused for an answer but none came. Are you the one who was standing in my room when I woke up?" She waited but no answer came, still. She turned off the TV and sat in silence. She knew someone was in the room, and she had his attention or the TV would not have come on in response to her asking for something tangible to convince her she was still sane. "Jesse, I don't know if it is you or not, but if it is you, I miss you so much." Tears welled up in her eyes. "I love you, Jesse. I will always love you. You've been in my life so long I don't know how to feel normal anymore without you and Ethan in it."

Just as she felt she was going to have another hard cry, she suddenly felt a soft brush against her face, and it felt as if her hair actually moved away from her face, but she wasn't sure. "Jesse, is it you?" Goosebumps covered her body like a blanket, and a surge filled her to the core. It felt as if there was a sudden draft. She sat, closing her eyes, trying to focus on what she was experiencing. A soft feathery touch and tingling sensation crossed her lips, and she opened her eyes hoping to see Jesse, but she saw nothing. She only felt an energy enveloping her, and whatever, whoever it was continued to calm her with his presence.

Just then, her phone rang and startled her. She hesitantly reached for it.

Hi, Mir," seeing her name in caller ID.

"Hi Sweetie, are you up or did I wake you?" She asked compassionately.

"I'm up and having some coffee. Thanks for setting the timer on the coffee pot for me."

"You're welcome. Do you mind if I come over?"

"I don't mind. I could use the company?" meaning it.

"On my way then," Miranda told her.

"Okay. See you soon, then," and ended the call. She scanned the room and sighed. "I guess this means we discuss this later," and went upstairs toward the bedroom. She changed out of Jesse's shirt and put on some white Khakis and fuchsia long-sleeve pullover. The looseness of her clothes was more significant than even a couple weeks ago. She brushed her hair and then made the bed, placing her decorative teal blue pillows neatly in the center propped against the white sham bed pillows atop the white down blanket.

The bedroom was large and spacious with the master bath adjoined to it. There were two large walk-in closets, one of which she found a pair of her flip-flops and slipped her feet into them. She walked over to the sink and forced herself to brush her teeth, then put on some soft powder pink glossy lipstick. She was not in the mood to bother with eye makeup. In fact, she had not been wearing any makeup since she had been crying so often.

Looking in the mirror, she barely recognized herself. Her face was thinner and her clavicles more prominent. She wondered who she was if she was no one's wife anymore and no longer a mother to a child. She knew she *was* in one sense but not that she could carry out the daily functions of those roles in everyday life now. The feeling was foreign to her. When she thought about it, it was overwhelming, and she didn't think she could cope with dwelling on it. She closed her eyes and took a deep breath and opened them again.

Downstairs, she picked up her cup on the coffee table and walked back to the kitchen and poured a refill and stirred in some creamer. She knew she had to embrace everything that was still the same in her life, and she had to take inventory of what those things were. They included even small things, like having to set the coffeemaker timer of a night so it was ready when she woke up. Something so slight could keep the flow going, even though Jesse was not there to do it for her anymore. It was taking a lot of willpower to do the smallest tasks. She had to fix her own breakfast and her own meals, though she had barely been eating lately. She would have to wash her own car, do the yard work herself, take her car to a garage for tune-ups and oil changes. Jesse had always done those things for her, and now he wasn't there. It wasn't that she couldn't or didn't want to do any of those things. She was most capable. It was that she and Jess had fallen into roles of who usually did what.

She found herself sobbing just thinking about how her life had been changed in the blink of an eye. Her eyes were constantly red and swollen. She couldn't imagine *not* needing to cry. It was an effort to care what she looked like anymore. She still had

Miranda, and she was a huge stability in her life; that had *not* changed. She knew Miranda was making every effort to try to cheer her, despite she had been moving past her own pain and losses. She was staying close, which Hannah was grateful. She appreciated how Miranda was encouraging her to process her grief and celebrate life. She had said to look at the bigger picture, not put her life in a box by only focusing on what was inside the box. She thought Miranda had been giving her the advice she, herself, had given to her when she was going through her divorce. It was now being returned to her. She was grateful to have a friend like her. Miranda had grieved with her, shed a thousand tears with her. Hannah was grateful Miranda had met someone, though she had been very sensitive in discussing anything to do with Alex with her the last three months.

She took another deep breath, closed her eyes, held it, and exhaled. As she started sipping her coffee, she pondered the vision she had seen that morning when she woke up. Was it Jesse who turned the TV on and who had caressed her face? The silhouette did not look like Jesse. It didn't "feel" like him either. This man had long hair and was stockier than Jesse, and Jesse did not dress like that. Reality beyond this earthy life was a mystery to her in some ways. No one truly close to her had died before. She was fortunate that her grandparents were still alive and had come to the funeral and spent a couple nights with her before driving back. She still had her parents, all her aunts, uncles, and cousins, everyone was alive, even though they all lived in Arizona and she rarely saw them. They had all come to the funeral.

She was born and raised in San Francisco, but her parents had moved back to Arizona right before she got pregnant with Ethan, which is where they were originally from. She and Jesse had roots here, and neither of them wanted to leave. She had no desire to live in Arizona. California was her home and had been Jesse's and Ethan's. A part of her wondered if she could stay in this house, but another part of her told her she had to stay, at least for now. A part of them were still here. Another part of her knew she would have to leave and live somewhere else.

The sound of the doorbell pulled her out of her thoughts. Miranda stood there smiling and holding out a bag of banana walnut ice-cream. "Your favorite," she told Hannah. She walked past her and set the ice-cream on the counter of the bar. She wore a wide grin on her face. Miranda had the theory that smiles and laughter were contagious, so she was always trying to spread it around in hopes she could create an epidemic. Hannah obliged her and pulled up a chair at the bar. Miranda set a plastic container in front of her and proudly told her, "I made cinnamon rolls this morning," obviously proud of how they turned out. "I ground the cinnamon myself, and I already did a taste test, and they are absolutely delicious. Have one!" It was not a question. It was like a parent telling a child, "You have to eat!"

Hannah took one and bit into it. "Really good, Mir," still chewing.

"I thought you would like them," smiling.

"You're so thoughtful," swallowing hard and trying to nibble smaller bites. She knew she needed to eat.

Miranda's smile softened as she became more serious, "I can't begin to imagine what this feels like for you, but when I try to imagine, all I know is I don't know how I would handle it without a friend like you." She was almost pokerfaced as she said it because she honestly didn't know what she would feel. It has got to be one of the worst things anyone could feel, a loss like no other in comparison, and I'm not going to be one of those people who says, "I know how you feel, because I don't. I only know it is beyond imagination. So, I'm going to be here for you anytime of any day, day or night, 24/7, ya got that?"

"I've got it," Hannah nodded, as she took another bite followed by a sip of hot coffee. "You're my person," she told Miranda.

"You're damn straight I am." Miranda knew if ever she was in a situation that her world was turned upside down, Hannah would be there for her without hesitation.

Hannah needed to talk about what she had been experiencing, and she trusted Miranda to take her seriously without judgment, "Something is happening, but I don't want you to think I'm crazy when I tell you," pausing, trying to figure out the right words to say it.

"Is it the dreams? Are you still having them?"

"No. It's strange. I haven't had one like what I described to you since I told you about them, the day…."

"Hannah, I've known you long enough to know you are one of the sanest people I know. You don't have to worry I'm going to think you're crazy but even still, with everything you've gone through and are still going through, you would be entitled to some crazy," touching her hand.

"Someone has been here with me, I believe. No, I know it," measuring her words.

Miranda appraised her and knew Hannah would not tell her that if she thought there was a chance she was imagining it. "What's been happening?" she asked, with trepidation.

"I've been sensing someone is here," Hannah told her, "someone concerned about me, someone I don't feel afraid of. This morning, though, I woke up and I saw the distinct silhouette of a man with long hair and something like a cape or a long piece of clothing draped over him standing in front of my bedroom window as the sunrays were coming in the window. I couldn't see the details of his face, but I don't believe it is Jesse, because Jesse didn't have long hair. After I came downstairs and got some coffee I sat on the couch and I felt a presence with me, so I spoke to whoever it is and asked if I was going crazy. The television came on, just like that! The remote control was three feet away on the coffee table, and I swear I hadn't touched it. Mir, something is happening and I don't know what to think. I don't know if the dreams I have had are related to this. I felt a hand brush against my face, and I could have sworn something touched my lips. I considered I was being delusional, but I did *not* imagine the TV turning itself on. I had to reach for the remote to turn it off."

Miranda didn't believe Hannah was delusional. She didn't believe she imagined it. Two people she loved and who were a significant part of her life were taken from her tragically and unexpectedly. Miranda believed in earthbound souls, spirit guides, a Higher Power, and the afterlife, and so somehow this did not surprise her.

"Hannah, you are not crazy! Don't even question that. Whoever it is either has unfinished business or is trying to communicate something to you, probably with the intension of comforting you. There's nothing to be afraid of. Sometimes when someone dies suddenly and tragically, they aren't ready to go. They may not even realize they are...."

"Dead?" Hannah finished the sentence, lowering her eyes to her lap.

"Yeah, I didn't want to use that word, but yes. The soul doesn't die, but the body does, so in truth, no one truly *dies*. I really don't like that word. It's the opposite of truth. Dead. There really is no such thing of a person dying. It's a false perception. Death is life. It's such a contradictory description of a life transition!"

Hannah continued, "Mir, when I was in the hospital, I had a dream that was as real as you and I sitting here talking right now. I dreamt that I ran to Ethan's room and he was there, and he was proud of himself for mastering a Rubik's cube, and said it was easy now that he figured it out. He told me that his daddy wasn't ready to leave yet, but that *he* wanted to

136

go, and then he took my hand and instantly, we were in a different place, unlike anything I've ever seen before, and it was so beautiful, and the more I thought about it, it seemed it was a place of Ethan's creation because what was in it were the things that he loved. It was as if the place had been designed just for him."

Miranda listened intently, feeling glad that Hannah had experienced and remembered this dream. "Go on," as she drew in closer giving Hannah her undivided attention.

As Hannah told her what she had seen in the dream, Miranda smiled with tears streaming down her cheeks. "He's in a good place, now Sweetie. Ethan is okay! He's still alive but just in a different dimension that we can't see."

"Hannah looked at her and agreed, "I know," half smiling but obviously very sad.

"You have to trust Jesse is alive, too, in a good place, and it would not be uncommon if it was him trying to reassure you and comfort you, to allow you closure, before he moved on and crossed over," Miranda assured her.

"I believe that, Mir. I really do."

Miranda took Hannah's hand. "You may never understand why this happened, but you can learn to accept it and move on from it, grow from it, and I truly believe you have someone, whoever it is, trying to help you do that."

"Thanks for believing me," Hannah told her, feeling relieved.

"Of course, I do," unequivocally, leaning in, raising her second and third fingers and pointing them directly toward both her own eyes and nodding. "I believe you completely."

Hannah nodded speechlessly.

"Let's get you out of the house today," Miranda suggested. "We'll go shopping, plan on getting some pictures, try to resume some normalcy. You need it, honey. We can go for a drive and just drive wherever, it doesn't matter, wherever spontaneity leads us. What do ya say?"

Hannah thought about it. She knew she desperately needed to get out of the house, "Sure, okay, I probably do need to get out of here a while. I've been feeling like I'm losing my mind."

Chapter Seven

The Road Trip

Miranda and Hannah stopped at a fruit stand and bought some grapes and bananas, so they could snack while on the road. Miranda drove along Highway 1 going north until they arrived in Mendocino. It was midafternoon. A quaint grill restaurant next to the ocean seemed like a good place to enjoy a glass of white wine. There were open windows from wall to wall with a mix of rustic and modern design with vaulted ceilings. The solid wood walls from floor to ceiling gave a blended atmosphere that felt inviting, spacious but yet cozy. The dining area was bright, allowing the sunlight to naturally light the room. The sunlight bounced off the ceilings throughout dispersing natural sunlight.

"I love this place," Miranda commented in awe, as she took it all in.

Hannah nodded, "Yeah, it's really nice," glancing around.

They sat next to a window and sipped their wine and watched the ocean waves roll into the shore. Neither of them was hungry yet so thought they would hold off on dinner. The sun was bright without a cloud in sight. Hannah tried to allow her mind to clear and take in the calming view.

"Why don't we lodge here tonight?" Miranda suggested. It's beautiful here and we can explore, take pictures, breathe in the salty air, and spend a couple days, or longer," she added. "I have Aristotle on a timed automatic feeding dish. With him being declawed, he can go outside and drink out of the fish pond, so there's no need for either one of us to hurry back tonight," trying to be persuasive. "It will be good for both of us."

Hannah smiled weakly, "I'd like that." The hollowness and anguish of not having anyone to return home to daunted her. She was trying to move forward, embracing the memories that she would always cherish, embracing her pain, attempting to heal while trying to gently let go without feeling guilty. She could finally accept the drastic change in her life. Her rational mind told her that's what she needed to do. Her heart felt like it had a heavy stone tied around it that plunged her to the depth of despair. She might as well have been at the bottom of the ocean she now gazed upon with reverence. The ocean that had always helped her feel centered and one with the universe was one she now imagined being swallowed up by it.

They checked into a room with two queen-size beds. Like the restaurant, it had the comforts of a mixture of modern and rustic design with vaulted ceiling and modern furniture. The wall hangings accentuated the rooms with a longing comfort. The large open windows provided them a perfect ocean view. Outside, there were wooden lawn chairs near the shore where one could lazily look out over the surrounding mountains. Hannah closed her eyes briefly and took a slow, deep breath, tasting the salty breeze. Pulling her camera out of her bag, Miranda took some photos of Hannah before she rejoined her.

"How are you and Alex doing?" Hannah asked. The winds blew her hair around her face prompting her to keep needing to tuck it behind her ears.

"It's coming along, but do you really want to talk about that right now, considering?

"I feel like I need to focus on the tangible as much as I can. I mean, look out there. It's so vast and infinite. To imagine my husband and my son out there, beyond that, so far away, where I can't see them, hear them, touch them, hug them, it's overwhelming, and I haven't been handling it well, not when I imagine it that way, anyways. It's like they are an entire universe away. It's really hard, Mir. So, talk about Alex. I don't want to keep feeling sorry for myself. Besides, I could use something cheerful. I don't want to become completely disconnected, you know? It would just be self-defeating. You haven't even mentioned him since I got out of the hospital. Talk to me! Really, I don't mind," she begged. She didn't want Miranda to stop living her life just because she had lost a large part of her own.

"Okay," Miranda started, "but you let me know if...."

Hannah interrupted her. "Mir, just tell me, please. I want to know."

"Okay. We talk on the phone every day, sometimes two or three times. He's been coming over on nights when I'm not at your place, and we play trivia, work puzzles, and have long conversations about anything and everything. We've continued to date, and it seems to be going okay; I mean we get along and have an amazing attraction to each other, so we'll see what happens, ya know." She forced her tone to be more melancholy to curtail her excitement of the new relationship.

"You guys should come over one night together and maybe we could just fix some popcorn or order a pizza and watch a movie. I don't want you to feel you can't bring him over," Hannah told her. "I know you don't want me to feel like a third wheel, and I don't want you worrying about it. It is what it is, and I know it's a part of life we all experience, so I'm determined to get through this because I can't keep feeling how I'm feeling. I have to *will* myself to get through this."

"He hasn't wanted to intrude. He's really sensitive like that. He asked about you all the time because he knows you're my best friend, and he's really sweet and understanding. Neither one of us wanted to dangle our relationship in your face. It didn't seem like it was the right thing to do. I would never want to do that to you. You have too much on your plate to process and work through."

"It's okay, really. Seeing you happy will do me good, and you shouldn't feel you can't share your happiness with me. It reminds me that life has to go on and is still meant to be happy. There is happiness all around, wherever you look, you'll find someone smiling or in love, and I don't want you to feel discouraged in sharing yours with me. I'm still your friend and as a friend, I am not going to treat your happiness like some kind of contraband you're not allowed to have. I'm not playing warden here. What I'm going through, I own it. It's for me to deal with. You're my friend but you don't own the problem. It's nice having you on my support team though," she smiled sincerely. I don't want to block out all else that can sustain me and being hush-hush around me makes me feel like I'm going to sink fast. So, come on, I need girl talk.

"If you're absolutely sure, then I will invite him to come with me. Just let me know when," she said, trying to be agreeable. Miranda didn't want to create conflict about it by disagreeing, but she knew she would tread softly when it came to bringing Alex around. "And if you change your mind at the last minute, that's okay, too."

"No, I need to be around people. I feel like I'm losing my mind sometimes, being alone. I always feel there is someone with me, and I can't live my life talking to a ghost! I'll go nuts and I don't think it's healthy for me, do you?"

Miranda weighed her reply carefully, "I think you need to be able to evolve towards gaining some closure and heal from this, whatever that takes, and if that means talking to Jesse's ghost, then like I told you before, I don't think that's crazy at all. I think it's natural to want to talk to them, especially at first, or maybe the remainder of your life. I mean, we are primarily spiritual beings, and for us to act otherwise, that's what is *not* natural!"

"I haven't actually sensed Ethan around. He just comes to me in my dreams, reassuring me he's okay, he's happy, and that helps, but you're right. I guess it's just a different experience for me. I feel out of my comfort zone with all of it, but at the same time, I don't feel scared or afraid. I just feel like I've lost a huge part of myself. They were my life. You know?"

"I know, sweetie, but everyone needs to feel a sense of individuality that is not dependent on others to determine or validate our happiness. Everyone should be able to be alone with themselves and enjoy their own company without feeling they can't function by themselves. Jesse and Ethan have transitioned to another place. They didn't divorce you or abandon you. They were promoted to a place of magnificent grandeur, and when it's your time, God forbid that be soon, you will join them. The end here is not the end there, and that is the way you have to look at it. When you start looking at just the moment, the now, it's overwhelming, but when you look at the grander scale, this lifetime is but a pin drop in infinite time, which is what we all live in," she emphasized. "Life should be celebratory. Every dimension of it," she added. "Keep reminding yourself we are all just at a pin drop between infinity and infinity. Say it."

"We are all just at a pin drop between infinity and infinity," Hannah repeated. "I don't know what I would do at this pin drop if you weren't pin dropped beside me," she said amused by the analogy, smiling.

"That's right, we stick together girlfriend," Miranda teased, starting to laugh.

Hannah smiled, and closed her eyes again. "I feel like I could sit here and just listen to the sound of the waves and seagulls all day."

"Oh no! We are going to walk around and get some fresh new pics! This is a great vacation spot. Might as well get some scenic snapshots in.

"Which reminds me, just because I took time off doesn't mean you had to stop working, too," Hannah told her.

"I don't work because I need the money, you know that. I work because I enjoy it. Besides, I wanted time off anyway. I loved them too, you know. I miss them, too. You guys have been like family to me. You're like my sister."

"Thanks, Mir."

"Just stating the fact is all."

After a couple of drinks, they decided to just walk around and do some light exploring. There was an old, gray barn near the shore where there was an old, wooden gray, rotted fence leaning over leading up to the barn. Miranda shot a few photos of it. "Let me get some pics of you," she told Hannah, who maintained her natural stance. She moved casually along the beach where they came to some tall rocks and a cove. Miranda shot one frame after another.

Finally, Hannah said, "I should take some pictures of you. Here, give me the camera." Miranda was as photogenic as Hannah. Being natural always resulted in the best photos. It was good therapy to be using a camera again. She was wise enough to know she had to push through her pain and grief whether she was in the mood or not. She willed herself to try. The more snapshots she took, the more she felt reconnected with life around her. She was grateful Miranda had suggested taking this road trip and had brought the camera.

Later they visited an art gallery in town and studied the different paintings, each section of the gallery being named after someone or having a different theme. Afterwards, they attended an antique car show and visited adjacent shops, first being a chocolate shop, where they bought a small bag of dark chocolate bark, another being a candle shop filled with inviting scents, and Miranda found an air freshener to hang in her car that smelled like lilac. Lastly, they visited a clothing store where they each bought a couple of summer fall dresses, a pair of jeans, sweats, hoodies, pull-over tops, socks, sleepwear, and a fresh pairs of underwear, since neither of them had packed a bag. They were both already wearing tennis shoes, but not knowing how long they would stay, they wanted to have a garment for whatever the weather was. The nights tended to be cool and breezy. Afterwards, they walked back to the car and put their bags in the trunk.

"Hey, I saw a pizza bar down the street when we came in. Sound good?" Miranda asked.

"Sure, I'm starting to feel a little hungry now. Are we walking or driving?"

"We can walk, it's not far, a couple of blocks maybe."

"Okay, let's check it out."

The thin-crusted sausage, pepperoni, mushroom, and black olive medium-size pizza and a glass of merlot hit the spot. Johnny Cash's *I Walk the Line* filled the bar. The band had talent. Every song they sang sounded like the original artist. Nearly every seat in the house was taken, and many were standing around and people watching. Miranda comically sang to some of the lyrics and moved gently to the beat. Hannah was thankful to have a friend that could actually humor her right now.

"Too bad they don't have karaoke. That would be so fun! Remember when we used to do Karaoke in college? It was such a blast!" Miranda giggled thinking about it.

"I remember being ousted for not being able to carry a tune," Hannah said woefully.

"What are you talking about? You have a beautiful voice! You just were shy is all," Miranda chided. After that is when Jesse proposed to you! You sealed his heart trying to sing that song, uh, what was it?" Miranda tried to remember.

"*Hero*, by Mariah Carey," Hannah reminded her.

"That's right, that's right. I thought you carried a tune quite well! You're throat just got a little dry a few times is all," she said still laughing and Hannah joined her.

"Remember that song, Jesse sang afterwards? He kind of sealed the deal too, you know," Hannah reminisced.

"I remember, alright. *This Guy's in Love With You* by Herb Alpert! Oh yeah, a song that would melt any woman's heart! That song was like from the sixties!" she added, shaking her head back and forth, "Good song! It was perfect."

"It was one the craziest and happiest nights of my life," Hannah said, "and really memorable," starting to feel emotional. "I miss him," she admitted.

"I know you do," was all Miranda could say. She watched her and could tell she needed to get out of here. "Hey, I'm getting a bit sleepy from so much wine. How about we go ahead and get settled into our room? What do ya say?"

"Sounds good to me," Hannah agreed, getting up from her seat.

They edged through a narrow path toward the door. Both the crowd and noise level had grown, and it was getting stuffy. Hannah followed Miranda through as they made their way to the door, excusing themselves as they squeezed by. There was a group of friends near the exit, some of who had drank themselves into inebriation. One was wearing solid black, long-sleeve knit pullover and black pants and had thick, wavy black hair, was clean-shaven, and looked like a male model with an ego. His buddy was a copper-haired guy with shorter hair and brown pullover sweater and jeans.

They were almost to the door when the one in black moved forward to grab Hannah from behind in a most ungentlemanly manner. Before his hand made contact with her, he was thrust down, sprawled out with his face against the floor. He hurriedly got up and looked around him. His nose was trickling blood from where his face hit the floor, leaving him considerably dazed and confused as to what had happened. Nearby onlookers were looking around to see who had pushed him.

His buddy with the copper hair was stupefied, "Don't look at me, I didn't do it."

The guy got back to his feet with effort, "Did you just freaking knock me down?" his high-pitched voice demanded.

"I swear, I didn't do it, man. I don't know who did," looking at the other patrons standing next to them.

Those standing next to him were puzzled, everyone looking at each other. Hannah and Miranda were never the wiser. By the time, he was back on his feet, Hannah and Miranda were both in their car, pulling out of the parking lot. The stranger and Jesse had been with them the entire time.

"How did you do that?" Jesse asked.

"Let's just say, I've had a lot more time to learn," the stranger told him."

"I wanted to punch his face!" Jesse told him.

The stranger's expression told him, "I already did."

As the women left to go back to the hotel, they were not alone.

Chapter Eight

Taking a Hike

The bags were emptied on the beds and clothes they had bought earlier were hung on hangers. Miranda sat in the middle of one of the queen beds after taking her shoes off and started nibbling on her dark chocolate bark. She patted the bed in front of her and told Hannah to come sit. She offered her the small bag of candy and Miranda purred, "It's chocolate time, oh yeah," with satisfying lust. Miranda's eyes rolled back and forth, as she moaned at the taste of her favorite candy. Then she broke out into song.

"What the world, needs now, is sweet choc-o-late ...."

Hannah couldn't help but grin at her. She had a natural gift for being comical and could easily have been a comedian. It was the way she approached much of life, but she knew when to refrain.

"Hey, did you see those chocolate drops they had in there?" she asked Hannah.

"I can't say that I did," Hannah said, as she took another bite.

"Well, they had milk chocolate, dark chocolate, sugar-free chocolate, and I was so tempted to get a bag of *them*, too, but gotta watch my waistline," she said teasingly.

Hannah was amused, because Miranda had never had to make an effort to keep her weight healthy. She simply enjoyed life, and dieting was not her thing. She always said, "If you think you are going to get fat eating foods you really like, then you will get fat. It's all in what you believe," and Hannah wondered if there was truth to that philosophy. Miranda never wanted the added stress of constant dieting, but she was by nature active enough she never had a weight problem. Miranda reached for another piece of candy.

"This has been a wonderful day, Mir. Thank you, truly meaning it. "I think I'm going to go take a shower." Her new solid light teal pajamas were laying on the bed, and Hannah picked them up and carried them in the bathroom with her and turned on the shower.

Miranda picked up her cellphone and called Alex. He answered on the second ring.

"Hey, Babe, how's the road trip? Where did you end up going?" He sounded relaxed with a lazy drawl.

"Mendocino. It's been nice. We're going to stay the night, but we've had a good day. She's smiling and even starting to laugh some, so that's good, ya know."

"Yeah, that *is* good," he replied.

"I'm just doing what friends should do. We spent the day walking the shores and taking some pictures. We walked around town. It's nice here, historical and small. She needed to get away from the city, and it seems to have been good for her so far."

"I think it's a good idea, Miranda." She heard him sigh lazily. "I miss you, Babe," he added.

"Miss you too," she reciprocated affectionately.

"I'll see you when you get back, then," Alex told her.

"Yes, you will," Miranda cooed at him sweetly. She heard a delightful chuckle in response.

"I can't wait for you to be back, Babe. You two ladies have fun, relax, and pamper yourself. You deserve it," he assured her.

"Thanks, I love you," meaning it.

"Love you, too," he told her. She blew him a kiss through the phone, something she often did before they hung up. "Back at you," he said, smiling.

After they hung up, Miranda reflected on how far their relationship seemed to have come in the last couple months. She had committed to not living in fear of "what if," because if she did, she could be blowing a second chance. She was going to reach for the stars and accept whatever happiness life would offer her, knowing she had to get rid of the wall she had built. She got her camera out and sat on the bed and started going through the pictures they had taken earlier in the day, not prepared for what she saw.

Hannah had stepped into the shower and begun washing her hair and letting the hot water wash down over her body, feeling she was trying to wash the emptiness away. Tears began to stream down her face, but the water washed them away. She lathered herself and rinsed her hair. Then she sank to the floor, weeping quietly. It seemed nearly twenty minutes had passed. She pulled herself together, not wanting Miranda to know she just had a meltdown, because she was trying so hard to cheer her up. She did not want her to feel she was failing. She had felt a calm being away from the city, in a less populated area, away from the house, away from everything, and she believed this had been good for her, but it was going to take a long time, if ever, before she felt she could feel happy again.

Maybe the day would come when she would have some semblance of a happy life again, but she couldn't even imagine that right now. Her happy, carefree life had been ripped from her. There was no getting it back. She turned off the water, grabbed a large bath towel and wrapped it around herself, and stepped out of the shower.

In front of her, on the steamed mirror was written, "I'm still here." Hannah stared at it. She turned full circle, looking around her. She saw nothing. She could feel the sudden acceleration of her heart as it began pounding in her chest. Hot tears flowed down her face, as she tried to grasp what was happening. The door had been locked, so no chance anyone was in the bathroom with her playing a prank, and she knew Miranda would never do such a thing. The only explanation was that there *was* someone there she couldn't see, someone who desperately was trying to communicate with her.

Hannah burst out of the bathroom with her hair soaking wet and the towel wrapped around her the size of a beach towel, startling Miranda.

"Mir?" she said, now standing frozen in place, tears still streaming down her face.

Miranda cautiously walked towards her, slowly, until she moved past her into the bathroom to see the writing on the mirror that was becoming covered with more steam, but still quite visible. Miranda stopped and stared at it and looked at Hannah.

"It was there when I got out of the shower. I know it has to be him. He's here. Jesse is here," Hannah said, almost in a whisper.

"I think you should see this," Miranda said cautiously, as she walked back to the bed and picked up the camera. "These are the pics from earlier today. Okay, I've gone back to the first picture, after lunch when we were sitting on the lawn chairs outside the restaurant. Now, start here and keep going," as she handed the camera to Hannah. "I think you need to sit down," and led Hannah to the bed closest to the bathroom where they both sat on the foot of the bed.

As she began scrolling through the pictures, Hannah stared in shock, her mouth nearly gaping open. She slid her finger across the screen rapidly from picture to picture. When she got to the end, she started all over. In the pictures Miranda had taken of her sitting outside earlier in the day, there was a semi-visible, white, transparent gas-like image in the form of a man sitting next to her with his hand placed on Hannah's forearm near her wrist. It was blurred without clearly recognizable features but definitely a man. She could faintly see the eyes, nose, and mouth, neck, torso, and limbs, though ever so faintly. Later, at the barn, the same image was standing beside her, facing her, as she looked out towards the sea, but in the next shot Miranda had taken of her at the barn, the same image had remained beside her, now looking down and reaching for her hand, but further in the distance, off to the side was yet another image, whose features were somewhat clearer but identity not recognizable. Hannah zoomed in and studied the images. There were distinct human facial features, hair, somewhat blurry but enough to tell they were both human and were men, by the way they dressed and their stature. The one in the distance had a brighter outer white energy force than the one closest to her, and his features slightly more distinct.

"We should enlarge these on a computer," Miranda said emphatically. "The hotel should have one. I think it is safe to say Jesse has stayed behind for you, sweetie. Who else could it be? and now the writing on the mirror! The question is, who is the second person?" Miranda queried, feeling puzzled. "You're not losing your mind, and here's the proof!" Miranda continued, her voice filled with compassion.

"Someone really is with you, Hannah. Someone who obviously cares a great deal for you."

Hannah continued studying the pictures, trying to enhance the details. She recalled feeling there was someone with them today, and at times, it felt is if her breath could just bounce off of whoever or whatever it was, it had felt so close. She had been feeling a lot of that lately, but now these pictures confirmed she was not imagining it. She really was not losing her mind, even though she still felt like it.

Miranda continued her train of thought, "The hotel should have a computer room for the patrons. I'll call the front desk." She got up and walked toward the hotel phone on the night stand.

Hannah once again could feel someone next to her, so she sat the camera down gently on the bed, and just closed her eyes. She focused within, and Miranda's voice drowned out as she was talking to the front desk clerk.

"Hannah?" she heard a faint whisper. "I'm here. I love you so much." She could almost swear it was Jesse's voice, the way he had spoken to her so many times when he had told her he loved her. Who *else* would be telling her this?

"Jesse?" she whispered, not even audible for Miranda to hear her over her own voice, still on the phone.

She felt a chill as if something gentle had touched her face, a tingling sensation like another energy field brushing against her.

"They said they do have a computer room we can use on the first floor. As soon as you can get dressed, let's go and get these enlarged," Miranda said urgently, after she hung up the phone.

The look on Hannah's face stopped her. "What is it?" she asked.

"Let's slow down. I feel really overwhelmed, and I just need to slow down and breathe." She was starting to hyperventilate. Don't rush me, okay," Hannah pleaded hoarsely, still staring straight ahead.

Then she looked at Miranda, "I've been feeling someone with me since they've been gone, having my TV turn on by itself, waking up to dreams, waking up to seeing someone standing in my room, writings on the mirror, and now to see these," recounting the events while pointing to the camera on the bed.

Miranda sat down next to her and didn't interrupt, as she listened.

"I just can't rush to a computer and blow these up to only magnify what I'm feeling. I just, just feel even more overwhelmed on top of already having been overwhelmed as it was, so let's stop right here and take it down a notch, for now, okay?"

"It's okay, Hannah. You're right. We're getting worked up and excited. I'm sorry," and hugged her.

Hannah closed her eyes and took deep breaths and slowly exhaled, trying to calm herself from shaking and dissuade the mounting anxiety, heart racing, and accelerated breathing she desperately felt she needed to gain control over.

The realization that the man she had fallen in love with, married, had a home and a child together with, neither of them were any longer here in a physical form. Their mangled bodies were buried in closed caskets, but yet, was this truly Jesse's spirit still with her? Was that what he looked like now, what she had just seen on camera? Her eyes were unable to discern an accurate image of him. Ethan had not looked like that in her dream. He looked like he had before. The realization hit her that a camera could only reflect this kind of image of Jesse now, without a physical body, not the image she had of him in her memories or in so many other pictures that she had of him in her wallet and at home, pictures of them together, *in the flesh*.

Then she had to wonder, could the other one be Ethan? His spirit could be an adult, even though he was a child when he died. All the thoughts were racing through her mind, but the fact that she had now seen these images on camera felt eerie and were etched in her mind. She wasn't sure if she should be comforted or utterly alarmed. At the same time, seeing these images proved she had not been imagining things she had been experiencing. She had not lost her mind, and the reality of it all came rushing in, flooding her, and she felt unable to welcome it, not yet, even though a part of her desperately wanted to and needed to. She wanted to run, shut down, close the shades of her soul and lock everything out until she could catch her breath and digest it all.

"I'm sorry," Miranda repeated softly with sincere remorse at having shown her the pictures immediately after what she had seen on the bathroom mirror. How had she not realized how Hannah might be feeling in the midst of feeling a bit freaked, herself. She thought she would welcome the evidence being presented that proved everything that was happening to her was real, that she was wanting to get to the bottom of it, the truth.

"We'll do whatever you want to do, whenever you decide what that is."

Hannah began, "It's too much to take in all at once. I don't feel afraid. I just feel like I'm caught between two different dimensions, each different from the other. I don't even know how to describe it."

She paused and Miranda waited quietly, still not wanting to interrupt her, seeing she was in deep thought and trying to find the words she wanted to say.

"All I can say is, my mind and my body are on overload trying to handle an energy brushing against me, trying to get my attention, a reality that is already hard to accept, and to even think that what I am seeing in those pictures could be the same man who made love to me, who I made love to, who was my husband and the man I woke up to each day, went to bed with each night, who fathered our child, who is . . . the man who liked to cook for me, who provided for us, who took me on dates, who I laughed with, adored, and who was taking me on a date that night, and I look at those pictures, and it just all comes flooding in on me, this is *him*, and the image is so different than the man I had been used to seeing every day. It's so different from all the other pictures I have of him." Hannah began to sob uncontrollably. "And I think about Ethan and the change in both their existences, the absence of bones, flesh, a body, how I remember them, but yet, I know they exist, and now I know I'm not imagining out of grief that Jesse is still here, trying to communicate with me. I try to imagine what he must be feeling to have stayed and to be so desperately trying to communicate with me, and the frustration we both feel at everything that has changed in each of our lives, both our lives! I just feel so much welling up inside me all of a sudden. I haven't even accepted the fact that they are gone, Mir. I don't know how else to explain it," Hannah said with tears free-flowing down her face. "I need to know what he's trying to tell me."

Hannah curled up in her bed facing Miranda, who could see her friend was having a meltdown and was panicking. Miranda decided the best way to calm her down was by *exuding* calmness rather than feed into the panic. In that vein, she casually laid down on the side of her own bed, placed her forearm up so that the cup of her hand supported her head in an effort to appear relaxed and in control. It was the best psychology she could think of at the moment. Her words were calm and relaxed as she spoke.

"Listen with your heart, and you will find out what he wants you to know," Miranda said and then repeated to emphasize, "Listen with your heart," now whispering. After a few minutes, Hannah had not moved or said anything else.

"Goodnight," Miranda said as she reached over and turned off the lamp.

At 7:30, Miranda was up, had pulled on a pair of pink sweats, a gray T-shirt, and a matching hoodie and walked downstairs to get some coffee and some breakfast. She returned to see Hannah still sleeping, so she set the coffee and oat muffins on the nightstand between the two beds. Ten minutes later she stepped out of the shower. There was no writing on the mirror, thankfully, she thought to herself. She had felt a little freaked out last night, not because she didn't believe in those kinds of things, but because she had never seen physical evidence that she trusted had not been tampered with, and besides, believing in it and actually seeing it took it to another level. The pictures left no room for doubt. She dried off and put her jeans on, brushed her fingers through her hair, and left the bathroom. Hannah was still sleeping.

She reached down and touched her gently, "Hey, there's coffee and banana walnut muffins if you're hungry," she said softly. Hannah stirred and opened her eyes. "Hey," she said. She focused her eyes on the coffee and muffin, then sat up Indian-style picking up the creamer and stirring it into her coffee.

Thanks. How long you been up?"

"Thirty minutes, maybe."

"What time is it?"

"It's about 8:00 now. How did you sleep?" Miranda asked.

"I was totally out. I don't even remember dreaming."

"Good. You needed the rest." Miranda continued, "Are you still up for hiking today?"

"I am. I think it will be good stress relief. Let's do it," Hannah said decidedly. She welcomed clearing her head with exercise, if only for a little while.

"I did some checking, and there is a scenic trail not far away. We'll have to drive to get to it though. It's probably at least four miles of hiking, but it is in some really steep, wooded terrain."

"Sounds good. Thanks, Mir, for this. For everything you're doing, truly."

Miranda smiled, "Don't thank me. It's good for both of us. It's good to get away." Miranda sat down next to her and put her arm around her. "We girls stick together, no matter what. We're a team."

An hour later, they had found the trail that could only be entered on foot or with a mountain bike, but the path was clearly defined, looping through primitive, steep terrain, the elevation of which rose quickly through a thick redwood forest that wrapped around mountain ridges and was home of pygmy cypress, pines, spruces, and fir trees. They brought only a small carry bag each to carry bottled water and a map. Cellphones were in their bags. It was cool and still early. The sun was peeking through the thick forest of trees from the east. The trail was uphill and narrow with unmarked paths that occasionally bifurcated into other trails.

The towering redwoods were beautiful and a good place to hook up with nature. "Come on, let's get started," Miranda started ahead of her. The trail did not seem steep at first, but after a couple of miles, they took a different trail off the beaten path, that met with steeper more rugged terrain. They stopped a few times for a break and to take a drink of water. Ferns were getting thicker as was a lot of the other brush. The trail was getting narrower. A couple of hours had passed since they had started but had finally come to a clearing. They had seen other hikers and bicyclists on the main trail but up here, they had not encountered anyone so far. They traversed on a little further, until they saw an overlook and, in the distance, could see a blue river. Looking down, they guessed they had climbed easily a couple thousand feet.

They stopped and straddled a tree log and gave their muscles a break. Hannah's felt the broad bark as she laid back against it and put one knee up, looking up into the opening amid the tree tops where she could see open sky.

"Can you imagine living in a cabin up here in a place like this?" Hannah asked. She seemed completely at peace lying there.

"I think I could imagine, yes. Boy, wouldn't that be different, no traffic, no horns, no sirens, no-one, just the trees and nature."

"Exactly," Hannah replied, still in her daydream. "I can see why people do it, move away. There is so much solitude, and I think I understand now why some people really need that, why it appeals to them. Funny, I had never thought about it much. I've lived in the city all my life, and it's what I've always been used to, but lately, I've felt like getting away. I felt like I wanted to escape, but right this moment, it feels like the wilderness is like a healing balm to the soul that is beckoning me. I feel connected here to something greater than I am. I love the silence and the quiet. It's so inviting."

She seemed like she was lost in her thoughts, drifting into a peaceful oblivion. There was a quiet majestic feeling and they both sensed it. Miranda closed her eyes and listened to the sound of silence.

"It is, isn't it? It's like the trees are nurturing and embracing us, reaching out to us in some strange way. Everything feels so alive up here, just so alive," she whispered in awe. "I believe trees and everything have a soul, and they communicate if only we pay attention and learn how to understand their language," Miranda continued.

"I never thought about that before, but I think that's what I'm feeling. I wonder what kind of soul a tree or a plant could have, or a rock, but yet, I do feel connected. It seems if we feel connected, they must have a soul."

"The Native Americans always believed so. I've always thought we could learn a lot from them, personally," Miranda said thoughtfully.

"Me too. When you're out here with nothing but silence and only the sounds of nature, it feels to me that the invisible energy is truth and love. A universe of truth, hidden in the silence like a much sought-after treasure. I think we tend to get lost from it and need to be reminded that it still exists."

"Yeah, it kind of does feel that way," Miranda agreed, as she laid back on the log and crossed her hands over her chest almost reverently. "Nature in itself is majestic," she said finally.

They laid there totally relaxed until some squirrels scurrying around in the leaves startled them.

"Look how cute!" Miranda exclaimed, watching them. Hannah climbed down from the log and walked up next to her.

"Looks like they understand the meaning of life more than most people," she said smiling, regaining her sense of humor.

Miranda nodded in agreement, and they began walking again.

Since getting up this morning, neither had mentioned what happened last night. Miranda really wanted to talk about it, but she wasn't going to push. Hannah seemed more interested in connecting with nature than disembodied souls for the time being. She pulled her camera out and hung it around her neck, now that they were high enough they had spectacular views from different points along the trail, she thought she may sneak in a few pictures of Hannah to see if anyone was around her. They continued walking until they came to another clearing where they could look down in all directions. The view was breathtaking. Miranda took shots of the mountainous terrain and small tributaries. The sky was clear and they could see for miles. The panoramic view was beautiful.

"We should probably head back," Miranda said, after being satisfied with the pictures she had taken. The sun was higher in the sky, and she had scheduled massage appointments for the two of them at 4:00. If they headed back now, they should return in plenty of time. After this hike, a massage would be greatly welcomed. The hike up had seemed to require use of every muscle they had.

Hannah gave Miranda a big hug, which she reciprocated.

"What's that for? Smiling.

"I really appreciate this. It's wonderful up here. Nice to have girl time with my best friend. This has been amazing for me. Thank you."

"You're very welcome. But hey, you came, so thank you!"

"It should be easier and faster going down than it was coming up, but it really felt great to feel some muscle burn again," Hannah admitted.

"A massage awaits us!" Miranda exclaimed. "You ready?"

"I would love to take a swim before turning in tonight," Hannah started walking toward the trail.

"Oh *yeah*!" Miranda said in agreement.

They started their descent going back down from the steep climb they had taken after they had left the main trail. Part of the path navigated near the edge where there was a steep drop as it winded down the mountain, slowly wrapping around the ridge they were on. They had reached a thicker part of the forest where very little sunlight penetrated into. They each picked up their pace a bit, almost at a slow skip, trying to avoid the rocks and tree roots that were scattered along the trail. They were focusing their eyes on the ground so as not to trip over anything as they navigated back down the trail. The descent was steep, and they had to balance themselves to keep from falling forward with gravitational pull. They had begun to maintain a controlled momentum and a steady pace, when suddenly Hannah heard a voice inside herself that was not her own, yell "Stop!" It was so real, so clear, so loud that she slowed to an immediate stop with Miranda nearly falling headlong into her, while trying to stop herself from falling and tumbling down the hill, but she was able to grab her footing and exclaimed, "What are you doing?"

"Did you hear that?" Hannah asked her in a hushed voice.

"Hear what?"

Hannah was looking back and forth wildly, to find the source of the voice that had sounded distinctly male when her heart nearly stopped at the sight of a large mountain lion ready to pounce, staring right at them.

"Miranda, don't move, don't move, just be still," Hannah ordered with urgency as calmly as she could.

Miranda turned to look in the direction Hannah was staring when she saw it hunched low and about to attack, "Oh my God!" she said feeling suddenly afraid.

"Why is it out in broad daylight?" Hannah thought out loud, knowing they were nocturnal creatures as a rule. It was uncommon for people to see them during the day, but there it was, and it must have been tracking them, she thought, but was obliged to attack when it saw they had accelerated their pace going downhill.

"Okay, I remember reading that if you are out and one approaches, to make yourself seem larger, unafraid, throw things at it, growl at it," Miranda said almost squeakily.

"Like you really sound like you could pull that off," Hannah scolded her. "Shape up! They can sense fear! You are going cause us to become dinner for it!"

Miranda realized Hannah was right, saw a stick nearby several yards away and hurried to pick it up, but she moved too suddenly, and the lion leaped into a run coming straight towards her. She grabbed the stick and looked back up, but the color left her face when she saw that it was already running towards her. She lost her footing and fell backwards down the hill, dropping the stick. It was coming directly towards her at lightning speed.

Hannah acted on impulse and began flailing her arms, yelling, growling as loud as she could to make herself seem ferocious and try to scare it off, but just as it got within a few feet of her, she suddenly felt herself being lifted and removed from its path and felt herself being set back down out of harm's away. She spun around and looked and the lion was still chasing Miranda, as she rolled further down the hill, still trying to regain her bearings. The camera was clutched in her hands but still strapped around her neck. Miranda could see it coming towards her and felt helpless to get her footing. When she finally stopped, she was lying on her back with her feet above and in front of her on the uphill. She instinctively tried to pull herself up into a sitting position in hopes of getting back up and gaining her footing, but before she could swing her legs around behind her and pull her body back uphill, she saw it jump in the air to attack. Instinctively, she covered her head with her hands, knowing she was about to be ripped to shreds. She felt her heart racing in her chest.

Seconds passed when she heard the animal land with a thud further down the hill from her, at least 20 or 30 feet. She rolled to one side, looking toward where she heard it land, and the animal was fully crouched down, belly to ground, facing downhill away from her. He was no longer focused on her. The animal was slowly starting to stand but stayed partially crouched. It seemed to be disoriented, looking around, making a growling, defeated sound. It looked back up the hill and locked eyes with her and then shook its head and walked away with its tail tucked, and once more turned and looked at them before it took off in a trot, advancing to a fast run in the other direction, away from them. Hannah was making her way as fast as she could towards her. Miranda stood up slowly, keeping her eyes on it. A moment later, Hannah was besides her. The two hugged each other tightly.

"Are you hurt?" Hannah asked.

"A few scrapes maybe. I'll probably have some bruises, but I'm okay, I think," sounding like she was in a stupor. She started rubbing the dirt off her hands and checking herself out, just to be certain. "How did you know?"

Hannah looked at her, "Know what?" she asked breathlessly.

"You told me to stop! Up there," pointing to where they had come from before they saw the animal. "You told me to stop!"

"I heard someone tell me to stop, and I just knew we had to. I sensed danger," Hannah answered her.

"You heard someone? Tell you to stop?" Miranda reiterated.

"Yeah," Hannah replied, "I did," feeling puzzled now that her adrenaline had slowed down. "All of a sudden, it was as if the voice came from within me, but yet I heard it clearly as you and me talking, only the voice thundered through my very being. It wasn't my own voice, but it seemed to have come from within and yet all around me. It sounded like a man, but not like Jesse," she said very puzzled. "Whoever it was, he was warning us, but then, did you see the lion when he jumped to attack you?" Hannah continued, recounting what she saw.

"I wasn't exactly looking!" Miranda pointed out, still a little shaky.

Hannah continued, "Mir, someone, something, I don't know, but I was trying to stop it from attacking you, and suddenly I was lifted and carried at lightning speed back up the hill and set back down, and when I turned and looked, it was jumping towards you, but just as I thought it was going to land on top of you, it just kept flying through the air. There is no way that animal could leap that far. It was as if something had grabbed it, kept it from attacking you, from landing on you, while it was still in midair and then just dropped it to the ground down the hill, away from you. I know it sounds insane but I know what I saw, and I know something stopped me from getting in the way, just like I know something stopped that cat from jumping on you." Hannah looked back to where she saw the animal fall to the ground. "That cat knew it too, I think. Did you see how it acted? It acted just as puzzled as we are right now," Hannah pointed out.

Miranda swallowed, still shaken. "It certainly seems that way." She looked around the forest and said, "Whoever you are, thank you," as she spoke to the unseen being, feeling nothing but pure awe as Hannah's recount of the last few minutes began to sink in. It had happened so quickly.

They found their bags they had dropped and a couple of large sticks and continued their trek down the mountain, fully alert now. Miranda felt a little sore and limped a little, but she didn't think anything was broken.

Behind them walked Jesse and the stranger. "How did you *do* that?" Jesse asked, feeling thankful his new companion had saved both Hannah and Miranda.

"Like I told you before, you have the ability. You just don't remember what you are and where you came from, but it will come to you when you are less disoriented by physical death," the stranger answered him. "There's much to learn, and we have an eternity given to us to advance our knowledge," he told Jesse.

"I didn't think we could pick up anyone or anything like I saw you do, now that we're not," pausing to say the words, "mortal anymore," Jesse said, wishing he did not have to accept he was not mortal any longer. "And Hannah heard you tell her to stop. How did you get her to hear you? Will I ever be able to get her to hear me?" he asked, filled with so many questions, not knowing she already had heard him.

"As I said, there's a lot to remember, and we never stop learning, but you learn more and remember more after you cross over, when you're ready, of course."

"I'm not ready yet," Jesse replied, not feeling closure with the life that had unexpectedly expired.

"You underestimate yourself, Jesse. You have all the power you need within. It's a matter of remembering how to use it. Even in mortality, the power is still within each person to embrace, to create the full life they desire, but because they don't remember, most feel life is what happens *to* them and not what they create. Everyone is different, some having progressed more than others, but ultimately, we are all creative beings, all connected, and even in immortality, we are still connected to those who remain mortal, just as they are very much connected to us. Thus, I have returned and you remain, even though we are no longer mortal. There is no separation of souls except by perception created through mortality. Once you realize this, you won't be afraid to cross back over and return."

Jesse thought about this. "Had you crossed over?"

"Indeed, I had.

"How did you come back?"

"As I said, we are all connected, by love, and we all have free will. We all have goals to achieve and purpose in what we choose."

"What did you choose?" Jesse asked.

"We make many choices but my choice for being here is, as I told you, I'm here for Hannah. I chose to help her."

Oddly, Jesse thought, he did not feel jealous. He only felt a desire to comfort her, but he appreciated this stranger was here to help her, and he seemed far more capable than Jesse was at protecting her.

"I guess I should thank you, then," Jesse told him, as they walked behind the two women.

Chapter Nine

Closure

Face down on the massage tables wrapped in large white towels, with their faces inserted in an opening with a view of shined hardwood floors, two Asian female masseuses who appeared to be in their thirties kneaded their muscles with deep massage from head to toe. Miranda was sore after the tumble down the side of a mountain, and there were some scrapes and bruises that had obvious tenderness that the masseuse was very careful not to massage as deeply over them, but otherwise, deep massage was what she needed right now. Every few minutes she groaned or flinched with pain, but it was a good pain, she thought. She had paid for an hour but now wished she had paid for more. She laid there thinking about what was going to show up on her camera, as they had not had time to check it before coming to their appointment.

"I'm sore in places I didn't even know I was sore, which I think is everywhere," Hannah admitted. "I think we should start doing this more often," feeling the tension release as the masseuse had started massaging her scalp.

"I'm just hoping I can move tomorrow," Miranda groaned with a gasp. "Ouch, oh that's tender," she said out loud, not sure how well the women spoke English.

"Hopefully, the massage will help prevent stiffness from that tumble you took," Hannah told her, halfway laughing.

"I hope so. Ah, it feels good. Eich! That didn't!" Miranda complained, clenching her teeth. The masseuse began massaging her feet slowly and deeply, and Miranda practically yelped, "Ah, that feels good and hurts like hell at the same time," trying not to hold her breath. Miranda could almost feel her face turning red. "I've got to relax!" she thought, "relaxing, relaxing, relaxing," she murmured to herself.

"Feet massage heal body," the masseuse told her in broken English.

"Oh, well I definitely could use that!" Miranda squealed in a high-pitched tone as every pressure point in her feet reeked of tenderness and raw, sharp, ripping pain.

"Heal organs of malady," the masseuse informed her, as she leaned in towards Miranda's ear.

"Malady, uh? I hope I don't have any maladies, but it definitely makes me forget I hurt everywhere else," Miranda screeched but laughed a deep, throaty laugh at the same time. Even the laughing hurt right now. "I know what else I need, and that's an Epsom salt hot bath!" she told Hannah.

Hannah had started to drift into her thoughts about what she had experienced on the hill, the way she had been physically lifted by an unseen being and the voice she had heard warning her of danger. She replayed it over and over again in her head. Miranda's voice sounded like it was far away, as her mind drifted to what had been happening, the mountain lion flying through the air, outstripping its own capability, and shaking its head in bewilderment when it landed unharmed. The fact that Miranda was safe, untouched by the animal was all nothing short of a miracle. She wondered if this other being who was not Jesse had always been with her or if he had come only before the accident, if he was a guardian angel or some kind of reaper. Whoever he was, she did not feel afraid of him.

When Hannah was a child, she used to be afraid to go to sleep at night with the lights off. She had feared some evil being, the devil maybe, would come and carry her away or paralyze her ability to breathe, and she would die of suffocation, because she had used to wake up in the middle of bad dreams feeling completely paralyzed, unable to scream, but that had not happened to her for a long time. There was nothing evil about this being. If there was, she believed she would sense it, but all she sensed was feeling loved and protected. She knew he was masculine by the silhouette she had seen of him and by the voice she had heard. It clearly was not Jesse's voice. No, she was sure of that. Would he reveal himself to her more, she wondered?

"Hannah? (pause) Hannah! Did you fall asleep on me? Hello over there!"

"Sorry, Mir, not sleeping, just lost in thought. You know you could also plug in your earbuds and download some meditation apps to your phone," Hannah added, remembering what she had started to say before her mind drifted. "There are some really good ones, and they've helped me to relax and let go of tension after my workouts. You should try it out," now feeling deeply relaxed.

"I may do that," Miranda replied, "Awe, that feels wonderful!" she told the masseuse now that she had loosened her foot muscles. "I never knew feet could be so tender when I hadn't even noticed them being sore in the first place. I must have been murdering them!"

Hannah managed to laugh at Miranda's way of expressing herself, which didn't go unnoticed by Miranda, who wanted to bring humor to an already tense situation. She wasn't counting but she always noticed when she could get Hannah to at least smile without faking it. Laughter was a bonus. She knew if she were in Hannah's situation, she would want

189

someone around who could make *her* laugh. Hannah had helped her get through a lot, and Miranda knew the value of that intuitive kind of friendship. It was in Miranda's nature to enjoy making someone laugh, despite the kind of day they had already had. For her, it was about being positive, because one thing Miranda had learned in life, being positive used less energy and had proven better outcomes for her, so she believed in turning a bad situation into an opportunity, even if by merely choosing *not* giving into negativity, and besides, being positive could be infectious.

After the first half hour, they were both feeling less pain and were feeling more relaxed, and the therapist was now focusing on Miranda's neck and shoulders while she moaned pleasurably. Hannah had been tense, but she was not the one that took a spill and gotten banged up rolling down a mountain. She knew it was wrong to laugh at Miranda, but she was so comically dramatic, and Hannah knew the massage must have been excruciating at first for her, but at the same time, it was probably just what she needed to prevent stiffness and soreness from setting in, so hopefully, she could enjoy the rest of this trip.

An hour later, they were at a seafood restaurant next to the shore. The décor was simple but elegant. The restaurant itself was small with mahogany tables and chairs, and there were candles that burned on each of the tables in clear sconces. They both took a table by the window overlooking the ocean. When the waitress took their order, Hannah ordered the salmon entre while Miranda ordered the sole. They each ordered a glass of white wine. Miranda decided it was best to wait until they were back at the hotel room to view the pictures they had taken while hiking. So, she asked Hannah, "Are you okay?"

"It's been really hard. Sometimes I feel like I can't breathe for this black fog filling the space where they used to be," she said, blinking her eyes to hold back the tears.

Miranda immediately regretted bringing it up, "Hannah, Jesse and Ethan are irreplaceable, so don't let a black fog fill a void they left behind. Fill it with happy memories in honor of them. You were so blessed, I know, but try to embrace what the new chapter of your life holds, and don't do what I did and build a wall around you, promise me, okay?"

Hannah nodded, trying to smile.

Miranda continued, "I know you love the house, and you built a lot of memories there, but maybe it's time to move to a new place. Make things fresh and new. You can't bring them back to that house, Sweetie, but you can take all those beautiful memories with you and keep them in here," pressing her hand to her chest.

"I know. I've been giving it some thought," Hannah replied. "I'm just trying to adjust the best I can. It's not like I've ever been through this before. It's all so overwhelming," fighting back more tears.

"I know. I know," placing her hand over Hannah's.

"I think the hardest part will be giving away their things, all their clothes, Ethan's toys. I honestly don't know that I'm ready for *any* of that!" tears starting to well up in her eyes.

"I'm with you every step of the way, and you don't have to do any of it alone," Miranda reassured her. "I just don't know if it's wise to put it off too long."

Hannah smiled sadly and nodded her head.

"You were willing to sacrifice yourself to save me today!" Miranda pointed out, "I want you to know, I would do the same for you, you know that, right?"

"I wasn't really the one who saved you," Hannah reminded her solemnly.

"In any case, I'm just glad someone was there! Watching out for us."

Only five feet away, from their table, unseen and unheard by anyone in the restaurant, was the stranger, while Jesse was pacing the restaurant, anxious for Hannah.

"I've been trying to place where I know you from," Jesse said. "I do know you, right? It really feels like I know you," rubbing his chin.

The stranger smiled at him almost teasingly, "As I've already told you, we are ALL connected, both in immortality and mortality, and those who are immortal remember those who remain mortal. We don't forget. Is that really what you thought would happen? That we would all be separated by a veil of forgetfulness? Never to remember anything about before you came to this earth or any part of your life or the people in it after you departed?"

"No, I'm just saying you seem familiar. Have you ever been mortal?" Jesse asked with curiosity, as the thought stopped him in his tracks.

"Yes, many times, but not for a long time. We each know when mortality is no longer necessary to teach us what we need to learn."

"And what is it that we are supposed to learn?"

The stranger's expression was kind and compassionate. "For starters, how to enjoy life without turning it into a negative experience. Life is meant to be happy, prosperous, but most imagine it as something to struggle through. Many focus on everything negative in the world while others try to embrace what is positive. What one imagines is what one gets in life. If you think you're sick all the time, then illness and bodily aches and pains will be what you experience, or the other way around."

"So, you're saying we, mortals, I guess I'm no longer a mortal," as an afterthought, "need to learn how to use our imagination differently?" Jesse asked, sounding puzzled.

"That is one way of putting it, yes. Your imagination creates how you experience life. If you live in fear, you *attract* what is fearful, but if you live with love and gratitude, you attract those things that make you feel surrounded by love and make you feel grateful. If one would change their perception of life and of their environment, their abilities, and even their existence, they could create heaven on earth for themselves. Right now, if you desired to be someplace else and imagined the experience as if you were already actually there and *believed* you were there, you would immediately *be* there. *That* is the power of imagination! Mortals tend not to realize how powerful it is. In mortality, it is *relearning* the power of imagination to obtain the life each one desires, but most do not use their imagination toward happiness but toward *misery*, creating their own hell on earth. I say, "relearning" because in immortality, we naturally know all these things. Life is simply art. Imagination is a gift. We each create our own masterpiece as we go," he told Jesse enthusiastically. "If you don't like the work of art you're creating, then create something new! It's simple as that! But sometimes what is simple, simply can't be processed as simple. It's *perceived* to be complicated."

"So now you're saying life is an art class?" Jesse proclaimed somewhat snidely, but then as he thought about it, he began admiring the simplicity of the concept.

"In a manner of speaking," the stranger replied, "and life is the masterpiece, and if you want to take it further, one's mortal body is also a masterpiece. One has to be careful how they perceive themselves because all the cells in the body obey the mind and transform the body into what the mind believes and perceives it to be. So, as a mortal, one should believe in health, not sickness!"

"I've never heard life described like that before," Jesse admitted. "I do like how you put it, though. I mean, it does make a lot of sense."

"Some are students and others are teachers, and to have both is necessary, and one is not more significant than the other," the stranger added, "Just a matter of different levels of advancement."

"It is one way of looking at it, yes, I definitely get it. So then, we are students and you're a teacher?" Jesse stopped pacing and focused on watching Hannah as she and Miranda were waiting for their meals to arrive, and then asked, "Why have Ethan and I been ripped from her life?" he asked quietly, wanting to understand. He had not felt any sense of time since the accident, but he knew time was what Hannah had, each day, each hour, each minute, missing her son and her husband and grieving her losses. Jesse didn't want her to go through that, to suffer that kind of grief, pain, and loneliness. It wasn't fair to her. He wanted her to be happy again.

"I know it hard to understand, but even for one to experience the passing of someone they love is an experience to remind them of life's infinite continuity. Mortals cannot avoid passing back into immortality. When I say we create our own reality, that is one reality that is unavoidable. I'm speaking in terms of what one does with their life and the decisions they make from moment to moment that effects the reality they experience, that forms their self-identity, their level of prosperity, their health, and their expectations in life. Death of the physical body is inevitable and unavoidable. That is a natural process of mortality. What one believes about it, however, may in turn determine the outcome of how they process their emotions. Look at us, here we both are, nonphysical but not *dead*," chuckling at the word, "but yet most mortals would say we're *dead*! Don't you find that interestingly contradictory? Do you feel dead? I don't feel dead!"

"To be honest, I feel more alive than ever!" Jesse admitted.

"Exactly. But most mortals imagine us as dead, nonexistent, or so, so far away, or so they *imagine*, and hence their mourning. If only they would imagine how close and very much alive we are, instead."

"Makes sense, I suppose," Jesse replied thoughtfully. "I would think how Hannah perceives mine and Ethan's passing would effect a certain reality for her as far as coping," Jesse said thoughtfully.

The stranger nodded. "They often imagine what they can't see doesn't really exist, and what they do imagine results in their emotions, and their emotions feed their imaginations, and so to advance, one must break that cycle from a negative one that brings sadness to a positive one that results in happiness and richness of life!"

"But Hannah has always been a positive person," Jesse pointed out.

"This is meant to make her stronger, and she will be challenged in her beliefs. It will also help her remember who she is and who we all are."

"And who are we?" Jesse asked.

"Connected, all of us, mortal and immortal, to something greater than us all!"

"I feel that. I do feel that!" Jesse said, as comprehension pervaded him, turning to look back to Hannah. "Connected!" The full meaning of the word suddenly was enlightening in a way he had not realized.

"I imagine myself in a time and place where the sunset is just going down behind the mountains and the rays are shimmering across the mountains for as far as one can see," Jesse closed his eyes.

"Are you imagining it as being real?" the stranger asked.

Jesse paused and then, "I do now," and when he opened his eyes, he was no longer in the restaurant. Surrounded by mountains as far as he could see, the sun casting shadows and reflecting glints of light onto the beautiful colors adorning them, it was a different kind of majestic than he had seen. The beauty and peace that surrounded him was astounding. His imagination had brought him here. "It's starting to all make sense," he said out loud, just above a whisper.

Moments later, he imagined himself with Hannah again, but when he transported himself to her, she was back in their house and no longer with Miranda at the restaurant. The stranger observed him.

"How long was I gone? It seemed like only a couple of minutes!" Jesse told him, while he looked at Hannah intently.

"Time does not exist in this dimension as it does on earth or in mortality. Time is given to those in mortality. It has no place nor purpose in immortality."

"Then you have no idea how long I was gone any more than I do?" Jesse was feeling anxious for Hannah, not himself. He had not wanted to leave her, and the fact that he was gone much longer than he realized suddenly alarmed him. He had not been there for her. If he could leave and think he was gone only seconds, what if he had been gone for years, he cringed at the thought of her feeling abandoned by him, more so than what he could help anyway. The fact that he no longer had a body to share with her, to enjoy one another physically and enjoy physical encounters in the way that people do, was beyond his control, but to be absent from her, he wasn't ready for that, and he didn't believe she was either. The feeling was like that of a parent that had left their child alone too long unattended only to realize they had done so, except of course, she was not the child, and he was not the parent. She was the woman he loved, longed for, and still wanted to be with. She would have felt his absence and that was not something he wanted her to feel.

"The sun has gone down six times and risen seven since you visited your sunset," the stranger told him.

"I only saw one sunset!" Jesse corrected, confused.

"You are in a different dimension now, Jesse. You created with your mind and imagination what you wanted to see and you were there. You experienced it because your mind and beliefs created it. Mortals remain in a dimension of time and space where the sun rises and sets in earthly time. It is not so for us. We can enjoy a single sunset for years in earth time. We can enjoy our hearts' desires because we remember who we are and our creative abilities. If who and what we are was remembered while in mortality, there would be no poverty, no struggling with debt, no sickness, no wars, and no stress."

Jesse considered this with awe. "It felt familiar, as if I had done it a thousand times, but yet ...." He began to realize the truth of what this stranger was telling him. Jesse also realized the dimension he had just departed in his mortal life and the one he had entered in immortality coalesced one with the other. They are separate but not separate, he realized. It was as if the puzzle was starting to form into a more fathomable picture of understanding. "You know, I don't see anything wrong with having no wars, no poverty, no debt and stress! But you're saying because when we are in mortality we don't remember who we are, we create sickness, poverty, and suffering?" Jesse asked.

"That is exactly what I'm saying. One either lives with positive attitude by the law of love or they live with a negative attitude under the law of fear, and that is how each form their perspective on life. What they expect life to give them, they receive. Until one learns to change what he believes, the mortal experience will not change. It is allowed for people to be homeless, for people to suffer, because it gives everyone opportunity to respond in a way to make the world a better place rather than being part of the problem. How often do people ignore those that suffer and are homeless?"

"People live their entire lives into old age without realizing this," Jesse reflected, feeling sadly enlightened about this. "Hannah always stopped and gave to the poor. She brought them food." He reflected sadly, "I never did."

"Yes. You will understand more once you cross over. Some people are more disoriented than others as they cross over, and then there are yet others who are not disoriented at all," the stranger pointed out. "It will come back to you."

"But I have to cross over and leave Hannah before I can remember everything you already know? Everything you're saying?" he asked sadly, not wanting to leave her.

The stranger's silence affirmed the answer to his question.

Jesse watched Hannah. She had a glass of red wine and was curled up on the couch reading. It was still daylight. He looked at the book cover and knew she was reading about experiences with earthbound souls that have passed. On the end-table next to the couch were four other books on the same subject. He looked at the time on the clock, and it was only 2:20 in the afternoon. "Is this a weekend?" he wondered, "Or has she stopped working?" He knew he had left her with a sizeable life insurance policy, so she could easily afford to take time off from work or never work again, if she chose not to. He had taken it out before they were married, when he knew he wanted to propose to her. Now, he was glad he did, more than ever. He could hear the words rise from the pages as she read them, as they were transformed into thoughts, and he could hear her thoughts. Instead of it seeming strange to him, it was an ability that also felt familiar, even natural.

He moved closer to her. She looked up from the book as if she were aware of his presence. Her energy field was strong as he caressed her cheek. Her sadness and emptiness he could feel in her heart, he would not wish on anyone. She closed her eyes and reflexively drew in a deep, quick breath in response to his touch. "I wish you could hear me like you used to," he said to her, but she did not seem to hear him this time, as she had at the hotel room, but then, she surprised him.

"I know you're here, Jesse. I feel you. It's like I can tell when it's you and when it's not you. You have your own distinct energy, and I feel you. I won't lie, this is the hardest thing I've ever gone through. Ethan has come to me in my dreams, but I don't really feel him when I'm awake. In my dreams, he is happy, alive, vibrant, and he's good, he's safe. He seems more grown up in how he talks and thinks, but he looks the same," and she let out a laugh as tears started to flow. Wherever he is, it's better than San Francisco," she said with another broken effort to laugh. I wish I were with you guys, that we were together again. It's not the same without you," and with that, she cried freely. Her words took him by surprise. He had not anticipated them.

"I miss you both so-o-o much." His arms were around her, embracing her, willing her to feel him. His faced brushed against hers, longing for his own body that he could touch her with. The penetrating energy of her soul was palpable. He willed himself to give her more energy, to calm her, give her strength. As the ocean calms after a storm, her body relaxed, and her stress calmed. He kissed the top of her head as if to impart to her all the love he had for her. Their auras had merged with one another's, with Hannah's energy increasing. Jesse was remembering his power within and how to use it. He saw the pleasure in the stranger's eyes as the goal was accomplished. Jesse had given Hannah all the energy he had to give.

Tingling to her core, all the way through the bone, covered in goosebumps made her shiver and her breath hitched. Once she felt the immediate warmth that followed, a joy, then a peaceful calm filled her being.

"You're okay?" She asked him. Then she heard him.

"I'm be okay, Baby." The tears fell, streaking her cheek.

"Don't worry about me, okay? I'm going to be okay. I love you always and forever, and nothing will ever change that. You hear me, Jess? You are always in my heart," she told him, and as she said it, goose bumps washed all over her body again. Her body felt weightless. Infusing her with every emotion he felt for her, her eyes opened for the first time, and she saw him. He was not even transparent or ghostly looking, just real as if he had never left, still wearing the outfit he was wearing the last time she saw him. The smile on his face, the love in his eyes gave her heart a leap. She felt a surge of electricity fill every part of her body.

"I love you, Hannah. For time and all eternity, I love you."

She started to touch him, but a glow now surrounded him, and his image slowly vanished. He had stood only two feet from her. The emotion of seeing him flooded her intensely with elation and tears at the same time. It allowed her closure she hadn't had before. She reached out and touched the space where he had been. The electricity was still there. She felt his essence, the lingering of his soul, and a moment later, it was gone. He had said goodbye to her and willed her to see he was okay. She stood in the space he had just occupied for a moment longer, closed her eyes and held out her arms and embraced the peace he had just left her with. She imagined him wrapping his arms around her from behind and tucking his chin into her shoulder. She smiled as more tears rolled slowly down her checks.

"I'm ready," Jesse told the stranger, who nodded in acknowledgment. "Take care of her for me."

"She will be alright," he assured Jesse. "And Ethan is waiting for you, as are others."

Jesse was finally at peace and his countenance began to glow a little more. He felt a lot of his energy had left him as he had given so much of it to Hannah.

"You will feel stronger once you cross over," knowing Jesse's thoughts.

The brilliant white light of energy that swallowed him from every side heightened his awareness, vanquished every mortal apprehension, accepted him with intimate knowing of every secret remembered and forgotten, filled him with celestial light and truth, restored every forgotten memory, healed every invisible scar, as it lifted him through a tunnel of enveloping, moving, living light, elevating him beyond all the cares of the world and out of the earthly dimension.

Ariel had been beside Erianthé watching a lamb and the rest of the wildlife, including a small black and white Shetland pony that was playing nearby. A moment later, Jesse held out his arms to Ethan, who ran to him, covering more ground than his tiny steps would have covered on earth, "Daddy, look, it's a McCaw and she's mine!" Joy and excitement poured through the light that filled his eyes, Jesse could not contain his own smile, gesturing to the Shetland pony, "Is that pony yours, too?" picking up his little boy. The McCaw was perched on Erianthé's shoulder.

"Yeah, that's Skyfire, she's mine too, and this is Kaliope," introducing his McCaw.

Another presence surrounded by a blue aura was approaching quickly, as if floating atop the ground. Each deliberate step covered fifty feet. Her long reddish, curly hair flowed down over her shoulders. Her garment was a mossy green silk, flowing loosely around her body. A brilliant white wrap hung down on each side of her neck to the hem of her dress. The soft, matching high-top slippers that laced around her ankles matched her garment. Her eyes were soft, golden brown, and her complexion was one of a soft, fair color, and her lips a rich natural color. She came to a stop in front of Jesse and introduced herself.

"I am Amara. I have come to accompany you on your journey," she said kindly, gazing into Jesse's eyes.

"Are you my guide?" Jesse asked her, mesmerized by her eyes and feeling he knew her and had always known her. Her familiarity was comforting. He set Ethan back down, and the McCaw moved from Erianthé's shoulder back to Ethan's.

"I am," she answered cheerfully. "You are now ready, I understand." It was not a question.

"Yes, I'm ready," Jesse answered quietly.

She turned and gestured toward the lamb that now led the way. Jesse took Ethan's hand, as they walked toward the hills in the distance with Erianthé and Amara closely behind them, all the animals followed. Their pace was slow but each step covered larger and larger distances, until they ascended into the soft white clouds where a bright emanating majestic light opened up and welcomed them. Then, the place that Ethan had created, folded upon itself and vanished, leaving nothing but a white light in its place.

Chapter Ten

The Voice

Warm, steamy water that looked like a sea of white, mountainous bubbles reflecting glimmers of flickering light covered her as she relaxed in the saline water. The lemon-scented bar of soap emitted its fragrance all over her body, picked up by the crystals of steam. Her body was small in comparison to the tub that was sized to accommodate two people with room to spare. Glowing candles lined the outer edge of the tub, illuminating the entire bathroom.

Her eyes were fixed on the steamed mirrors, wondering if a handwritten message might appear. Minutes of more staring passed but nothing happened. Her mind wandered back to the hotel, after she and Miranda had finished getting their massages, then Miranda's eagerness to view the pics they had taken while they had been hiking in the forest. The ghostly images in the photographs blew her mind. Both of them had looked at them so many times, studying them, that she had every snapshot memorized.

Miranda had been holding the camera to her chest when she fell. She had hit the snapshot button inadvertently in an effort to keep from dropping it and to keep it from banging against anything when she fell. The camera had continued snapping one bursts after another, in the process of her fall and rolling down the hill, which had been mostly on her backside. The bursts had been continuous from the moment she began falling, until she had rolled to see the lion had not landed on her. She had gripped it so tightly that she miraculously hadn't dropped it, completely unaware of what she had filmed or that anything *had* been filmed at all. Neither of them knew until they returned to the hotel later that night. She recounted, in slow motion, the flashbacks of everything that happened along with everything she had seen on Miranda's camera.

The flashbacks replayed in her mind just as Miranda's camera had captured it. Two ghostly images appearing as solid light in the form of human males in close proximity to where I was. One was closer to me than the other, just like near the old barn in Mendocino. Everything changed quickly on the mountain when Miranda had begun falling. The bursts of frames became longer as she had pressed harder to hold the camera.

The figure who had been standing further away from me had his hands on me at my waist. I was midair, feet off the ground being swung around before I was set down at least 20 feet up the hill! He was moving so fast, faster than the naked eye could conceive she was sure of, based on the pattern of his movement captured in the bursts. The other image appeared to be moving towards me but not as fast, his arms reaching towards me. His image had been blurrier. Another burst of frames was of the tree tops, when she had actually fallen backwards and was on her back side facing upwards. She hadn't braced her fall or grabbed anything for holding on to her camera.

The mountain lion was over her, midair, frame by frame, his head, his neck, and then a white ghostly image wrapped around him, clutching it like a vise, carrying it through the air further away from where Miranda lie on the ground. He had control of the animal, holding onto it, redirecting its landing far away from her. She had seen it happen with her own eyes. It could not have leapt that far or that high on its own. Mountain lions can't fly like that. It was as if gravity defied itself just as the animal's calculation should have placed it landing it on top of Miranda. Her own memories played parallel in her mind with that of the picture frames, as if playing out in her mind from two vantage points simultaneously. He saved her. He saved us both, she knew.

Jesse's spirit that had appeared to her earlier, looking as if he was real again, in the flesh, mortal looking but then he faded and disappeared before she could even touch him. His eyes had communicated his adoration for her, his essence, all his love for her. Love was infinite, she realized, never-ending, and beyond death, he loved her still and wanted her to be okay. He had wanted her to see he was alright and did not want her to grieve and be unhappy. He had communicated in thought that he knew Ethan was alright, too. Though she embraced what he had wanted her to know and was so grateful he had come to her, knowing she felt stronger because of it, the fact remained she still missed both him and Ethan, and she didn't want to *not* miss them, *not* think about them, but when would it stop hurting so much, she wondered.

She closed her eyes and tears seeped through her lashes. She pulled herself down beneath the surface of the water, listening to silence, feeling tranquility as she imagined a baby felt in its mother's womb. She thought she could lie there and let herself go, not come up for air, then she would be with Jesse and Ethan, and the idea became quickly, more impulsively appealing, as she imagined seeing Jesse and Ethan again, running towards them. She had no fear of death at all. She was letting go.

"Hannah," a voice thundered in her chakra, deep in her soul, piercing it but yet, at the same time, felt gentle as a whisper.

Again, she *felt* the voice speak to her. "Hannah, get up," it commanded her with a voice of authority.

She thrusts herself out of the water breathlessly. Someone was in the house! He had walked in on her! She wiped the water from her eyes and looked around seeing no one. She pulled the drain stopper and heard the roaring slurp of the water running down the drain as the tub began to empty. Hesitantly, she stood in a crouched position while she grabbed a large powder blue towel, quickly wrapped it around her.

Moving toward the door on her tiptoes, she peaked into the bedroom, her eyes searching for any sign of someone in the house. The rapid thumping of her heart felt like it was coming out of her chest. The bedroom was empty, and she exhaled, realizing she must have been holding her breath, afraid whoever it was would hear that too. One step, then another, no one there.

"Is anyone there?" she squeaked almost at the volume of a whisper. Nothing. The room was silent.

She inched backwards to the bathroom door and grabbed another towel to wrap her hair. Tiptoeing cautiously, trying to peak through the door once again before proceeding back to the bedroom to get some clothes to put on, she encountered the feel of his presence. His intensity grew, almost taking her breath. She felt the force of his presence drawing near, almost as she would bump into him, he was so very close. She slowed her step, checked her towel, assuring it was securely wrapped around her, only aware of him shadowing near and around her.

The voice she heard had not been Jesse's. Jesse's voice had been baritone. He was gone; she just knew that, somehow. This voice was deep, much deeper than Jesse's. It possessed authority and command. It sliced through her soul like lightening but thundered with clarity. It did not sound like a thought or something she imagined. It came from both inside and outside herself, ever so audible to her ears, from beside the bathtub, no, inside her being. Her ears had been filled with water and the voice resonated from within. At the same time, it sounded only just inches away, so close, so commanding, it had shaken her to her very soul. Yet, it was soft and gentle as a whisper at the same time.

She no longer felt afraid, as she believed it to be the unseen being who had surfaced in her life with Jesse's passing, the being that had been standing in her bedroom when she woke up one morning a couple of months after the memorial service, the same being that had been the second ghostly apparition in the photos on Miranda's camera. Whoever he was had just stopped her from drowning herself in her own tub. It *was* him. She *knew* it with every fiber of her being. She needed to find out who he was, why she was important to him. His presence gave her peace and she felt unafraid, now that she *knew* it was him.

He was inches away, as she could feel the warmth of her own breath hovering close to her face as if bouncing off of an invisible shield that must be his essence. He was so very close. She felt him and wanted so much to know who he was, as his energy felt very familiar to her, so very uncannily familiar.

Shadows cast across the room from the lamp. "I know you're here," measuring her words, speaking slowly in hushed tones, pausing between each question and sentence, hoping he would respond.

"I heard you," she continued gently. "I know you're real. Who are you? Will you talk to me? I should thank you, for protecting us out there. It was you, wasn't it? I know it was," lowering the volume of her voice. "Are you sent to me because I lost my son and my husband? Are you the one Ethan saw when they left that last morning before the accident? The one he saw standing next to me? There's a connection there, isn't there? With their passing and you being here? I sense that's why you're here. I could be wrong, but I don't think so."

She closed her eyes hoping to focus more, hear an answer within, or even open her eyes to see his image again, but when she opened her eyes, there was nothing. Only the feeling of his presence.

The stranger listened to her and desired so much to reveal himself to her. He stood close to her as she spoke, could smell the lemon fragrance she had bathed in still lingering on her skin. He had come knowing her earthly husband and son were departing their earth life, that she would be too weak to handle it, and thus, he had been staying close to impart strength to her, peace, comfort, but he knew her thoughts as she sank under the water, and he knew she had decided to stay under the water and allow herself to drown so she could be reunited with them. It was not her time to leave her life and return yet.

He knew he must stay with her and keep her from anymore impulsive mistakes that would result in harm to her or her premature return. He was committed to protecting her. She had an advanced soul, not as advanced as he was but more advanced than many and had no fear of *death*, a word that only applied to the physical body, but not a word that was favored by those in immortality. With the sudden and unexpected loss of both her husband and child, he needed to keep her from impulsive, irrational efforts to end her earthy life. He knew she appeared strong on the outside, but on the inside, she was fragile, often trying to hide it as a weakness, not wanting to burden others, always wanting to be strong for everyone else, but now he was here to be strong for her and to help her heal and to not self-destruct.

When Hannah opened her eyes again, she saw nothing, so she walked to her bedroom and found a sleeveless, solid pink gown that came to her ankles. She started to put it on but looked around the room, and said out loud, "I would like to change in privacy, so would you please just respect that at least?" The stranger turned and went to stand by the window, looking out of it. He knew he would not be leaving her, not now, maybe not ever during her mortal life.

Once Hannah had her nightgown on, she walked into the bathroom and towel dried her hair and fluffed it with her fingers. She walked back to the bedroom, crawled into bed, and pulled her covers around her but didn't lie down.

"Whenever you are ready to reveal yourself, I would like to meet you," she said quietly. Her eyes searched the room. She still felt his presence but now she felt him draw closer again. Her voice softened more and more, almost to a whisper, as her mind drifted back in time.

"When I was a little girl, I remember feeling a presence with me sometimes. One night I woke up from a dream. It was a happy dream. I was playing with my best friend, a boy, but I woke up from the dream, I saw someone, a man with long golden-brown hair standing at the foot of my bed. I didn't feel afraid at all. I remember he smiled at me, and I asked him if he was an angel. I don't remember anything after that, but I never saw him again. I wasn't afraid then and I'm not afraid now. Funny, I just now remembered that. I had totally forgotten. Maybe that's why I have always believed in angels and spirits, but I don't recall ever having another encounter like that, not until recently." She paused, then continued. "Was it you I saw as a child? I was only four years-old," she whispered with a hint of a smile, "but I remember it; it was so real. Why am I just now remembering that after all these years? I don't think I ever told *anyone*. I don't even think I ever thought about it anymore, either, almost like my memory of it just vanished, but I remember it now, vividly. I know it wasn't a dream and I know I didn't imagine it. I *know* I didn't," she continued in a barely audible whisper.

Hannah held a pillow to her chest and sat there hoping for a response but none came. She tucked the pillow behind her head and sat back and reached for one of her library books she had been reading and pulled her knees to her chest and read a couple of chapters of Why Spirits Show Up in Our Lives. Something stood out at her.

Sometimes spirits that visit us can be someone we have known in previous lifetimes that we have a mutually close attachment with, or they can be someone who has passed from the current life and return to act as guardians. There is also a theory that some spirits who visit someone may be that of a soulmate who did not incarnate into the same lifetime and instinctively feels protective of the other soulmate, as those who are immortal are aware of their loved ones on earth and their circumstances or events about to happen so will reenter a loved one's life to either warn them or act as a protector. This has not been scientifically proven, but there has been evidence and testimony that strongly suggests this as a possibility.

She sucked in her breath, "a soulmate?" Something about the familiarity she felt with the essence or energy of this spirit and how he had been there since Jesse and Ethan had died rang loudly in her mind. She had never considered it. Could it even be possible? "I thought Jesse was my soulmate," she thought. "Could we have more than one soulmate? I always thought we only had only one," her mind raced. She had not spoken these thoughts out loud.

The stranger perused the books on her bookcase that was built into the wall in the bedroom while listening to her thoughts. He already knew the contents of the books she was reading from beginning to end, every word that was written in them. She enjoyed historical literature, philosophy, romance, as well as some art history. Revealing himself to her could affect the rest of her human life, he considered, and she was too young for that to happen. She had chosen to incarnate again, even though he had not. He had respected that, but now that he had returned to protect her and offer strength to her, he found himself not willing to leave her.

Her sensitivity to him should have been anticipated, but she is more advanced and sensitive to the immortal dimension than he realized she would be as a human. It would be unfair to reveal to her who he is or his significance to her, or would it? She would have a chance to keep her life normal and reestablish new and normal relationships during the remainder of this life she had chosen. He knew in time, her earthly life would end but preferably not before she has lived a long one and learned all she had desired to learn in this lifetime, and he wanted her to live it to the fullest.

He had found her to be open to his presence, when he had not intended to reveal himself to her, but when he had intervened to keep her and her friend from being attacked, he had judged her safety took precedence over her not knowing he was there. Now that she knew, he didn't think he had the will to hide himself from her.

Hannah laid her head on the pillow thinking about the memory of the stranger at the end of her bed as a child. Was it coincidental she had just then remembered seeing him? She decided it wasn't a coincidence. It was as if the memory was given back to her as a gift. She couldn't help but wonder if it were not this Being that had unlocked it. Was it a memory they shared? Had he wanted her to remember?

With so many unanswered questions, one thing she was certain of was the familiar sense she had about him, but the other feeling that accompanied this familiarity was an unconditional love, as if he is someone she *had* loved, even still loves, someone that she loved in another time, but when?" "Could this really be happening to me? Is this even possible?" she thought to herself, starting to feel groggy. The more she thought about it and tried to fight sleep, the sleepier she became. She turned the lamp off beside her bed. Within seconds she was drifting, slipping into a dream.

In her dream, she was running, holding onto a kite that was sailing through the wind high above her, and behind her about 200 feet was a little boy, her own age, skillfully managing his own kite. In the dream, she knew him and felt a closeness to him. He had blonde hair that came down over his forehead that blew freely in the wind. He was a very handsome boy, she thought. "Look, it's staying up! We did it!" She stopped running and followed his example, moving closer to him now. Both kites rose above them high in the sky. The sun was bright and the sky was clear. They were out in the open, surrounded by mountains. It was a different era of time judging by how she and the boy were dressed, but she was unsure when, but perhaps the eighteenth or nineteenth century.

There were no adults around and she could see no houses or structures for that matter to gain any clues from the architecture. Just tall stout trees in the distance that looked like they had spring blooms. She could feel the strong breeze on her face that had carried the kites high above them.

"Isn't it amazing?" she thought out loud. The boy looked at her smiling in agreement and looked back up towards the sky. She had moved to within twenty feet of him. His eyes reached her again, still smiling, his gaze holding hers for a moment longer, filled with the same joy she felt herself. They genuinely enjoyed each other's company. The breeze picked up a little more and they began running together, shouting joyfully and playfully at one another, as the kites soared higher and higher. In the dream, she felt a love for this boy, not a brotherly love, but strong friendship that made her heart swell. They had a bond that was special, filled with trust and respect.

"Come on, let's go to the mound!" he exclaimed and changed directions running towards the crest before them, but before they topped it, she woke up.

She laid there, eyes open in the night, only the moonlight illuminating the room. She looked towards the window reflecting on the dream. This was the same boy she remembered in a dream she had as a child, whom she had been playing with. Now, she had just awakened from dreaming of this same boy, only they were a few years older, about nine or ten, but she instinctively knew it was the same boy. In the dream, she knew him, loved him, was enamored with him. He was her best friend. It was as if his name were on the tip of her tongue. She had known it but neither of them had called the other by name in the dream, but after waking up, she realized she had no idea who he was or what his name was, only that he was someone she had loved in another time and another place and someone who had been a significant part of that lifetime.

It was clearly a first-person dream in which the girl had been herself, not one in which she was the spectator. She felt mystified and curious, feeling the same feelings for the boy in the dream upon awakening in the present that she, as a child in that lifetime, in another dream, had felt, except now she was awake, in another era and another lifetime.

She was feeling the same enamor towards this Being that had been hovering around her, and the more she realized she was not hallucinating and that he was real, the more her feelings seemed to intensify, the less alone she felt. Lying there looking out into the moonlight, she felt she was in a paradox that drew her into another lifetime with this boy and the relationship she imagined she had with him as another person and the unknown relationship she had with this Being, who clearly was out of Time himself.

Then, there was Jesse. Is it possible that her soul was in love with each one of them, all occurring at different overlapping times, perhaps even simultaneously, a reality that had not clearly presented itself but had inferred itself upon her? With the dream and sleep state still lingering, and as her conscious state began to alter slightly back into a light sleep of semi consciousness, the thought presented itself to her, "Could time fold and exist simultaneously? Is it possible time is not linear at all?"

Her mind was drifting back as if she were being hypnotized, and in her mind's eye, she was an adult, looking into the eyes of a man that was holding her in his arms, flashbacks of memory as his lips pressed against hers. She felt herself respond passionately, reciprocating the feelings she knew he felt for her. She was deeply in love with him. As he pulled back and looked into her eyes, he had a striking resemblance to the stranger who had appeared at the foot of her bed many years before. In her soul, she knew this was the little boy grown up she had dreamt about before. She knew him, loved him deeply, longed for him. She became aware within the dream that she was dreaming of the man she had been dreaming about repeatedly, before the accident. Then, the dream drifted as she fell further into a deeper sleep.

At dawn, Hannah awoke, lying still curled up on her side, looking out the window where the moonlight had come through as she had fallen asleep, now replaced by the rays of the morning sunrise. She did not move, just laid there, looking out, straining to remember the dream that now seemed even more vague to her, as the fitful night's sleep banished its remembrance from the morning light, yet she knew a part of her past life had been revisited upon her, just a moment of it but something significant. It seemed she laid there for all of a half hour, trying to remember, make sense of everything, tie it all together, but there were too many missing pieces of the puzzle.

She decided she could use some coffee to help her clear her head. She raised up and was about to put her feet into her slippers, when she felt him in the room and instinctively knew his eyes were on her. She suddenly became aware of the sound of her breathing and her heartbeat softly thumping, then goosebumps swept over her skin.

"You're here," she said softly, and slowly turned but sucked in her breath as she beheld him.

He was standing on the opposite side of the room, intently watching her. He did not look like a ghost at all but appeared to have a mortal body. He was beautiful and ruggedly handsome. Every molecule and atom in her body quickened at the sight of him. The power of his presence penetrated her, filled with perceptible and unmistakable love and emotion that was the most unconditional love she had ever felt bestowed upon her, a love that felt infinite and eternal. He had the same face of the man who she had dreamt of so many times. It was him.

His brown eyes rested upon her attentively, as if he knew everything about her. He had such a knowing look in his eyes that seemed to pierce and elevate her soul. Even Jesse had never looked at her like this. Her skin warmed and the goosebumps disappeared. A peace was washing over her, as if he had discerned he had alarmed her and caused sensations in her body that had felt like a sudden burst of ethereal feathery lightness. He was taking inventory of every breath, every beat of her heart, every surge of hormone, and had willed her body to relax, leaving her with only awe, restoring her ability to reason and comprehend the moment she now found herself in. She could recollect no memory of him from this lifetime, but instinctively her soul remembered him and knew him and was not afraid of him. His presence had given her comfort, and seeing him sent healing into the brokenness inside her. His warm eyes revealed he had a kind and highly intelligent spirit. His features were resplendently attractive. She recalled her dream from just the night before. It was him who held her in his arms, and she immediately imagined the feel of his arms around her now.   There was an inert silence between them, and then finally he spoke.

"I'm Jared."

Chapter Eleven

Familiar

His voice was gentle with a deep quality, but its familiarity made her feel her heart and breathing had momentarily stopped. His words rolled smoothly from his lips with punctuated deliberation and clarity.

"Don't be afraid, Hannah," he said comfortingly.

She took in his soft brown eyes that pervaded her, his perfect skin, and muscular form. His gentle demeanor left no room for fear. It should have been disconcerting that he knew everything about her, but instead, she found that to be comforting. Something about him *felt* familiar, *more* than familiar. It was as if she *knew* him, though logic dictated otherwise. She had no memory of having ever met him, as her mind raced to remember, only to have no recollection of him at all. Yet, paradoxically, she instinctively sensed she knew him very well.

There was a command about him that could lead an army. His air of authority was both intoxicating and sobering, but with her, he conveyed a soft, tender, and protective stance that was not commanding towards her at all. His appearance was exceedingly clean, unlike that of anyone she had ever seen. He was angelic, yet something about him was earthy. His hair flowed like silk to his shoulders. Judging by his attire, a very ruggedly designed, rich-brown outfit that included a vest, a long coat, and boots with buckled straps, made of high-quality material that she could not identify, because it didn't look like anything she had ever seen before. It was some of the highest quality material she had ever seen. It was apparent to her he did not belong to the present era, but then he seemed not to belong to any. The calmness of her own voice surprised her.

"I'm *not* frightened," she responded.

"It was not my intention to reveal myself to you," noting the gallantry in his voice.

"But yet you have," she nearly whispered, unable to look away from him. Stammering, as realization began to settle, "It was *you* that was captured in the photographs and *you* that has been with me, since…I didn't think spirits revealed themselves like that.

"An immortal seldom appears in a photograph, but it does happen." Nodding towards her camera on the dresser, "The images you saw confused and frightened you," he stated apologetically. It was careless of me," he admitted solemnly. He paused only slightly, reading her. "It is what you desired of me though, is it not? To see me?"

Hannah's lips parted slightly, trying to keep her mouth from falling open, "It was you that protected us from the mountain lion, wasn't it?"

He nodded, "Yes."

Where did she know his voice from? He had a slight accent she was trying to place but couldn't. Perhaps it was that he sounded so eloquent and spoke so distinctly.

"Why have you come? And why have you continued to stay?" Part of her felt as if she had been swallowed into a dream, yet she knew it was not a dream. She knew that this *being* was in fact standing before her, discerning her every thought, every emotion and was real, not a figment of her imagination!

236

His gaze did not fall from her as he assessed her and waged his reply. "I'm here for *you,* Hannah," and she could see compassion in his eyes.

Then, the question that had haunted her, "Did you know they were going to die?"

"Yes," he said gently.

She felt a slight quiver in her lips so she pressed them together before she spoke again. "Was it Jesse that was the other," needing to pause to compose herself, "image in the photos? Were you with him?" Her heart thumped inside her chest and her insides seemed to flip flop, anticipating his answer.

"He stayed to make sure you were going to be alright," he replied.

"And now?" not sure if she wanted him to answer, though she thought she knew.

"He needed you to release him, to feel you would be safe, and you gave him that, Hannah. He and Ethan are together." His tenderness comforted her like a warm bath that washed away the clutter in her mind. She nodded in response, accepting what she already believed to be true, trying to detain the tears, as she felt a surge of pressure within her eye sockets that expanded the capillaries in her eyes, turning them red.

Why are you so familiar to me?" she probed.

"Life is infinite and interconnected, Hannah, not just confined to the reality you know and see now. We *are* eternal beings, having formed many relationships and made contracts with others regarding those relationships *before* coming to earth." He moved closer to her.

As he did so, she felt the energy between them increase, which caused her breath to hitch before she replied.

"I've always believed that to be true," she told him in almost a whisper, looking up at him, gazing directly into his eyes, "but what *am* I to you?" she pressed.

He hesitated. He was already overstepping a boundary he should not have crossed. He had come to her from another dimension, a parallel universe, someplace not of this earth. She moved to sit on the end of the bed, but he did not move from where he stood. His eyes followed her intently.

"What *am* I to you?" she asked again softly, as a feeling of significance overwhelmed her, touched her in a way that she had never known, despite how much her family and friends loved her and had always made her feel loved and valued. This was far more reaching. "Was it you that took them? Ethan was my baby," she sobbed uncontrollably now. "It took so long for me to get preg...," her voice tethered as her chest heaved, and the tears rolled as if the dam had suddenly broke, "pregnant," she managed to say. "Now, my only child is gone," not holding back the tears as they poured down her cheeks and all the way down her throat. She could feel the salt burning her skin, the taste of saline as they flowed across her lips, dripping onto her top. Her stoicism had abandoned her.

His empathy was palpable and shadowed every word, "You *do* know me," he said. "I did not take them from you. My desire is for you to be happy, not ripped apart and in pain as you are now. Everything within me rebels against seeing you hurting." His face was etched in pain as he spoke. He then paused to allow her to absorb what he was saying. "I have presented myself only because they *were* taken. That was *not* at all my choice, but it *is* my choice to be here with you *now.*" He paused. "If you would prefer that I leave?"

"No, please don't! Don't go. Please," she hastened, not able to think about what his absence would mean to her now that he *had* revealed himself.

She thought back since Jesse and Ethan had passed. Her life had been ripped apart, and a deep void had left her devastated beyond words, but then she had started to feel less alone, but now, looking into Jared's eyes, she felt hope, a glimmer of healing, and an unconditional love that felt eternal. His presence had been a source of comfort to her.

Even Jesse had never elicited such fullness in her being. As with any marriage, they had their share of challenges, and there had always been a measure of compromise, but it had not been as difficult as it is for some. The physical attraction had been strong, but yet they had also been each other's best friend. It had been a relationship of trust and attraction, and yes, love.

The love she felt now from Jared superseded anything she ever remembered feeling. Yet, she thought, it was not an unfamiliar feeling or an unnatural one. It seemed more of a *forgotten* feeling that simultaneously existed parallel to her existence on Earth whether she remembered it or not. It felt ethereal. She felt as if she had one foot on Earth and another in immortality, if that were even possible.

The realization made her feel she was being submerged in an unfolding reality that was now more real to her than her life had ever felt to her before, even more so since she could actually *see* him in human form. There was no denying he was real, exuding his magnificence, standing before her, as human looking and real as anyone she had ever seen. Her soul felt quickened as an invisible energy surged through her. He had unveiled his mysterious presence to her that permeated her to the marrow of her bones, lessening her grief and numbness, if only for now.

He gestured towards her bookshelf in observation, "You're interested in philosophy, I see. Plato, over two millennia ago, wrote something about relationships, turning to look at her."

"It' been awhile since I read it. Are you an admirer of Plato, then?" she asked.

"I knew him, yes."

"You *knew* him? You say it like your friends with him," intrigued.

"I've met him, attended some of the philosophical gatherings from that era of time," he said casually, which elevated her jaw-dropping astonishment and curiosity about him even more, but *he* was merely answering her question.

"Wait! You knew Plato?" she persisted.

"I did, actually," he said with fondness of his memories, still taking in her collection of books. When he looked back at her, she was gaping at him but quickly recomposed.

She cleared her throat, but before she could say anything else, the doorbell rang. She turned toward the sound of it and then looked back at Jared anxiously. The goosebumps vanished almost instantly, and she was caught back into the moment of her surroundings.

"It seems we have a lot to discuss. Don't go away! Please, stay," she pleaded, as she turned to make sure he was still there before she hurried out of the room and down the stairs, leaving him standing there looking after her with one eyebrow arched.

He was reflecting on a memory of her from another time, in another place, when he called her by another name.

Miranda's smiling face greeted her when she opened the door. "I have a surprise," she sang out, holding up two tickets. Hannah stepped aside to allow Miranda to enter, who was still dangling the tickets. Certainly, any other time, Hannah would be happy to see her, but her timing could not have been worse! Nevertheless, she tried to conceal her anxiousness and regain her composure.

"Shakespeare?" Hannah guessed, trying to smile while her tension mounted, wanting to get back upstairs to her other guest.

At this moment, she wished she had not answered the door, looking over her shoulder towards the stairs, biting her lip but made a concerted effort to hide her anxiousness, still trying to reorient herself from the interruption of her conversation with a ghost she had left waiting in her room, who she hoped would still be there when she returned upstairs. Then again, he could be anywhere and be unseen. After all, he was not confined to a room, she knew that.

"Focus!" she thought to herself. She tried to engage in Miranda's excitement. She knew she was a huge fan and she loved plays; they both did. Going to a play was the last thing on her mind right now, as was just about everything else. Trying to pull off acting was not her strong suit, but the occasion required it until she could override the anxious feeling that was beating against her like a torrent of down-pouring rain and hail. "He has a ton of patience," she reminded herself. "He has no sense of time, so the wait will be nothing to him, literally," continuing to alleviate her exasperation. Miranda's voice pulled her back into the moment.

"Not quite," Miranda answered. "Beethoven, one of my favorites, she nearly sang, hugging herself with her arms crossed over her chest as she swayed back and forth in a dance, as if she had just tasted chocolate for the first time.

"I loved the music but I've never been to a symphony," Hannah told her. "What night are the tickets for?" she asked, trying to sound enthused.

"Next Friday," she said whimsically, and "Girlfriend, we are going to wine and dine! I've reserved a limo, too, so we can enjoy all the winetasting we want," she said excitedly.

"Thanks, Mir. That's really nice. Where is it playing?"

"Berkley. You will have an amazing time, I truly believe it," Miranda said imploringly. "You look great, like you're actually sleeping again. I just thought it would be good to do something really fun, to keep living, ya know?" She furrowed her brows, realizing Hannah was more than a little distracted. "Wait. Something's going on, isn't there?"

When Hannah didn't say anything, Miranda pressed, "Do ya wanna talk about it?" It almost didn't sound like a question. She became more serious and put aside her sanguine animation.

Hannah stared at her a moment, let out a sigh, smiled somewhat contradictorily. She felt anxious about leaving him like she did to answer the door, and it was tearing away at her, despite her logic purporting to the absurdity that he would be bothered by the interruption. She reminded herself, "He's a ghost!" If he was going to stick around, this interruption wouldn't change that, she reasoned.

"What's been going on?" Miranda pressed, cautiously.

Hannah hesitated, trying to decide how to proceed but just dived in. "I saw him."

"You saw Jesse?"

"No, yes, I mean Jess is not who I am referring to just now," she clarified hesitantly, giving her time to let this sink in. I saw Jess, too, but he's gone. He crossed over. He was saying goodbye," her mind drifted as she reflected on that experience, then continued, "The one who I think I've been feeling near me, that saved both of us from that cat while we were out there hiking. I saw *him*. He came to me and I saw him," she said resolutely.

It wasn't that she didn't trust Miranda. She did wholeheartedly, but it was that this felt sacred to her, like something she wasn't sure she wanted to share with anyone, including Miranda. She had already opened her mouth, so she had to tell her something.

Miranda almost seemed to hold her breath. "Who is he, do you know?"

"It feels like I do, but no, I don't know. He looked as real as you and me. We talked just as you and I are right now."

Miranda's tone was even more serious now, "What did he say?"

Hannah became more thoughtful, as she was still absorbing what he had told her before Miranda had so *inconveniently* rang the doorbell. She got up to pour a glass of water. Miranda followed on her footsteps anxiously. Hannah drank the entire glass of water. She offered a glass to Miranda, who took it without breaking her concentration. Miranda gestured to Hannah to continue with the story. Miranda could feel an adrenaline rush as she leaned closer to Hannah, who was now leaned against the kitchen counter composing her thoughts, trying to decide what she would and wouldn't tell her.

"I get the feeling I *know* him, not in the typical sense. I mean I feel like I know him from another lifetime, like I've known him for eons. It sounds insane, I know."

243

Before Jesse and Ethan's accident and their passing, she and Hannah had never had any conversation that bordered the subject of spirits or ghosts. She knew this was not something most people were accustomed to experiencing on any level, let alone *seeing* an immortal being, yet she sensed no confusion or doubt in Hannah's tone in *what* she saw. But now, this went beyond white blurs on a photograph. This was taking it to another level.

"Maybe he's your twin soul. I am pretty certain Alex isn't mine, at least fairly certain anyway, but you don't always meet them in every lifetime. Sometimes we are separated from them for entire, or multiple, lifetimes, which supposedly is to help us develop inner spiritual strength. For them too, of course. Maybe that's who he is," Miranda conceded thoughtfully with a measure of amazement.

"I don't know," Hannah mused with a faint quality in her voice. "It's not something I ever gave much thought to, not seriously anyway. I always thought it was a myth."

Miranda's jaw dropped, still reeling in her own thoughts. She leaned back and bit her lower lip and tightened her face. "Actually, that would explain a lot. That's the one explanation that actually does make sense," she looked at Hannah solemnly.

"How do you mean?"

"Honey, his protectiveness of you has been obvious, and there's the fact he didn't really allow you to be aware of him until you were, well, alone, so to speak. I don't know, it's a gut feeling, not like he's just an ancestor, ya know? She got up from her seat and started pacing the floor slowly.

"Keep in mind I don't have personal experience with this, seeing how my relationships haven't worked out so well in the past. I've done my share of reading up on this, and from what I know about it, there is

244

a strong, intense energy between them, an overwhelming attraction on a soul level. Some people do find their twin in life, and some don't, but we do get to experience a lot of lifetimes where our paths cross, and we even marry them, just not *all* our lifetimes. Also, the lifetimes we don't meet them can be very lonely for some. It's like we keep waiting for the right person and keep searching but end up settling or just staying alone. Most of us marry *a* soul mate and are really happy together, but fewer find their twin soul. It doesn't mean they aren't out there, just that they may not be incarnated the same time *we* are, and even if they are, there' no guarantee they end up together. What if he is your twin soul? If he is, he's moved heaven and earth to be here for you," she intrigued. "Can you imagine?" and then shivered violently, rubbing her skin quickly to warm herself. "Look at me," she shivered again. "It gives me goosebumps just talking about it!"

Hannah hugged herself. "Yeah, I have them, too. I don't know," she murmured thoughtfully. "Feels like a draft went through." After a pause to consider this, she asked, "So, you really don't think Alex is your twin soul?" Hannah asked.

"Not really. We get along but I think he's just a soul mate, not a twin soul."

"How can you be sure?"

"I think we can know in our heart, but a soul mate is someone we knew in other lifetimes that we feel a bond with or familiarity with. I believe you and I are soul mates, and we are best of friends and have been a long time, but remember how it felt like we had already known each other for ions when we met?"

Hannah nodded.

"We have multiple soul mates, but we only have one twin soul." Miranda paused, as she thought about how to describe it, then continued.

245

The relationship is very intense. When their paths cross, there is the feeling like they were never truly absent from each other." Miranda continued, "I'm no expert, Hannah, but I have read a lot about them, and I've spoken with people who have talked about what it felt like for them when they met theirs for the first time. One would have to experience to really know, but I didn't feel that kind of intensity with Alex. We both felt some familiarity but that was it."

"It was like that with Jess, too, just familiar. I love Jesse, I really do. He was never anything but good to me, and we had a very close bond, but what I felt when I saw *him*," Hannah took in a slow, deep breath and slowly exhaled, "surpassed anything I ever felt with Jesse. It was indescribably intense, but I figured it's because he's ...," she paused, "a spirit."

"I can tell you this much, you're not crazy. We both saw the photos, and there were two, not one, personages on them. There's no question something is happening. So, don't be afraid to talk to me about it. Okay?" Miranda raised her hand in front of her face and was pointing two fingers at both her eyes now. "This is me standing here. I told you, I *believe* in this. No matter how much you may feel like you're losing your mind, and I suspect that *is* what you're wondering, you are one of the sanest people I know, so when you feel like you want to talk about this more, and I sense you don't right now, just know I'm your friend."

Hannah was processing what Miranda had told her. Her eyes scanned the room, wondering if he was listening. What if he was, she thought. Was that what he was getting at, bringing up Plato? Miranda was right, it would explain a lot, she thought.

"I think you're right. This is more intense than anything I've ever experienced. I mean, I've met people that seemed familiar when I had never met them before, but this is different." Hannah paused trying to finish her thoughts as she reflected back on seeing him. "It's just the vibes I'm getting. I can't explain it," she relented, not wanting to disclose what Jared had said to her, and anything she would share with Miranda right now would be left open-ended, since the conversation she had with him had been interrupted. She had to wonder how many other people out there at any given time throughout the ages had ever experienced what she had experienced already today. Was it, in fact, more common than anyone knew? Had people had experiences like this and were afraid to talk about them? Hannah decided to hold off on some of the details until she knew more, herself.

"Just know this, Miranda said smiling, love has no boundaries, not even between heaven and earth,"

"You really believe that? That this is really a possible explanation?"

"I do," she said with conviction.

Jared was standing out on the deck that overlooked the underground swimming pool and the skyline above the Pacific. A smile pursed his lips. He listened as the two women talked and appreciated Miranda had reincarnated with Hannah once more and was a friend who was not only supportive but a believer in what Hannah was confiding in her. She needed a friend like that, he thought. In truth, everyone needs a friend that believes in them and who can be trusted. That is what aids embodied souls through their journey on Earth. Otherwise, life on Earth would be unbearable, as it is one of the most challenging planets to incarnate.

Hannah and Miranda had been best friends over many lifetimes, he knew, just as he had known Jesse and Ethan had been a part of many of Hannah's lifetimes, much of which Jared had shared in, as well, when he was still incarnating. He reminisced all the times he and Hannah had crossed paths, but Jesse had not recognized Jared immediately upon disembodiment, despite the many times they had known one another in other lifetimes, but he wouldn't until after he had crossed over and his soul's memories restored to him.

Jared, on the other hand, possessed all his memories of every lifetime. He knew Hannah intimately better than anyone, and he vowed he would do whatever he had to in order to ease that kind of pain for her now. He had hoped she would not return to mortality again, though he had respected her desire to do so. He hoped this would be the last time.

"So, I wanted to ask you if you would like to go for a slice of pizza and then take in a run and burn off the carbs?" Miranda suggested. "It would be another step towards getting some routine back in your life, and I miss my running partner," she pouted.

Hannah thought a moment and said, "You're right, I have been totally off my routine. I'll get dressed and we'll go. Sure, let's do this. It will be good to run again." She agreed.

Miranda followed Hannah upstairs and was pleased to see it was tidy as ever, thinking that's a good sign. No chip or candy wrappers, empty bottles of liquor, and no pill bottles on the nightstand. She was coping better than she feared. The house was spotless.

A few weeks ago, things would have been a lot different. Hannah had gone over the edge, and people are known to turn to vices when they are grieving or overwhelmed with stress. She had been afraid to leave her side, but now those fears were allayed. She had been texting and calling to check on her every day after Hannah had wanted to spend some time alone, but today, she had created an excuse to stop by unannounced to see for herself.

Miranda smiled to herself. "This ghost really has a positive effect on you, that's for sure," she thought out loud, out of Hannah's

248

earshot while she was in the bathroom brushing her teeth. Unbeknownst to her, not out of Jared's earshot. He stood 10 feet from her.

He smiled at Miranda's spoken thought, agreeing out loud, having muted himself for neither of them to hear. "Of course, I'm good for her!" he said as he adjusted his collar and brushed his sleeves, feeling humored. Of course, he had been interjecting his thoughts and opinions behind the scenes without being seen or heard, on myriads of occasions with no one the wiser and considered himself quite capable of entertaining himself, if necessary, but he often found mortals entertaining, as well, but other times they engaged in considerably alarming behavior, in which he had intervened when someone's mortality was at risk, or he had witnessed bullying of innocents, but never had he allowed anything to distract him from Hannah's wellbeing.

"I'm ready," Hannah announced after she had tied her hair back in a ponytail and put on sunscreen, followed by a sports bra, light blue sports top, and matching shorts, revealing her toned legs. "I'll grab a bottle of water for both of us," and started down the steps to the kitchen.

Miranda looked around the room one last time, imagining the ghost revealing himself in this room, and then turned and followed Hannah, who was now grabbing two bottles of water out of the refrigerator, handing one to Miranda, who had worn gray sports capris that came just below her knee with a gray and white tank top. She pulled her gray headband out of her purse and put it on. They each had an arm band that they packed their IDs and credit card, which was automatically something they always wore when they went running. Hannah grabbed hers off one of the key hooks in the kitchen where she always hung it and filled it with what she needed, and Miranda pulled hers out of her purse and they both strapped them on.

They stretched out their hips, legs, and feet for the next five minutes, for which Jared narrowed his eyes and hiked his jaw in amusement of the way they pretzeled their bodies. Once sufficiently stretched, "Let's go!" Miranda exclaimed, happy that Hannah was finally running again.

Once their feet hit the pavement, they paced themselves at a steady pace, running in place when they had to stop at the red lights, until they made it to Chelsey's Pizza. It was one of their favorite places to get pizza on the go. They had a wall with autographed photos of several celebrity patrons that customers were drawn to while they waited. After they each chose their slice, they stepped outside and ate as they walked.

"That really felt good!" Hannah finally said after she swallowed her first bite. "I didn't realize how much I missed it," tearing into another. After finishing off their slices, they drank some water and started running back towards Hannah's house. When they were halfway there, Miranda suggested, "I've been thinking, we should plan another trip, maybe go someplace where we can swim with the dolphins or go snorkeling, or we could go scuba diving. What do ya say?"

"I'm not really feeling compelled to scuba dive, but I've contemplated going whale watching. I don't know about a small boat. I'm not sure I can bring myself to do it," shying away from the idea, unwilling to commit.

"I didn't realize you had an aversion to being on a small boat," Miranda admitted, stopping to catch a breath. "Is it like a phobia of being on one?" She started recounting the times when sailing had been brought up in the past, and Hannah had dismissed it so nonchalantly that Miranda had not suspected it was for any other reason than conflict of time with family and having other plans.

When they made it back to Presidio, they broke into a brisk walk going uphill until they finally made it back to Hannah's. They unloaded their arm bands and took two more bottles of water, and both drank half the bottle before saying anything else. Finally, Hannah spoke, "Thanks for getting me out. That was good," as she began stretching her legs out.

"You're welcome," Miranda replied. "I'm glad you agreed," doing her own calf stretches.

They walked out to the deck and sat down. "The breeze feels good," tilting her head back and lifting her hair off her neck. "I'm alright, you know."

"Are you?" Miranda asked.

"As well as anyone *can* be, I suppose. I never wanted to bury my child, Miranda, but I can't go back and save him *or* Jesse. The way I see it is I have two options, to be selfish or to be selfless. If I don't take care of myself, even if I have to force myself to do it, I would hurt people who love me very, very deeply. I don't want to be a part of hurting people. Or, I can choose not to hurt people I love."

"You are a wise woman, Hannah Barstow," smiling slightly, as she leaned in and gave Hannah a tight hug. "I love you, ya know," hugging her a moment longer.

"I love you, too," returning the hug. When she released her, "Miranda's eyes had a pool of tears that had not spilled. She smiled at Hannah, feeling relieved she had assumed positive reasoning.

"Hey, I'll call you tomorrow, but I better get home and get a shower. Alex is coming over for dinner tonight," she told her.

"In that case, you two have fun," Hannah replied.

"Call me if you need me?"

"I will. I promise," Hannah answered.

Miranda held her gaze another moment, "Okay, I'm out of here," as she headed towards the door. "Don't forget, next Friday night," Miranda reminded her.

"I won't forget. Say hello to Alex for me," Hannah called out, watching after her until she was in her car.

Inside, still facing the door as she closed and locked the deadbolt, she froze still. She felt him near, moving closer, the energy from his presence flooded her, again. She didn't know if she could get used to this, despite how natural it felt even though it didn't. She hesitated, slowly turning. He was standing only inches from her.

Chapter Twelve

An Amused Ghost

Hannah almost fell back against the door but steadied herself. He was looking into her eyes, as if she were the only person in the universe that existed. His eyes had symmetrical beams of light, like stars that shown with piercing light that penetrated back at her own gaze. The faint celestial glow dimmed as he assumed the appearance of a mortal. Her body felt as weightless as speckles of dust floating through a sunray that had breached the shadows. Gravity seemed almost absent. Surprise had overwhelmed her when she turned and saw him so close, his passion palpable, so immortal, looking into her eyes like he *was* mortal. A current of energy surged through her entire body. Collecting her senses, maybe it was the change in lighting as she had closed the door, forcing her eyes to adjust from the bright sunlight. The curtains were pulled, casting dark shadows throughout the room. Maybe her heart rate had dropped too quickly from the run, but she didn't feel dizzy. She was trying to rationalize why she felt a sudden but brief change in her, her what? Equilibrium? Her molecular substance? Her mind was racing. His eyes continued to assess her, imposing upon her soul, yet she invited him. He leaned in slightly closer. For the first time, she felt she understood the true meaning of intimacy, as she had never known it before. She thought she must be having a spiritual orgasm, if that were even possible, not sure how to describe it. Jared could read her well and knew what she was feeling. He stepped back only slightly, then took another step until he was several feet from her, and she could feel the charge of energy lessen just enough that she could finally manage to speak.

"I was hoping I would see you again," she croaked, still feeling his intense energy that had subdued her.

"I didn't mean to overpower you like that. I have to remember to be more careful," he said apologetically. He started to move closer but then stopped himself, mindful of her mortal fragility, keeping his distance to allow her to regain her composure.

"It was good for you to you run again," he told her sincerely, feeling genuinely pleased she was making progress.

"Again? You say that as if you've watched me before. I mean, I haven't run since ..." She stammered, taking in the scope of what he just said. "How long have you been watching me?" she paused, feeling a lump in her throat forcing her to swallow hard.

"I've always been aware of the course of your life. I never had cause to make myself known to you before now. You've made choices that have been good for you," he continued nonchalantly, "so there was never any reason for me to make you aware of my presence." He recollected the times he had intervened to protect her, once from a bully at school who had been jealous of her, a rapist on the football team, a serial killer/rapist as she was jogging through Golden Gate Park after dusk, something he frowned upon as he thought of it, and then he had kept her from slamming into a tree at Lake Tahoe while she was skiing, but she didn't need to know any of that. The important thing to him was that he had protected her from real harm.

"You did enjoy the run?" he asked, pressing forward.

"I did, yes," her mind still reeling. "It felt really nice to hit the pavement, again," beginning to compose herself but then began to blush, as she recalled what she had been thinking while she was out with Miranda, which he immediately recognized she was trying to conceal something from him he already knew. He was amused by her, broadening a grin that accentuated his dimples, which in turn left her blurting the first thing that came to her mind, as if the conscious part of her brain seized and lost momentary control of Freud's id.

"I just kept imagining you running along beside me, given how athletically fit you seem, I figured easy for you, right? I mean," realizing how outlandish that must have sounded coming out of her mouth, spoken to a man who did not even possess a physical body. His dimples had made her forget momentarily, and if that was not enough, in an effort to hide her embarrassment and regain her poise, she continued without a hitch and blundered again, "But that's ridiculous. You don't even have tennis shoes. I could just imagine someone seeing you out there, running along beside two women and have a jaw-dropping moment and lose their fresh latte to the pavement. Can you imagine?"

Now she was really feeling foolish, wondering why she had just started nervously blurting. It was not like her at all. She had always considered herself composed and was not in the habit of speaking before weighing her words.

"Oh! I didn't just say that! She was about to profusely apologize but stopped quickly, wanting to completely silence the flow of words before she choked on her own foot.

He studied her as if watching a comedy. "Ah, you find that amusing, do you?" straightening his lapel and lifting his foot outward in front of him, turning his foot this way and that, observing his boots.

"I suppose I could turn them into proper shoes for human running activity," continuing to consider his footwear, arching his eyebrow, something he did when he was perplexed by her ongoing ability to continue to take him off guard.

"I didn't realize you would have a sense of humor," she admitted, relaxing a little.

"Witnessing the stress, she had just put herself through, he wanted to put her at ease. "Even immortals have a sense of humor. But just so you know, you are the only mortal who can see me."

"I suppose that's a relief," she replied sheepishly. I never thought about the immortal world or God like that, having a sense of humor," smiling back at him with genuine sincerity. "Duly noted." She curled her nose as she sniffed her shirt, "I really need a shower to rinse the sweat off and get into a clean change of clothes. I'm feeling a bit ripe right now. Do you mind?"

"I don't mind."

"Thank you, I appreciate that," and turned towards the stairs, reflecting on how strange it was asking to be excused from the company of a ghost. When she glanced back over her shoulder, he was gone, which gave her pause. She was anxious to get out of her drenched, sweaty outfit and to wash the dried salt from her skin, so she went straight to the shower and stepped in before the water had even warmed.

Twenty minutes later, Hannah emerged cautiously, peaking out, grabbing a towel and quickly wrapped it around her. She grabbed another towel to finish drying off before walking into the bedroom. She looked around the room but still did not see him, nor did she sense he was there, so she opened her spacious walk-in closet and ran her fingers along her dresses until she decided which one she wanted to put on. It was a cream-color, long summer dress that had extra short sleeves that exposed her firm, slender arms, a large-rounded neck that buttoned down the front, which hung on her loosely. She towel-dried her hair, brushed it out, and put on some soft pink lip gloss. When she scoped her room, she didn't see him, so she went back downstairs. Still, there was no sign of him. She was confident he hadn't gone anywhere.

Feeling a little hungry after the run, Hannah pulled some cheese out of the frig and put some on a small plate, added some almonds, and poured a glass of sauvignon blanc that she carried to the living room, where she curled up on the couch. She nibbled slowly at the cheese and took a sip of the wine. She still didn't see nor feel him. Perhaps he was waiting for an invitation, knowing that she had gone to bathe. It was obvious he came from a time era when gentleman would have made themselves absent for a lady about to undress.

"Jared? Where are you?" she spoke softly, looking around the room, that was filled with sunlight from the west. Then, he was there. She closed her eyes at his immense energy that always foreshadowed his entrance, moving in on her. The sensation forced her to hold her glass of wine midair, steadying her movement, before bringing it to her lips, she focused on her senses and what his essence felt like. She reopened her eyes and saw him. His voice was gentle, "Are you ready now?"

"I am," she replied. "Would you like to sit down," she offered, motioning to the seat beside her.

"I'd prefer to stand, if you don't mind."

"Alright," she answered in compliance. "Tell me again, how long have you been with me, here, "she clarified," in this life?"

He walked around the room, slowly, observing, touching glass décor that were molded in the shapes of vases, bowls, and other abstract shapes she had bought in Mexico after having watched how they were heated in the fire and shaped into beautiful shapes, she had chosen several pieces to bring home, some clear with a vibrant color while others were soft pastel with a white color. She also had some figurines of dolphins perched on pedestals on each side of the open doorway that lead to the dining room that he took particular interest in, as if feeling for their energy or history of being made.

"I was with you when you departed to come to Earth, and though I didn't choose to reincarnate again, I began monitoring you while you were in your mother's womb. I wanted to make sure nothing was causing you distress. Sometimes I would sing to you." He said it without embarrassment or shame or any reservation.

"What? You would actually sing to me? While my mother was pregnant with me?" Her eyes filled with tears that did not flow and her smile turned into brief, involuntary laugh as she tried to imagine him singing to her while she was still a fetus in her mother's womb. In that moment, Hannah knew she could not fathom the love he must have for her.

"So, angel singing is *real*," she noted outloud. "You accepted the role of being my guardian angel? Is that what you're telling me?"

"I'm not officially assigned to you, no, but I do choose to be involved in your well-being."

"And you can do that? Immortals can stay close to people they love or are attached to on Earth?"

"It's not uncommon," he said casually. "It's different with each soul, what they choose to do. Some are not ready to leave the earth's atmosphere at the time of their passing, so they stay until they're ready. Others leave immediately and cross over and stay until they reincarnate, *if* they choose to reincarnate again, that is.

"You're saying we have a choice whether we reincarnate?"

"Everyone has a choice. But we tend to see things more clearly when there and choose to do what is in the best interest of our development, unlike when we are mortal." He smirked, "Mortals have a tendency to be self-sabotaging at times. Then there are those who cross back into the earth's atmosphere when someone they care about is in danger or going through a difficult time. They may come to warn or comfort them. Each situation is different."

He paused as he picked up a picture frame on the shelf. It was of Hannah with her parents, taken of them when she was a small child.

"Ah yes," he said, gazing appreciatively at the images as if reminiscing. "Your mother seemed to sense me at times, but she didn't know for sure, nor was she certain that anyone was even there," he smiled at her as he looked up from the photograph. "You were three years-old in this picture, in earthly years. Of course, there is no sense of time in mortality." He set it back down and continued speaking. "Those who leave the earth in passing are not disconnected from those they leave behind. Each one's experience is based on what they choose to focus on once they depart their mortal life. Most processes are similar for everyone, but yet there are differences based on one's faith and expectations immediately upon their earthly departure. There is a lot of freedom once one re-orientates to their immortality. It is an atmosphere of learning, creativity, joy, and peace."

He looked at her tenderly with compassion before speaking again. "I know you don't remember, but it's quite an amazing place, really."

He stopped moving momentarily and looked directly into her eyes, reading her internal responses, as he described to her what she had forgotten. She was hanging on to every word, imagining the reality he was recounting.

"And, contrary to the freedom we have," he continued, "there is also an immense amount of structure and organization."

"But what you're explaining, is it why I feel this overwhelming connection to you?" Something in her soul was resonating, as if the soul itself remembered, even though her brain didn't. She was mostly talking to herself but trying to process this one piece of information that seemed to expand to a larger picture, a greater purpose for him being here now.

"Have there been other lifetimes you have been with me, I mean, like this, without a physical body?"

"No. This is the first time I have ever presented myself to you, as I am now, while you have been mortal." He moved closer to her now and sat on the large cherry coffee table opposite of her, so he could look at her face-to-face. He touched her hand, his energy surging into her.

She closed her eyes as she felt it. He had a glowing light in his eyes, as if there were a shining star of sacred knowledge that he possessed. He was the most resplendent being she had ever seen. She felt her mortality in his presence. His effect upon her was so very familiar, so natural, yet nothing like anything she could ever remember experiencing. She felt so comfortable with him, despite he was an immortal. She looked into the depths of his eyes, searching them. They seemed filled with more light, more love than any pair of eyes she had ever looked into before.

"How is it, when I look at you that you look so real, like you are mortal, but just like that, you can disappear? I mean, obviously, your body is not flesh and blood, or you couldn't do that. I've read that even angels walk amongst us and sometimes we think we're looking at a human being and it's *not*. People have seen them and thought they were real, but …."

Jared interjected, "What am I made of?"

"Yes," she replied, almost in a whisper.

"Energy. It's what forms each of us. It's what forms the Earth, the universe, and everything in it. Storms! It's what thrust the waves through the ocean. It's what forms matter. It's what forms light. If you've ever studied physics, you learned energy can never be created nor destroyed. It can only be transformed, and thus the earthly body is one form of transformed energy while the spirit is another form of transformed energy, and when one passes from mortal life, their energy is transformed from the *mortal* body to the *immortal* one. Youthfulness is recreated.

Fatigue is turned to vibrancy. The old passes away and all things become new. That's what transformation is, but regardless of what any form of energy is transformed into, its substance is very real. I am *no less* real than you are. The mortal body was not intended to last for an eternity. Just because the human eye cannot see the spirit, unless the spirit allows it, it does not mean it does not exist. The human eye cannot see air, but it exists.

"I do remember studying physics, actually, but I don't recall the professor actually using the soul or a spirit as an analogy. I still find the matter of you being human and I am human, but both created of different kinds of substance still amazing, but you're right, it does make better sense using that analogy," she told him appreciatively. She felt like a student, again, listening to him speak.

Everything about him interested her. His perfect form made her wish he *was* mortal but willed herself to dismiss the thought, knowing it was impossible. Discerning her thoughts, he turned away.

"It's impossible to have a physical relationship," he said, anticipating the obvious would come up, and it had. Her disappointment did not escape him.

"I know," her eyelashes covered her eyes as she diverted them to the floor, acknowledging the elephant in the room.

"Always be honest with yourself, Hannah. I would know if you weren't. It's important you're always honest with yourself concerning what you can bear or not bear as far as my presence in your life, in that I have allowed you to see me. It is self-defeating to long for me to have a physical body," turning again to face her.

"I *am* being honest, I promise," she told him, meaning it, as she looked up at him.

"If it ever becomes more than you can bear, I'll know."

"Speaking of what I can't bear," smiling sheepishly at him, "then, would you stop electrocuting me!" feeling the need to lighten the tension. "I might as well tell you before you read my thoughts," she blurted out. I do welcome how I feel in your presence, but it is a bit intense at the same time. It's like everything inside me is just leaping inside my body!" She watched his expression, as he seemed humored and were about to erupt in laughter. "It kind of tickles," she conceded as if she had exaggerated, "but it feels just feels like you're electrocuting me!"

Jared's laughter was intoxicating. "Do you have any idea how delightfully comical you can be, Hannah Barstow?" obviously amused.

"So, spirits not only have a sense of humor, they laugh?" she noted, pleasantly surprised.

"Not only do we laugh, but we laugh often! We are happier than mortals by hundred-fold if not more!" his eyes sparkling and dimples deepened.

"So, you are saying we embodied souls are a miserable bunch, are you?" she added teasingly, finding it impossible not to laugh with him.

"I would never say that," he said wittingly. "You're putting words in my mouth!" She could see he was enjoying the banter, which she found most intriguing.

"But you thought it, didn't you?" she teased, her smile broadening.

His eyes seemed to glow as he gazed upon her admiringly. "Not in those words, no," he jested, slightly flabbergasted, but I would say you've summed it up accurately, yes, but there are exceptions" he quickly added.

"Well, I'm sure I'm not counted among the exceptions," she admitted. "I like that I'm seeing you laugh," feeling she had seen him laugh thousands of times but only said, "When you touch me, it really is powerful, a new feeling for me, but I kind of feel revved by it," she said reflectively.

"You told me it electrocuted you," somewhat bemused, noting her contradiction, raising his eyebrow and crossing his arms.

"It does but, but it's different," trying to explain. She began pacing this way and that, further amusing him, searching for words to describe it. "It's not painful; it just feels *different*, not in a bad way, just takes me off guard because it's so unexpected. I mean, *this body,*" pointing at herself, "has never experienced it before. It's like a total body tickle that swallows me whole. It's not a *bad* feeling," she stammered to clarify, realizing she sounded like she was complaining. "I'm sure I could get used to it," pausing to look at him, but then almost flirtatiously, "I mean it is a rather *charged* feeling," eliciting an intrigued look from him. He was enjoying this, she could tell. "It would just be nice to know when to expect it, is all." Her rambling captivated him as he feigned a perplexed stare, arching one eyebrow. His reaction was not lost to her.

Tilting her head, she locked eyes with him, "A baffled ghost," she thought out loud, assessing his stare. "Interesting."

"Pleased to see you still have your humor intact, Hannah Barstow."

Midafternoon, Hannah drove to the florist and bought pots, soil, and seeds to plant more Birds of Paradise, which was her favorite flower. She loved the beauty of contrasting colors of orange and purple and blue and gold. She made sure to pick up some mulch to put around her existing plants, which she had planted around the house after they had moved in. These would go on the balcony where she could keep an eye on their anticipated blooms before putting them in the ground.

Jared watched her on her hands and knees, as she toiled with pruning and laying the mulch. She was every bit as elegant as these magnificent flowers she so loved. They had been her favorite flower in other lifetimes, as well. In his eyes, she was like a flower, and he could see her starting to bloom slowly after a devastating storm.

The last of the mulch had been laid and the winds picked up. Before she had gotten her garden tools and empty mulch bags picked up, it began to rain. She hurried to get to the garage and out of the rain, but by the time she was inside, she was drenched. She threw the bags in the recycle bin and took her shoes off as she entered the house. After washing her garden tools at the kitchen sink, she dried them and left them on the counter while she pulled her wet clothes off and threw them in the washer before running a warm bath. The warm water felt good after the chill from the wet clothes. She had not checked the weather forecast, as she routinely did when she got up. "Jared!" she thought out loud. That's why she hadn't known it was going to rain.

"Where are you?" she asked.

"Do you seriously mean to blame me that you were not better informed it was going to rain?" she heard him ask.

She sunk a little deeper under the suds that floated like mountains of crystallized bubbles atop the water, as if she had been scolded.

"Yep," she squeaked in response before emerging her head to wet her hair.

"Mortals!" she heard him exclaim with a quality of laughter. Once again, she noted, Jared was amused.

Chapter Thirteen

Journey to Farallones

She was running up a hill. The boy was ahead of her, looking over his shoulder laughing, "Come on, I want to show you something." They were each pulling kites that danced high above them in the breeze. They topped the hill and as they did, there was a herd of elk grazing. They were the largest creatures she had ever seen. A few of the elk stopped to take notice of them, but the boy motioned her to be very quiet, putting his index finger to his mouth. They sat down on the grass to watch them.

"They are magnificent," he told her with awe. This is one of my favorite places," he added.

"They are beautiful," planting her eyes on them, wondering what it was like to be one of them. She looked beyond, further in the distance and saw a large stone house. It seemed to stand out, perhaps because it *was* so large, and thought rich people must live there, but just as she thought it, she felt the tug of the kite as the breeze picked up and she looked up at it almost giggling. She watched it gracefully jump around and then laid herself back on the grass, looking up to the sky, moving her arms and legs as if she were an imaginary snow angel but without the snow. "This is the best day ever," she told him, continuing to watch her kite soar high above her. His face lit up with a broadened grin, seeing how happy she was.

"Do you think we will be friends forever?" she asked him.

"Of course, we will!" he told her, as if it were the silliest question he had ever heard.

"I hope so," she answered thoughtfully.

Hannah bolted up in bed, startled, as if she had been sucked back through a time capsule. There was a dim light from street lamps coming through her windows. The dream had seemed real, just as the last time she had it. She noticed she was breathing faster than normal. She had felt the boy being torn away from her as she awoke. She tried to go back to sleep to finish the dream, but an hour went by, and she gave up. She slipped out of bed and walked to the sink to get a glass of water and splashed water from the facet onto her face. She needed to clear her head and knew she couldn't go back to sleep.

A run would do her good. The sun would be up soon. She slipped into a gray sweatshirt and a pair of navy spandex, tied her hair in a band, grabbed her cellphone, and stepped outside.

The brisk air gave her pause, as she took a moment to inhale its crispness. Everything was still damp from last night's rain. The streetlights were still dimly lit in the dawn sky that was still bejeweled with a slight hint of the night's darkness. She took off at a slow pace but gradually her muscles welcomed the old routine. She ran faster, varying her pace, not to overexert herself. The exercise did not involve distance as much as it did incline that made the workout more intense. As the blood pumped faster through her veins, she focused on the adrenaline rush, every sensation in her body, every burst of energy that pushed her for more. She topped a hill, breathing hard, but pushing herself up the hill reminded her of how much she loved the run.

She had spent a lot of time in the house since the memorial, and though Miranda had made successful efforts to get her out of the house, she had not truly gone anywhere by herself or without being prodded with encouragement. She came to a circle not far from her house where there was a gate that opened into a wooded area, where she descended down dirt steps through trees and bushes where it opened onto the beach. Straight ahead was the Golden Gate Bridge and the entrance to the bay. The beach offered an expansive view of the Pacific.

At this time of the morning, the beach was vacant. A soft burning glow rose behind the mountains where the sun would be coming up but hadn't broke the skyline yet. She sat down on a grassy mound above the beach and watched the ocean waves, feeling lost in the tide, reflecting on the recurring dream. She had been alone since waking up. Jared had not unveiled himself to her yet, but she was grateful for that, appreciating some time for introspection. He probably already knew what she needed and wanted and was obliged to give it to her. Nothing about her seemed to be secret from him.

Her mind wandered, looking out over the ocean, as she drifted back to the dream, trying to re-envision the faces of the two children, but no sooner had she begun to remember bits and pieces, she could see a cruise ship approaching. It seemed to tower above the sea like a floating castle with what appeared, from a distance, to have at least nine levels of windows from the bottom level of portholes to the sundeck. She watched it journey closer to the bay entrance. From near the front of the bow, she saw it was a Grand Destiny, the decks filled with returning vacationers, who appeared no larger than small ants against its colossal size. She guessed there were close to 3,000 people on board, if not more, enjoying the last moments of their voyage, as the ship entered the bay and crossed under the Golden Gate. She imagined being on it, the joy and rush of excitement and even a little disappointment as the cruise returned to its port, remembering the first time she and Jesse had gone on a cruise to Alaska.

She reminisced watching the whales and dolphins swimming alongside the ship and allowed her mind to take her back. The memories sparked a sudden desire to go whale watching. It had been a couple years since she and Jesse had gone whale watching at Point Reyes where they had seen a family of blue whales with their calf during the month of January. It had been so windy and cold, and the wind had nearly cut like a knife. Jesse had opened his coat and snuggled her into it against his warm body to shield her from the cold wind. They had both taken turns watching them with the binoculars. Every year, they had gone whale watching, but only from land, sometimes from higher elevations like Fort Funston and most years they had seen them except for two, but the experience of watching the hugest mammals on earth grace the sea was still breathtaking.

They had talked about taking a boat out this year, something Jesse had hopes she would be willing to do, so that they could see them close up. It was October. She knew if he were still here, Jesse would still want her to go through with the plan. He had always tried to encourage her to go out, but Hannah had a trepidation about going so far out on smaller boats. A cruise ship had been the only way he could get her out on the ocean to experience being on the water and the wonders of watching marine life. He would be thrilled for her to rise above it.

She thought about that for a few minutes, and knew she had to make up her mind to overcome her fear. If the boat sank, she would be with Jesse and Ethan again, and then the thought that took her by surprise, Jared, the idea of which did not repel her in the least. She considered that to be the worst that could happen, even if it meant she had to be eaten by a shark to get there, but by then, the freezing sea would already have numbed her body, she would never know, probably just float into the white light and there they would be, waiting for her. She bit her lip, as she pondered a few seconds longer.

"What the hell," she decided. Here goes nothing, or maybe everything. She would do this in honor of Jess's memory and everything he had wanted her to enjoy. Maybe his spirit would join her, if only briefly, to whisper in her ear, "Aren't they amazing, Babe? I'm glad you did this for yourself."

She sprinted back to the house. Despite that she was out of breath when she got there, she ran up the steps to the bedroom and got on her laptop in hopes that there would be room for her on the next tour to Farallon Islands. She had always imaged what it would be like to go but knew it would mean traveling 26 miles from land in a small boat.

"Please, please, don't be sold out," echoing her thoughts anxiously under her breath. After choosing the option for only one ticket, "Yes!" she exclaimed, then quickly grabbed her wallet and added her credit card information and printed her confirmation. Bold excitement flooded her with a rush. Spontaneity had always been a part of who she had been, and she welcomed it as a sign she was making progress with recovering to a point she could function and go on with her life. The spontaneity made her feel alive, but this was more. It was adventurous. She would do it in celebration of their lives in honor of the happiness they would want for her. Ethan always loved seeing her smile, which she did just thinking about his little face and how he would always grin back at her when she *did* smile. She could feel a healing force sparking inside her. This was something she *had* to do! She had to do it for *them,* to see in her mind's eye they were smiling down on her from heaven, maybe even giving each other a high five.

She hurriedly turned the water on to the shower so it would be warming, removed her spandex and sweatshirt and got in. It hit her, "Miranda! She had just mentioned yesterday doing something like this together. If I survive this, I might have to do it again, then," she rationalized. She didn't want to waste time feeling guilty she was going without her.

Ten minutes later she was brushing her teeth and applying lip gloss before retying her hair back in two hair ties, one for a ponytail at the top and another halfway down to keep her hair from flying into a tangled mess, anticipating the ride was going to be windy. She quickly slipped into a pair of leggings with jeans over top, a cotton long sleeve shirt with a turquoise pullover sweater over the top of it, anticipating the icy winds further out from land.

"I'm going to do this," proclaiming to herself. She was feeling wondrously giddy and pleased with herself to be living in the moment. She searched the closet for the binoculars. After she found them on the top shelf, she hung them around her neck, sucked in a deep breath and exhaled slowly. "I can do this," boasting self-confidence and then descended the stairs almost running. She grabbed her keys hanging in the kitchen and put them on a belt loop hook, tucked her credit card, license, some cash, and her cell phone into her cell phone carrier, after which she hurriedly rushed to the coat closet, grabbed a waterproof jacket with a hood and thick lining.

Before going out the door, she stopped and turned, looking around the house. "Jared, are you coming? It will be fun," she said coaxingly, looking into thin air. She did not see him, but she felt him and sensed his smile and approval. She smiled to herself, and at him, then hurried to the car.

Fifteen minutes later, she found a parking space at the pier. She had been headed to the parking garage when a car had pulled out of a parking spot along the street just ahead of her, so she whipped in, paid the parking meter with her credit card, and ran the rest of the way where she presented her ticket confirmation to attend the whale watching tour to the Farallon Islands that was scheduled to leave in 15 minutes.

She walked quickly down the pier towards the *65-foot* catamaran, where the waiting whale watchers were gathered while crew instructed them on what to expect on the trip. Once everyone started boarding, she was given a lifejacket, after which she found a seat behind the cabin at a table next to an older couple who smiled at her as she sat down. She then promptly hooked her cellphone case to the belt loop of her jeans as she settled in amid the other patrons who had already boarded, immediately appreciating the boat was not yet filled to capacity.

There was one other couple that boarded just after she did, which made her feel a little better that she was not the last one to board. The older couple she sat next to seemed excited as she watched them holding hands, smiling at one another. The woman had short, dark hair with faint auburn highlights. She had a squared face and brown eyes framed by long eyelashes and natural tones of makeup and warm-colored rouge that accentuated her high cheekbones. She wore dark shade of orangish-brown lipstick that matched the colors she wore under her jacket. She appeared quite slender despite the bulk of her jacket, and the gentleman accompanying her, she assumed was her husband, appeared maybe ten years older, was tall, athletic looking with peppered color hair and a mustache that suited his face very well with Sinatra eyes. He was strikingly handsome for someone of his age, which she thought might be seventyish, and together, they were a very attractive couple. Hannah could picture their younger versions being the high school prom king and queen.

Noticing her, the woman turned to Hannah. "You made it just in time," the woman said to her smiling. Glancing at her partner and back to her, she added, "We got here at 7:30, but you didn't miss much. We go out every year and it's always the same orientation speech," she said. "We've pretty much got it memorized."

"So, you two are from the city, then?" Hannah asked, curious.

"We live in Mill Valley, lived there for the last thirty-five years. It's more our rhythm, if you know what I mean, but we enjoy coming into the city and living close by, going to the opera and theater, and we shop here, of course; I mean, there's a lot of perks living so close by, but we're retired and the traffic is something we prefer not to deal with any more than we have to," she said, waving a gesture of nonsense, stifling a laugh.

"Oh, I agree! I'm Hannah, by the way," introducing herself.

"It is lovely to meet you, Hannah. I'm Trudy and this is my husband, Sam," gesturing towards the gentleman sitting beside her, "Yes, we've been married forty-two years now," Trudy told her, smiling at her husband with a spark in her eye that did not escape Hannah's notice.

"Hello, Hannah, a pleasure to meet you," reaching out to shake her hand. "Have you been out to Farallon Islands before?" Sam asked, being politely conversational.

"No, I haven't, which now that I think of it, surprises me since I've lived in San Francisco all my life."

"You're in for a treat then. You'll love seeing all the sea life out there. Oh, and by the way, if you starting feeling seasick, I always bring a bag of ginger candy," patting the zipped pocket of his jacket." A lot of people aren't prepared for that, and you see them gripping the railing and losing their breakfast over the side of the boat. It's no fun. I was seasick our first time out, so after that, we come prepared and always bring a little extra for others."

"Thirty-one years ago, Sam and I were at Muir Beach one morning, very early at the crack of dawn, and the water was cold as ice, but silly fools we were, we dared each other to get in and see who could keep from running out of the water first. It was the middle of summer, and we often did go to the beach and walk around the overlook. It was so romantic, and still is, but anyway, I don't know what possessed us. I was turning blue, and Sam was laughing at me for yelping every time a wave hit nearly knocking me down. In came a large wave that I knew was going to be chest high on me, if it didn't swallow me completely."

"I was just about ready to turn and make a dash back to the beach and wrap myself in the beach towel, when all at once, Sam and I were surrounded by a family of dolphins that seemed to have come in with the tide. They had swum right up to us, didn't they, Hun," eliciting a nod from Sam. "Neither of us had even noticed them until they were right upon us, because we were both acting like such fools and so entertained with one another. There they were, though, swarming all around us. Sam's lips were blue as berries, but something about those dolphins coming up to us like that, we forgot that we were cold. Then, they took off after several minutes."

"We both ran out of the water and sat there on the beach snuggled up under two heavy beach towels watching them swim around and jump in and out of the water. We could hear them frolic and play for about twenty minutes, until they swam so far out we could barely see them. We were so excited, we ran back to the car and got in, sand and all, and hurried back to tell nearly everyone we knew, not even having changed out of our wet clothes first," she recalled, laughing and nudging Sam playfully, who was nodding his head, reminiscing the memory with obvious joy, chuckling.

"Well, it would have taken away from the moment, if we had taken the time to go and change first," he said teasingly for emphasis, his countenance filled with charm, as he looked upon his wife with complete adoration.

"I suppose you're right. I never thought about that," she said with a deep throaty laugh.

Sam continued, "Every year since then, we do *this,*" gesturing his arm out toward the Pacific, "in hopes we will see more dolphins. Of course, we enjoy the whales too. They are the most fascinating creatures," he stated musingly. "We still go out on the beach in the summer and wade in the water, but we've never had them come up to us like that anymore."

"You know they are the only other species besides humans that call each other by name! They mate for life, too, very loyal creatures," Trudy informed her.

"I did not know that!" Hannah replied, genuinely intrigued.

"Yeah, yeah, you should look it up. Very interesting," Sam concluded.

"Oh, looks like we're moving," Trudy turned to Sam feeling excited. The boat had begun to pull away from dock and was slowly edging out into the marina where they would go twenty-eight miles out to sea towards the islands that were a national refuge and habitat to many wildlife. Trudy and Sam shifted their attention towards the surrounding seascape for a moment long enough to give Hannah a chance to excuse herself and move towards the side rail and take in the salty air, as the breeze began to pick up. She watched as they moved towards the Golden Gate where they were surrounded by sailboats that were already out, people living and enjoying life, and just as they passed under the bridge, she felt him near her.

"I'm glad you're doing this," Jared said. His voice was felt as much as heard. He watched the breeze against her skin, saw the light in her eyes, and put his hand to her hair. Despite the breeze, she felt his energy brush her and reached up and touched where his hand had been. "You're not alone," he told her. "I myself am quite fond of the sea," he smiled, and when she turned towards his voice, he was there, smiling at her.

"Can anyone else see you?" she asked sharply, tensing for a moment but quickly recomposed herself.

"No," Jared answered reassuringly. "Only you."

Relaxing her stance, she recomposed herself and looked out over the ocean, and without looking back at him, "If people think I'm talking to myself it will draw attention!"

"I hear your thoughts," he pointed out, amused by her reaction to him. "Besides, no one can hear you over the wind." Hannah was conscious of the joy she felt having him with her, glad that he had accompanied her. She had clearly accepted his presence in her life, and in fact, had come to welcome it.

"Did you give me the idea to do this today?" she thought silently, feeling the breeze blow across her face, could hear it pounding past her ears. She didn't feel cold with her layered clothing.

"And if I did?" he asked her.

Hannah smiled nervously. "If you know me so well, then you do know I have had a fear of being out on the ocean in small boats?" she said almost silently that only Jared could hear her. She avoided looking towards him so as not to appear she was talking to someone imaginary. She looked toward the sea with her back to the other passengers.

"I do know," he affirmed.

"Well, I trust you would have forestalled this impulsive notion if you knew I would not be safe," she told him. "Given that you have been so devoted to my safety and well-being, I'm trusting you with my life." He heard the humor in her thoughts.

"If you are going to ever be free," he spoke slowly into her ear, "you must face your fears and not avoid them."

"I don't even know why I've had so much reserve in the first place," she said, as an afterthought. Nothing has ever happened that could have caused me to be so afraid of being on the ocean on a small boat, at least not that I remember." She was holding on tightly to the railing until her fingers were turning white under her fingertips and knuckles. "There has just been something about the open sea, being so far from land, I don't know why," she queried to herself.

"I mean, I feel perfectly safe on a cruise ship but not a smaller boat. I may never know," she said curiously.

Jared knew why and remembered like it was yesterday. As he looked out on the expansive horizon, he remembered the ship that they had been aboard during the eighteenth century. They were three miles from land, when a massive storm had culminated unexpectedly. The waves had grown rapidly, causing the boat to thrash out of control. Water filled the deck as the boat creaked loudly from the strong winds tossing it back and forth. There had been lives lost, though hers had not been one of them. The boat was eventually washed ashore, but not before crashing into a large rock structure closer to land where the remaining crew and passengers had barely made it to land alive. The fear had remained with her, embedded deep into the subconsciousness of her soul, having become a phobia that held no connection to her current life. It was a soul memory from centuries ago. It pleased him she was facing it rather than let it continue to paralyze her. If she were going to seize into an onslaught of panic, he would be with her when and if it happened.

The waves were slightly up from light winds, slapping against the hull, but otherwise the day was bright and clear. Jared watched her intently. She had closed her eyes and was relishing the breeze against her face and the beautiful scenery all around her. The sound of her heart was steady, and her breathing was even, but he would know if she was in distress. He focused keeping her from thoughts that would invoke fear by keeping her absorbed on the beauty around her, the peacefulness of the sea rather than imagining its ravaging tempest.

"Do you know how many different species live in the sea?"

"I've no idea," she admitted. His eyes seemed to be taking in the scope and depth of the ocean, as if he could see beneath its surface all the lifeforms and hidden secrets.

"Nearly a third of a million, many of which the earth's scientists do not know about. Humans are the most intelligent species on land, but did you know amongst the cetaceans of the sea, which you know as the whales, dolphins, and porpoises, they are capable of transmitting and receiving 20 times more information than mortal humans while using only one of the senses? Their souls are tightly connected to the human soul and to the universe. They create the music of the sea," leaning in towards her affectionately. "Their melody is so beautiful, so peaceful," he continued as if he were listening to a symphony with the utmost appreciation.

"The ocean is also symbolic of the human soul, forgetfulness, knowledge that is hidden; it's an 'other-worldliness,' a search of truth. One must dig deep to find what they are looking for, discover treasures within, the same way one must search within his soul to find truth, what is real and what isn't, that the things we fear most are nothing to be feared at all but are worthy of love and embracing. That's when the healing takes place."

Hannah clung to what he was trying to tell her, looking at the ocean all around her, imagining its depth and the similarities it had with the soul. The big sea monsters, the monsters under the bed and in the closet, all seem to correlate with the fears hiding deep within the psyche. Truly, the unknown was the most frightening.

She was finding it easy to understand the analogy and the connection of all things. She sensed all life and matter on earth was in some form one big symbolic analogy of the spiritual flow of life. As humans, we tend to choose one of the opposites to center our lives around, keeping our lives out of balance and only fractionally cognizant of the imbalance we create. The mental health field calls it "dysfunction."

"The psyche really *is* like the ocean," she reflected. Lights were coming on, synapses were firing, as she became more aware of what Jared was telling her.

She was grasping what he wanted her to understand.

"Our knowledge is as vast as the sea," he said as he stole a glance from her, but then looked back to the water below as if seeing what was not visible to the human eye, "but one does not remember most of what they know, and what one knows is never truly lost to them. The task is to rediscover the hidden treasures that are yours and have always been yours, to define yourself more and more and embrace what has been given to each one of us, mortal and immortal alike. The only difference is that mortals struggle to remember who they are. Immortals just know, maybe not immediately after they leave the earth, but once they return home, everything they forgot is restored to them.

Hannah's attention was on Jared, lost in his words, shutting everything else out, her mind drifting to her own insightful interpretations. Without any warning, a large humpback whale breached the surface a few short feet from the catamaran. It swam underneath the boat, missing direct contact with it by what seemed to be a mere two feet, if not inches. Hannah felt as if her heart had stopped, and no sound passed her lips as the gush of oxygen filled her lungs. The other passengers displayed mixed reactions between calm and reverence to frantic fear the boat was going to capsize. Most were speechless at first.

Jared came behind Hannah and stood against her, placing his hands on her shoulders to steady her and help her to focus on the awe of this amazing creature. He whispered in her ear, "It senses your heartbeat, your feelings. Don't be afraid of it. Its calculation is perfect. It knows how close it can get without bumping the boat. It will not compromise the safety of anyone aboard." He could feel her shoulders relax, her breathing and heart beat slowed to normal pace.

She was not sure if he was communicating a truce with this creature, but she trusted him.

"I'm fine, just a little startled is all," she told him. "What an extraordinary creature," she said in respectful awe.

Just then, the passengers noticed there were two other humpbacks that were swimming near the boat on the other side, seeming to want to join them. At first, they were spyhopping, exhaling air and steam from their blowholes, but afterwards, breached the surface and swam along beside the boat. The one that surfaced first looked to be all of fifty feet long, while the other two were slightly smaller, probably 40 to 45 feet. Voices were reverberating all around them as the other passengers delighted in getting to see and be up close and personal with these gentle giants, and everyone had their cameras out, including Hannah who was able to take a few really good pictures. She noticed the larger of the three had swam up close to the side of the boat where she and Jared were standing and seemed to be looking right at them, holding their gaze.

Hannah captured one solitary picture of that moment. That's all she needed. After about twenty seconds it swam away and breached once more thrusting most of its body out of the water and diving beneath the surface. Hannah and the passengers watched, as it passed underneath their boat to the other side. Once the humpbacks had gotten far enough away from the boat, the catamaran picked up speed again and continued toward the islands. A school of dolphins came close, some of which were jumping in and out of the water next to them. Everyone was taking pictures and filming. The excitement of being graced with their presence was palpable. The whales were further in the distance now but close enough to still see to get decent pics as they surfaced. Hannah watched with her binoculars. Eventually the whales were out of sight.

As they neared the islands they began to reduce speed. Hannah used her binoculars and could see the sky cranes with their big mooring balls, used to lift boats carrying scientists that worked on the island. She could see the many elephant seals and sea lions basking in the sun and swimming in the open waters, perched on the massive rock that was a part of the islands. Western gulls were flying atop the island with some diving for food. The seabird colony was amazing with so many different species of birds, but one specie that Hannah thought was most striking, fine-tuning her binoculars to get a better look at the tuft puffin, which is black with a thick red bill and red feet with a white marking on its face that reminded her of a white Zorro mask wrapped around their heads. She watched them dive for pray, catapulting out of the water with a small fish or squid, taking them back to their nests. She found them to be remarkably beautiful and secretly wished she could see them in the winter when their plumage would turn a brilliant blue, but coming all the way out here in the winter was not something she imagined herself doing.

A family of dolphins was swimming near their boat and seemed to want to say hello and greet everyone as guests to their domain. Two large Mola molas surfaced nearly 15 feet from the boat, which is an ocean sunfish. As they got closer, she set her camera to zoom in on the seabirds, the sea lions, and dolphins. A blue whale surfaced less than a football field away. It gracefully and repeatedly emerged and would resurface again almost in slow motion. After a couple of minutes watching it, another one surfaced, as if coming straight up from the deep and then swam alongside the first.

All attention was now on them as they commanded the undivided attention and awe of everyone aboard. Each time they surfaced, a fountain of steam would thrust forward from their blowholes with a loud whoosh. They possessed patience as they moved, gliding through the deep blue water with a majestic presence, in no hurry to get anywhere, no anxiousness, no fear, no aggressiveness, just a magnitude of peace and contentment, as if they knew who they were, what they were, and lived their lives simply *being* what they were created to be.

They seemed to be going in no particular direction, but then after a few minutes they turned and were getting closer with no deliberation to do so, it seemed. Everyone was trying to predict which way they were going, and some talked nonstop between themselves.

Hannah looked at Jared who was watching her and knew his focus was on her reaction to the largest creature to ever inhabit the earth. She was in *its* domain. He turned and observed the whales briefly and then looked back at her. She was not sure which was the greater miracle and more fascinating, but knowing she was the only one on the boat that could see him was just now sinking in. Realizing the love that was being shown her from this massive, infinite universe was humbling. She felt privileged to have had *that* miracle bestowed upon her. She felt chosen in a way, privileged to experience all she was experiencing. She felt noticed and acknowledged by something, someone, greater than the massive power she felt surrounding her out here in the Pacific. She felt loved beyond anything she had ever known.

Something was flowing through her she had never felt before, not like this, to the magnitude she now realized. She smiled at Jared and then almost broke out into joyous laughter.

"I have never felt so alive! Thank you!" she only relayed to him in her thoughts. He received them clearly and smiled back at her.

He stretched out his arm toward the blue whales, and he held his hand in a manner as to invite them closer. As he did so, they turned and swam directly toward the boat, not moving any faster than before, but began swimming towards them, as if upon command.

Hannah was dumbfounded when she realized what was happening. No one else knew, of course, there was an invisible being onboard whose command was summoning them to come closer. Nevertheless, everyone's excitement, both visibly and audibly, increased as they realized the whales were coming in much closer.

"How are you doing that?" as she raised her camera and began taking pictures of them. When the whales came within fifteen feet of the boat, Jared lowered his arm back to his side. They lazily frolicked in the water, diving and coming back up until one was so close that when it sprayed from its blowhole, some of the passengers near the railing were showered with it, as the wind blew the steamy mist in their direction, only escalating their excitement.

The whales were migrating towards Baja, so they must have seen a hundred gray whales at a distance, which took Hannah's breath away, not to mention the hundreds of sea lions, fur seals, elephant seals, porpoises, Cassin's auklets, elegant terns, and brown pelicans, amongst so many other species one does not have the advantage of seeing inland, so much. Their populations were much higher out here. There must be tens of thousands of species out there that most humans never see, never know exist, she thought to herself, feeling grateful that she got to see a few in their own habitat, uncaptured by man, living free in the world.

The day had truly been unforgettable and as the catamaran was headed back to the marina, Hannah felt free of the fear that had gripped her for as long as she could remember.

The question raised itself, "Did I have to lose my child and my husband to experience what I experienced today?"

The more the question posed itself in her mind, she told herself, no, it wasn't all about her. They had eternal purpose, and their crossing over was about them and the happiness and joys that awaited them, wherever they had gone to. It's about everyone their passing has affected, too, Rachel, Kyle, Danny, people Jesse worked with, people who loved them. My parents. They lost their only grandchild, their only son-in-law. I'm not the only one who has been hurting, so no, it's not just about me, she thought. In some way, their passing would make each one stronger and teach us something about ourselves," she chose to believe. She owed it to herself to look within, to know her Higher Self. She believed Jared was there to make sure she did just that. He saw her as she really is, stripped of all mortality, flesh, and weakness. It was up to her to discover the spirit within and let it shine rather than snuff its light out. Maybe we owe it to each other, in this life.

She wondered if others have someone there for them, keeping them afloat, helping them rise above their grief. Yes, Hannah decided, they did, but whether they could actually see that being, as she was able to see Jared, she didn't know. She had to trust that grace was a gift available to all who were willing to believe, be open to it, and embrace it.

Chapter Fourteen

Reflection

The catamaran docked at the pier and once secured, everyone was making their exit in single-file, still discussing between themselves different sights and wildlife they had seen, their favorite creatures, imagining a life at sea, and the fact that only scientists were allowed to be on the islands, which most people didn't even know existed in the first place. Some were still recovering from seasickness.

The sun was now high in the sky, and although there was a haze across the sea, the sky was clear, and the breeze inland was moderate enough to impose the need for a light jacket. Despite most were glad to return and be on solid ground again, there was the widespread inner longing to still be out there, taking in more of the experience they had immensely enjoyed. There was an air of euphoria, as Hannah stepped off the boat, being assisted by one of the crew onto the walkway. She was in no hurry to be anywhere, so she took her time, as she headed the direction of her car.

Jared walked closely behind her, smiling as he discerned her euphoric mood and thoughts, while she was completely unaware of him. He chose not to distract her while she reflected on the day's experience. He remembered the times while he had been a seaman that he had witnessed such other earthly wonders, and the last time was when he was a physician with Hannah by his side, as they journeyed from Wales to America. He had not reincarnated since. This was a new beginning for her to witness the earth's beautiful creatures in this life, having no memory of ever seeing anything like she saw today before. In spirit form, he remembered the details of the many lifetimes they had shared, as well as the ones they didn't. This time, he had chosen not to return with her, but neither had he known how much she would need him.

She had not even realized until she passed the restaurants, surrounded by aromas of fish, sizzling burgers, and fresh-made breads on the pier, that she was hungry. Once in her car, she turned on the engine, and the time on the dashboard said 4:11. She stared at it realizing how quickly the day had gone by. For the first time, she noticed her stomach was growling. She unclipped her phone case from her belt loop and set it on the magnetic dashboard mount. She had missed a call from her mother and two calls from Miranda. She made a mental note to call them after she got home. She couldn't wait to tell them about her tour to the Farallones, not sure that she could even describe everything she had seen with any justice. One would have to experience it for oneself to even begin to understand what it was like.

She drove towards Presidio feeling lost in her thoughts, Jared being there with her today and the couple she had met. Then, she remembered the dream and was wondering about the connection, if any, the dream had to Jared. Everything seemed so interconnected, she thought. Today, she had felt as free as the kite she had dreamt of. She would never had conceived of having such a wonderful day without Jesse and Ethan. Her life was taking a surprising turn she could not explain or fathom ever being possible.

Suddenly, she felt the car brake and come to a stop, only to see a skateboarder crossing the street in front of her at a red light. There she sat, completely unaware of coming upon the intersection. Her mind had been elsewhere. She had goosebumps covering her body and felt a rush of adrenaline, and as it quickly sank in, he was there.

"You really do need to pay attention," he told her.

"Did you …?" not able to finish her question. "You scared me senseless!" She took a deep breath realizing he had stopped her from hitting someone, possibly killing that skateboarder, who had seemed oblivious that he had almost been hit, that his life had been in danger at all. She looked around at the other traffic and pedestrians. No one was staring at her or cursing her.

"*I* scared *you* senseless?" he countered with a puzzled expression. "I think you scared yourself!" correcting her. It might behoove you to thank me that you won't be arrested for hitting that boy," pointing out the obvious.

"I didn't know you were in the car with me, so how do you do that?" she asked, feeling a little flustered and embarrassed. She was grateful though.

"Simple, I just put myself in the driver's seat and pressed the brake."

"But I'm sitting here!"

He looked at her, entertained by her astonishment. "You and I both, while you were, shall we say, absent."

She gaped at him.

"The light?" he pointed, redirecting her attention.

She looked again, and it had turned green, and the driver behind her had tapped his horn, thankfully without blaring at her with it. With every previous thought in her mind having come to a complete halt along with her car, she proceeded forward and did not speak a word to him until she had parked in the garage and had closed the garage door. She turned to say something to him, but he was gone. All she felt in that very moment was gratitude that he had been there in that precise moment.

"You know I'm grateful," she shouted into thin air.

Once inside the house, she still did not see him. She hung her jacket in the closet, then washed her hands and retrieved two leftover pork chops and vegetable tray from the refrigerator she had prepared the night before, accompanied by a glass of white wine. When her stomach had stopped growling, she rinsed her hands, put on a long powder blue sweater that she kept on the coat rack, and carried her glass of wine and walked out on the deck and sat down in one of the chairs.

She and Jesse had enjoyed the view and many intimate conversations sitting in those chairs, day and night. There was a table between them she sat her glass on that supported a large umbrella. There were blue and purple checkered throw rugs in front of each chair. Large hanging baskets of plants hung with flowing greenery on each corner from the balcony above. There was an array of candles sitting on the table, as well as on two candle stands in the two distal corners that they had often burned at night. She didn't want to let those memories put an overcast on the thoughts she was having of today. They were some of her favorite memories, in fact.

She needed to allow herself to be happy and reflect on the new memory she made today and make room for the joy she had felt out on the ocean watching the whales, the ocean life, and the many species of birds. Life around her was so amazing. Today had felt epic for her. In her mind, it was as if the universe's puzzle pieces were falling into place, and some of the pieces were magnetically drawn closer to connecting pieces, but it was an infinite, ginormous puzzle. It was easier to see a piece snap into place when she was in state of such joy, as she was now. When she was hurting and grieving, it all closed in on her, and she couldn't see more than what her mortal eyes would allow her to see. When she was feeling truly happy, feeling joy and gratitude for life's experiences, the universe opened up to her and life was expansive, infinite, and forever. Every suffering and every confusion seemed like a distant star you could barely see amongst so many others that shown so brightly until it faded out and was no more.

The universe handed each one of us the kind of puzzle that would take lifetimes to figure out, millenniums perhaps, but with each journey, each experience, more pieces would become connected and begin to form something discernible. She took a sip of wine and was once more lost in her thoughts.

Over an hour passed. Jared sat in the chair next to her, but he remained invisible to her. She needed this time to herself, he knew. He did not want to intrude. Today had been liberating for her, and although he had been there witnessing her experience of it, he found wisdom in letting her reflect on it on her own.

He occasionally projected thoughts in her mind to help her see the bigger picture of life, but a discussion was not what she needed from him right now. He sat quietly discerning all her thoughts. She was the same soul he had always loved and would love without end. Every memory he had of her that spanned over eons were never dimmed with time.

There was no forgetfulness of anything where there was remembrance of love.

He watched her for a while, aware of every thought and memory she was feeling. He was pleased with the progress she had made today and wanted to give her privacy and more time to reflect. He stood up, took a step forward but stopped and turned to look at her once more, then crossed through all physical matter as he ascended past the trees and crossed into the parallel unseen world.

Chapter Fifteen

A Symphony

At 7:01, Hannah emerged from her house adorned in a navy meshed long dress with three-quarter sleeves, a fishtail hem, and a jeweled neck that accentuated the 14-inch white gold chain and half-inch diamond pendant with matching earrings. The latter, Jesse had given her for their five-year anniversary. A long navy, embroidered cape hung from her shoulders to offset the evening chill. She wore navy four-inch wide heal sandal with a strap above her ankle that matched her crossbody wallet that hung to her side.

The limousine chauffeur held the back door open for her, and she gracefully entered and sat next to Miranda who was wearing a charcoal gray dress that conformed to her body and was loosely pleated from the knees down and black coat that hung just above her knees. Her black stilettoes were open-toe patent leather revealing black polish on her toenails that matched her fingernails. She wore a matching set of black onyx jewelry and wore dark red lipstick.

"Hey, girlfriend! I hope you're hungry. We have pizza and pointed to the to-go box sitting on the opposite seat. There's wine in the frig, pointing to the mini refrigerator. They had everything they needed to sit back and relax and enjoy a luxurious night. Miranda was flipping the bill for all of it.

"Wow, this is really nice," she said, taking in the amenities that included blue neon lights. She checked out the frig and found a bottle of pinot grigio.

"I had the complimentary champagne replaced with white wine," Miranda said, her eyes gleaming as she smiled at Hannah.

"All the better!" and poured two glasses and set them in their respective glass holders and helped herself to a slice of pizza. "This is really good," careful not to get any on her dress and held up her glass, "Let's toast to our friendship."

"To friendship," Miranda said and touched their glasses together. "I told the driver to take the longest route, as long as we are there by 7:45, so we'd have time to eat and finish a glass of wine.

Hannah glanced toward him and noticed Miranda had the privacy partition raised.

"So, what's been happening?" Miranda asked. "Anymore visitations?"

"Actually," signaling her to hold on while she swallowed, "Yes. He's always there, and he allows me to see him. He stopped me from hitting a boy at an intersection earlier today. I'd probably be sitting in jail right now!"

"He's seriously watching out for you! He's not playing around!"

"No, he's not," Hannah agreed. "Oh, one other thing. It was spur of the moment, but this morning, I took a boat to the Farallones. I mean really spur of the moment. One moment I was sitting on the beach, and the next I was running as fast as I could to get an online ticket and rush down to the dock before it sailed. It happened that fast. I know we talked ...."

"Oh, my word! You did it! You—went—sailing!" Miranda's astonished look of surprise and thrill seemed to exude from her pores, she was so ecstatic, stomping her feet on the floorboard and doing a dance in her seat. "Yes!" She took Hannah's glass out of her hand and placed it in the glass holder and gave her a long hug. "I am so-o-o proud of you," staring into her eyes. "This is huge for you."

"Yeah, it kind of is," she admitted, "It wasn't planned or I would have called you, and we would've done it together," she started to explain.

"Don't you dare apologize. "Look at us. Right here. Tonight." And all this after you were on a boat tour at the islands! We have got to celebrate! She did a search for the song, Celebration by Kool & the Gang and played it. Miranda immediately started bouncing and singing to the lyrics. Her giddiness was infectious, and Hannah chimed in with her. They sang and shoulder danced to a couple more songs before they arrived.

The chauffeur came around and opened their doors for them and they filed out of the car and entered the symphony hall. It was so grand. Hannah could do nothing more than surrender to her fascination, though it was not Miranda's first time there. One could not help but revere the architecture, acoustics, lighting, and the overall beauty. Their seats were in the box seats to the right of the stage. They had only been in their seats a few moments before concertmaster came onto the stage, and the musicians began tuning their instruments. Afterwards, the conductor came to the stage.

Throughout the symphonic performance, there was an atmospheric magic that arose from the ensemble. Hannah felt goosebumps blanket even her scalp with a couple of the soloists' performances. She saw Miranda rubbing her arms, so she knew she had experienced the same thing.

Hannah thought about how each performer had been practicing and perfecting their talents since childhood, the hard work, self-discipline, passion, and dedication. Each one had contributed to the collective experience for every patron tonight. She tried to imagine what the entire world would be like if all human beings were that dedicated to a talent or purpose that edified someone else, even if one person.

Back in the limousine, Miranda played another song, and again, they both shoulder danced and sang together to the tune the entire song, *I Hear A Symphony*. Miranda asked the driver to just drive for two hours. Going through San Francisco along the city streets, they opened the moonroof and stood up so they could look out while singing to anyone who was listening, mostly pedestrians who looked on with humored pleasure while others waved them on.

"I'm glad we did this," Miranda said as she started to unwind.

"Me too. It's been so lovely. Thank you, Miranda," Hannah said appreciatively.

"You bet."

"This day has been absolutely magical for me. I needed to be able to step out of this cocoon of death that had swallowed me. I have to accept they are on the other side and give myself permission to stop grieving and start celebrating life. They're *alive*, Mir, just ...."

"And don't you ever forget they're alive," Miranda admonished her. "And so is their love for you! Even still." Miranda kissed her cheek. "You have so many experiences waiting for you, yet to come."

"I know. I think I have to make them happen, though," she said conclusively.

"That you do," Miranda agreed. "You owe it to yourself."

Hannah stepped out of the limousine as the driver opened the door for her. She was thoughtfully smiling as she entered the house, locking the door behind her. Nightlights illuminated the entrance. The evening had been grandeur. She took a deep breath as if to breathe in the day that was now concluding. She reached down and pulled off her heels and carried them to her room. Undressing, she felt him approach her from behind. She was getting use to his powerful energy when he drew near, and she welcomed his presence.

Jared's hands rested on her bare shoulders. He discerned the change in her, the quiet acceptance, as she began to heal. He had watched her throughout the evening and witnessed a deeper transformation. She was letting go of the last threads of emotional paralysis that kept her from moving forward. A new fabric of liberalization was weaving its new thread into her mind and soul. She was giving herself more and more permission to live and laugh without feeling guilty. There was a knowledge greater than hope that she would see them again, whole and smiling at her, catching up on one another's experiences on the other side. She was disengaging the delusion that their existences were truly separated, except by a singular delusion called *mortality*. The insightful reality of their continuance in life so parallel and near to her own had grafted firmly within her knowledge of what she considered to be true. She embraced its quiet comfort.

She turned but did not see him, yet she knew he was there. She pulled her white gown over her head and then slipped into her robe and slippers. She was not yet sleepy, so she lit candles in the living room and sat down to enjoy the quiet companions of peace and stillness, watching the small flames inside the crystal fairy lamps evenly dispersed near the center of the room.

It felt so good to feel silence in a good way, a way that rendered a feeling of peacefulness, a silence that didn't feel lonely or imperious. Was it unnatural? *Perhaps* it was more natural than the lack of it. It didn't feel suffocating or monopolizing. It felt bigger than she was. She had decided it was a companion that belonged. It was welcoming and alive but quiet, not noisy or imposing, nor was it strangulating to the human soul. There was no element of loneliness in it. It did not scream at her with blaring sadness. It was like a quiet clear sea that carried her afloat, drifting with one peaceful wave after another. She felt light, not really thinking about anything, as her thoughts had cleared her mind.

It was if her soul was being observant and mindful of a power that everything in the universe bowed down to, whose unseen presence made everything in the house, every object, every furnishing, the walls, even the invisible air, seem as though they were filled with energy that loved her. A color felt like an entity with purpose and voice that communicated its energy to her.

Everything felt alive but quiet and soft, as if at peace with itself, sharing with her a quietness that seemed healing, encouraging, and inviting, yet she felt a distinct awareness she was the one doing the inviting.

Everything exuded quiet understanding and knowing with no judgment, yet power beyond imagination was in every molecule of the air she breathed. It seemed to paint and correct everything she perceived into censorship of purity and wonder. Every fear and every perception of loss held in the balance was vanquished. Taking it all in, she wanted to embrace it, accept it, not run from it. She sensed a recognition of the energy that surrounded and permeated her. In doing so, fear also seemed nothing more than a delusion.

She didn't want to move from the room or turn her focus to any other task. She took in everything she knew to be her home, aware of the most minute details of everything her eyes beheld, the expansiveness of the room with high ceilings and arches, the soft tan and gray colors, the large ceiling-to-floor bay windows that gifted her with a view of the western sky beyond the large, sturdy deck, the polished mahogany hardwood floors covered by a square of soft tan carpet occupied by the large, symmetrical coffee table that was surrounded on three sides by two cream-color perpendicular couches with two complementary chairs and a hanging chandelier that provided the room with a moon-like golden glow.

An open area faced the gray-stoned fireplace that supported a large hanging TV above it and exterior book cases on each side. There was an elongated cherry Chip and Dale dining table in the adjoining open and spacious dining and kitchen area, and a booth that was enclosed by the open bay windows, also on the west side of the house. There was an island for food preparation lit by a hanging chandelier in the center of the kitchen, the light from which bounced off the taupe-color painted cabinets and stainless-steel appliances. The open space between all three rooms was expansive and seamless.

As she took in every detail of her earthly home, it was as if her soul was seeing everything in molecular detail. She slowly sat down in one of the cream and light gray plaid high-back chairs facing the window where the sun had gone down, appreciating its firm but soft comfort. The stairs were to her right behind the bookshelves that lead to three bedrooms and two full bathrooms on the floor above.

Without turning, she reached behind and pulled the gray crocheted throw around her that her mother had made for her and closed her eyes. Her higher Self had emerged, and her awareness had been sharpened. She was acutely aware of her surroundings, yet they remained a delusion that had no place in the immortal world. She realized sleep was setting in and felt herself drifting obliviously into another level of consciousness. Then, she slept.

Chapter Sixteen

A New Chapter

The neighbor's Schnoodle's irksome barking alternated from whimpering to annoying howling. It continued less than a minute. She checked the time; it was 8:23.

"Wow, I must have really been out of it," thinking out loud, orienting herself to the fact she had slept in the chair. She had not even taken the time to change into her pajamas or get into her own bed.

The last thing she remembered was pulling the throw over her and turning the lights off. The tea candles she had lit the night before had long since burned out. She stood up and stretched, noting she was a little stiff.

An unsettling feeling came over her, as she became increasingly aware she had not seen Jared since yesterday on the boat. She whipped around, jolted with alarm, hoping he would be there, patiently waiting for her to wake up. Nothing.

"Jared?" No answer. "You there? Anywhere?"

After a pause, no response was forthcoming. She didn't sense he was anywhere near her. She stared at nothing, trying to think. What had changed? She called for him, again, but was met with silence. She rushed towards the kitchen, the sunlight peaking in, looking around, as if he might suddenly appear from wherever he was watching her from.

Upstairs, she stopped in the doorway to the expansive master bedroom that took up the entire west side of the second floor with the guest bedroom on the east side and a full bathroom that separated it from the bedroom that had been Ethan's near the top of the stairs. Her full queen-size bed was still perfectly made, having not slept in it.

She paused when she came to Ethan's bedroom door. Her hand touched the door handle but she hesitated, taking a deep breath before turning the handle. She had expected a tsunami of emotion to swallow her as she stepped inside, but she was met with a manageable wave, instead. She would not allow herself to give in to more.

"It's time," she thought out loud. Monterey Bay was an area she had often thought she would like to live if she weren't living in San Francisco. It was smaller and quieter, slightly warmer climate, and possessed a different quality that she felt she needed at this point in her life. It was exactly what she needed.

Searching Google, she found a reputable realtor and immediately dialed his number. The thumping of her heartbeat in her chest was not ignorable, and she noticed she was holding her breath as the phone began to ring. On the third ring, a male voice answered, Smith and Cowles Realty, this is Matthew Cowles. How can I be of service to you today?" Five seconds longer she held her breath, not sure whether to speak or hang up, but after those five seconds, she found her voice.

"Hello, Mr. Cowles, this is Hannah Barstow. I'm in the market for a house in your area, and I would like to meet with you, today, if possible," afraid she would change her mind if she put it off, despite her better judgment. Everything inside her was propelling her to do this.

"Sure, Ms. Barstow, I have several properties available. Have you looked on our website at our listings?"

"Honestly, I have not. I very much like the area. I'll be coming from San Francisco."

"Okay then, tell me specifically what you have in mind, and I'll be happy to accommodate your interest."

"I'm interested in something with an ocean view, spacious but not overly large, a lot of shade trees, patio or deck is fine, a garage, secluded but not necessarily isolated from neighbors or community, and lastly, quiet. I would really like to be in a quiet area. Also, I would like something that has a security system installed, of course," she added.

"Absolutely. I could schedule an appointment for 1:00 to show you some properties. Will that give you enough time? I could show you what I have today. There are several properties I believe will suit your needs."

"Okay, sounds good. I'll plan on meeting you at 1:00, then. I have your address."

After hanging up, she felt a whim of excitement. Not the kind of excitement that comes with going parachuting or hand gliding for the first time, nothing that compared to yesterday. This was a subtle excitement that comes with long-term change. Change is always scary, she thought, regardless of whether it's perceived as good or bad. It was still change.

The oatmeal took all of 90 seconds in the microwave, and she scrambled a couple eggs on the stove and ate them with a glass of pineapple juice. After a quick shower and putting on a pair of faded jeans and a pink pullover sweater with a white tank top underneath, she was on the road, making one stop at Starbucks for a large blonde coffee for the road to take care of her caffeine fix before getting on the 280 going south.

The drive was relaxing. The weather was sunny with only a few cumulous clouds that sailed the sky like colossal fluffy ships minding the stratosphere. Her mind was made up she would sell the house and leave San Francisco. A quieter, smaller town with a slower rhythm would be good for her, and it would be that much closer to her family.

She wanted to stay in California, as Arizona didn't really appeal to her, despite that being where her family lived. She had always been fond of the central coast. It would be a good change for her, she thought, having a small-town address. She was at a point in her life she needed introspection, where she had no memories of living with Jesse and raising Ethan. Those memories would stay with her, she knew, but living in the house where those memories were associated was not something she could keep doing.

Yesterday, the trip to the Farallones made her feel alive, separated from grief, from everything associated with pain and reminders of loss. It was a bifurcating path, and she had chosen to experience the empowerment of her choices rather than feeling disenfranchised by them. The exhilaration of choosing that one new experience and facing her fears had felt so empowering that she wanted to make more decisions that would make her feel she was in control and not just a passenger of life. That one choice had made her feel more alive inside, not because she was happy, because she wasn't, but because she had responded to an idea without someone coercing her or just going along with someone else's suggestion or having someone else making choices for her. This decision had come from within rather than some external voice telling her what she needed.

She thought of Jared and the dreams she had been having. Something she intuited gave her inclination to believe somewhere, in another time, Jared may have left her with a similar void she had felt months earlier, or perhaps the other way around, or both. "What if?" she had thought more than once since he had manifested himself to her. Yet now, at this conjecture in time, his very real presence gave her a deep joy and assuredness of our eternal existence, something she always had believed in but now had no room for doubt. His energy brought with it an infinite familiarity that felt more real than anything she had ever known. Yet, he was not a physical being, not anymore, anyway.

It was imperative she make the choice to turn the page, to dawn a new chapter in her life. She owed it to herself to explore it, make it what she needed it to be, and trust that it would be more than she imagined but all she could hope for. Jared had made life more tolerable, but she had the distinct feeling he was there to guide her into making changes that were going to help her regain footing her in life again, making it possible for her to move forward.

To think that he would stay until her dying breath in old age was probably not how the universe planned his visitation, if the universe had anything to do with it at all. Maybe he was acting on his own. Perhaps he had gone rogue to try to save her. Well, that was probably stretching it. That was the most egotistical thought she could ever remember having.

She wondered, if angels, spirits, whatever one would call them, really have that kind of power to take off from Heaven without permission or being instructed to do so? Who was she to know the answer to that? she wondered. Was she that desperate for significance? She laughed mockingly to herself, feeling the need to back up from that thought, and pull herself together, but then, again, she tried to remember when was the last time her thoughts were really *together*? What had been rational about her existence at all since...? She couldn't go there, wanting to refuse being drawn back in. Why was this all hitting her again? It was as if a sudden storm had blown in.

She leaned against the wall in the hallway and felt herself slide to the floor. She pulled her knees to her chest and closed her eyes. The thoughts wouldn't stop racing. "No! I can't stay here!" Stop! Just stop! Please just stop!" and then the dam broke and she cried relentlessly until she willed herself to stop. Crying made it hard to breathe, so she pulled herself up to get a Kleenex. The decision to initiate voluntary change was also met with emotional challenge, as she was facing now. She knew she had to recognize it for what it was, process it, and continue to execute what she had realized, since yesterday, would be a much-needed gift to herself.

After she had gained her composure, she stared at herself in the mirror that hung in the half bath. She kept staring.

A huge part of her heart, the love she felt, all that energy she gave in loving her husband and son had departed with them to accompany them on their journey to the afterlife and had left her feeling empty and fragile. They would always have that part of her. It could also be that the depth of love they felt for her had spilled over into the spillways of her soul, if that were even possible. The overwhelming emotion had simply seized her because she missed them so much, as they had been before when she could wake up each morning and see them, touch them, and hold them. She hadn't *wanted* to adjust. If she adjusted, what did that say about her? What normal person can heal from this?

The less memories that filled her mind, the more she had felt she was building a wall to insulate herself. The more the memories did flood her mind, the more helpless she had felt to feel a normalcy that included happiness and joy. Either way, there had been no normalcy. Nothing about her or her life had felt normal anymore. Last night she saw things clearly in her mind, and this morning when she woke up, it seemed to her as if during the night, while asleep, in an alternate state of being, she had made her mind up and awoke knowing what she had to do. She had to redefine what normal was to her, as she learned to redefine herself. Moving was her attempt to do that.

She arrived early so she spent a few minutes driving through town looking around. She had been here many times and had always felt drawn to the area. It was a wonderfully quaint community, full of culture, no high-rises or skyscrapers, away from interstate traffic, and most of all, quiet. She arrived five minutes early at the realtor's office.

Matthew Cowles was a middle-aged man, casually well-groomed, a few inches shorter than Hannah with slightly thinning hair, who wore a wedding ring, and greeted her professionally with a smile and warm handshake.

"Mrs. Barstow, here are the listings I thought you would be interested in that sound closest to what you told me you would like." He handed her four. After viewing the detailed descriptions and photographs of each property, she wanted to see the ones on the north side of town first, being familiar with that area.

We can take my car," he told her, which was a Volvo, Hannah guessed was not more than two years-old. As a professional courtesy, a bottle of water was in the passenger cup holder, which she thanked him when he had offered it and began sipping on it.

"Each time I have come here, I have been in awe of the town and thought if I ever moved from San Francisco, this was the perfect place to live, retire, make a life," lost in the scenery as he drove, imagining herself living her day-to-day life here.

"I like it," he told her. "My wife and I moved here from San Diego. We've love it here. Our kids have been happy. It's been the perfect life, that's for sure. I think I can provide you with just the right home that you feel is a good fit for you."

"I'm counting on it," was all she said, as she imagined herself living a completely different life.

They spent a little more than two hours viewing each of the properties north of town, each of which she liked very much. There was one in particular she liked the best, and she could very easily choose that one, but there was one more on the list to see before she would make a decision. They were all well-built with excellent constructive engineering, she was sure of that. She wasn't going to draw this out. She was going to allow spontaneity be her guide and let it take her on an adventure. Where she moved to was already decided, it was just a matter of choosing the house.

"The last property is just south of here a few miles," he told her. Matthew Cowles had a good sense about people, and he sensed Hannah was running away from something, a pain she could not bear anymore. He sensed she not only wanted but needed this move to happen.

It reminded him why he was passionate about his job. He not only made a good living, he was making a difference for someone else, and this was an area that many sought to live. For some, it was an escape, a new leaf, starting over, whereas for others, it was a matter of retirement or getting that big promotion that made them want to ascend to an elite status. Not for this woman. She doesn't care about that, he decided. He suspected she was searching for solitude. Therefore, he chose not to chatter too much so as not to annoy her. When he did speak, he focused on what she needed to know, and was thorough in answering her questions without rambling.

Matthew Cowles kept his demeanor professional and left personal out of the conversation, which he often included to build rapport, but she did not seem approachable in regards to small talk or being personable. He would respect that. He would not state the obvious just for the sake of conversation. Anything he told her would be informative. His vibe was that was all she wanted from him, nothing more. She did not seem the least bit arrogant. No, it wasn't that at all. Yes, he felt intimidated by her, but not because she intended him to feel that way, he told himself. In fact, she struck him as being very humble and reserved. Why was he so unnecessarily analytic? It was hard to take his eyes off her. She was elegantly beautiful. She had inner beauty that was distinct. He picked up on that almost immediately. She was not superficial either.

He had always been analytic of people. It was why he was successful at his job. He didn't apologize for it, but sometimes he did think he overanalyzed. He was determined to deliver to her the house she needed.

In some cases, it was not just about the commission alone but compassion. There were the rewards that came with knowing you helped someone else attain their own desire and see it to fruition when the house someone loved became their own.

It took just over 10 minutes to get there. It was off a narrow, less traveled road, high above the sea with a view of the aqua-rich colors and creamy white capped waves that rolled in like foam stretching as far as it could reach before a horizontal gravity pulled it back to its own substance of where it came, an infinite sea of abundance that never allowed a wave to stray before bringing it back to itself. The incoming tides reminded her of infinity. The ocean could easily be seen through the thick of trees that lined the street while driving under a canopy of branches that provided privacy between neighbors who enjoyed a comfortable distance from one another. They turned off Highway 1 onto a narrow road that directed them uphill until they saw below them the warm blue ocean; its waves seemed as if they were welcoming her.

"It's beautiful up here," Hannah spoke in awe, thinking how different it was from living in the city. "I could really get used to this," not taking her eyes off the view. The car slowed as Matthew pulled into a driveway where there was a garage sitting next to the road.

The property was in a clearing that had several tall trees lined by meticulously trimmed bushes and shrubs. The perpendicular A-frame roof of the house was covered in sable brown concrete tile over sandy-white color stucco. The front of the house faced the ocean, so the entrance was accessed through the eastern side. There was a balcony upstairs that faced the west with an entrance between floors on the north side where there was a walk way. When you entered on the landing, there was a half flight of stairs going to the second floor and another half flight going to the first floor.

Once on the first floor, the living room was spacious, with an open deck facing the west, where one could look down over the beach and out over the ocean. The master bedroom and full bath were on the east side of the house, and on the south side of it, perpendicularly, there was a large kitchen, laundry room, and another half bath.

There was a sitting room on the west side of the kitchen that had large windows on both the west and south side that one could sit with a 180-degree view to take in all the scenery where there were colorful foliage, grapefruit and lemon trees, and a walkway that circled around a flower garden.

Upstairs, there were two bedrooms and a bathroom that separated them, each having two vertical windows on two of the walls but only one having a balcony that also was on the west side.

"Matthew," she said solemnly, "This is exactly what I had in mind when I called you," she told him. "This has my name on it," standing on the upstairs deck taking in the view, before turning to go back downstairs to view the kitchen again, opening the stove and refrigerator to look inside, noting that the appliances were like new.

There was a walk-in closet she could hang her broom and mop and had ample shelving for storing food or to be used for any other storage. She would have to bring her own washer and dryer, as the house did not come with them. The paint was fresh, a dark beige throughout the house, with the trim being a few shades darker, providing a comfortable atmosphere.

Matthew thought she possessed a hushed fascination with the property that he eyed very intently. "If you prefer seclusion, this may be ideal for you," he affirmed.

"Where are the current owners?" she asked.

"They are in Connecticut. They have decided to sell their California home rather than maintain it any longer. There have also been some health problems, I believe, and travel back and forth has become a hardship. They just put it on the market last week."

"I see."

"I'm interested," she said resolutely.

Raised eyebrows, he nodded approvingly. "I had a feeling you would like this one."

"I do. I absolutely love it."

They returned to his office where she made a firm offer. The paperwork for her offer was drawn up and signed before she left. The sellers were given five days to accept or reject it.

Afterwards, she drove through town and found a restaurant where she ordered fish tacos and an ice tea. She ate them heartily, feeling as if she were famished, ordered a tea to go, and continued to drive up and down the streets one more time before leaving to go back to the city.

As she drove back, the mountains seemed to be saluting her. Her smile in return was genuine. She felt gratitude for small graces and the mysteries of how they come to each one of us. She would sell the house in the city, and the money would be enough, she thought, to cover the cost of the new house. Jesse had left her with enough to provide for her the rest of her life if she managed it wisely. Knowing what a frugal person she was, she didn't foresee that would be an issue.

Before she was home, she called Miranda and told her what she had done.

"Get out of town! Are you serious?"

"I'm very serious," she answered solemnly, standing by her decision.

"I'm speechless. I mean, wow! Congratulations, Hannah. I am so-o-o-o happy for you," and meant it. "What lit your fire, anyway?"

"I think finally accepting and being open to change and trusting in something bigger than I am, something bigger than my life and even bigger than the world. Not everything that happens in life is our choice, but I think it's important to recognize the choices we *do* have."

Miranda nodded, "I think you're right."

"I'm surrendering to a power far greater than I can conceive of to take the helm and lead the way. It seems more preferable than resisting it, at this point," she conceded.

"This will be so-o-o-o good for you," giving her full support.

"I think it will be. I *need* a new chapter in my life. This is an open door. I'm stepping through it."

"It's all going to work out. You're going to be alright. I'll miss you when you move though," Miranda pouted.

"I know. I'll miss you, too, but we'll still see each other, and we can FaceTime. We'll figure it out."

"Don't worry about me. I'm just happy for you. You deserve this. I'll just have to commute, that's all there is to it," she said resolutely.

"I'm glad you support me on this. It means a lot," Hannah admitted, meaning it.

"Of course, I do. You're going to be alright," Miranda told her, wanting to reassure her friend.

"I know," Hannah replied, and for the first time, Miranda believed it to be true.

"It's good you have Alex. Is that working out alright?"

"Yeah, actually, it is," sounding surprised at her own admission, though she was still uncomfortable flaunting a happy relationship in front of Hannah.

Hannah stopped her, "I am so happy for you. Really, I am. Have fun with him. Enjoy him. Live and be happy loving and being loved. There is no greater gift in this entire world!"

"But you had the perfect life," she began, and just like that, it's gone."

"Miranda, you deserve to be happy, and I smile inside knowing you are for once happy, at last. You deserve to be both loved and in love. So, don't hide him from me! Oddly, it feels good to see other people happy and being loved. Despite everything, that's how I feel. It would serve no purpose, even for me, let alone anyone else, if I secretly desired others to be lonely and miserable because I've been feeling that way. I know I've tried to hide that, even from you, but it's been hard, and I know my life will never be the same, but something tells me it doesn't have to be the same in order for me to find new meaning and purpose. Maybe even be truly happy, again. I don't know, but I have to be open."

"It's good to hear you say that. It sounds like you really mean it."

"I do," she said. "It's the only way to think. Otherwise, I couldn't bear it."

"I know," Miranda replied in almost a whisper.

"I'll talk with you soon."

"Soon."

The next day, Matthew called her. "Good news. The sellers accepted!" He could feel her broad smile and joy through the phone, reverberating in her voice.

"That really is good news! Thank you so much. I mean it. Thank you for showing me the house."

"I'm glad it was what you wanted, and more importantly, that it worked out," feeling humbled by her gratitude.

After they hung up, a sharp panicked feeling struck Hannah that stopped her in her tracks. She wondered if Jesse was letting her know he didn't approve of her moving. It was almost a sick feeling that left her confused. How could something she felt so sure of suddenly be met with doubt. It was if something inside her was screaming, "No!"

That night, Hannah didn't sleep. There was a dark cloud looming over her. It ripped at her and whispered guilt. "How could you?"

"I'm doing this," she whispered back. "I *have* to do this!" If it had been Jared, she knew he would have just come to her, appeared to her, but this was not Jared. This had a name. It was called Memories. Then another cried out, and its name was Abandonment of where those memories were made. This was her turning her back on Jesse and Ethan, the voices accused. Then another voice surfaced, and it had a name. Traitor! Her mind reeled as the voices tormented her. They resounded from unseen recesses of her mind. She bolted out of sleep.

"Liars!" she screamed back at them. "I loved them," she cried. "I'll always love them." She sat in her bed and cried in the night. The voices had seemed real. Strangely, Jared said nothing in the matter. Neither did she seek him out. She was not in tuned to his presence, though he was there. He placed his hand on her head. The voices quieted and she drifted back to sleep. It wasn't necessary that she see him. It didn't change the fact that he was there.

Less than a week later, they met for the closing. Hannah and Matthew met at the attorney's office, and after an hour of grueling signatures, it was a done deal. The owners were able to sign electronically without having to be present for the final transfer of ownership.

The movers had already been scheduled and would be packing and transporting her belongings in two days. Everything was happening fast, but she was not going to allow mixed emotions to stop her from moving forward. She had FaceTimed her parents and told them and gave them her new address, and although they knew it had been a tough decision for her, they agreed it was best.

"You guys should come visit once I'm all moved," she had told them

"We'd like that, and in the meantime, if you need anything, anything at all, let us know," her mom insisted. "Promise us that."

"I will, Mom, I promise."

"We love you, sweetheart," her mother's voice was quiet with emotion.

"I love you, too. I love both of you. I'm going to be okay. Promise. Try not to worry so much."

After ending the call, she went to the frig and pulled out a pitcher of freshly brewed iced tea. She slowly took a small sip as she moved to the bay window and pulled her knees to her chest, propped her feet up on the seat and watched two hummingbirds and a squirrel outside the kitchen window. Her mind was filled with anticipation of the new reality and the changes it would bring to her life.

Her imagination was met with welcome, as she imagined living in a different house, taking walks through a different town, meeting a different population of people. She was swept away in her thoughts, as if she were already there. The voices tugged at her but she fought them back. Another voice inside told her she *had* made the right decision.

She sipped her tea and wondered if there would be hummingbirds at the new house. She would take her bird feeders and bird bath. She inwardly hoped she would always be surrounded by hummingbirds. They fascinated her with their tiny wings that moved almost indiscernibly and sustained them midair so gracefully. Their tiny statures were filled with a grand, yet silent energy that gave beauty to life and the world. She was lost in watching them move silently around the bird feeder, occasionally distracted by the squirrel moving up and down the nearby strawberry tree, nibbling freely at the fruit.

She had always taken animals and creatures for granted, but since the trip to the Farallones, she felt even more connected, not just to nonhuman life but to everything around her. Perhaps it was that she felt more *aware* of being connected. It was a feeling she found herself feeling hungry for, as if creatures were healers in and of themselves of the human race. It was an idea she pondered in a, "What if?" manner of thinking. Summarily, there was no denying she was drawing off the energy that the wildlife seemed to have offered her as a benevolent gift, which she graciously accepted.

There were small packets of melba toasts on the table that had been ignored, but she picked one up and opened it and began to nibble small bites, taking another sip of tea. She swished it in her mouth, rinsing the dry toast from her palate. She let it settle on her tongue before swallowing, savoring the refreshing taste.

A gush of energy swept around her followed by a calming peace. There was a movement of dangling energy that was perceptible to her eyes, almost like swimming oil in a dessert that glimmered, as she felt an increase in her own energy level heighten very quickly, and then, he was there, in front of her, his eyes filled with peace and delight. He smiled and his energy radiated even more, as if joy and happiness made his essence shine brighter.

"Jesse?"

Chapter Seventeen

Questionable Sanity

The dust appeared suspended within beams of light, casting a reflection of sunrays throughout the room. Jesse looked the same as he had the last day she saw him alive. The glow that emanated from him made him even more beautiful than she had ever known him to be. His countenance was soft, filled with love. He looked as if he could see right through her, just as Jared did. She could not pull her eyes away, as he sat down across from her. She wanted to reach out and touch him but abstained from doing so, afraid the very act might cause him to disappear and leave her feeling disillusioned.

"I need for you to know it's okay to sell the house and let go of things that we no longer have need of anymore. Ethan and I have gone to a glorious place, and you can be at peace knowing that, and you *will* see us again! Until then, you are free to move forward in your life without feeling guilty. I want you to be happy, Hannah. I would never want you to deprive yourself of that. Live your life and be happy."

"I'm trying," was all she could say. His hand softly brushed her cheek and then he faded away. She lifted her hand to her face, as if she were trying to save part of his essence. The emotion she felt seeing him, again, was indescribable, feeling his love, seeing him whole, not dead, not lying in a casket, not buried in the ground, to see him alive and not broken. There was not a scratch on him, despite neither of them had been able to have an open casket because of the extent of their injuries. But there he was, unscathed, shrouded in an ethereal light. She felt her lip quiver as his image faded.

She reached out to touch the space he had just occupied, across the kitchen table, and an energy pulsed up her arm. She got up and sat where he had just been, wanting her body, her mind, and her soul to *be* in the same space he had just been seconds before. She felt a heightened energy lingering, dissipating, but she waited until it was completely gone. All she felt was peace.

"Thank you, Jesse," she whispered. "Thank you."

Outside, there were two hummingbirds hovering just outside the window facing her. Behind them, perched on a limb was a white turtle dove with its eyes set on her. She watched it, not wanting to move for fear it would be frightened away. After a minute, it turned and flew away, and the hummingbirds began to move away from the window in different directions, going about their more normal activities. It was as if they were witness, she thought. The more intriguing fact was that turtle doves were not native to California. Now, she was even more convinced that animals are in tuned with the spirit world, even a part of it.

More birds were gathering around the bird bath. She watched them frolic and fly to a nearby branch or the top of the fence and return. They seemed unaware of her. Then another one came. A quail flew down, followed by a blue bird, a goldfinch, and a few others she didn't know, but the gathering of birds intrigued her. All she could do for the next half hour was watch them out of curiosity. Some were eating from the birdfeeder. They were taking turns in the birdbath. She watched them. She had never seen that many birds at once outside the window. There must have been thirty or more. When no others flew in, and the ones that were there had begun flying away, she called Miranda. "Can we meet?"

Twenty minutes later, Hannah was outside on Miranda's deck telling her what had transpired. The day was sunny and bright. The privacy fence blocked some of the light breeze. She was wearing a red sunhat, a pair of green cargo shorts, and a red and green print tank top and was cleaning her fishpond.

Miranda listened while she completed her project and rinsed her hands with the water hose before she sat down on the full-length lounge chair and motioned Hannah to sit in the one next to her. Hannah had tied her hair in a ponytail and had kept her sunglasses on, which covered most of her upper face.

She was not as warm-natured as Miranda and wore a pair of faded straight-leg jeans with long-sleeve gray cotton square-neck top that hung just below her beltline and a pair of blue tennis shoes. She pulled her knees up and leaned her head back, as if absorbing energy from the sunrays.

"I tossed and turned all night, just restless. Having a little trouble sleeping, or staying asleep, anyway. I had fallen asleep feeling so determined, but I woke up in a panic, and all I could ask myself is, do I even know what I'm doing? After that, I questioned whether selling the house was the right thing. I just starting feeling anxious about everything!"

"I don't think it's unusual to have mixed feelings," Miranda said.

"Maybe not." Hannah wanted to agree. "Then, this morning, Jess came to me to tell me it was okay to sell the house.

"You saw him, again?"

"He knew. I thought he had crossed over. I was sure of it." Hannah stared at nothing. "He wanted me to know," her voice trailed. "Mir, how is it that I am able to see and hear what others can't?"

Miranda listened intently, as Hannah spoke, without interrupting her. She put her hand on Hannah's, "It's a gift that has been given to you," she answered. "Don't question it, Hannah. Embrace it. It's given to those who can receive it. Not everyone can, sweetie."

"Do you know of anyone else who has experienced anything like this? I know death is a part of life and everyone is touched by it, but I don't recall ever hearing about anyone having experiences like this. I mean, sure, sensing someone around them, yes, but seeing and hearing them, as if they were still …. I've just never personally known anyone that talked about having these kinds of experiences."

"You probably do and don't know it. It happens more than anyone realizes. Sometimes it is so subtle, and someone may not realize who they were speaking with until after the fact. Sometimes unseen beings appear to us as human and mortal-looking as you and I are. And, a lot of people simply *don't* talk about it. It's personal to them."

"I agree. It is definitely personal," Hannah agreed. "It's not like I am willing to talk about it to anyone else. You're the only person I've talked to about it."

"Exactly. Visitations are always with purpose and meant to give someone what they need. It's something one's departed loved one feels they must impart to them, so they will be able to have comfort or move on, and it may be that it also gives the one who is departed comfort or closure before they move on, depending on what it is. Most people are unaware how often it happens, because the ones that have these experiences *don't* talk about it. It's just too personal."

"But do you *know* of anyone else?"

"I do," nodding. "My aunt saw my great uncle two days after he was killed, hit by a car crossing the street. My mother saw her great grandmother after she had passed. She was a young girl but had been very close to her and was inconsolable. My grandfather was visited on a couple of occasions, too. So, yes, I do know people who have had experiences, and that's just a few of the stories I know of with *my* family," she pointed out.

"Wow. That's pretty incredible," Hannah said.

"I know it greatly impacted the ones in my family that had those experiences. They have a keen sense of mortality, but even more, a sense of *immortality*. Then there are ones that didn't see anything but experienced interventions if they were in danger, or really needed help with something, and they witnessed miracles right before their eyes," so just because they aren't seen doesn't mean they're not there. I grew up always believing we're never alone."

"Me too," Hannah reflected. "I've always considered myself ordinary, but nothing has been ordinary lately," she reflected. "I've thought about seeing a hypnotherapist to try to see if any sense can be made of the dreams I've been having.

"Be very careful who you talk to, Hannah. Know who you're confiding in," Miranda advised solemnly. Just because someone has a license to treat or offer therapy or professional opinion does not mean they will consider you to be sane or understand or even believe you."

"Doctors believe in science. If they cannot mathematically or scientifically explain it, if they do not personally believe in it, then they call it hallucinating! It's bullshit in my opinion. Sure, people do hallucinate when they are schizophrenics, spaced out on drugs, or having chemical withdrawals, but if a person sees a loved one while they are under hospice care and nearing their own death, I believe they are more sensitive to who's around them, waiting to meet them from the other side."

"Practitioners may *only* believe that *you* believe it and think that they need to correct *what* you believe, so out comes the prescription pad. It could do more *harm* than good. Be *very* careful who you go to."

Hannah sighed, "Yeah, I suppose you're right."

"And sweetie, I don't think you need a therapist. I believe you are saner than most people on this planet."

"Thanks, Mir, I guess I needed to hear that."

"Think about it. We all know the universe exists. It's been proven that it does, so no one argues that. Most people believe in an afterlife. So why is it when the universe or the afterlife openly acknowledges *us*, we think we are going crazy and losing our minds?"

"You have a point. It's just for me, it *keeps* happening, not just isolated incidences."

"I still don't think you're crazy! Need I remind you, again, I was in Mendocino, too?"

"No, of course not," wincing a smile.

"We both know we were not alone, and there's the pictures to prove it. Lots of pictures!"

"Do you think that I'm one of those people who are more tuned in than others?"

"I definitely *do* believe that!" Miranda assured her. "Is Jared still communicating with you?"

"Not for a few days. He just stopped. I don't know. Maybe he's moved on. Maybe he was here just to get me through the most difficult part," she conceded. It was not a welcome thought, but what if it was true, she wondered.

"Let me remind you, time is different for them! It doesn't exist. Don't put him on your timetable."

Hannah considered this. "You're right. You're absolutely right. Nothing like the wrong conclusion to derail someone," finding it a little easier to see the humor now that she had been thoroughly validated and reassured.

"Okay then. Are we good on you no longer believing you're delusional or need a therapist?" looking at her expectantly.

Smiling, "Yeah, I'm good," as she took her first sip of sea. "Wow, this really is good!"

"It has a coconut almond mixed with black tea leaf. Glad you like it."

"Yeah, it's really good," taking larger gulps.

"Now, tell me about this move you're making!"

Hannah explained how the decision had come about and how spontaneity had all played out the last couple of days. When she had finished telling her, Miranda just replied, "Good for you! Don't be surprised if I don't visit you *really* often."

"I'm counting on it," Hannah assured her.

Chapter Eighteen

The New House

The next week was filled with movers packing everything in the house. Miranda and Alex had come over and helped with cleaning the house, changing furnace filters, sweeping cobwebs and dust from chandeliers, high-to-reach ceiling corners in the vaulted ceiling, pruning some weeds, wiping down the stove, oven range, and refrigerator. They followed her to the new house, so that they would be there before the movers.

It had been a challenge for the moving truck to make it up the small, narrow, and steep road to the house, and they had to block off each section of the road for traffic, leaving only one option for people who lived on the street to go out, which meant, they could not pass by her house, as the road was only wide enough for one vehicle. The movers had to plan very carefully their entrance and exit routes so as not to make any sharp turns, but they had managed it, which Hannah hoped had not already put her on the bad side of the neighbors before she even got unpacked.

The next afternoon, a couple of neighbors stopped by with home-baked goods as a welcoming to the neighborhood and introduced themselves. Alex was closest to the door when they paid their visit. He was wearing a gray T-shirt that revealed his muscular, tanned arms, which hung loosely below the belt of his faded jeans. His hair was a little mussed, and he had two days of stubble. His smile obviously took the women off guard.

"Uh, hi, I'm Sarah, and this is Nikki," putting her hand towards her companion, as she introduced her. Neither could hide their goggle eyes as they looked Alex over before composing themselves. "I live next door," pointing down the street, and Nikki lives on the other side of me," blushing before she continued.

Sarah was a tall red head with hair that hung to her shoulders with bangs and green eyes. She dressed in beige slacks and sweater with a long white blouse underneath that hung below her sweater. Her makeup color was that of natural-warm tones with pale lipstick. Nikki had short ash-blonde hair cut in a pixie who was tiny as a toothpick, who wore fawn-color leggings and a pink, long-sleeve sweater that hung below her hips. Her makeup was cooler tones and more heavily applied than Sarah's. Both women had freshly done nails and each was wearing designer tennis shoes, presumably were walking buddies, and this was a stop before their walk.

"We brought some banana muffins to welcome you to our neighborhood," and held them out for Alex to take.

"Why thanks," he said, already wanting one.

Hannah and Miranda came up behind him, and immediately the goggle eyes disappeared, replaced by cordial smiles, as Hannah introduced herself.

"Hi, I'm Hannah. I'm your new neighbor," reaching to shake hands. "And this is Miranda, and I see you met Alex. They are here helping me get unpacked." There was a hint of disappointment on their faces that was quickly disguised as they introduced themselves to Hannah.

"Hey, I apologize about blocking the road with the truck. There seemed no other way…"

"Oh, that's fine. Not a big deal at all," Nikki said.

"Welcome to the neighborhood and *our street*," Sarah said. "Where are you moving from?" smiling at Hannah.

"I'm coming from San Francisco," she informed the ladies.

"Oh, well, hopefully you will enjoy the change that comes with living here. Much different," smiling broadly at Hannah and glanced at Alex and Miranda. "Do you guys live in San Francisco, also?" she asked.

"Yeah," gesturing towards Miranda, "We both do," Alex answered, as he spoke.

"Again, welcome and hope you enjoy," pointing towards the muffins Alex was holding. "We'll get going so we don't hold you up, but it's really nice to meet you and, again, let either of us know if you need anything," Nikki added, as they moved away from the door.

"I'll do that, and thanks for the muffins," Hannah said, waving as they turned and walked away.

Alex couldn't wait to have one after the door was closed and then handed the bowl to Miranda, who helped herself.

"Smells good," Hannah took a long whiff, before taking one. "Yum," she purred, as she bit in.

"Wow, really good," Miranda agreed.

Alex finished his and said, "Okay, back to work."

"With Miranda's and Alex's help, Hannah had most of the larger pieces of furniture in place, and furniture for the upstairs attic furnished as a spare bedroom with a full-size bed she had bought specifically for it, along with an antique cherry dresser and small lamp, end table, and a sitting chair. She had sold Ethan's bedroom furniture in a garage sale she posted online and sold many of his and Jesse's clothes and personal effects. The rest, she donated to a homeless shelter.

She bought another queen-size bed set for the second-floor spare bedroom, and Alex had been the strong arm that helped get a lot of the bigger furniture moved into place the way she liked it. She and Miranda had helped, but it took two of them on one side helping him. Together they managed. The delivery men had gotten the new bedroom furniture upstairs. By the time everything was put in place, it had started to look like a home.

Alex had gone to buy a six-pack of beer for himself, but they all had one after the hardest part was done. Hannah told them she would work on the small stuff a little at a time, so everyone could relax after a lot of hard work.

"You guys, thank you so much for all your help. There's no way I could have done this on my own. I really appreciate both of you. She held up her beer as a toast, and they held up theirs, "To friends," Miranda said.

"Hey, no thanks needed. Glad to do it," Alexis spoke up.

"That's right, no thanks needed. So how about we order a pizza and take a breather," Miranda suggested. "I'm starving."

"Good idea, I like everything but anchovies, so whatever you guys prefer is fine with me. I'll leave it up to you," Hannah said.

Miranda opened an app on her phone that told her what pizza places were nearby, and after looking at the online menu, she called it in. When the doorbell rang a half-hour later, Hannah said, "I've got this," and paid for the pizza and gave the delivery boy a generous tip.

"Hey, do you already have your television service turned on?" Alex asked.

"Hmmm, no, I don't. They are supposed to be here tomorrow to install it. I do have a Blu-ray/DVD player though. It should be in here, as each box was marked with contents by room."

Alex got up and started reading the boxes and found one that was marked. He opened it and found everything he needed to hook up the Blu-ray/DVD player to the TV, which was a 60" curved screen Jesse had bought before he passed, which almost gave him the feel of being at the Giants' games he loved to watch. Hannah had barely touched it since.

Miranda found the DVDs and Blu-rays she had packed, and they started putting them on the shelves of the entertainment center in alphabetical order. They found her CDs and added them to the collection in alphabetical order, as well.

"Johnny Cash!" Alex commented, holding up a CD. "Now that's some music I can get into."

"Alex Carmichael! I didn't know you liked Johnny Cash!" Miranda exclaimed. I thought you were more of a soft rock and pop kind of guy."

He looked at her like a deer in headlights. "I am, but gotta love the Cash," he said smoothly in the deepest voice he could muster. Miranda could not help but laugh at his teasing grin, picking up a pillow that belonged to the living room couch and threw it at him.

"Go ahead and put on the CD," Hannah told him," enjoying this.

"O-oh yeah, putting on the Cash," popping the CD into the player. Folsom Prison Blues started playing, Alex sang along with it in a deep baritone voice that took Miranda by surprise. He could do that slow hum perfectly, and *his* voice should be on a CD, she thought.

"I didn't know you could sing like that!" she said, dropping her jaw, as he came up and wrapped an arm around her and sang the next verse. She was loving it.

"My man can sing!" as she swayed her hips toward him.

When the song was over, Alex turned the stereo down, so that it played in the background. Hannah actually laughed, finding them entertaining.

She was so elated for Miranda, seeing she was so happy with him. He seemed good for her. She had seen a transformation from pretending to be happy to truly being happy since Alex had come into her life. To watch them, one would think they were made for one another. She started putting some dishes, pots and pans, and silverware away in the kitchen. Miranda pitched in and helped her.

"You guys go well together," Hannah commented to her. "He's a hoot, just like you."

"Oh yes! We hoots flock together," Miranda chimed and then started laughing at her own comment.

"Well, he's a keeper, so hang on to him," looking over her shoulder at Alex, who was unpacking some of the boxes in the living room. "He loves you."

Miranda turned around and leaned against the sink, "He's the best thing that ever happened to me, guy-wise. I think I *will* keep him," admiring him as he set things out and put them in place.

"Hannah, is this okay?" He had started arranging some vases and the artificial flowers that go in them.

"I like it!" adding a thumbs up. "He's got some talent with arrangements," she told Miranda under her breath.

Looking at him as if she was amazed all over again, "Yeah, he does, doesn't he?"

"You're in love."

Miranda looked at her and hesitated, "Pretty obvious, uh?"

"Yeah," chuckling, "pretty obvious," as she put glasses away.

The day had gone by quickly, it seemed. After they had put the rest of the dishes away, Hannah wanted to give them some privacy, so she told them, "I have the bed made with fresh linens in the spare bedroom, so you guys can go to bed anytime you're ready. I think I'm going to get ready to turn in, so I will see you in the morning?"

"You will." Alex replied assuredly. "We'd like to stick around and help you unpack a little if that's okay."

"Of course, it's okay!" Miranda insisted, before Hannah could respond. Miranda proceeded to give Hannah a sisterly kiss on the cheek with a big hug.

"I love you," she said, as if Hannah did not already know.

"I love you, too. I love both of you. Thanks for being a lifesaver for me with all this," scoping the rooms. "I couldn't have gotten so much done without you. And it means a lot to have good company around."

"Hey, no problem at all, we're happy to help, anytime. Get some rest, and we'll see you in the morning," Alex told her. "We probably will be turning in soon, too."

"Okay, then. Goodnight," looking at them once more before turning to go toward the stairs.

Hannah tied her hair up and stepped into a warm sudsy bath. The warm water was relaxing. She grabbed the bar of soap and a washcloth and pulled her feet up to wash them. She inhaled the steam from the water, washed her face and ran the soap over her body. Part of her wanted to go to sleep lying there, she was so exhausted. Instead she got out and found some pajama's packed away and put them on and literally crawled into bed.

She felt her body relax and took a deep breath and exhaled, letting go of tension from a long day's work. They had gotten a lot done, and she began thinking about everything she needed to work on getting unpacked in the morning. She could hear the faint music and quiet talking between Alex and Miranda with an occasional quiet burst of laughter and some giggling.

He had definitely been good for her, she reflected, thinking back over the years, all she had gone through. The divorce had been so hard on her. She had watched her try to be strong and stoic and use laughter and joking as a concealer to the pain she buried inside, and Hannah often had suspected she would cry herself to sleep at night, and then, she seemed to have turned off all of it, like closing a book she had just finished. She started a new chapter in her life and buried herself in work, and she stopped talking about it.

It wasn't until she met Alex that Miranda had allowed herself to become vulnerable again. Then, she began to wonder where her own life would take her now that Jesse and Ethan were gone. She went from being a wife and a mother to being widowed and single. Everything had just changed in the blink of an eye, and being honest with herself, she had no desire to put herself out there and start dating again. She didn't know if she ever would, but then again,

Miranda didn't either. Life had proven plans don't work out the way we think sometimes. Not that it's not smart or wise or good to make plans, but always be on notice that plans can turn on a dime and change in a split second.

She needed to set goals for herself. A life without goals is like a house without lights on, void of life. It's something that had been ingrained in her by her parents, and so she had always tried to have at least one long-term and one short-term goal in progress at any given time, sometimes more. And she had always made sure she rewarded herself when she accomplished one, something else her parents had taught her.

Jesse had lived by the same principal. They had set goals together and celebrated each time they reached their goals and set a new one. They were a great team, and now, she was going to have to think of what she wanted to put on her goal list now that she was in a new house in a new town. Her eyes grew heavy and she turned the lamp out. Falling asleep in a new place was not a problem. Every muscle in her body relaxed, and she felt all the tension leave her just as she drifted into a swift wave of unconsciousness.

A glow softly lit the room as Jared stood next to her, keeping her unaware of his presence. She was already drifting into a deep sleep. Soon, she would be dreaming.

Chapter Nineteen

Wedding March

I am looking out the upstairs open window. It is spring and there are fresh pink blooms on two cherry trees and new leaves adorning the enormous trees over the property. I see the angel oak tree I have so loved to climb high into its branches and stay for hours sometimes, as if it had a soul that soothed my own. I can see the hedge of blackberry bushes off to my left. The soft breeze on my face is relaxing, and I can hear birds chirping and whistling. There are horses grazing and running playfully in the field, but I can hear the sound of neighs and snorts from around the corner of the house. We have guests, I realize.

The spacious upstairs bedroom I'm standing in is the room of a large manse, and servants are preparing a dress for me to put on. They summons me to come along and begin dressing. The dress is a creamy white.

First, an undergarment is placed over my head. It has long, loose sleeves with ruffles around the wrists and the neck is ruffled and low cut. The women are chattering with conversations amongst themselves about the dress. There is intense excitement in their tones as they speak.

Next, I am fitted into a stay that covers the top of my shift. As they tighten it, I start to feel as if my breath is being choked off. It's so tight. Once they are satisfied with the adjustments of my stay, a hooped petticoat is lifted over my head and fitted around my waist, followed by a satin petticoat and a laced apron. An off-white gown was placed over my garments fashioned from a silk material. Then a separate garment used to flatten the stomach was hooked onto the bodice of my gown and to the stay beneath. I was finding it increasingly uncomfortable, as if my oxygen counted on them loosening the stay.

"It's too tight," I complained.

An older, attractive, middle-aged woman ordered servants to loosen it just a smidge, and I felt it loosen just enough I could breathe a little better.

"Balance yourself on me, dear," one of the servants ordered me, "Raise one foot, that's it," as I lifted my right foot, slipping it into a tan shoe that was actually more like a low-cut boot with a metal buckle across the top. Everyone was making a fuss over me.

A shallow hat with a wide brim and a flat pink ribbon around it that hung off to one side to my shoulder was carefully fit on top my head. I was escorted to the full-length, Victorian mirror near the corner of the room. I'm studying my reflection, realizing I am a bride gowned for a wedding.

I look different but yet I'm me. It is my own consciousness looking back at myself in the looking glass, but my hair is blonde, tied back loosely behind my head and hanging along my neck in soft waves. I am not as tall. All the women gathered around are plain looking, some with their hair in buns while others wore long puffy locks of curls that flowed down their backs. They are all talking at once and full of chatter and observatory remarks.

"Isn't she beautiful?"

"What a beautiful dress!'

"What a lovely bride you are! I so long to be a beautiful bride like you."

"Come along, Dear. You don't want to keep the groom waiting," a woman was saying to me, as she smoothed out my dress and pinched my cheeks to elicit color in them. As I take note of her, I know she is my mother. Her eyes are beaming with joy and sentiment.

"Are you ready?" she asked with knowing anticipation, "You'll be just fine," her eyes are telling me she is fully approving of this marriage.

The ladies were exiting the room, and it is just me and my mother. She takes my hand and leads me to the door, then hesitates and turns towards me.

"My darling, Elizabeth," tears of happiness filling her eyes, as she carefully wiped them away. "I...I am so very proud of you. He is such a wonderful young man who I know loves you very, very much. You have surely chosen well." She wiped more tears, as emotion swelled within her. "You're such a beautiful bride." Her voice cracking, she pulls out her handkerchief and blots her eyes gently. I can tell she wants to say more, but emotion prevailed over speech.

"Are you ready?"

I nod yes, and she puts her arm around me, and we walk toward the top of the staircase. I realize the sound of organ music is emanating from a room below. It's the Wedding March.

As we descend the stairs, I can see into the opening of another large room. There is a gathering of people dressed prestigiously. I am nearly descended to the first-level floor and nearing the entrance of the room. A large crowd is now turning, one by one, then as if all together, everyone is looking toward me. Their expressions are reverent but beaming and happy. I am met at the doorway by my father, who I immediately recognize him as such. His smile is emotional, like my mother's. I slip my arm into his elbow, and he slowly escorts me forward amongst the crowd, who are now seated on both sides. I am looking into each of their faces for any recognition, and although I know that I know them, I couldn't determine *how* I know them.

My attention is drawn front ahead of me toward where I am now proceeding, and there is an elderly man, tall, slightly plump and balding, holding a Bible. There are men and women gathered around him in formal attire, all watching me with anticipation and smiling, but my eyes froze as I recognized the one nearest the center. It is him. Oh, my beloved. It is him. My heart leaps.

Jared never took his eyes off her as she dreamt. He thought back over his own, vivid clear memories of the many lives he had shared with her, lives she had no memory of. He watched her rapid eye movements, as he imparted his memories into her dreams and helped her to remember her own memories. Dreams and time were healing her, as had his presence. Love was healing her, and he had no shortage of it.

He watched over her to keep the nightmares at bay. He would prove to her there was more to *life* than the senses that cause mortals to wail and grieve when they become fixated on earthly finite senses and fall into depression and despair as they tend to be short-sighted. For as long as she was mortal, he vowed she would never be alone or ever *feel* alone. "I shall not forsake you, ever," he bent over her and whispered into her ear as she slept on.

The scene changes. I am in a room lit with candlelight. There is a bed, a very large bed. It is a solid mahogany four-poster bed with white brocade curtains and coverlet. The curtains hang from the canopy and are tied to the posters. I see a brown Victorian couch at the foot of the bed. The room is spacious with tan wall covering. The room is furnished with Dutch Renaissance wardrobe and a large dresser. A table sets near the head of the bed against the wall where a candle burns. In front of the couch on the wooden floor is a large embroidered rug that has rustic colors with flecks of midnight blue along the edges and center of it. There are long, narrower rugs of similar design on each side of the bed. Large windows are opposite the bed with long flowing wine-colored drapes. The light burns softly in the room.

He is helping me out of my clothes. His hands are soft and gentle. He sets my pieces of clothing on the couch and picks me up in his arms and carries me to the bed. I feel myself sink into the feather mattress, and I feel the soft feather pillow under my head. He strips out of his clothes and lies down next to me. His lips are soft. His arms wrap around me and rolls me over on top of him and he presses me to his hard body. I feel so much overwhelming love. This is a man who knows everything about me and loves me unconditionally. I feel it. I am so deeply in love with him. I feel that too. Then everything becomes a blur and then nothing.

Hannah woke to the sounds of seagulls outside the window she had opened before getting into bed. She heard a small bird chirping in a nearby tree. A faint smile crossed her lips as she awoke refreshed and remembered the dream. She laid there unmoving, reflecting, trying to remember as much as she could. She played it over in her mind.

The house was quiet as she thought of Miranda and Alex being there. She couldn't hear anything. They must still be asleep. She pulled the sheet over her head and willed herself to go back to sleep and dream again, but she was awake, too awake to sleep. A pervasive peaceful feeling filled her with tranquility. Peeking out from the sheets, Jared was there. There was a gleam in his eye as he watched her. A soft smile lit his face.

"You've been busy."

Chapter Twenty

Outside My Body

Hannah leaped out of bed to run to him and was almost about to throw her arms around him, when she stopped abruptly, pulling her hands back to her sides, looking down at them, taking note of her pink pajama shorts and top that did not cover her bare legs and arms, her mortal flesh, and reminded herself he had no physical body. The difference between them felt extremely acute in the moment, as she saw an aura of golden stardust-like energy between them. She felt it as if it had touched her skin and permeated to her core, and the fragrant change was pleasant but not in an earthly way that she could place, but more it was the absence of pollution. She felt her mortality fade from her conscious awareness, as he imparted to her a magical sense of her own immortality. All her senses had elevated beyond what she had ever known.

He had not revealed himself since she had returned from the Farallones. Tilting her head up towards him, she looked into his eyes and saw no judgment. His eyes told her he knew everything she was thinking and feeling. His smile was gone from his face but not his eyes that now penetrated hers. Neither of them moved. They were inches apart. He appeared angelic, which is what stopped her in her tracks, a reminder this cannot be a physical relationship.

If anyone had ever told her there was someone that loved her more than Jesse had, it would have been unfathomable. The eyes that looked back at her were filled with love she could never have imagined possible. It was all she could do to resist the urge to reach out and touch him, but yet she felt *touched* by him in a way that no mortal could touch another.

"I've missed you," she whispered softly.

"I didn't leave you, Hannah."

"Why did you disappear? Why have you not answered me?" she asked with trepidation.

"I want you to realize your own strength, apart from me, not because of me. You were doing that. You broke free and stepped outside the box. I just let go of your hand and took pleasure in watching you."

"Please don't let go, again, Jared. Please don't disappear like that. I thought you had crossed back over."

"I'm immortal, not absent," he reminded her. "Just because you can't always see or feel me near doesn't mean I'm gone from you."

"It felt like it. I always *feel* you right before I see you, and I have felt nothing since the day we were on the boat.

"I haven't gone anywhere, Hannah. I've been with you."

Since he had begun speaking, with all her senses acutely heightened, both physically and spiritually, she could not only hear his voice but *felt* it, instinctively bringing her hand to her chest, as if it had somehow separated her body and soul, having the magnitude of thunder but the softness of a gentle whisper.

"What's happening? I feel as if I've stepped outside my body. Everything in me feels so heightened. She started at nothing as she focused on the feeling that felt it did not belong to the five senses she was accustomed to experiencing. This was so very different.

"After one has crossed over from mortality, all the senses are greatly heightened, no longer dulled by the physical body. When someone from the spiritual realm communicates with a mortal, the mortal becomes connected to the senses of their Higher Self. With you, it's far more intense for both of us," he explained.

"With me?"

"Yes, remember when we talked about Plato?"

"You, you said you knew him and met him, but we were interrupted," she recounted.

"Plato was extraordinarily insightful in the subject of twin souls. He wrote:

"And so, when a person meets the half that is his very own, whatever his orientation, whether it's to young men or not, then

something wonderful happens: the two are struck from their senses by love, by a sense of belonging to one another, and by desire, and they don't want to be separated from one another, not even for a moment."

"That's how I feel about you," she whispered. "I can't bear the thought of being separated from you. You are the reason I have been able to cope at all with losing Ethan and Jesse. I don't even want to think how much worse it could've been…would have been, if not for you. I might not have held on."

The soft, compassionate way he looked at her reinforced his words that he had come to her so that she could bear it, that he was there to protect her and support her, to help her heal. The entire experience since that day to now had been surreal and otherworldly. She had often wondered how it was possible that she had been able to smile, to laugh, to have any kind of joy at all to any increment or fraction, but she knew it was because of him and his love for her and the love she felt for him. Perhaps also because both Jesse and Ethan had come to her and showed her they were in a good place, and Ethan had been so happy in the dreams she had of him, which she knew in her soul he had come to give comfort to her.

Life was sometimes unkind, but then its graces and gifts restored balance. She had accepted those, and Jared had helped her tilt the balance back, but so had the things he had said to her, the kindness of his words. How powerful words are, she thought. His had been a balm to a deep wound. But most of all, it was his love that had made life bearable.

The fact that he was immortal definitely had an effect, because Ethan and Jesse were now immortal, and to see so much life in an immortal being, so much love, so much power that went beyond what a mortal person could be capable of was a lifegiving gift they had imparted to her, one she had never imagined possible. Otherwise, she did not know if she would have held on. It was him that stopped her from drowning herself in an effort to join Ethan and Jesse.

Jared's energy increased and rose to a higher level, and Hannah could see him in all his immortality, the glow of his auras. There was a fragrance in the air that intensified to another level that was indescribably clean smelling. Every part of her body was covered in goosebumps, and every organ, every synapse of her brain seemed to respond, as if to a magnetic field, and her hearing and vision became acutely perfect, as she found she could hear breathing and heartbeats from another room in the house, birds outside, and as she looked around the room and out the window, she could see individual feathers on every bird in sight, could see their tongues as they opened their beaks, and as she walked closer to the window and looked down, she could see bugs on the ground and every detail of the foliage. She looked up and could see birds that were so tiny as they were so far away. She could see minute details of their form. Everything was so crystal clear.

She turned back to Jared, and saw the details of his form, every strand of hair, every eyelash, every fleck of hazel and brown color in his eyes that she had not noticed before. He was so flawlessly beautiful. Everything within her felt empowered, alive, and so much love bursting between body and spirit. He looked glorious, but he slowly then began to dim his energy until he resembled a mortal man. As he did so, she felt her senses slowly return to normal. It was a feeling that no one would ever forget in a lifetime if they never experienced it again.

She was still reeling in the magnificence of the experience. "I could never have imagined…," trying reorient herself. She had fallen speechless.

Jared's eyes never left her. She was the focus of his attention, always. She was the center of his purpose of being. He had given her a glimpse of what their relationship and their existence in the spiritual dimension, apart from the mortal body, was like after crossing over after death. Not the near-death where one is resuscitated but when they cross over into light.

"That's what it's like to be immortal?" she asked with amazement.

"It can be, especially if you are with the one you have always been meant to be with, but being immortal, one's senses are magnified beyond anything possible with a physical body. You only experienced a part of what it is like. All the senses converge into full capacity, unhindered by flesh. We see everyone's energy field and their auras. We feel what they feel. Every sense is so far beyond what a mortal can experience.

"But I experienced it just now, with you. I'm human. I'm mortal," she countered.

His smile was like a high for her, "Yes, but it's because I wanted you to experience it, and it's because of who we are to each other that I was able to impart all I am to you, allowing you to experience it to the level that you just did. I wanted to show you what real life is. Earthly life has its limitations, some that people place on themselves with their belief system and hindrances of fear, unworthiness, lack of confidence, and all the reasons they come up with to say, 'I can't,' but there are no limitations with immortality. That's what I wanted to show you."

"I just wish I could hold you," she told him. That seems to be a very big limitation for me," she complained sadly. "I want you so much," and with that, Jared knew the genuine helpless she felt, and this was not imposed on her by anything other than their different states of being.

He had the power to transform himself, his energy, into a physical body, but he would still be immortal with only the delusion of a physical body. Even if he remained that way, it defied all laws. The only way to become truly mortal is to be born. The only reason he would do that was to be with her, but that would create a substantial age difference, so it wasn't going to happen. Entertaining the thought was futile. He could not compromise the greater good for either of them. He knew unerringly that to even entertain such thoughts proved a weakness within himself neither of them could afford.

"I'm sorry, Hannah," he replied. You can reach out to me, but it would not feel like touching a mortal, and I know that's what you want." He, himself, wanted to touch her as a mortal man and wished in that moment that he was.

Hannah's eyes bore into him. "What we just experienced felt far better than being mortal. We'll get through this, I know we will. But right now, I really have to pee!" and she darted off to the bathroom and closed the door. He heard her shout, "One of the many downsides of being mortal!"

Jared's laughter was heard only by one of the three mortals in the house. If Miranda and Alex were able to hear Jared, they would have awoken with a start and bolted up in bed, so loud was the roaring laughter that Jared laughed, but they still slept. From the bathroom, Hannah yelled, "Stop laughing!"

When she came out, she marched past him, not at all embarrassed, "I'm hungry." Jared had not stopped laughing.

Chapter Twenty-One

Blind Date

In the kitchen, Hannah found some eggs and turkey bacon and located where Alex had put her skillets. The toaster oven was already out and plugged in with a loaf of bread next to it. She turned on the burner and put the bacon in the skillet and then prepared the coffee and turned the coffee pot on.

"You always have had a way of humoring me," trying to stifle his laughter, as he appeared at her side. She had dressed knowing Alex was there, having slipped into some kaki brown shorts and a light blue tank top. She was wearing sleeper socks that she often used as house slippers.

"We are not alone in the house!" she reminded him just above a whisper.

"Must I remind you no one else can hear me unless I choose for them to, which I do not?" quickly suppressing his laughter but not his humor, which relieved her so that she relaxed somewhat.

"But they can hear *me*! So, stop talking to me so that I will stop answering," reproaching him, trying not to look at him for fear Miranda or Alex would walk in and wonder who she was talking to.

"They were up very late. I assure you they have not heard a word that you've said," poising himself to recover from her admonishment. When she looked towards him again, his glow was gone. He looked mortal except so exceedingly clean, but the fragrance was still present, however, not as prominent as it had been during what he had revealed to her minutes earlier. In that moment, it seemed as if he bore the fragrance of heaven. She stopped and looked at him. Reaching out slowly, she put her hand where his arm was, and she not only felt energy but saw a light around her hand as their energy touched. Her hand passed through his sleeve. She stared and slowly pulled it away. Their eyes locked for only a moment before she turned to go about finishing breakfast.

"Tell me when they wake up so I don't have to explain myself, okay?" She set the butter and grape jam out. A part of her wanted to ignore him, and another part of her could not bear the thought of him not being with her. Turning him away was not easy. It was crazy, insane, she thought, to have feelings like she was having for a ghost! But everything about him felt good, embracing, and welcoming. There was nothing sinister about him.

"I won't allow you to embarrass yourself, I assure you."

"Thank you," she sighed with relief, then turned toward him with unrelenting curiosity, "Jared, where do you go when I can't see you?"

"I don't go anywhere that is away from you," his voice soft and reassuring. If I want to change my surroundings to see other things while you are otherwise occupied, I bring them to me. I create what I want to see, but it is not away from you, only in a different dimension that I cannot share with you," he explained.

"Like what?"

"For instance, if I want to read from the library, I imagine the book I want to read, and it manifest in my hand."

"What library? Are you talking about just any library on earth?" amazed at this newfound possibility. She imagined having library cards from all around the world that she could check out an e-book. Any book she could think of would be accessible to her. The idea was appealing.

"Yes and no," he answered carefully. There is a library on the other side that contains books not written by any mortal. It contains an infinite amount of information to teach us how to overcome our weaknesses," pausing to let his words sink in before he continued. "The books are not written in any earthly language. Although I can't describe it to you more than that, I assure you the library very much exists.

Hannah's jaw dropped and she stared at him, as just the idea of an immortal library and immortal books written in immortal language peaked her curiosity even more. "So, everyone that ever lived has access to these books?"

"Yes, everyone does, once they cross over, of course. Sometimes, I read. But in answer to your question, I can read from the earth's libraries too. Mainly, I enjoy reading philosophy and learning how connected mortal philosophers are to truth or how far off they are from it. Many of them are very advanced souls, so it does make for interesting reading. I also enjoy poetry and music and will often create my own symphony and spend my time listening if I am so inclined.

"Wait, did you happen to attend the Beethoven Symphony that Miranda and I attended recently?"

"Of course, I did! You didn't think I would miss it, did you?" His voice was filled with surprise.

"I wasn't aware of you being there. I didn't feel you," she said in quiet astonishment. "I was on a blind date with you?" She laughed at herself. "Get it? Blind date? I couldn't see you," starting to double over with laughter.

"I assure you I was there, and I found your attempts at musical talent to be quite entertaining, as did most everyone else that shared the amusement," arching his eyebrow at her.

"That's not nice, Jared," staring at him in mocked surprise with a spatula in her hand.

He stepped within inches of her and cupped his hands around her face. "You were lovely, Hannah," and his face was within only a few inches of her own. She swallowed hard, wanting time to stand still.

"As I was saying," pulling back only slightly, "There's many activities I can engage in while never really leaving you. I simply bring what I want to be engaged in *to me*. I create a different surrounding that is invisible to mortal eyes and mute to mortal ears," detailing his activities. "That night, "I enjoyed *your* symphony," he said joyously.

Feeling her breath flow through her lungs, again, "You're describing a parallel dimension," still intrigued by the concept of his activities.

"I am," he smiled.

Hannah was letting that sink in when Jared informed her, "Alex is awake."

"You better go listen to your symphony or find a book to read then, because this day is about to get busy," she added with dry humor, then smiled wittingly, as she stirred the scrambled eggs into the skillet before grabbing a loaf of bread and placing some slices in the toaster oven. She heard his laughter, but when she turned, he was gone. She was sure he was still there, just invisible as the feel of his presence could still be felt next to her.

She heard the footfall of Alex descending the stairs before he appeared in the kitchen. She listened for a second set of footsteps, but none followed. Alex approached the coffee pot looking for a cup. He was wearing faded jeans and the same gray T-shirt.

"Hey, good morning," he said groggily.

"Good morning. You hungry?" She watched him as he poured the hot liquid into a cup. She could see why Miranda was attracted to him. He was tall, solid, looking like he worked out. His hair was short, dark reddish brown, and he was clean-shaven with a squared jaw, and now had another day of stubble that was starting to look like a beard. He reminded her of someone who had been in the military, but it was probably just his manners and the way he carried himself.

"As a matter of fact, I am," taking a sip of coffee. "Looks good and smells delicious," eying the eggs.

"How did you sleep?"

"Oh, sound as a baby in the womb," not looking up but turning to go sit at the bar. He sipped at his coffee while Hannah continued stirring the eggs before turning the burner off and checking the toasts. When he spoke again, he sounded a little more awake.

"This seems like a good move for you, Hannah. It's private but not too far away from neighbors or community. Great location, good view of the ocean." He paused before continuing, "Feels like it could be a place one could heal their soul. I would love to have a place like this," he told her.

Hannah turned and was about to agree but hesitated, realizing he was not finished with his thoughts.

"I don't know if Miranda has told you, but I lost a brother to a car accident several years back. A little over eight years now. It's tough. I know," opening up to her.

"Yes, she told me," she admitted softly.

"There's not a day that goes by I don't think about my him," he admitted.

Hannah could see his eyes were far away. He continued to sip his coffee. She was not the only one in this room that knew what it felt like to lose someone close, and it gave her pause.

"It's good you made this move," Alex continued. And this place," he stood up and walked to the window and looked out. "It's great. How did you come by it, anyway?"

Hannah noted he had made eye contact and was looking at her expectantly. She set the plates down on the counter and gave him her undivided attention.

"It was rather odd, now that I think about it," recalling the morning she called the realtor. "I hadn't planned on moving, but then, something inside, something that felt larger than life came over me. It was like," she searched for the right words, "an enthusiasm that gave thought to what I needed to do, and it felt right*! So right!*" lowering her voice with conviction. "In my mind's eye, I could *see* this house. *This house!* As if I was being drawn," reflecting on the experience. She paused a moment before continuing and then admitted, "I did have moments of confusion afterwards, though. I started feeling guilty, so very guilty, as if I were abandoning Jesse and Ethan," she reflected as if it was now a mystery. "It passed, thankfully." She smiled without further explanation but continued her train of thought. "I know it sounds senseless and crazy, but a few hours later, I was here looking at houses, and the moment I saw this house, it was uncanny how identical it looked to what I saw in my mind as I imagined it. There's no rational way to explain it, really."

Alex listened intently before saying anything. She wondered if he thought she had been impulsive and foolish. His response came as a relief.

"It sounds like it was meant to be, like a guiding force that was leading you. Everything fell into place too easily for it not to be," he replied. "Think about it. Pretty amazing if you ask me," pouring more coffee and leaning against the counter. "No, you finding this place was no coincidence," he assured her.

"I don't think it was either. For whatever reason, I feel I belong here," her voice clearly denoted wonder and acceptance of a divine intervention that had lead her here and resulted in her being the new owner, as if the house had just fallen into her lap.

"You're going to be okay. You know that, right?" His smile was compassionate, almost knowing. Hannah realized he was speaking from his own experience and appreciated his sincerity and support.

"I will be," she agreed, returning the smile and nodding, then hesitated. She needed to know, needed to ask and started to stop herself but didn't.

"Did you have any *experiences*, I mean after your brother passed?" The question felt awkward after the words were out, and she wanted to retract it but yet, she still felt she had to ask, "I mean ...."

"Yeah, actually, not that I've really talked about it, but I did," pausing to reflect. He did not seem bothered by the question. He knew what she had been through and understood why she was asking. Miranda had confided in him knowing he could be trusted.

"It was after his funeral." Alex smiled while tears filled his eyes, prompting him to quickly wipe them away. He breathed deeply through his nose and wiped a sniffle as he tried to compose himself before he continued. "I was having a really tough time, was in my room sitting on my bed, staring at the floor really, and I just wanted to know why. *Why?* I looked up and he was standing there, just looking at me. I couldn't move," he recalled, "wondering if I was imagining seeing him standing there, but yet I knew I wasn't," trying to hold back the tears that started to flow. After a moment, he continued to speak, forcing a smile. "He spoke to me and he told me, 'I'm alright, Alex. Go to sleep. I'm alright.' That's what he said to me. Then he smiled at me. I don't even remember lying back on the bed. The next morning, I woke up and I had slept all night. I've missed him, more than I can put into words, but I know he's alright. It gets me through each day." He bit his lip and took a deep breath before looking directly at her. "Hannah, *they're* okay, too."

His words were heartfelt and touching, and she welcomed them.

"Thanks, Alex," smiling at him through restrained tears. "I know they are."

"We'll always miss them," Alex continued, "but we both know we have to keep living to honor their lives with love. I think a way of doing that is accepting the love they still have for us and to allow them to witness the continuing *life* in our own souls instead of the collapse of our being. I can't help but think it helps them to see us making the choice to live and at least see us making an effort at continuing to do that. I don't think it is any comfort to *them* to watch us fall apart, you know?"

"You're right, I don't think so either," Hannah answered.

"I like to think those who have left us only in body have not left us in spirit, and that they witness the choices we make, and that out of love for them, we should embrace life. It's a gift and one I'm sure those who have departed realize all too well." Alex paused and seemed to be in deep thought before he spoke again. "I believe it would cause them sadness to see us throw it away and forfeit any measure of happiness we can still have. I imagine in my mind where they are, and I see them very much alive and living."

"It helps me to imagine seeing them happy," Hannah said, "not suffering, more than it does to focus on their mortality being taken from them and grieving over memories and life cut short. It's too painful to dwell on. It takes effort, believe me, but it really helps me to take that approach. It gives me a lot of comfort and makes every day more bearable,"

When she looked up at him, he seemed to be looking at her with admiration.

"You're absolutely right. It makes a big difference how we think about it," his expression more relaxed.

"I smell food," Miranda murmured as she sat down at the table, oblivious to what Alex and Hannah were discussing, as they quickly recomposed. She was still yawning, wearing the same clothes she wore the night before. Her hair was uncombed, and she pulled her knees up and laid her head on them and was trying to blink herself awake.

Alex poured her coffee and set it on the table in front of her before leaning down kissing her head.

"Good morning, Babe," which she responded with a yawn, "Mornin' to you too," she managed to say through another yawn. He ruffled his fingers through her black hair that hung in curls around one side of her face, where she had pulled it around her neck, "Wake up sleeping beauty," sitting down across from her.

"Getting there," Miranda murmured in a gravelly voice, allowing her lips to broaden into a sleepy smile. Her blue eyes were noticeably bloodshot. "The waking up part, that is."

"Ah, but always a beauty," he added, broadening his grin revealing a perfect set of teeth.

Hannah set the table and filled some glasses with orange juice before sitting down with them. They were still goggle-eying each other, which she found delightfully entertaining.

"We'll clean up the kitchen for you, Hannah," Miranda told her as she scooped food onto her plate. "This is so good," closing her eyes as she slowly chewed the toast. "I love this jam," rolling her eyes.

Both Alex and Hannah chuckled, obviously getting a kick out of her. "What? I'm famished! Moving really works up an appetite, ya know?" eying both of them back and forth.

Hannah laughed openly. Miranda's manners would be the pink elephant of an elite gathering, but that was part of what made her so likeable. She didn't care what anyone thought of her. Her love for life was captivating. She could be so childlike at times and other times astounded Hannah with the wisdom of an old soul.

It was obvious from Alex's expression, he admired and appreciated the same qualities in her.

"Good for her," Hannah thought of Miranda. She has a man who really gets her and from what Hannah was seeing in Alex's eyes, someone who is going to stick around.

By late afternoon, most of the remaining boxes were unpacked and things organized and put away. The house was looking like a lived-in home and had a comfortable feel to it. The boxes that were not unpacked had been put in the spare rooms out of the way until Hannah could sort through them. She didn't want them to do anything else. They had done so much already, and it was time to call it a day.

They had a long drive, and she didn't want them rolling in at midnight or after being exhausted. They all sat in the living room and curled up with a glass of wine and kicked their feet up and enjoyed one another's company. She made some to-go coffee for them with some of the muffins that were left over that Sarah and Nikki had brought over. Afterwards, she walked them to their car and they said their goodbyes.

"Text me when you get home," Hannah insisted.

"Don't forget you can track us through your phone," Miranda reminded her, "in case I forget to text you," waving good-bye.

Hannah had forgotten about that feature and made a mental note to check it.

She watched them drive off, then turned and looked out over the ocean, which she could see from the drive way. She could see the white caps on the waves rolling in, but the sound was lost in the breeze at the distance. The sun was still up. She could smell the salty air, as the breeze blew lightly against her face.

It was nice, she thought, to live somewhere that houses were not nearly touching and the neighbors were separated with distance, not on top of each other. San Francisco was behind her now.

Chapter Twenty-Two

Warning

It had taken a week, but Hannah had committed herself to the remainder of the unpacking and organizing, getting up before sunrise and in bed shortly after sunset each night, as she carefully balanced her work with her sleep. Even then, it had all been physically taxing. She placed two porch swing beds with baby blue pillows for added décor on the covered deck that extended the south and west sides of the house. She had been so exhausted she had grabbed a warm throw and laid her head on the pillow. The sway of the swing being blown in the gentle breeze relaxed her, and she drifted to sleep. An hour later, she was fully refreshed.

The hanging Japanese wisteria plants and new crimson red cushioned furniture to lounge in had given a nice effect to the back patio. She could soak up sun, while she admired the flower garden and birds feeding from the feeders and bathing in the bird baths. Inside, the house was shaping up. Scented cream color candles were placed in every room that smelled of cotton linen. Palms or ficus floor plants accentuated almost every room. Wall hangings were leveled and hung at measured distances between walls and at eye level.

There was a shop she found in town that sold décor, so she bought a few impressionist copies specifically for the bedrooms, and then she had found three other pieces that were originals, which she hung two in her own bedroom, one of which was a watercolor painting of wings that reminded her of angel's wings.

The second painting she hung in her room was of a blue whale emerging its body out of the water as the golden sun reflected a rainbow of colors into the surging water that fell onto sunlit hues that surrounded its body. To her, the whale had always represented something majestic, larger than life, full of force, but at the same time, mortal and vulnerable.

The third was a painting of a dove with radiant rays of light that beamed outward, which she hung in the living room near the kitchen entrance where she would always be walking past it. Just looking at it was moving. Everything inside and outside the house was coming together.

She had bought a large rectangular red, pink, and orange rug with patchwork design and placed it over a cream rug that was slightly larger, giving it a border effect. A solid watermelon color quilt served as a foot runner to her bed over a white down blanket that matched the rug perfectly.

The guest bedroom had a blue and green theme for which she found a painting of a dolphin swimming amidst the ocean plant life, in which there were mixtures of red and sea green. The new artwork had blended with the color themes she was creating for the rooms, and she had appraised the end result with satisfaction.

While having a bowl of oatmeal and blueberries, she browsed the web for things to do nearby, as well as shopping centers in the surrounding area. She studied the Google map on her iPad to get a feel of direction around town. She enjoyed her sense of space around her home and not being crowded in anymore. As soon as she finished her oatmeal and coffee, the only thing she wanted to do was take a warm shower.

She had seen banners placed over downtown streets advertising the town farmer's market today. She had made a note to check it out and get vegetables she wanted to make soup. It seemed forever since she had made homemade soup. Jesse had been more of a meat and potatoes guy, so she was in the habit of cooking three-course meals, but she'd gotten lazy lately with cooking. Stopping by the Farmer's Market would lend opportunity to pop into a few shops.

"Be careful, Hannah," he warned. Jared was standing behind her as she was applying some makeup. His reflection was absent in the mirror, prompting her to turn. His tone was solemn and sincere.

"Why do you say that?" searching his eyes, seeing her own reflection but his countenance revealed concern, which alarmed her. When he only looked back at her without answering, she asked again, "Jared, what is it?" she whispered. "Am I in danger?"

He could read her far better than she could read him, but he had her full, undivided attention. She could feel her heartbeat in her chest and everything around her felt like it went void as she waited, one second after another.

"You're vulnerable and it's only been a short time. You are an attractive woman, and men will desire you. Be careful who you let into your life and how soon," he cautioned. "Sometimes it is not so much who as it is the timing."

"Do you mean someone who would hurt me?" she conjectured.

"If you use poor judgment, which vulnerable people often do, then yes," his eyes filled with pain.

"What do you know, Jared? Tell me."

"I can't protect you from your own choices, but I can offer you some guidance in hopes you will exercise awareness, which everyone should do anyway. Sometimes people who are vulnerable do not make the best choices for themselves. The look on his face was solemn.

"So, you see me as vulnerable?" she asked, surprised.

"You are, Hannah. You need to focus on yourself and not get involved in another relationship so soon. You owe it to yourself to know who you are apart from anyone else and to learn to enjoy your own company. People who can't do that go into relationships strictly because they are lonely. Loneliness can lead to poor judgment in choosing a mate."

"I think I've always been comfortable with who I am," she countered.

"Who would that be, Hannah?"

"I, well I," stumbling over her thoughts. The weight of what she realized was in the next words that she spoke. "I'm...I was a wife and mother," lowering her lashes, realizing now what he was conveying to her. "I was," she concluded.

"When one is no longer in a relationship, sometimes they forget who they are not anymore. It often results in what is commonly referred to as the rebound. On the other hand, it can result in people never moving on to develop a healthy relationship with themselves and never having a healthy relationship with a new partner. I admonish you to see time as your friend and not your enemy. Take time to redefine yourself and love who you are before you invite another relationship into your life." His eyes bore into hers gently and lovingly. There was nothing selfish in him, she realized.

"But I'm not looking for anyone, Jared. She searched his eyes, which were clear, liquid pools of brown and hazel with a beam of light shining through them, reminding her of a lighthouse shining its light out to sea warning a ship's captain to turn the other way. His unfaltering eyes seemed to be telling her just that, to turn the other way. "You see something about to happen, don't you?"

"I can't protect you from everything, no matter how much I would like to. I can't."

"Is that the only reason you look at me so gravely? Is there anything else you need to tell me?

All I can do is caution you. I only ask that you be mindful. You're vulnerable, Hannah.

"Okay, I understand, Jared. You would be there to keep me from doing something stupid, right?"

"Emotions are powerful. Once you open yourself up to something, it's not easy to turn away. Just know you are not yet ready to pursue a committed or physical relationship with anyone, as it would lead to demands and expectations for both involved that you are not prepared for or may regret, and yes, result in mutual pain that you will not be ready to handle and may reflect on later with regret and remorse. Right now, you're making progress. I have no desire to see you sabotage that. Time is a gift, Hannah. Remember that. Use it wisely."

She was taken back by his impromptu concern for her. He must foresee something she hasn't, yet at least. "I understand, I do. I appreciate your concern, but Jared, I'm not thinking along those lines, at all."

"Perhaps not as we speak. Again, I remind you, be careful and give consideration to your decisions pertaining to new relationships before you commit to them," he told her again. "The time will come when it will be right for you, but not now."

She looked at him steadfastly for what seemed like half a minute, then nodded. "Okay, I promise, Jared. I'll be careful. I promise."

"Don't ignore the still quiet voice within your soul. Pay attention to it. I am not a replacement for it. Nothing is. It's a gift given to all, though many ignore it. That's all I'm asking," he told her, and relaxed his stance considerably.

"You won't leave me, will you? You'll stay, right?"

"I'm never really gone, Hannah. Haven't you figured that out yet?" arching his eyebrow at her. "I explained that to you. Remember?"

"I mean really leave, not just invisible but not *with* me," she pressed, emotion swelling in her. Her throat felt as if it might close, as if the worse thing to fear were looming over her, which was losing him from her life.

"You're speaking of abandonment. That won't happen. It is not possible for you to *lose* me. Do you not understand that?" He leaned closer to her, and his energy merged with hers, giving her reassurance she found herself needing. This conversation had made her uneasy, yet she also was grateful to him. He watched her, knowing his words had alarmed her, but he could not in good conscious withhold this warning from her. He had seen how men looked at her and discerned their desires, unaware of the trauma she is still healing from, nor would some relate to what she had suffered if they had never experienced it in their own lives, and if she engaged in a relationship too soon, it would not be fair to either her or the other person. He knew she would soon be met with the challenge. Now, it was up to her to heed or ignore the advice he just gave her. He hoped she would heed his warning.

She turned back to the mirror and stared at herself, feeling conflicted. He was behind her but had no reflection of his own in the mirror. Then, she set her makeup back down on the vanity that she had been holding and walked in her room and sat on the end of the bed. She looked up at the painting of the wings she had just hung yesterday. They reminded her of herself, a butterfly spreading its wings and flying.

That's what she had been doing, learning to fly, to go on with her life. That's what he wanted her to *keep* doing. It concerned her that he was afraid that something, or someone was going to interfere with that.

Relationships were always a gamble that had risks. Perhaps he only wanted to decrease her risks. She knew he didn't intend for her never to meet people or seek out new relationships. He's not selfish like that. There was nothing selfish about him. She had not given any consideration to seeking out another relationship.

He foresees something, with someone, someone in particular, she thought. Duly noted, she told herself. For now, she didn't want to dwell on it. She picked up her purse from the dresser and walked out the door to go to the farmer's market to pick up some vegetables for a soup and salad she planned to make.

Chapter Twenty-Three

The Girl on Rollerblades

The turnout for the market was larger than Hannah had expected, and there were a lot of college students since it was near the college, but then, she wasn't sure what she had expected. It was in the sixties, so she wore a long and loose brown sweater over royal blue button up blouse and jeans with brown ankle boots.

The fruit and vegetables were ripe with fresh smells that wafted in the air. There was a troubadour playing a violin who was very gifted with her instrument and danced as she played. A small crowd was gathered around, and as a few would walk away to finish shopping, more would come in their place.

There were stands selling food and drink, and some providing free water in Dixie cups. She gathered up supplies of condiments, homemade pasta, teas, scones, avocados, blueberries, oranges, melons, lettuce, tomatoes, asparagus, carrots, celery, grapes, and cherries. She had filled two large bags and took them to her car but wanted to go back and get some cheese spread and fresh bread.

She had these items packed away in a bag and thought she would look a little longer, and then she'd walk over and listen to the violinist and offer her a contribution before leaving.

She walked by a table that sold dates, figs, seeds, and nuts and debated whether or not to buy some figs and almonds but only chose the almonds. Satisfied, she walked along paying more attention to the people that were there. To her unease, she found there were men staring at her, men walking with their wives or girlfriends, men holding a tub of grapes or a melon who were not paying any attention to the task at hand or the person they were with. Some turned away when she made eye contact with them, but a couple of them just smiled flirtatiously.

She remembered Jared's warning and made a conscious choice to ignore them, but she was also now conscious of them staring, which caused her to feel awkward. She came upon a booth that was selling strawberries and decided to add those to her purchases. This would be the bulk of her groceries for the upcoming week. She had everything else she needed for salad and to go in the soup at home. She paid the vendor and turned to leave, but a pit-bull on a leash was approaching and vied for her attention.

"Hi there! Aren't you a beautiful dog," she cooed at him. "Oh, you like me, do you? I like you, too!" petting him.

"He *does* like you," the woman holding the leash observed. "He loves to meet people and make friends," she told her, smiling, as they both watched him beg for more attention.

"What's his name," Hannah asked?

"Pascal."

"Well Pascal, do you shake?" Hannah held out her hand and Pascal put his paw in her hand. "It's a real pleasure meeting you, fella," and pet his head once more. He really is a beautiful dog," she complimented.

"Thanks. He's a lot of company. Do you have a dog?"

"No, I've considered it, but recently moved here and just settled in. Haven't made that leap yet," she confessed.

About that time, Pascal seemed distracted, so the woman bid her farewell and continued on. Hannah was watching them walk on, thinking how much she would enjoy a dog, but immediately talked herself out of it, not wanting any added responsibility just yet.

She turned to walk toward the violinist but glanced one more time at the dog when her feet were knocked right out from under her. There was no grace she could add to her fall, which had plummeted her right off the sidewalk and onto the curb. The pain was sharp, wrapping around her ankle like a vice. The side of her body hit the pavement with a jar. Her head came within an inch of hitting the asphalt before she gained control. The raw skin on her elbow and wrist burned. People ran toward her from different directions coming to her aid.

"I think my ankle is broken," she winced.

"Lie still. Just lie still," a male voice spoke, stooping down to help her. He appeared to be assessing her for injuries. "Where do you feel pain?" he asked.

"In my pride," she wanted to say, but thought better of it. "Mostly my ankle," she answered.

She was sprawled out and trying to get up, but he stopped her.

"Lie still, lie still. He unzipped her boot and slipped her foot out of it, while she sucked in a rush of air through her gritted teeth. "Oh, that hurts," she pressed her lips tight and clenched her jaw.

"You don't want to have that boot on when it swells, he told her. It will be harder to get off." He palpated her ankle, which elicited an, "Ouwa!" She yelled before she could stop herself, and began sucking in breaths, as he continued to assess her injuries. The pain shot deep into the ankle, as he palpated, despite that he was very gentle. She could feel the pressure from the swelling that was quickly increasing.

Sucking in a deep breath through her teeth, she attempted to move thinking she would maneuver herself to get back on her feet.

"I am so sorry, are you okay?" came a teenager's remorseful voice. "I didn't mean to run into you, I really didn't!"

Looking up, she saw roller blades two feet away from her line of vision, which was, at the moment, level with the ground. Looking upward at the person wearing them was a frantic, young girl with earbuds in her ears," the culprit, she guessed.

"I'm so-o-o sorry," she continued, "I didn't see you, I really didn't!" The genuine concern on her face made it hard for Hannah not to be forgiving.

"We need to make sure nothing is broken before you try to walk on it," he told her.

Still speaking to the girl, "I'll be okay, as soon as I can walk at least," gritting her teeth. "No worries, kiddo, just be careful, okay. Try to pay attention to where you're going." With an effort to use the uninjured leg to thrust herself up, "I've got this!" making another effort.

"Just lie still a moment," the man assessing her injuries insisted.

She wondered if he was a paramedic. He seemed to know what he was doing. For the first time, she noticed he was not so hard on the eyes.

"Your ankle is swelling quickly. It's already showing signs of bruising. It could be a sprain or it could be a fracture. We won't know until we get an x-ray. You shouldn't be putting any weight on it," he chastised her.

"But…I think if I can make it to my car, I'll be okay. I did have a bag in my hand." She looked but didn't see it. Frantically, she addressed the spectators, "Does anyone see my bag?"

Embarrassment outweighed the pain. She wanted to go home and start the day over.

"We'll get your bag and anything that fell out of it. Don't worry, the man told her." His voice was soothing.

"I have your bag. I picked up everything that fell out, so it's all there," she heard someone say, before she saw the bag being set down a couple feet from her.

"Is there anything we can do?" she heard an older woman ask as the man, who she now was looking at, was assessing her elbows and wrists for mobility.

"No, I can manage," she heard him respond to the woman.

There was no bleeding through her sleeves. He then assessed for bleeding or lumps on her scalp, which he didn't seem to find any. He raised her sleeves to check her elbows, when she said the left elbow burned and found a scrape but nothing that required suturing.

"You're going to be alright. You'll need an x-ray of your ankle, though," his eyes were stern but warm, as he now spoke to her. "Let me help you up, slowly, very slowly, that's it. Lift your foot off the ground and keep it up," coaching her as he eased her up.

When she was finally upright and standing, he kept his arm around her waist, "Hold on to me," he instructed her. "Would you hand me her bag?" he addressed a little girl standing closest to it who handed it to him.

He supported her weight on the left side, instructing her to hold her leg, so that she didn't put any weight on her foot. "I'll be your left leg," he assured her, and you lean on me and only use your right foot, okay?"

"Okay," she agreed, thankful for his help. She wanted to get a better look at him, so she looked him in the eye when she responded to his instruction. He had blue eyes and dark brows and lashes and sandy blond hair that was combed back, kind of like Elvis but without the sideburns, and as she looked down, she glanced at his physique and noted he was quite muscular looking through his khaki pants and gray polo shirt. The modest tan on his arms and face gave him a young appearance, perhaps mid-twenties. It was hard to tell how tall he was since she was unable to stand up straight. At the moment, he was standing taller than she was. He looked like he could have been a college quarterback.

"I'm taking you to get an x-ray. You need to make sure that ankle is not fractured," he spoke with authority, leaving her little room to argue. "My office is nearby, so I'll take you there and do the x-ray myself. My car is just up ahead, nodding his head in the direction he was taking her," looking at her as if monitoring her for pain. They walked slowly and he struck her as someone with a high level of patience, as slow as she was hobbling along.

"This is really very kind of you," she said to him. "I feel bad spoiling your day like this," being honest.

"You're not spoiling anything." He looked at her and his smile was contagious. "Really, you're not," he reassured her.

A moment later she heard the squelching of his door electronically opening on his BMW, as he pressed the key lock, after which he opened the car door for her, still supporting her balance. He shifted to get out of her way so she could sit down in the car, which required a little hopping and shuffling, but she finally managed it. He closed her car door and put her bag of produce he had been carrying for her in the back floorboard. He was in the driver's seat next to her in half a second it seemed.

Before putting the car in gear, he looked at her and asked, "Besides your ankle and scraped elbow, are you okay?"

"Mostly embarrassed," she confessed, "but yes, I think I'll recover," trying to smile appreciatively. His smile was enough to assure her that she would be.

His office was less than a mile away, and he pulled around to the back door. It was a professional building that had a sign near the road that identified it as a medical office building.

"Sit still just a moment and I'll be right back in two seconds," he assured her and was already out of the car. A few seconds later, he came out with a wheelchair and rolled up next to the car door, which he opened for her. It seemed a little easier getting out of the car and into the wheelchair than it had been for her to pick herself off the pavement.

He wheeled her to the x-ray room where he gave the technician orders, and Hannah was then positioned on the x-ray table for three sets of x-rays.

"How in the hell did this happen?" she moaned as she thought about how this was going to impact her the next several days, perhaps longer. She refused to cry. She had cried enough to last a lifetime.

"Why?" Jared, where are you?" she whispered. She closed her eyes and took deep breaths to control the pain. Each time the tech had her to change positions to reposition her ankle, she winced with sharp pain.

Afterwards, she was wheeled to an empty exam room where she sat in the wheelchair until he had read the x-rays. The exam room was painted a light mossy green with tall windows and closed miniblinds, and like most exam rooms she had ever been in, it had a sterile quality to it.

"Why wasn't Jared there? Where was he?" A palpable dread loomed over her. She searched her mind trying to define it. She had always believed things happened for purpose. One's life could be turned upside down in the blink of an eye, but she'd always believed there was a silver lining if one just searched for it and believed in it. The fact that Jared did not stop her from being hurt this morning...but she had to remind herself, he was not her guardian angel or spirit guide. He had protected her before, but her life had been at stake and so had Miranda's. An injured ankle was hardly life-threatening. It would slow her down a bit, however.

She looked down at her ankle and noted the swelling had gotten worse and the bruising was becoming more visible. There was a tap at the door before a medical assistant stepped inside with a hands-free blue icepack with Velcro that could be wrapped around a leg or arm.

"Hi, I'm Michelle. Dr. Hurley asked me to bring this in for you to put on your ankle. He wants you to apply it for 10 minutes." She gently applied it to Hannah's ankle, which she elevated on the second chair in the exam room the physician normally sits in. The cold slowly increased as it penetrated through layers of flesh, and the weight of it was slightly uncomfortable but tolerable.

"The doctor will be in with you shortly," Michelle told her and smiled before leaving the room. She was an attractive girl, probably twenty, obviously pregnant, Hannah guessed around seven months.

Her mind reflected back on her own pregnancy, the visits each month to the obstetrician, feeling Ethan move and kick inside her, and the moment she went into labor. It had been 7:15 in the morning, when a sharp pain woke her up. Jesse had taken leave of absence with the approaching due date. She nudged him to wake him up, "Babe?" and he was instantly alert. He knew without her saying anything else, it was time. An hour later they were at the hospital. She remembered how methodical he was. He didn't panic like so many men do. He had really impressed her that morning.

In her mind she replayed everything, the drive to the hospital, being wheeled to the labor room, Jesse right by her side during the entire labor, coaching her. She could not have wished for a better partner.

"Good news. Your ankle is not broken. It's just a really bad sprain," Dr. Hurley was saying, bringing her out of her reverie. She had not even noticed him walk in.

"That's a relief," Hannah agreed. "So, no cast then," feeling thankful.

He pulled up an extra chair in the room and unwrapped the icepack. "No cast," he announced in agreement, but you will need crutches for a week or so. Michelle is getting a pair for you." His hand was warm on her foot, as he palpated the swelling. His touch was gentle, but there was some tenderness that made her flinch.

"You'll have to keep an eye out for kids on rollerblades," he teased and smiled. Michelle knocked and came in with a pair of crutches and handed them to him. He thanked her, and realizing she was dismissed, she left the room.

He handed her a prescription for Lortab. "Take this if the pain is unbearable," he told her. Otherwise, just take ibuprofen every four to six hours and that will help with inflammation associated with it. He took the crutches and set them in front of her.

"Grab hold of them and pull up," he instructed, as he steadied them for her while she pulled herself up. Hannah positioned them under her arms and tried to get a feel for them.

"How does that feel?" he asked, observing her attentively.

"Good, I think," looking up at him, wishing she could rewind to two hours ago.

"Be sure you use them, even short distances. Okay? And, I'm going to send the icepack home with you. Apply it for 10-15 minutes about 4 times a day for the next couple of days.

"Okay, I'll be fine, thanks," she replied warmly. For reasons she wasn't sure, her eyes went to his left hand. He was not wearing a ring. Why did she care, she wondered, feeling a little alarmed that she had been curious and had purposefully looked?

"Thanks, for all your help. It was definitely an awkward moment," she admitted, still feeling embarrassed.

"I'm just glad I was there."

"So am I," she admitted. "I guess you will be taking me back to my car?" she asked, unabashed.

"Yes," he teased, "I will be taking you back to your car," taking pleasure in her blatancy.

"Oh! What do I owe you for your services, Dr. Hurley?"

He looked up, making eye contact, "You can call me Brad. Nothing. You don't owe me anything. Just glad I could help," he responded resolutely.

Okay, well, then I suppose all I can do is say, thank you," smiling back at him politely.

Brad drove her back to her car and helped her into it. Once she was behind the wheel, he handed her his card.

"Call me if you have any problems. There's a podiatrist next door, and he can apply a medicated wrap if the swelling doesn't start going down or the soreness doesn't ease up. I don't anticipate you will need it, though, as long as you stay off it and use the crutches. Keep your foot elevated to ease swelling. Don't forget to ice. Otherwise, plan on seeing me back in 7 to 10 days. Deal?" he concluded.

"Deal!" she agreed. "Thanks again."

"You bet." He closed her car door. Hannah was thankful it was not her right foot or she wouldn't have been able to operate the pedal. She started the car and pulled out. He watched her drive away before turning back to his own car.

Hannah had planned on seeing some of the shops, but right now, she just wanted to go home. The day had not gone as planned, at all. Driving back, she questioned why she had wanted to know if he was married, why she had made a conscious effort to look at his left hand to see if there was a ring on it.

"Why do I care? Why am I even acting interested?" she mumbled to herself. "Besides, even if I was, I could tell it wasn't mutual," grumbling this time. She shook her head no, as a gesture of scolding herself.

"Just put it out of your mind, Hannah Barstow. Don't even go there," she ordered herself.

She hadn't even felt Jared with her today after she left. She thought of the warning he had given her. She recalled all the men that stared at her. Gloom was taunting her after the accident, as if some negative energy making her feel anxious. No, she decided. It wasn't the collision with the girl on roller blades. It was more than that. For the rest of the afternoon, she couldn't get her mind off of it.

Later, she was sitting on the barstool in the kitchen with her crutches propped against the bar, having a bowl of soup and browsing her iPad but then closed out of it and set it down, really not into looking at anything.

Her ankle was hurting, and she needed something for pain, *and* she needed to prop her foot up.

Closing her eyes, "I just can't believe how this day has turned out," grumbling to herself, *and* to anyone who might be listening.

"Jared, are you here?" feeling downhearted.

She looked everywhere her eyes could see but didn't really feel tuned in. Her pain was too distracting. She took hold of her crutches and put one under her left arm and took the bowl and spoon to put in the sink. She managed to get the other crutch and hobbled to the steps. The bedroom was upstairs. There was a half bath on this floor, but she was realizing it was going to take a lot of effort to get up the steps. She stood at the bottom and felt daunted by the task of climbing them. One step at a time, she thought to herself, trying to maneuver the crutches, realizing she was going to have to figure out how she could do this with the most control over her balance. The last thing she needed was another fall.

"I could really use some help, Jared," she mumbled under her breath, sure he could hear her. She took one step at a time, getting the hang of how to use the crutch. If she kept her balance she would be okay, she thought. Halfway up the stairs, she felt him. His presence moved in on her fast. She felt the goosebumps all over her body. She continued to move forward but felt an energy, like a magnetic field in the presence of metal, that came up from behind her. It moved fast and felt charged, and she paused her efforts to keep propelling herself upward.

"I'm here," his voice came. It was gentle and compassionate.

She didn't turn but spoke back, "Where were you today?" she wanted to know. "I mean, chivalry from *you* would have been nice. Perhaps I wouldn't be sporting a pair of crutches and a sprained ankle. Being knocked to the ground by a kid on rollerblades is definitely not my finest hour," she complained, grumbling under her breath.

She stroked her fingers through her hair in a gesture of frustration. She asked herself if she was angry at him, but she knew she wasn't. She didn't understand why he didn't stop the girl from running into her. That was exactly what was wrong. She knew he tried to give her insight, but he seemed hesitant in what he could tell her. She decided she was just frustrated with the situation itself more than she was with him.

"I can't stop everything unpleasant from happening. I know you want, maybe expect, me to do that, but I can't. Sometimes small inconveniences are the way you are protected from worse things happening. You don't always see the path you're on or what an inconvenience may have caused you to avoid. He moved in front of her. He wanted her to see him.

"Do you not think I would do everything in my power to protect you? Sometimes, things like what happened today, or your car not starting, or having a tire blowout, those incidences *are* what may actually be protecting you! Few people consider that, but it *is* true." His countenance was sad.

"I know. You're right, I know that. Yes, it *is* the situation that's frustrating. I'm not upset with you, I'm really not," being truthful. "I want to understand more than I do. I'm just really in a lot of pain with this, and I need to get upstairs and take some ibuprofen and prop my foot up. I might as well plan on being an invalid for a few days," she complained, trekking further up the steps.

"I won't let you fall," he promised.

"Thanks," she whispered just as she reached the landing.

The irony of the situation she now found herself in was like a pink elephant in the room. A new house, new town, all in the spirit of moving on, healing, making a positive decision for herself and her well-being, only to be run down by a kid on rollerblades that now has left her temporarily crippled. The more she thought about it, the funnier, more ironic it seemed to her, and the more she felt humored by it, if only to keep from crying. She laughed without knowing why she found humor in it, and the more she considered it, the more humorous it seemed. Laughing seemed to lighten her perspective *and* her mood. Every thought seemed to elicit a chain reaction of more laughing.

"I'm losing my mind. This is so nuts!"

"You're not *losing* your mind, Hannah," Jared interjected, amused at her. "You're simply frustrated."

His eyes read her, knew her, and she understood he was being supportive in a get yourself back on track sort of way. He watched her as if monitoring her sanity, she thought, but in truth, she knew better.

"Okay, I know that. I'm just venting," shaking her head as if it was all unbelievable, everything, since Ethan and Jess had *left her*. Her life felt foreign to her with each passing day. Moving was a hope that she could shake off the dust and reestablish her sense of security and normalcy, but she found herself wondering if this was an omen, and she had been misguided.

"Why *did* this happen?" she asked him.

He smiled, "Sometimes what happens just isn't about fate, Hannah. Sometimes things happen because of laws of nature."

She stared at him, speechless.

"Not the answer you hoped to hear, I see," responding to her unthought out words.

"No, it's not that. Honestly, I don't know what it is. I just feel like, I feel like I just need life to make sense. I *want* life to make sense! But it doesn't always, especially when things don't go as I would hope. I know that sounds like blatant overthinking, but I don't know," her voice trailed and she looked at nothing.

"Life does make sense. Just not to the mortal mind that doesn't see with absolute clarity and sees nothing past the present. What one anticipates is not always what unfolds, and what one does *not* anticipate is often what does. What matters is how one responds to what does happen, regardless of how much or how little they understand it, like it or don't like it. It's a matter of practiced perspective."

Reading her thoughts, he knew she didn't want to discuss the matter any further.

"Honestly, I've never had to *think* so much in my life about how I react or what I feel about anything! And right now, I just don't want to think anymore," and with that, she cleared her mind of everything.

Seeing that her mind tuned him out, Jared left her to her thoughts.

Chapter Twenty-Four

Redefined

Hannah spent the following three days absorbed in a book, a memoir that was about a journey of self-discovery and spiritual liberation. She paid very little notice of Jared's presence. He watched her read, often standing behind her, peering over her shoulder. Other times he stood in front of her, just watching her and adoring her. He hid himself from her so that his presence was not distracting, but she was aware he was there. His presence was very much felt, like the warm, glowing feeling that makes one feel safe and loved.

She continued reading. As much as she wanted to give him full-time attention, she knew for whatever purpose she had chosen to return to this world and be reincarnated and suffer the unimaginable and unthinkable losses this life had bestowed upon her, she had eternity to give Jared her attention. She was still alive, and therefore, she should be living her life as a mortal, not wasting time wishing she could be immortal to be with him or wishing he were mortal to be with her. No, there was a reason she had wanted to return, and so she determined she would focus on living and on her mortality. Life was meant to be lived as long as one was living. She aimed to live it.

She had every confidence Jesse and Ethan were living theirs in their immortality. She would see them again, too, and she knew that. If anything, their deaths had taught her to be aware that these years she has lived, that they had also lived, and short lives as they were, theirs had not been all there is and then no more. This profound experience had taught her to be conscious of the reality of the spiritual realm and all its power and consciousness and good will towards all human beings. It had led her to more mindful, conscious living, not just taking life and happiness for granted. Happiness, she realized, is something we create for ourselves, not just something that falls from the sky like manna. It is not something that is just gifted to us, but something we must strive for and create for ourselves.

She had depended on Jesse and Ethan for her happiness. They had been her world. She had never once considered happiness was something she had to create from within, that it was a state of being, a state of mind, that it was birthed by choice. She had believed happiness just *was* a thing in and of itself that either one had or they didn't. Now, she believed it was a choice. Jesus had said, "Where your treasure is, there your heart will be, also," and Proverbs stated, "As a man thinketh in his heart, so he is."

These statements resonated within her. Happiness was not in wealth, designer clothes of the latest fashion, name brand shoes, a fine home, fancy car, or anything tangible. She had always had a measure of all these things and took them for granted. More and more, precept upon precept, the concept of happiness was being redefined in her life, because it was no longer in a family life. It was in being creative with one's own life, starting with now, doing something with one's talents, setting goals, and following through with them, never giving up, and always, always being mindful of one's higher power and higher self.

Happiness was in believing in one's self to accomplish whatever one set their mind to do and to always be doing it and working towards it. Happiness was recognizing one's connection and worth to all humanity, to all life, to the universe, and with something greater than what one can see when looking around themselves. Happiness was not connected to a thing but to the heart, mind, and soul, but most importantly, again, it is a choice. Once that choice is made to believe in and pursue it rather than reject it, a portal to the divine seems to open up, and the universe seems to respond, "You found the key."

She read book after book, knowing that this activity would keep her off her ankle, and she would heal faster. She had chosen to take in the ideas and discoveries of sages and learn as much as she could while her ankle was healing.

At night, she burned candles and meditated, and all she asked of Jared was that he be silent so she could listen. He was silent. She focused on her healing, not just of her ankle but of her soul. She knew she had been acting out the motions of trying to move on with her life, do things to take her mind off the day her life had forever changed, the pain she still remembered as unimaginable and unfathomable, yet she experienced it and endured it. It was still a process and she knew it always would be for as long as she remained in this life.

After three days, she was thankful for the girl who had knocked her off her feet. What a gift the girl had given her. The mishap gave her time to absorb richness through her reading and meditations, which she now understood she was so hungry for. She was taking advantage of time to be still and listen to something other than her id, ego, and superego. There was a stillness in her being now that was peaceful.

"Thank you," she whispered, speaking to all that was higher than she was and that had provided her with the love she had been given by friends, family, Jared, and the universe, and for the love she had shared with Jesse and Ethan for the short time they were on earth. She was thankful and mindful of the unseen power that had lifted her and held her up and guided her through.

On the seventh day, Hannah drove to Dr. Hurley's office to return the crutches. She was going to just leave them with the receptionist and be done with it.

"Hi, Bridget," noticing her nametag. "I'm Hannah Barstow and I was here a week ago with a sprained ankle." Before Bridget could respond, merely getting in a quick nod, "Do you mind letting Dr. Hurley know my ankle is recovered, and that I would like to thank him for his kindness, and let me leave these with you," showing her the crutches. She handed Bridget her address and insurance card.

"I don't feel right that he didn't charge me for his services. I know, he just happened to be nearby when I fell," remembering she was literally knocked off her feet rather than just fell, "so he didn't charge me, but he went over and beyond, so would you please ask him to charge my insurance for his services so that he can be paid? I'd feel better if he did."

She was pulling out her wallet and handing the receptionist a check, "Please put this on my account," she asked.

Bridget was looking up the account on the computer and said, "Mrs. Barstow, I don't see you have an account in the system. Could you hold on a minute?" and rushed from her desk and disappeared.

Less than two minutes later, Michele appeared, who recognized her immediately, and Hannah noted she was still very pregnant.

"How's that ankle?" she asked cheerily, standing in the doorway to the waiting room.

"Better!" Hannah rushed to answer.

"Come on back," and gestured for Hannah to grab the crutches. She followed her to an exam room and saw a glimpse of Dr. Hurley coming out of another room where he had just seen another patient. Their eyes met just before she entered the room Michele had taken her to.

"Looks like you are going to have that baby any day now," Hannah smiled, trying to make conversation. She had not planned to see him.

"My husband is in the service, so I would rather be here than home by myself in case I do go into labor. I'll be in good hands," she said purposefully. "I'm staying with my parents for the time being, since I'm so close to the due date, but they work during the day, and I don't want them to take time off work when I can just be here instead."

"Sounds like you have your bases covered. That's smart," Hannah commended her.

"Yeah, my husband is on board with it, and it's taken a weight off everyone's minds to know I won't be by myself when it happens. If I'm between home and work, it's not very far, and it would be manageable, I think, so now it's just a matter of when nature calls," rolling her eyes.

"Best of luck and early congratulations," Hannah smiled at her.

"Thanks!" she replied, sincerely appreciative and left the room. "Dr. Hurley will be in to see you in a moment."

A moment later, Dr. Hurley did enter the room. "How's that ankle?" he asked, sitting on the stool and rolling it towards her. "Let me take a look."

She raised her foot for him and he put his hand under her lower calf for support while palpating her ankle. "No swelling and minimal bruising," he noted.

"Well, it seems you've done all the right things to take care of it," looking at her as he let her leg down.

"I indulged in a lot of reading," she laughed.

He smiled and held her gaze a little longer than necessary. "Well, you're welcome to keep the crutches, and there's no need to pay me," he said resolutely. "I'd prefer you didn't. I merely responded to a damsel in distress, like any gentleman would, so there is no charge."

"That's very kind, but you did go out of your way," she reminded him.

"One doesn't need to be paid for being kind, Hannah," his eyes melting into hers.

"Alright, as you wish, and thank you, again," she resigned.

He paused and seemed to be contemplating. "I would even be honored if you would allow me to take you to dinner sometime," his voice sounding hopeful.

She remembered Jared's words, to be careful. "Now is not a good time, Brad." She contemplated what to say next. "My husband and son were killed in a car accident this past summer, and the timing isn't right for me to start dating right now," she wanted him to understand, though not wanting to completely discourage him either.

"My word, Hannah," he gasped, embellished with genuine heart-felt sympathy. "I had no idea!"

"I know. I'm processing it all, and I still need some time."

"Definitely, I totally understand," he rushed to agree, still feeling the awkwardness of the flirtation. There was no way he could have known.

"I'm considering getting away, taking a trip, soon," she added.

"That could do you some good, go someplace fresh. I can't even imagine," he admitted. "Any idea where you might go?"

"I'm still working that part out, but someplace I need a passport," she said with a hint of mystery, trying to put him at ease with her smile.

"By yourself?" he asked curiously.

"I don't think I'll be alone," she wanted to say, expecting Jared would be with her throughout the entire trip, but it's not what she said. "Yeah, I guess so," she lied.

"Well, in any case," not sure what to say, "I just ask that you are careful. Beware of strangers!" he warned, trying to sound lighthearted, but in truth, he wished she were not traveling out of the country alone.

"I'll be fine," she assured him, knowing Jared would not let anything happen to her. "Again, thanks for everything," she said again, more sweetly.

When she started out the door, he said, "Do you know when you're leaving?"

"Probably after Thanksgiving," she answered thoughtfully.

He half smiled and half grimaced. "Don't forget to pick up your check from the receptionist," and looked to Michele to make sure she did.

Hannah sat in the local coffee shop and connected her tablet to Wi-Fi. She sipped a cup of green tea and nibbled at a blueberry scone. On the library website, she searched for more e-books. She had taken a greater interest in Rumi, Gibran, and many modern-day authors, some fiction and some nonfiction. Once her ankle didn't feel as stiff, she wanted to ease into jogging again, and had already gone on a couple short runs and then would come home and ice her ankle as a preventative measure.

The thing that she pondered most was how her life had been redefined. It was a process that was still unfolding. If anyone would have told her a year ago how much her life would change, she would have reacted in horror and disbelief. It would have been unfathomable. She would probably have thought anyone was a lunatic that would have said such a thing.

Now here she was trying to remember what it felt like to be that woman again. She had felt secure and happy then, but yet she had depended on Jesse to be her rock. He had been her foundation, and she had never imagined life without him or Ethan. It would have been impossible to imagine. She had faith, she had thought, but never had it been put to the test like it had been when she found herself alone. Yet she *knew* she wasn't alone at all. Her life had taken on a different perspective, and she had acquired a different viewpoint about *the living* and what it meant to be *alive.* She had a greater curiosity about what separates us from beyond death. Before, she had never given serious thought to this mystery. Yet this very mystery was the reality of life itself beyond the small dot on the infinity timeline. It was deserving of contemplation.

There were a couple days she saw she had a missed call from her mother. She would be so into a book and think about calling her back and turn the ringer on her phone up so she could hear it if she tried calling again, but Miranda had called instead. She had been diligent to remind her she was there for her, trying to keep her focused on day-to-day living. Almost every other day, she FaceTimed Hannah, and they would talk for an hour.

"Tell me about the doctor," Miranda asked. "Is he safe territory?"

"I don't know, but I'm not rushing into anything regardless. It feels different, and I'm not sure he's in my comfort zone," she decided.

"I hear ya. You know it took me awhile to go out again, so I completely understand if it doesn't feel right."

"I don't know what it feels like to me. He's handsome. He seems nice. But other than that, I don't know that it's anything more than a physical attraction, which isn't enough," she pointed out.

"It's not enough, but that's usually how it starts," reminding her. "It's going to be a challenge, I mean, given everything that you've had happening in your life, I think it's going to take so much more than just a good-looking guy to rock your world," Miranda told her.

"I'm sure it will," she admitted.

"Nobody is going to replace Jesse, you know that, and no one is going to know you like Jared does, especially given who he really is to you. The timing sucks that he shows up without a body! It's going to be hard for you to lower the bar for a mortal guy to have a chance, but if you don't…"

"I could spend the rest of my life never letting anyone else in," Hannah finished.

"Yeah, and all I can tell you is even though it took a while, I'm glad I let Alex in. Keeping that wall up can make us lonelier than we may even realize if we don't get that rush of fresh air that hits us in the face to wake us up, which is kind of what it was like for me."

"You still think he's not your twin soul?" Hannah asked.

"Naw, I still think we're just soulmates, but I love him, and I'm happy being with him. It feels meant to be. Just not that yin and yang other part of me feeling."

Sounds so much like how it was with Jesse, now that I have a feeling to compare it to," Hannah said. "There are just different degrees of love, it seems."

"There are," Miranda agreed. "Listen, Thanksgiving is coming up, so why don't you plan on spending it with us. Alex's family is having us over, but they said to invite you if you weren't doing anything else."

"Honestly, I haven't thought about it, Mir. I'm not sure right now."

"Well, I don't want you to spend it alone. You know you can come here, if you're not going to go to Arizona. Just do one or the other, okay?"

"Thanks," Hannah replied noncommittedly.

"Okay, well Alex just got home, so I'm going to get off here. Let's get together soon," Miranda said before Alex appeared on the screen and waved hello and said, "Hey Hannah!" She waved and watched him kiss Miranda.

"Love you, bye," Hannah told them and ended the call, smiling. She truly loved her friends.

Chapter Twenty-Five

Holidays Past and Present

Hannah had just gotten home from going to the market, where she had gone after going to the AAA. She had asked that they book a two-month trip for her. She had done her research and knew where she wanted to go and what hotels she wanted to stay in. Thankfully, she didn't have pets to make arrangements for. She loved dogs and cats both, and eventually, she may still adopt a rescue animal, but she'd give it more thought later. Right now, she was appreciating that she had the freedom to just go, leave, to wherever for as long as she wanted. It was a part of taking charge of her life. She started putting the groceries away.

It was two weeks after her ankle healed, and Thanksgiving was in a couple days. She had never spent Thanksgiving alone, but she was not in the mood to drive or fly to Phoenix. It wasn't that she particularly wanted to be alone at Thanksgiving, but she had come to realize being alone was not necessarily a bad thing. There were benefits to being alone with one's self. Maybe she would do what some people did that didn't like the mess and cleanup, just go out for Thanksgiving at a restaurant.

It would be easier to let her parents think she spent it with Miranda and Alex and for Miranda to think she had gone to Phoenix. She was not in the habit of being deceptive, so she thought she would come clean after the holiday that she had just decided to stay home at the last minute.

She had just finished putting away the meat and produce when her doorbell rang. Looking through the peephole, she saw her parents standing on the other side. She had not expected them, but it was a pleasant interruption. Throwing open the door, she fell into their arms.

"Wow, I am so happy to see you! Why didn't you tell me you were coming?" she asked wearing a grin from ear to ear.

"Well, we wanted to surprise you! And to see this new house of yours," her mother answered, looking around appreciatively. "Darling, this is so charming!" she exclaimed as she started to walk around, as if to initiate a self-guided tour. "Nate, look at the view!" as she opened the doors to step out on the back patio overlooking the garden and the ocean beyond.

Her father put his arm around Hannah and walked toward the patio. "Your mother has practically had her girdle twisted about coming," he told her. "She wanted to surprise you by coming to spend Thanksgiving with you. She doesn't want you to be alone. Wouldn't take no for an answer. You know how she can be," he explained. "I hope we're not intruding," he said almost wearily, obviously feeling they had.

"I'm just glad you're here," still smiling, and meant it. "This is such a wonderful surprise," kissing his cheek before stepping out on the patio with her mother who was examining the flowers.

"It looks like you brought starts of the plants you had at the other house with you," she noted. "Do you have the hummingbirds, here?" she asked.

"Actually, yes, lots of hummingbirds. I love to come out and watch them. They are so amazing, and did you notice I made some additions to the Birds of Paradise, too," she pointed to the new plants.

"I see that," her mother said. "You had a lot of hummingbirds at the other place, too. I think they're trying to tell you something."

"Like what?" Hannah asked curiously. She knew her mother believed that when an animal crossed your path or hangs around, there is a spiritual meaning to what they are trying to show you.

"Such as you should focus on taking time for yourself to try to enjoy life, at least as much as you can. They encourage you to play," she said, looking at her daughter encouragingly.

Her dad stepped in wondering if the timing was off for her mother to be telling Hannah this. "You sure have a beautiful view from here," her father spoke, looking out at the ocean and around the property. "Not as crowded as before," he added.

"*Much* more private!" Hannah agreed. "It's peaceful.

"Well, let's see the rest of the house," her mother instructed excitedly, turning to go back in. Hannah allowed her to lead, and her father kept up. Hannah showed them all the rooms, pointed out the new artwork she had bought, and showed them the spare bedroom.

"Where's your luggage?" Hannah asked, noticing they hadn't brought any in.

"Oh, it's in the trunk, just a couple suitcases. Is it alright if we stay a few days?" her father asked, teasingly, putting his arm around her shoulder, still feeling guilty they didn't call ahead in the first place.

"Nate! Of course, it's alright! Isn't it honey?" addressing Hannah.

"Yes! Don't worry, Dad," she chuckled. "Hey, you guys hungry?" figuring they must be. "Did you fly or drive?" realizing she didn't know.

"We drove," her mother answered. "We were in the mood for driving. It's such a nice drive. We left yesterday morning and got into Los Angeles by late afternoon, spent some time walking around Beverly Hills and Santa Monica, and spent the night and left there early this morning," she explained. "It's been a nice getaway," she added.

Her father was smiling at Hannah, as if to say, "I hope our unexpected arrival was really okay," but when Hannah beamed at him, she saw his smile broaden as if relieved. "Yeah," he said slowly, "It's been a relaxing trip, and it's been nice to do something spontaneous," he admitted, "and we rather thought it would be nice to spend Thanksgiving with our only daughter, although I think your mother has had this up her sleeve for a while," he chuckled.

They had sat down in the living room. Her mother was still looking around at how nicely the house had been decorated, seeing pieces of décor she hadn't remembered and admiring Hannah's taste and personal touch.

Her dad was paying more attention to Hannah. He had always had a fatherly knowing, and from what he could tell, she genuinely was proving to be stronger than he had thought. Inwardly, this was a tremendous relief for him. The house seemed well maintained, dishes washed, furniture dusted, and floors clean. She was keeping up with things, including her flower garden, and that was a good sign she was functioning and not wasting away in depression. Despite that he had not wanted to barge in unannounced, he knew at Kathleen's insistence that they didn't call ahead, they would get a good sense of how she was doing with no pretenses.

His daughter had always been a meticulous housekeeper and even as a child, her room stayed spotless. Even back then, she was quick to do dishes or run the vacuum. She had very high standards for cleanliness. She never left her bed unmade. If she had not been doing well, he would have known, and so would her mother. He knew his wife well enough to suspect that was exactly why Kathleen had not wanted to announce their visit. It wasn't until now that it dawned on him why she probably insisted on it. She always had been a wise woman, and he admired her for her level-headedness and insight.

"Speaking of spontaneous, "I'll be taking my own trip soon."

"Really?" her father asked, sounding pleasantly surprised with peaked interest.

"Yes," she beamed, thinking both her parents would be relieved she was taking the initiative.

"Where to?" her mother asked, curious.

Hannah sucked in a breath before she began. "I'm planning on going to Thailand and then to New Zealand," clasping her hands, as she let them process that.

"Are you going with friends?" her father quickly asked before her mother could speak, but saw her eyes turn from him to her.

"I'm doing this by myself, actually," pausing before she continued. "I really think this is going to be good for me. I'm really making a lot of effort to move on with my life, and I'm thinking it would be healthy to have some adventure and to do a little traveling." Both her parents had a flummoxed expression, but yet one of delight. Her father had leaned forward with intent interest, taking obvious pleasure in this news.

"Once I get there, I'm just going to take it day by day, immerse myself into a different culture, and see another part of the world," she explained.

"Wow," her mother replied and leaned in to give her a hug. "You're doing better than I thought, I mean, honey, that's fantastic!" she proclaimed, looking at Nate, who was smiling. Both her parents had always encouraged her to experience as much as she could in life.

Her father agreed, "Good for you! Good for you," he echoed. "I think it'll be good for you." Hannah could see the joy on his countenance, as he took in the news. He always had encouraged her to reach for the stars, to do what made her happy, and had always supported her in new experiences. She had always appreciated that about him. He was so wise, thoughtful, and insightful, not the anxious type.

"It seems the timing of our surprise visit worked out, then," her mother said. "Just glad you hadn't left yet," she almost bellowed with a loud chuckle, relieved they hadn't made the trip to find her already gone.

Her father nodded in agreement, "Yeah, it seems to have worked out. Well, how about I get the luggage out of the car?" he suggested, almost out the door.

"It's good to see you doing well," her mother said after he had walked outside. "I needed to see that for myself, you know? I didn't want to give you time to put on airs if you weren't," she admitted, and it's almost Thanksgiving. Then, Christmas after that, and we hadn't heard from you like we always have at Thanksgiving. We even tried calling but there was no answer and you didn't call back. I decided we had to come. Your father didn't want to come unannounced, but like I said, I needed to see for myself. He was just going to have to suck up to it," she informed her daughter.

"It's okay, Mom. I'm okay, really." She still saw concern in her mother's expression as her eyes seemed to search hers for truth.

"Actually, Miranda started getting me out of the house after the funeral, and she's been there for me, even since I moved here, she FaceTimes me regularly, doesn't give me time to feel sorry for myself, and I've pulled through. It's all been one day at a time, but I trust they are in a good place, Mom. It's the trusting that I think helps," she concluded.

Her mother nodded and put her arm around her. "I'm relieved," meeting her eyes for a long moment. Your father didn't want me making a nuisance of myself and pressuring you, but I can't help but worry about you."

Her father walked back in with the luggage. "I'll take them to the spare room, if that's alright," he said to Hannah.

"Sure, Dad. Do you need any help?" she asked.

"Oh no. I can manage. It's nothing," he replied from halfway up the stairs.

They had dinner at an Italian restaurant later that evening, after it had already gotten dark early. While they placed their order and were nibbling at the warm bread and butter, Hannah thought it would be selfish of her not to share some of what she had experienced with them. They had grieved and mourned over losing a grandchild and their son-in-law, who Hannah knew they loved very much. They had thought the world of Jesse. He was like a son to them. She had been filled with her own grief and had not been in a state of mind to share anything with them that she had experienced after they passed. She felt prompted now to tell them.

As they were making light conversation, Hannah vaguely heard them making comments about what a nice town, how much quieter it was, how glad they were she had made the move to someplace quieter. When there was a pause in the chatter, she spoke up.

"Mom, Dad, something happened I feel like I need to share with you," looking at each of them, as they both stopped to listen, giving her their undivided attention. Her father wiped butter off his lip, and her mother stopped just as she was about to say something else. They seemed to discern the gravity of what she was going to tell them before she had said anything at all.

"What is it, honey?" her mother asked.

"Remember when I told you earlier that I knew Jesse and Ethan are in a good place?"

"Yeah, sure I do," she answered softly.

Hannah paused and looked at her napkin and then back to them. She began to fidget, stirring the ice in the glass and focusing on it as she spoke. "I've had dreams where Ethan comes to me. They feel so real. In one of them, he took my hand and took me to a place that was so beautiful." She took a napkin and wiped a tear from her eye and allowed a moment for her throat to relax. "It was real! What I saw, seeing him, it was all so real. I just wish you both could've seen what I saw. He looked so happy and peaceful, and it gave me a lot of peace to see him like that. I've dreamt about him other times since then, too. It's like he's coming to me, reassuring me and showing me he's okay."

When she finished telling them about Ethan, she looked up at them. Her mother had tears streaming down her face, and her father's eyes were moist. She saw him take a deep breath and look at nothing. She saw relief on both their faces. She realized they needed to hear this. She had withheld it from them too long. Her father inhaled, and she could tell his nose had started to water as she heard him suck in his breath. She saw him fidget for his handkerchief. Her mother just kept wiping her eyes with the napkin and then she smiled and let out a quiet laughter of joy.

"I'm so glad you told us," she said, her voice cracking. Hannah realized she should have told them this at the house where they would not feel so conscientious of anyone taking notice, but it was too late.

"I saw Jesse, too."

They're eyes turned back to her. "His spirit actually came to me. I saw him. He told me it was okay to sell the house and be happy. He said he and Ethan are okay and for me not to grieve for them. This has been what has helped me know I'll be okay," she confessed to them.

Her father put his hand on hers. "You needed that," he said softly, his voice cracking. "I think it helps all of us to know you had those experiences," his eyes still damp. "It's an invaluable gift you've been given. Thanks, Hannah, for sharing it. He took a moment to recompose, then smiled at her with complete trust and gratitude in what she had shared.

Her mother wiped her eyes again, "I bet my mascara is all over my face," feigning a laugh, "but I am so glad you told us. Why didn't you tell us before? It's been hard for all of us," she admitted. "It just really helps knowing…" pressing her lips together. She couldn't speak without breaking down crying, needing to pull herself together.

"I'm sorry I should have told both of you. I think I was afraid of sounding crazy."

"No, not so. We would never have thought any such thing," her mother chided.

The food arrived, and they all tried to switch gears for appearances sake, though if anyone had been watching, it would have drawn a solemn respect from any onlooker. Hannah quickly scanned the patrons, and no one seemed to be paying attention. Thankfully, the atmosphere was dim with candlelight ambience. If the waitress noticed the tears, she didn't let on.

"Everything looks good," her dad smiled at the waitress, "Thank you."

Hannah did not tell them about Jared. That would have been too much information and served no purpose. It was meant for her and no one else. Miranda knew only because they were best friends, and because Miranda had been there when things started happening. It seemed Miranda was supposed to know, had been allowed to know.

Just as she started to take a bite of vegetable lasagna, she heard a whisper in her ear, "They needed that," Jared said, approvingly. She turned slightly towards the direction she had heard him, but he had not appeared. With the goosebumps they were all feeling, as she recounted her experiences to them, she had not noticed his presence until just now. It gave her comfort to know he was with her and that he was supporting her decision to tell them.

The next morning, her father had gotten up first and had taken a walk, something he always did when he got up. Her mother had cooked French Toast and bacon and had coffee ready. Hannah wandered into the kitchen.

"Something smells good," sniffing the aroma.

"I hope you're hungry. Your father went for a walk. He should be back soon," pouring coffee for Hannah and setting it in front of her. Hannah sipped it and went to the refrigerator and got an ice cube from the icemaker and put it in her cup. She took another sip.

"Did you guys sleep okay?" she asked her mother.

"Yeah, it's a comfortable bed. I think it's more comfortable than ours at home," she appraised.

"I doubt that," Hannah jested.

Her father returned from his walk and said, "Smells like breakfast is ready," sounding chipper.

"Hannah set the plates and silverware. Her mother set the food on the table.

"It's nippy this morning," he said, "but the sun is shining. It's a beautiful day." His words seemed to set the mood. Nothing else was said about what she had shared with them at dinner the night before. There was a quiet acceptance and a noticeable lifting

488

of tension between them and with her mother especially, who had a tendency to be overprotective and sometimes overly motherly. She seemed less anxious, Hannah thought, wishing again that she had told them sooner. They deserved to know.

That evening, while her mother was in the shower, her dad asked, "Sweetheart, Christmas is a few weeks away. You're going to come home and spend it with us, aren't you?" His eyes searched hers hopefully.

The question stopped her in her tracks. "I hadn't even thought about Christmas," she said, truthfully, despite that she had noticed Christmas lights that had been put up around town and neighboring homes. She had ignored them as if nothing about it applied to her.

His eyes were gentle and understanding. "You should come. We really want you there," he said. "I suspect you'll *need* to be there," he added.

She looked at him and sighed. "That means I have to acknowledge my first Christmas without them. It almost seems easier to go on as if there are no more Christmases," she said more icily than she intended.

"I know," he whispered. "But please don't do that. Come stay with us and let's all get through it together," kissing her cheek and putting his arms around her. She hugged him with a sudden need for her daddy's arms to be around her.

"You remember when you were six-years-old, Santa brought you that shiny red bicycle? That's one of my favorite memories of your Christmases," he reminded her. "Do you remember that?"

She nodded, smiling emotionally as her eyes dampened. "I remember. I also remember that was my first year I got Barbie dolls, and Mom had even made them homemade outfits so that they had a pretty big selection of outfits," smiling at the memory.

"Remember your own childhood and those memories as Christmas approaches. Try not to be so grown up this year," he said. "Let's celebrate happy memories that are always with us. Sometimes, we need to just remember those things that have the power to carry us across the bridges we must cross."

"I'll be there," she promised him.

"That's my girl," he said, and kissed the side of her head.

Hannah always felt her father had a magical way of comforting her. In that moment, he had done just that. He had carried her past painful remembrances to memories of a time when her life was carefree and Christmas had been magical. In that moment, she was that little girl again.

The following day was Thanksgiving. Hannah had called Miranda that morning and let her know her parents had come to be with her for the holiday and to see the new house, and not to worry since she wouldn't be spending it with her in San Francisco. Her father offered to help in the kitchen, which he had always been one to do, but her mother told him to go enjoy something on TV and just relax. It was his turn to take a break. Her mother had put the ham in the oven at the crack of dawn, smothered it in pineapple. They had buttered baby red potatoes with parsley, green beans with ham broth added for seasoning, cranberry sauce, homemade bread from the market, and blackberry cobbler with vanilla ice cream.

Her father offered a blessing on the food as they joined hands. When they all said "amen," they noticed Hannah was staring at her empty plate and then looked up at them, one at a time.

"You alright, Hannah?" her mother was first to ask. They both waited for her to answer, looking at one another and back at their daughter.

Hannah nodded. "Yeah. I'll be alright. It just kind of hit me is all. I'm fine."

Her mother glanced out the window, and said, "Oh, I see a hummingbird." She smiled and looked at her daughter.

Hannah turned and saw it. "Point taken," and smiled at her mother, as she scooped some potatoes onto her plate and passed them to her dad. Her parents looked at one another a brief second and began filling their plates. After a few bites, her dad noticed Hannah was watching the bird.

"I like hummingbirds," he told her. "They are adaptable and can go long distances, can even fly backwards, but they have a lovely sense about them, so elegant," further commenting.

"Hummingbirds encourage us to reach our aspirations and embrace empowerment and resiliency. They represent being *free*," her mother informed them, placing her hand over her chest for emphasis. "They've always been my favorite bird."

"Mine, too," Hannah said. "I've always thought they were so graceful and mesmerizing, but I guess now I know why they're fascinating," still watching it. It truly did seem to be sharing something with her, as if it was trying to impart to her a shared resilience and quiet love. Was it her imagination based on what her mother had said? She decided she would accept the communication as real between the bird and herself. Somehow, she found comfort in the possibility. She thought back to the whale, how it had raised its head out of the great water and looked her in the eye, like it could see her soul. There was something to this, she thought. She felt compelled to share that experience with her parents, which enraptured them.

"Really!" he father exclaimed. Actually, I'm not surprised that it happened, but I am surprised I'm just now hearing about it. That's a once in a lifetime experience most people will never get," he stated. "I've seen whales out at sea, but I've never had one get so close and look me in the eye!"

Her mother shivered and wrapped her arms around herself, "That just gives me goosebumps! You know, I'm starting to realize how it is you've been so strong and how you're adapting far easier than many could imagine, including myself. But to receive so much grace and to experience and recognize the gift of what has been shared with you, I absolutely find it amazing. I *really* find it amazing!" She laid her hand on Hannah's arm. "This has been a gift, but what I'm finding so remarkable is that you are tuning in rather than away, and that is what I believe is making the difference," searching her daughter's face as if she needed her words to sink in, not just for Hannah, but it was something she was realizing herself. This is what had been happening with their daughter. She was finding grace in small things, although having a whale look you in the eye was not such a small thing. She felt the goosebumps cover every inch of her flesh, as she imagined what that must have been like for her.

That night when she got into bed, both her parents knocked on the door and came in. It reminded her of when she was a little girl. Her dad told her a story of a sailing adventure he and his mother had gone on before Hannah was born. "It was nothing like what you experienced, but we did see a lot of whales from afar, but that was a magical day for us. It was the day I asked your mother to marry me," he told her.

"Mom, Dad, I've never heard this story before," her eyes beaming with warmth and fancy at the story. "How come you never shared it before?" feeling a treasure had been bestowed upon her. "How come I didn't know about the day you proposed?" still smiling with grand curiosity.

"Oh, I don't know," her mother began. "Life happens, and sometimes I think we forget to remember some of our prized moments in life, but even still, sometimes we forget to share them because they happened a lifetime ago. I don't know," she said.

"I'm glad you shared it with me," Hannah said. Her parents could see a light in her eye that sparkled brightly as she had listened to the story. They each kissed her and her mother even tucked her in. More memories of her childhood came to her mind, and as they turned off the light, Hannah felt a peace and glow inside she had not felt since she was a child. A part of her didn't want them to leave, didn't want this feeling to end. If only she could hold on to it.

Two weeks after her parents returned home, Hannah had completed her Christmas shopping. Miranda and Alex had driven down from San Francisco and spent the night, and they had exchanged gifts a couple days before Christmas. There was no tree, only the lighting of candles. They played instrumental classical Christmas music and enjoyed one another's company, had a Christmas dinner of a homemade chicken and vegetable casserole and splurged on calories with red velvet cake and cream cheese icing with butter pecan ice cream and bourbon balls. They shared a bottle of wine and talked about their favorite childhood Christmas memories. It had been heartwarming, and something about talking about their own childhood memories kindled a nostalgic reminiscence that almost made her feel as if she was there again, in another time, when she believed in Santa Claus, when life was simple and felt secure and her mind was innocent again. She found herself wanting to go back in time more than twenty-years ago.

That night as she brushed out her hair after undressing for bed and brushing her teeth, Jared was with her. She felt him. His presence was so strong though he had no reflection in the mirror. She finished brushing her hair and turned. His smile warmed her.

"We have had some wonderful Christmases, you and me," he told her, as if he, himself, was reminiscing. His eyes were like a warm glow that held her gaze and he smiled lowering his eyes.

"Your smile looks sad," she said, feeling curious, wondering if he was.

"Only thinking it would be nice for you if I had a body right now," he answered softly.

"Knowing you are with me, that I'm able to see you and hear you, I feel I have you, Jared," she told him.

"You will always have me, Hannah. All the love I feel for you will always belong to you. No one or nothing can ever take it from you."

"I believe you," she told him. "What was your favorite Christmas we shared together?" she wanted to know.

"I have more than one," he smiled again. "You were with child, and I had felt the baby kick from inside your womb. It was a moment of joy that was unequal to anything else. I never knew so much love for you as what I did in that moment during my mortal time on earth," remembering the experience.

"You're feeling nostalgic, too, I take it."

"I suppose I am," smiling as if his mind were someplace else.

"Tell me about the baby," she asked of him.

"The baby was a beautiful little girl. That was not the only time we had family together. I rather enjoyed being a father, and I was a good one," he informed her, somehow surprising her that he made it a point to say so.

"I have no doubt in my mind you were," she whispered.

His eyes bore deep into her own. They were filled with kindness and gentleness. "I am not privileged to tell you who your descendants are," he continued.

"I understand," pausing to look at him. "I think it would be quite strange for me to know anyway," she admitted, with a hint of awkward laughter.

"I was on many occasion very much a mortal, Hannah," he said as if to remind her, but there still remained the sense of sadness in him.

"Are you regretting not having incarnated again," she asked, suddenly curious. The silence before he answered seemed longer than it was.

"No," he finally replied. "Only that you chose to," and his eyes fell away from hers.

His answer to her last question was quickening. It pierced her. It had left her speechless. Something about it revealed his vulnerability in his feelings towards her. Had her mortality become a weakness for him, she wondered. He had proven to her that love transcends the divide between mortality and immortality.

"I bid you goodnight, Hannah," he said and when she looked up, he was gone.

She drove to Arizona and spent a week with her parents and visiting some of her relatives. She had spent an emotional Christmas with them, which only made her more anxious to leave on her trip. Christmas had felt unbearably void without Ethan and Jesse, especially Ethan. It would have been worse had she not been with her parents, so much worse. They talked about Christmases past, Hannah's, their own childhood Christmases she had not heard about, and it seemed to help her get through it. It somehow felt like time folded on itself, and she was back in another time. They knew she needed that to get her through Christmas, but she also thought they needed it, too. Having each other was what they all needed, so they could *all* get through it.

The following week, in the afternoon, she drove to San Francisco on New Year's Eve.

Alex answered the door with a big smile and gave her a warm hug. Miranda rushed to her and squeezed her in a bearhug.

"I'm so surprised to see you," she squealed with joy. "Five more days," she squealed. I bet you're so excited!" Miranda was giddy as usual.

"I am very excited, actually," Hannah replied.

"Tell me again, where are you going?" I am going to have to google these places, pulling up her notepad on her phone.

"I'm going to Thailand and will be visiting Doi Inthanon, Chiang Mai, and Phang Nga. I want to see the mountains, go to the temples, seek out the healers, and just learn from them. I need this spiritual journey," she told her. Just saying it made it feel more real to her. She was doing this! "After that, I am flying to New Zealand. I just want to see it, *be* there for a while.

"I can totally see you moving there," Miranda said thoughtfully.

"Just taking life one day at a time. I seriously doubt I will be moving anywhere else anytime soon."

"I hope not!" Miranda teased half-heartedly.

"I'll take lots of pictures. I promise. It's going to be beautiful, I just know it. I can't tell you how I've been looking forward to traveling abroad. It feels like what I need right now," she told her.

"Getting back into photography, then?" Miranda asked.

"For now, that's a big fat yes," she affirmed.

Just then, the doorbell rang. "Japanese," Alex exclaimed, as he headed toward the door to answer it, again. "Ah yes, smell it already," he smiled at the delivery boy, handing him a tip, who offered an expression of surprised gratitude as he looked at the bill. "Have a good evening!" he waved and hurried off.

"Let's dig in," he told the two women, as he set the boxes on the dining table and opened them. "There's plenty to go around," getting another plate for Hannah and scooping food onto it. Miranda set three wine glasses on the table while Alex hurried to get a bottle of wine from the frig they had put there an hour earlier to chill. He opened it and filled the glasses.

"Let's make a toast," he held his glass up. "Let's toast to friendship," and they all clinked their glasses together, "To friendship," they all agreed. Then after taking a couple bites and the first sip of wine, Alex surprised Hannah.

"Is Jared still with you?" He asked most seriously with warmth and sincerity. His eyes were fastened upon her.

Hannah looked at Miranda, who bobbed her head to mean, "Yes, I told him about Jared,"

It occurred to her that over the holidays she had not been paying as much attention to Jared, having been distracted by parents visiting, nostalgia, Miranda and Alex visiting, memories flooding her, and getting prepared for the planned trip. He, being selfless as he is, was not imposing on her uninvited. He was giving her the time she needed to process, plan, host, and be alone with her thoughts. This rush of realization unsettled her. With only a moment's pause, she replied to Alex.

"I feel him. I know he's there. I've been so distracted, preparing for the trip, so much I'm trying to get done that I've not been having as many conversations with him, but I know time is not an issue with him," she said thoughtfully, almost as if trying to make an excuse for neglecting him.

An insidious feeling of guilt for her withdrawal from him had been nagging at her for days, maybe weeks when she thought about it, but now she felt it acutely. She found herself wishing he would appear at her side, knowing only she could see him. Then, no sooner than she had wished it, she felt him near her, but he did not appear. She found herself trying to force back the quickening of sadness, as one forces back the need to vomit when they realize they ate something that wasn't settling well in their stomach. She took another bite and washed it down with another sip of wine, sauvignon blanc. She savored the flavor and hoped it would quieten the feelings stirring within her.

Alex continued, "Jared's not monitoring lapses in time. He's only attentive to you. You are his sole priority while he is with you, and if you still feel him and know he's there, then how much time passes between conversations with him or seeing him is not important. It sounds like you're doing better each time I've seen you, and Mir here has noticed the same thing. That's what's important," Alex continued.

"That's true," Miranda agreed. "I don't think he will ever leave you as long as he knows you need him. That ghost loves the socks off you!"

"Ya think?" Hannah blushed.

"I think!" Miranda affirmed.

Alex held his glass up, slightly bowing his head in agreement. It was undeniable, Hannah thought to herself. They were right, and she knew it. She so cherished their friendship, glad Alex was her friend, too.

That night, they laughed, told ghost stories, respectfully not at Jared's expense, while they enjoyed one another's company. Miranda told a ghost story of a man cleaning fish near his barn, while his old dog lay lazily nearby. He kept hearing his wife calling for him from inside the house. She had died years before, so he thought surely he was imagining it. When he kept hearing her voice call him to come inside, he finally decided to check it out, thinking possibly a relative had stopped by. His dog followed along after him and they both went inside. He searched the house but no one was there. He lived too far from other houses, so no one was anywhere nearby or close enough to be within earshot, so he knew it wasn't coming from a neighbor's place. Once he was inside the house, he never heard it again. Shaking his head, he thought he had imagined it. It occurred to him it might have been the cowbell that was hanging from the porch, but the wind wasn't blowing and it hung still as a statue. "Old boy, did you hear it?" he asked the dog, but the dog was old with cataracts, losing both its site and hearing. The dog just looked at him. Convinced he had imagined it, he started to go back outside, but stopped himself and closed the door as he stepped back inside. There was a mother bear and her young cubs approaching the barn. As he watched from the window, they found the fish he had been cleaning. From where he saw them round the barn, he would never had seen them until they were upon him. Whether it was his deceased wife or an angel, whoever, he knew the voice calling him to come inside had saved his life and probably that of his dog's.

Alex scratched his chin. "It could be true, you know. Things like that happen with ancestors or departed loved ones saving another family member. I believe in that wholeheartedly.

"You don't have to tell me, I know things like that happen, all the time, more than we know or hear about!" Miranda emphasized. "I showed you those pictures from the trip Hannah and I took to Mendocino," she reminded Alex, who nodded, remembering.

Alex appeared to be remembering something and furrowed his brow. "Hey, did you gals ever hear the story of the ghost in Golden Gate Park?

"I don't think so," Hannah replied thoughtfully, trying to remember. Is it a true story?"

"Not that I remember," Miranda answered.

"Okay, well, I remember my granddad telling me about it, when I was a kid. He loved to tell stories," he added, "but then I remembered it again a few months back and so I googled it. It happened in 1908 and was on the front page of the San Francisco Chronicle."

Hannah and Miranda both leaned in closer.

"Some guy was partying with some girls one night, and they were all loaded up in his car. Some mounted police had stopped him for speeding through the park. When he stopped them, he saw the guy and all his lady friends seemed scared to death and looked like they had all seen a ghost. They had seen something, alright. They all told the police that a woman, who they described as a ghost, had stopped right in front of their vehicle flagging them down. She was wearing a white robe, which was shimmering white, and she had long hair.

Given their demeanor, the police officer demanded they take him to the place where they had seen her, but the women refused to go back. They were still freaked out. When the man took the Mounty back to where they saw her, nothing was there.

The earthquake two years before in 1906 had destroyed a lot of records the police had, so I believe it was impossible to really go back and investigate all the deaths at the park, since there had been so many were suicides.

The story I heard is that right after the earthquake happened, there had been a couple girls who reported they saw a baby floating in a nearby lake, so the legend is that it was a mother trying to save her infant. Must've been pretty convincing for the San Francisco Chronicle to publish it," he added as an afterthought.

"This was when?" Miranda asked.

"It came out in the San Francisco Chronicle in 1908. True story, supposedly," Alex said.

The story resonated with Hannah. She wondered if ghosts or incarnate spirits are still here because they need to save someone else who is still living? Is that why Jared is still here? Is he still trying to save her? Does she still need saving? Do I?" she asked herself.

For a moment, her mind circled around this thought, but then she dismissed it. She had been proactive and making every possible effort to save herself without burdening someone else to do it for her. Was she doing a good job, she wondered. Was she on the right path? She didn't linger on that more than a few seconds, as her primary belief was that she was doing *something* instead of nothing, and so what more could the universe ask of her? It seemed to her the universe was giving back to her, and that was enough for the moment. One day at a time.

"I can't say I have ever heard that story in all these years I've lived here," Miranda admitted, genuinely surprised.

"Neither have I, that I can remember," Hannah replied, with a puzzled expression. If the story *were* true, she could sincerely empathize with a spirit of a woman trying to save her child, as she would have done anything to save her own, and her husband's. But she had not died trying to save them, but if she had, would she be haunting partygoers in San Francisco, too, she asked of herself? Clearly, it was time to refocus on her trip to Thailand and New Zealand. Enough ghost stories.

It had been a couple hours since she had a glass of wine, and she had only drunk one glass. It was still only 10:00, but she decided against waiting until morning to go home. If she stayed until the New Year rang in, it would put her getting home later than she wanted to. The full moon would make for a relaxing drive home. She had been in the mood for a drive when she came, and she was in the mood for one now.

"Guys, I've had a great time, but time for me to take off," she told them. She knew they would invite her to stay, but she wasn't having it.

"Oh no, why don't you stay? It's New Year's Eve. Spend it with us," Miranda pouted. Besides, it's getting too late to drive all the way home, especially on New Year's Eve."

Hannah kissed her cheek and gave her a long hug. "Not tonight. I am actually looking *forward* to the long drive home. I love you guys," she told them. Alex stepped forward and gave her a hug.

"Nice seeing you, Hannah," and stepped back, letting Miranda finish saying her goodbye.

"I leave in five days, so we'll see each other before then. Maybe while I'm gone, you and Alex can come check on things for me." It was not a question.

"You know we will," Alex assured her before Miranda could say anything.

"Right, we'll just make it a vacation of our own, won't we Babe?" Miranda nudged Alex, who smiled mischievously,

"You bet!" he teased.

One last hug and Hannah was on her way home.

Chapter Twenty-Six

Snake and Curly

On the drive home, Hannah felt him. She felt something changing between them. It was not a growing apart type of feeling. It felt very much eternal and lasting, that forever feeling, knowing this relationship between them was never going to end and would last for infinity. No, what she was feeling felt different, like the elephant in the room different, the mortal/immortal difference. Sure, mortal/immortal relationships were always amongst us here on earth. They existed. Widows and widowers who don't want to move on and still feel their departed spouse lingering, but the one left behind didn't tend to see and be able to touch the ghost of the departed, did they?

When Jared appeared to her, she could feel him, well, almost. She could feel his energy. The thing was, she could see him as if he were mortal, as if he had a flesh and blood body. That was not something

513

common to humanity, was it? She'd never heard of that happening to the extent she had experienced it. She knew we have been warned we entertain angels unaware, but often, we don't know it's happening, at least not until afterwards. From everything she knew and understood, which was limited really, she believed Jared had defied the rules in the extent in which he had revealed himself to her. He never claimed to be an angel. Yet, to Hannah, he might as well be.

He was advanced and could qualify as a spirit guide, but he chose to be exclusively with *her*. There was something in the whole scenario that was so comforting and had given her so much restorative strength and energy that had helped her to heal, but something inside her spirit told her that even though her relationship with Jared was eternal and would last forever in the spirit realm, there was this vibe lately she had been getting that she had to let him go until the time came that she departed this life and her mortal body.

All this was weighing heavy on her heart, though in respect to her life, she now felt free, freer than she had felt, *ever*, that she could remember, and she truly had tried to remember. He had helped her. His presence had made a monumental difference in how she had been able to handle everything that had happened. She didn't want to let him go, but in her soul, she knew she must pursue her life's journey, and he would always be alive in her heart and her memory.

She was concerned how this would affect her being able to be in another relationship. Would she see him in her mind's eye, or in actuality, standing at the foot of her bed while she had someone else by her side? Would he always be there, reminding her he loved her? He didn't seem the jealous type, but he was protective. He had feelings, too, and she didn't want to hurt them. She loved him, more than she thought was possible to love someone. If he was flesh and blood, she would not hesitate to marry him and make a life with him, which she had every confidence would be a wonderful, happy, and amazing life, euphoric even.

With him, she was safe, protected, loved, and cherished. No one would ever be able to be to her what he is and has always been and would always be.

The glimpses he had shown her in her dreams were always accompanied by that grand agape love, so sweet, so coupled with romantic quality and attraction that was mind blowing. She didn't know if she could love anyone else even close, but if she could love someone as much as she loved Jesse, it would be enough. She had to choose happiness, choose to love, choose to live her life as fully as she could. Otherwise, she would wilt inside, and her life would be no more than inhabitance of an empty shell with no lights on inside. That would be so much worse than choosing the pursuit of happiness.

Jared was silent while she thought through all of this. Even still, how much love she felt from him prevented her from wanting to address this with him in spoken words. She knew that he already knew. She knew he well understood and probably agreed. Perhaps he was just waiting for her to be ready to let him go.

She saw him in her peripheral vision and glanced over. He was in the passenger seat, watching her quietly.

"Hey," she said to him in a whisper, as if he were just waking up from a nap. "I had a feeling you were along for the ride."

"I didn't come for the ride, Hannah," he answered, amused. "I assure you my transportation is superior to this car or this ride," continuing on, almost arrogantly.

Hannah erupted in laughter. "Is that a fact? Perhaps you should be the one taking me for a ride then!"

He didn't laugh, but he did smile at her and only said, "Not now." The stoicism in his voice was distinguishable, so she stopped laughing. She knew she was stalling.

"I love you, Jared," she told him. "I don't ever want to be apart from you, and never seeing you for the rest of my life *feels* so unacceptable to me, so unbearable."

"You'll never lose me," he reassured her. She believed him, but yet, there was the issue of *time* and the sorrow that was often its companion.

"I know," she said. "I know."

With everything she felt was pressing to discuss with him before she left on her trip, she did not feel the need to talk right now. Everything was understood. Of course, there was nothing stopping him from accompanying her on her trip. He didn't need a passport, money, a ticket, food, or any of those things. He could just be with her the entire time, if he so chose to be, and she would not stop him. She would never stop him from being with her. She desired him, always.

Once someone comes into your life and you fall in love, whether it's a child, a friend, a partner, it's almost impossible to imagine life without them. There was no need for words right now. She drove in silence knowing he knew every thought and every feeling in real time. When they came to the closest major city before getting to her house, she pulled into a liquor store.

"Don't stop, Hannah. Go home," he told her.

"I'm going to pick up some wine, Jared," and got out of the car. He was on her heels.

"Can't you just listen to me when I ask you not to do something?" he demanded. His tone took her off guard.

"It's just a few bottles of wine. I'm not drinking and driving, Jared!" She pretended she was brushing the shoulder of her jacket rather than looking over her shoulder at Jared as she entered the store. She didn't have ear buds in, so she couldn't suddenly pretend she was talking on the phone, either.

The store attendant didn't seem to notice and greeted her with a flirtatious smile. He looked to be in his early twenties, short, stocky, and looked like he could be a wrestler. Her beauty did not escape him as he watched her walk past the counter, grabbing a basket as she proceeded. She smiled back to be polite, conscious she was being closely followed. Jared was inches behind her.

She scanned the shelves for the types of wine they had in stock and chose one she liked and placed it in her basket and was in the process of choosing another, when the door chime rang as it had when she had entered the store, notifying the attendant there was a customer.

Two men walked in but she didn't pay any attention to them. She continued perusing the selections. She chose one and started toward the counter and was pulling out her wallet. She set the basket down and was counting her cash when a hand reached for her wallet and helped himself to the cash in her hand, "I'll take this, Darlin'. I think it feels a little heavy for you," he told her. She stared in disbelief.

He was taller than Hannah, but not as tall as Jared. He was muscular but not husky. She noticed a tattoo of a serpent on his wrist as he took her wallet and cash. The word "snake" stuck in her mind. His mannerism reminded her of a snake with his greasy blonde hair and bloodshot eyes that gazed at her like he was trying to mesmerize her with his glassy, dilated pupils. He appeared lanky and sickening and slithery the way he spoke to her.

She immediately understood why Jared had warned her not to stop or get out of the car. Why had she not listened? She turned to look for him. He was right beside her, but neither man had acknowledged him, and he did not look to her like someone these men would want to reckon with if they could see him. His eyes burned fiercely. The man behind the counter had his hands up, already surrendering, his eyes displayed the full circle of his blue corneas with room to spare, but he said nothing.

She felt something poke her from the other side. It was the other guy sticking his gun against her ribs. She didn't know he had rounded back and snuck up on her. He was heavier, dark curly hair, black eyes, tattoos on his neck and face. His curls made her want to call him Curly. He smiled at her and used the barrel of the pistol to pull her hair back to get a better look at her face.

"You're one fine-looking lady," he said seductively, giving her a cheesy grin. She glared at him while he looked her up and down. "You look like a classy lady, don't you think she looks classy, he spoke to Snake."

"Oh yeah, she's classy, alright. Snake walked around her, he too, looking at her from head to toe. He slid his hand along the length of her hair. "Did you dye your hair?" he pushed his face up in hers, and she smelled his breath. She wrenched her nose thinking Pepe Le Pew may be a better name for him. The foul stench of his breath was nauseating. She flinched her head back away from him. He retreated. He was toying with her, wanting to see fear in her eyes, but he saw none, which seemed to anger him and he glared back at her. Curly ordered the attendant to open the cash register, which he did. Snake continued to stare at her, growing angrier by the second.

"You think you're high and mighty, don't you, Bitch!" Curly raised and aimed the gun at the attendant and cocked it. The poor guy now looked on helplessly at his assassin, as urine soaked his jeans all the way down his legs and formed a pool on the floor. Curly's finger tightened on the trigger.

Snake raised his hand to slap Hannah across the face with all the force he could muster. There was a deafening explosion of shattering shards of glass as the gun went off. A sudden force blew past them, rocking them on their heels, as if air had been sucked out of the space they occupied like a vacuum. The magnitude of it caused Hannah to lose balance, forcing her to grab the counter to gain footing. The sound could be heard of raining glass hitting the sidewalk and pavement outside. The glass door that had only just been there, completely intact, was the shell of an empty frame. All that remained were small slivers of extruding glass. Once the raining shower of glass ceased to fall, only then was there a moment of utter silence as if deafness had fallen upon them.

The two men who were standing beside her not more than five seconds before had been absent from sight for the last four and nine/tenths of those seconds. They had vanished in a single instant. Hannah turned on her heel scoping a 360 of the store, but she didn't see Jared. She felt her heartbeat in her chest, could feel it pounding in her eardrums. "What just happened?" She mouthed the words but no sound came out. Nothing but silence.

Fear gripped her as she thought of the store attendant and the gun that had been aimed right at him. The gun had gone off. She had heard the single shot. She didn't see the attendant standing there. She ran to look behind the counter, and there he was. He was crouched down on the floor with his head between his knees, covered by his arms, sobbing. He was alive. She looked for signs of bleeding. He had to be bleeding. The gun had gone off. There was no blood. She kneeled down to him.

"You're okay, she cried. You're okay! Look at me! You're okay!" He looked at her, peeping from behind his arms that he had raised to shield his face and slowly relaxed them. "You're okay," she said quietly, again," trying to catch her breath. He nodded quickly, realizing that she was right. He checked himself and slowly stood up, peeping over the counter.

"Call 911!" she ordered him. "Now!" and she made her way back around the counter. Her purse and the money she had pulled out of it were laying on the floor. She picked up the money and her wallet and put the wallet back in her purse. The two bottles of wine were still setting in the basket on the counter.

She heard the attendant, whose nametag she now saw on his shirt, "Mark" call 911 reporting an attempted robbery and a gunshot. His voice was unsteady.

When he hung up, he asked, "What happened? Where are they, those guys, where are they?" His eyes scanned the store, and he saw the shattered glass, most of which had covered the sidewalk and parking spaces outside. There was almost none on the floor. He slowly walked around the counter and stood next to Hannah, who was staring. It had happened impossibly fast. Mark could not pull his eyes away from all the shattered glass.

"What happened?" he repeated in a whisper. Hannah looked beyond the door and saw two men, who she immediately recognized as Snake and Curly, on the ground hundred feet from the door, across the parking lot. They were not moving. Then, they heard sirens.

Chapter Twenty-Seven

Someone Watching Over You

Two firetrucks, five police cars, and two ambulances arrived on the scene in under five minutes with deafening sirens and enough red lights to light an entire city block. Mark stood near the entrance with Hannah, in surreal disbelief, dumbfounded but so thankful he was still alive.

"I heard the gun go off. It was pointed right at me. I heard it go off," he said more than once, stupefied by the turn of events. The cold wetness between his legs drew his attention to his trousers, where he saw that he had peed his pants. Notably, he was embarrassed but not ashamed. It was not what anyone was going to be paying attention to anyway. Hannah told him, she would have peed her pants, too, if she had not stopped a few miles north of town for gas fill-up and made use of the facilities, which was not true, but she said it to comfort and alleviate his embarrassment.

He still was unaware the men were lying across the parking lot. As far as he was concerned, something had scared them off and they ran. All he knew was that they had vanished. The liquor store door did not face the road, as it was in a strip mall, at the end and around the corner, so the store was essentially out-of-easy-view from passersby who didn't already know it was there, which made it a perfect target for a robbery. Around the corner and facing the street was a real estate office, an insurance office, and a beauty salon that were closest to same end of the strip mall as the liquor store, and they were all closed. The gunshot would not have drawn any attention from that end of the building. A grassy vacant lot separated the store's parking lot from a pharmacy drive-through, but the drive-through was closed, so no one was passing through. This had been an attempted robbery of convenience.

Hannah, as attractive as she was, had been a nice surprise Curly and Snake hadn't expected. The surprise they didn't see coming and had been their gravest mistake, however, had been Jared. Hannah summoned him in her mind. Electricity pulsed through her, making the hair stand straight up on her body as he responded to her, letting her know he was very much present. She turned and saw him, his eyes deadlocked on hers. He was still filled with rage and indignation, but his concern for her overrode any anger she saw in his expression.

"I'm okay," she relayed to him without speaking, and her body relaxed as she exhaled a long breath.

He nodded in acknowledgment. His eyes were pervading, showing only concern for her wellbeing, then turned his attention to Mark, who was visibly quaking where he stood. Jared seemed to relax, and as he did, she saw him place his large hand on Mark's shoulder. In a matter of seconds, she saw the quaking ease and then stop. In the silence of their minds, she whispered, "Thank you."

There was a barrage of questions upon arrival of the response team, as they cautiously entered store and surrounded the building. Was anyone injured? How did the door shatter? Who fired shots? What did they see?   Did they have a description of the assailants? With this question, Hannah pointed to the two forms that lay across the parking lot, still not moving.   Mark began running his hand in the shape of a cross across his chest.

"Oh Mary, mother of Jesus!" he seemed to be praying in a trembling voice. "I didn't see them. I kept thinking they escaped! What the hell happened to them?" He was sieged with utter bewilderment. Then he put his hands to his head as if he were trying to keep every last ounce of sanity from escaping his mind. Jared merely stepped closer to him, and he seemed to relax again.

The officers asked for their names and ID, which both Hannah and Mark handed them and waited while the officer took down the information, before he continued to question them. Several others were outside where Curly and Snake laid lifeless. At the conclusion of the questioning, the officer noted Mark's trousers to be soaked down both inner legs and as an act of compassion, patted him on the shoulder.

"If either of you prefer, one of our officers can drive you home here shortly" he added, speaking to both of them. "I understand if you don't feel up to driving."

Mark told them he lived close by and thought he was good to drive. Hannah smiled and thanked him but declined, as well. The officer then nodded, and told them if they changed their mind, let him or one of the other officers know.

Minutes passed, but it seemed longer. Jared never left her side. Paramedics were loading both the men onto stretchers, and Hannah noticed they each had oxygen masks on their faces and collars on their necks. The sheets had not been pulled to cover their heads. They were alive then, she realized. She wasn't sure how she felt about their lives being spared or lost, but she sighed with relief, nonetheless, as the two unconscious men were loaded into the back of separate ambulances that left only minutes apart of the other with sirens and lights activated.

The first unmarked car arrived with two out-of-uniform officers, who spoke to an officer outside before they turned and looked towards the door. Hannah couldn't tell if they were looking at her or the absence of a glass in the doorframe. They began to walk towards her. The second unmarked car arrived, and a man and woman emerged from that car. The first two unmarked officers entered the store, carefully stepping over the glass. Once inside, they approached both Hannah and Mark, introducing themselves as Detective Duffy and Detective Hunter.

Detective Duffy was tall with athletic build, middle-aged with thinning, sandy-color and gray hair, clean shaven, and had kind blue eyes with lines on his face. He stayed with Hannah while Detective Hunter, who was not as tall but muscular, sporting a blonde crewcut with hints of gray, and who Hannah imagined to be a retired Marine sergeant with his air of authority, took Mark to a separate location in the back of the store where he would be questioned. Hannah had a good idea what Mark would say, as he really hadn't seen anything once Jared took over, though he hadn't even seen him. The police lights were still blaring outside like blinding strobes.

"Ma'am," she heard Detective Duffy say, bringing her out of her reverie. "Would you mind telling me everything that happened since you arrived here at the liquor store tonight?

"I'll do my best," she complied.

"Please try to relax and take your time. Start at the time you arrived, and I'm just going to take down notes." His pen and notepad were in hand. Hannah began recounting the details from the moment she pulled into the parking lot. Jared stood behind her, close enough she felt his energy dancing against her own energy field. She was comforted by it rather than distracted. When asked if anyone had been with her, Jared immediately spoke, "No." She heard him and replied, "No, I'm alone. I was on my way home from visiting some friends in San Francisco and remembered I was out of wine at the house. I stopped here to get some," she explained.

"What are the names and addressed of your friends you were visiting?" She told him, and he jotted it all down.

"Was there anyone else inside the store besides the store employee, who was just standing here, when you arrived at the store?

"No, not that I saw. The store was empty as far as I could tell."

"Did anyone else enter the store besides the two men that attempted to rob the store?"

"No, it was just the two men. They attempted to rob both me and the store, she clarified, explaining how they had put the gun on her and how she had her wallct out to pay for the wine and had pulled cash out when one of the men had taken it from her. What she explained next made no sense. "Well, all I can tell you is that one of the men had a gun pointed at the store attendant, Mark, she corrected, who had both his hands up, except for opening the cash drawer when they ordered him to, then he put his hands back up and stepped back. The other guy was drawing his fist back to punch me, after calling me a bitch for not being afraid enough of him, and I braced for the punch, but it never came. There was sound of gunshot and a loud, unnerving shattering noise, and then they were gone. The glass door was just gone, smashed out. The two men were nowhere in sight," her voice trailed, remembering how fast Jared had been when he had grabbed the mountain lion, "and I looked for Mark and found him squatted down on the floor, frightened out of his wits. When I assessed he wasn't shot or injured, I told him to call 911. Only afterwards did I see the men lying across the parking lot while I was staring at the door, or what was a door when I had walked in, anyway." It was so much to take in, she thought but continued. "We both were too shaken to move from where we stood. We stayed in one spot until the police and first responders arrived. Detective Duffy listened carefully, taking notes.

"Did you at any time see any explosives?"

"Explosives!" Hannah reiterated, wondering why on earth he would ask that but then realized they were thinking an explosive may have knocked the two men through the glass door and across the parking lot. She knew they were trying only to make sense out of what had happened. "No, I saw nothing like that, but if that were the case, wouldn't it have caused injury to all of us? We were all standing within inches or a few feet of each other. I didn't hear an explosive or see one. I only heard gunfire, once. I thought it had hit Mark, but it seems to have only hit the ceiling, looking up at it curiously. Detective Duffy followed her gaze.

"You're sure there was no one else in the store besides you, Mark, and those two men?" he asked again, glancing back at the hole in the ceiling.

"It was only the four of us," she insisted.

"Did you notice any cars pull into the parking lot after you arrived? Anyone that may have been sitting in their car?"

"No, I didn't."

"Okay," he concluded. "That's all for now." He looked exasperated. She also gave him her number and information from her driver's license. He told her he would contact her if they had any other questions. Detective Hunter interrupted and said the store employee had access to the video surveillance and suggested they take a look at it. This almost alarmed Hannah, remembering how Jared had shown up on video camera before. At the same time, it would prove there were no other mortals in the store, even if it did freak them out as they watched it, over and over again with disbelief. She knew they would have no choice but to clear her or Mark of any wrongdoing. They would literally be chasing a ghost. She wasn't sure how she felt about that. She almost felt like she was obstructing justice, but who would believe her? No, she was not going to admit to knowing a ghost had thrown two men through a glass door and clear across the parking lot. Besides, she didn't see it. It had happened too fast for her eyes to see it. She hadn't even seen a blur as Jared swept the men away. They were gone in the twinkle of an eye. And even if she had seen it, what could they do to him? Nothing! It happened before she could blink, let alone turn her head. The responsibility to solve this would fall upon the police, namely Detectives Duffy and Hunter. They will conclude whatever they will, but she had no more information to offer them.

She waited with an officer in the front of the store while the two detectives went to view the surveillance video. She suspected them to have ash white faces when they returned. The officer who waited with her asked questions, too, as this was already proving unusual and mysterious. She did have one question though, and she asked him. "Are those two men dead?"

"No. They were unconscious and banged up is all we could tell. Probably concussions," he guessed. "They had already robbed another liquor store tonight and had shot and killed the clerk and a customer when we were dispatched here. We figured it was the same guys, and according to the video surveillance at the other store, these are our guys." There was no emotion in his voice, only curiosity that something didn't add up at this scene. Hannah had no visible sign of struggle or injury. Neither did the store employee. There was no sign of residual explosive, either.

Several minutes passed and Detectives Duffy and Hunter returned from the back of the store. Mark was with them. They had obtained three surveillance videos for evidence, one with a view of the cashier counter up close, one from the back of the store, and one over the door outside that showed cars in the parking lot, who came in and left, and even half the lot across the parking lot. There was a look of bewilderment, but the ashen white face belonged to Mark. Two officers were ordered to stay with him while he called his boss and closed the store. Again, one of the officers offered to give him a lift home if he wanted one. Hannah was free to leave but was offered a ride home, as well. She declined but thanked them for offering.

Detective Duffy spoke as she started to get in the car. "You're one lucky woman, Ms. Barstow. Those are very dangerous men. We can be thankful *something* stopped them before they did much worse. I would venture to say you have someone watching over you."

She regarded him for a moment. He seemed sincere, and she suspected him to be a man of faith by how he said the last statement. "We were fortunate," she agreed. "I understand others were not so lucky tonight," she said with humility, thinking of their families. "I'm glad you have them in custody, at least."

He nodded. "Be safe," he said and watched her get her in car and leave. She saw in her rear-view mirror he had gone back into the store.

The remainder of the drive home was quiet, but not completely silent.

"Jared," are you alright?

"Yes. You're safe."

"I am, thanks to you." She paused. "I'm sorry I didn't listen. I thought you just didn't want me to buy the wine, but you knew, didn't you?"

"Yes," was all he answered in response. There was no, "I told you so" or "Why can't you just trust me," type of response forthcoming. He did not chastise her.

"Are you upset with me?" she asked him, given that she had not heeded his warning."

He smiled lovingly at her. "I am not angry. If you had not gone in, the store attendant, Mark, would have been taken and the two criminals would have been free to do more harm. Instead, Mark's life was spared. It was not his time."

"Why are you so troubled then?" she asked.

He hesitated as he seemed to be in deep thought, very troubled in fact. "Hannah, I am so focused on you that I didn't consider anyone else when you pulled into the store. I knew it was about to be robbed. I only thought of you, not that there was a purpose for you stopping there in the first place. I'm slipping. If you hadn't stopped, I would not have been there to save Mark, and it was not his time to go. He would've left his mortality prematurely, many decades before he should. That kind of error is unacceptable on my part."

"Perhaps if you had not been there, another immortal being would have come to save Mark? Since he was meant to be saved?"

"Yes, perhaps, but there was no one else there. The concern I have is I didn't consider it, and that is something I should have considered. I'm so in love with you that I made a mistake that almost cost a man his life when it wasn't his time to go."

A light turned red and while stopped, she looked at him. He was not looking at her but turned and gave her his full attention. The connectedness between them had grown stronger than ever. She was becoming familiar with him all over again. It was a renewal of the familiarity from lifetimes on top of lifetimes. The bond between them was strengthening. For her, he represented love in its purest form. He was her twin soul, the love of her eternal life. It was impossible to imagine life without him in it after he had come to her, revealed himself to her, and shown her a love not of this world, a romantic love, an agape love. How could she ever settle for anyone else, she wondered. She wondered if it was possible to love anyone again. She had loved Jesse almost as much, but not as much as she knew she loved Jared. If she could even love someone else almost as much as she loved Jesse, it would be enough, she thought. After all, she had loved Jesse almost as much as Jared and had been happy, not knowing love could be any greater than what she had.

She thought she had had it all, the best life had to offer. She would have not known love could be any greater, any purer if Jared had not come to her and revealed who he was and the love he had for her. The best seems to await us after mortality, she thought. She knew Jared would wait while she lived out this life. He would be waiting for her when the time came.

This gut wrenching feeling was lurking. It's the same kind of feeling she had when her grandmother had passed away when she was 16 years-old. It had been impossible to imagine life without her grandmother in it. She was her best friend in all the world. They were so close, and she had spent so much time with her from her earliest memories. Then, her grandmother was diagnosed with lung cancer that had metastasized to her brain. She had been given six months at best, and Hannah had spent as much time with her as she possibly could. The day her grandmother told her she wanted her to have her jewelry box and all the jewelry in it when she was gone, and began telling her the history of each piece, Hannah couldn't take it. She told her grandmother she didn't want to talk about it because of the reason she was telling her in the first place. Weeks went by and her grandmother deteriorated. Hannah found it impossible to imagine living another 50, 60, or 70 years without her grandmother being there. She couldn't even imagine living one year, not six months, or even a day without her grandmother in the world. The only comfort she had when her grandmother passed was knowing that all the years of pain from osteopenia, fibromyalgia, and the cancer was over, and that she was free to enjoy a new body, a new existence that would offer her true happiness.

Now, she was feeling that unimaginable absence of the being she loved as her eternal companion becoming an inevitable reality that she would be forced to accept for perhaps decades to come. Of course, she knew she would see her grandmother again, just as she knew she would see Ethan and Jesse again. Even if Jared did have to leave her for now, she knew she would see him, too. This was what she disliked the most about being mortal was the separation. It was the most impossible thing to imagine, losing someone. Being visited by Jesse and Ethan, not to mention Jared, gave her so much hope, so much comfort that what we perceive as the end is really not the end at all. The light turned green and she proceeded. She was three minutes from home.

Chapter Twenty-Eight

Explanation of Dreams

She brushed her hair and washed her face free of makeup. Her pajamas felt comfortable and loose. Once she was ready for bed, she put on her housecoat and house slippers and poured a glass of pinot grigio. She took her glass and walked onto the deck and sat down. Jared was sitting across from her in the opposite swing.

"I wish I could offer you a glass of wine," she told him, almost being serious.

He appreciated her humor, "We've enjoyed many glasses of wine and brandy together, Hannah, in many other lifetimes.

"I hope it won't be the last," she replied quietly. "There is something romantic about sharing a glass of wine with one's mate," she admitted, smiling at him.

"I don't disagree." His eyes seemed to drink her into his soul. She loved that he was so attentive to her. After all, there were 7.6 billion people living on Earth, and Jared was focused on loving *her*. She was the love of his universe, and he was the love of hers. This was a knowledge she hoped she would never forget.

His eyes sparkled as if from a deep inner light not of this world, as he once again seemed to be looking into her soul, reading her, knowing her, filling her with his love and his energy. She wondered why everyone couldn't experience this kind of love. There would never be divorce, domestic abuse, battered wives, abused children, not any of that. It wouldn't exist.

"If life were so perfect, Hannah, mortality would be futile," he said, knowing her thoughts. This took her less by surprise than it had previous other times. She had come to find comfort and intimacy in him knowing her thoughts rather than alarm.

"How do you feel about me taking the trip?" she wanted to know.

"It will be a positive experience, rich with discovery and self-reflection. You will be better off for it.

Thanks for saying so," then paused. "You'll go with me, won't you?" She held her breath without realizing it. She had been dreading asking him this, but at the same time, she wanted to know.

"Do you remember I told you I am not going anywhere that is away from you?"

"Yes," she remembered.

"I'm not going to leave you. You are never going to lose me," he promised her.

"I guess I just needed to hear you tell me, again. It's been a long day. I'm just tired."

"I can see you're tired. Get some rest, Hannah," he told her.

"I am going to." Then she said what had really been on her mind. "First, tell me about the dreams, about the life we had. Are the dreams about different lives we shared or one in particular? I want to know," not looking away from him. It was a direct question that she trusted he would answer. If he didn't want her to know, he wouldn't be using the dreams to remind her, she reasoned to herself.

He returned her gaze as if searching her eyes for readiness to know. Once he saw what he needed to see, he answered.

"They are of the most recent life we shared," he began. "It started during the Revolution in Europe. We lived near Cardiff, Wales. I was born 1776 and you in 1777. You and I met in 1783, very young we were. You didn't live far from my grandmother's, north of town. My father had taken me to spend the summer with her at her bequest. I was fascinated by the hills and enjoyed going out exploring, finding animals to play with or talk to," pausing as he thought about it. "Sometimes I just watched them. That's when I stumbled upon you. You were playing fetch with your dog near your house. You had a border collie. I introduced myself, to both you and your dog. You called her Polly."

"There was an instant bond between us," he reflected. She listened without interrupting him, mesmerized by the story that was unfolding. "I asked you if you liked flying kites, but you said you never had. After that, I asked my grandmother if the next time we went to pick up supplies, I would like for her to get one for you, too, so we could fly them together. I had a wonderful grandmother. Two days later, I had another kite to share with you, and after that, we became best of friends. We roamed the hills flying our kites, and I could hear you laughing. On the way to show you where I lived, we saw a small herd of elk, and we stopped and just quietly watched them. They were fascinating animals to watch, especially for two young children." He smiled as he looked at her.

They were fond memories of childhood innocence. He remembered how pretty she was and her excitement of having a new friend. As he looked at her now, he still saw that innocence in her, the same soul he played with more than 200 years from the time she was now in was reflected in the eyes he gazed into now.

Hannah was intrigued and listened thoughtfully before she commented, "In the dream, I remember seeing a big stone house from where we saw the elk.

What significance does that have?" she wanted to know.

"That was my grandmother's house," he answered. "I was taking you there."

"You lived there?" feeling surprised. "That must be why it stood out in my dreams, seeing it on the hill," she remembered.

"Yes, I spent many summers there. Every summer, I would come visit you and we would roam the hills, fly kites, take picnics, and occasionally, we came across a herd of elk. Those were happy memories.

"What was it like in those times, with the revolution going on?" she asked. "As kids, were we even aware of it?"

"We were from educated, middle-class bourgeoise society. My father was a physician, and I followed in his footsteps. Your father was a banker. Your mother was an impeccable seamstress, and she was well-educated in matters of philosophy. My mother inherited her father's clock business, as she had spent most of her young life with him in the shop and had learned nearly all he knew about the repairs and fine workings. Her brothers had both studied law in London and had stayed there and opened their own firm. Neither wanted to give up law to come home and manage a clock company after their father passed on. She was quite happy with the work and her relationships with people of Cardiff. Even as a woman in that time period, she had won their trust and respect as a clockmaker. The people had watched her grow up at her father's side.

We grew up in an age when Mozart's compositions were fresh and new, so our families often attended operas and concerts. We attended Shakespeare plays. Even in our own homes, we had harpsicords and piano. My mother played violin and the harpsicord. My father played piano. I myself, learned to play all these instruments. Your family possessed a harpsicord and a piano, as well, so you and I would play together when we visited one another as years rolled by. We even would dress up and pretend we were actors in a play in which the two of us played different characters in Hamlet, Romeo and Juliet, Macbeth, and King Lear."

"Really? Just you and I learned lines and played all the characters in Shakespeare *pretend* plays?" Hannah startled.

"Mostly, yes, but sometimes we'd get someone interested enough to participate."

"Like who?" she was curious now.

"We had siblings and cousins, but you and I lived in a world to ourselves. Sometimes we could even coax our parents into taking part," he reminisced.

"I'm in wondrous awe," her voice filled with excitement, showing every bit of it as her eyes sparkled with the smile that lit her face.

"Yes. You were quite astute at acting, but you were also quite adept playing the violin. Your family always had a family night of various entertainments, and you were quite the storyteller. All throughout your stories, you would pause to play a tune for effect and then continue on with more of the story," he recounted.

"Oh, you mean like movies today have background music for special drama effect to build excitement or suspense?"

"Exactly so," he laughed.

"Sounds like a happy life," she smiled. "Pray tell more," she pressed him.

"It was," he agreed. "The industrial and revolutionary era were not without problems. There was much hardship in the face of all the changes. It was difficult for many. Those who lived nearer to cities were forced to conform to the new machinery. The industrial age brought very long work hours that was difficult for all but especially women and children. Even children were forced to work 12-hour days. The work place was cruel. For many, it transformed the laborer into a common slave.

"Why?" Hannah was appalled. "How could they force anyone to work like that? It's not humane!"

"No, it was not humane. The truth is, employers didn't trust people to show up, so they simply didn't let them leave. They squeezed as much work out of them as they could, except to let them go home and sleep. They were, in fact, slave drivers in every sense of the word. This took its toll on the health of the laborer. People became sick from exhaustion, had more accidents, and suffered unnecessary deaths. It kept my father busy, creating long hours for him in his medical practice. It was ultimately what inspired me to become a physician, myself," he added. "Industrial machinery alone gave rise to many injuries, notwithstanding compounding that with lack of sleep and rest people suffered from," Jared frowned as he remembered."

"Then, there was the shipping industry and railways, and as transportation became more efficient, it of course, replaced the use of horses. Canals were built and the shipping industry took off. It was an era of many changes and modernization. Many women worked in the textile industry. Of course, there had been uprising, too, because the machines could produce more fabrics than one could by hand. Machines replaced people and left many without jobs and a means to support themselves.

Your father forbade your mother to work in a textile factory. She had the luxury of being a domesticated seamstress, but she also made clothes for people in town who paid her. Occasionally, she made clothes for peasants and orphans at no charge. With so much poverty, as machines put people out of jobs they knew, even my father didn't charge everyone he treated. The rise of capitalism was beginning and with it came its pros and cons. The lower class found it difficult to get ahead, just as they still do in current times. In that era, when we were young and growing up, the people of that time didn't enjoy the protection of labor laws, as they do in current times, so there was a lot of suffering around us. In the cities, poverty gave rise to slums. Laws in that time protected the capitalists, not the laborer. Some laborers were literally locked in and not permitted to leave work until the end of their long shifts. The poor especially lost faith in the revolution."

"This was largely why both my mother's brothers went into law. My older brothers studied either law or banking. I was the only one of my siblings who studied medicine. Most of my family were either in law or finance. My father and I were the only two in my immediate family that had the stomach for medicine. We each viewed the revolution and industrialism and the burdens that were born out of it from differing viewpoints. Hence, we pursued our own strengths in how to better mitigate much of the harshness it bore upon humanity and society. Being in those professions gives one power to either help or harm the downtrodden, and I did not have the stomach for being on the side of harming them."

Hannah had listened with intent interest. Contemplatively, she said, "It's what makes the modern world so difficult, isn't it? Life is so hard for so many people," she commented painfully. "The poor are always with us, but then, so are the rich. In that respect, the world has not changed. It's just that there are exponentially many more who are poor than who are rich, as there always has been."

"True," he agreed, "Social injustices and death and sickness have been constants throughout time, and those make mortality very difficult. There was also heavy gambling that destroyed families, just as there still is today. People make choices that hurt themselves and the ones they love or their neighbors. Many people are not connected to their Higher Self, and they let their carnal minds have free reign to live life on a whim, engaging in impulsive, destructive behavior, but this too is part of being mortal, to learn to harness one's carnal mind and be of a higher mind and nature. People hurt people, just as they have all through time. There is a myriad of angles in which suffering and hardship defines and redefines each person as they go through mortality. They are all common to mankind, yet one has a tendency to feel alone with their own suffering. No one is alone. It's up to each one to search within themselves for their own resources, though it may not always come in the way one hopes or expects."

"As spirit beings, there are imparted strengths and gifts within everyone, and it is up to each one to open their minds, reach within, and allow the inner being, the Higher Self, the soul within, whatever one chooses to call it, to rise instead of suppress who each one is meant to be or has the potential to become. One must be careful what propels their expectations, whether it be trust and love or bitterness and fear. For one grants the heart's desires, while the other one denies them. It is paramount to know thine self, so that one knows what propels their expectations."

Hannah nodded. "That's a lot to think about but definitely worthy of ponderance." After a pause she interjected, "I also dreamt of my wedding. Were we married in Cardiff?" she asked assumingly.

Jared smiled. "Yes, at your family's house in 1798. You were so elegant and beautiful." She smiled in response to his words. By then, I had gone away to Birmingham and graduated with my medical degree. While I was away, we wrote letters to communicate. Once I returned back to Cardiff, I went into practice with my father for a while. It was then that we were married.

"I assume you gave me a proper proposal and that it was not a forced marriage," she teased.

"I assure you, it was a proposal that was most dignified and truly romantic. The town's people nearly thought you were walking on water for the following month, you were so aglow and your step so light, your chin held high, yet your humility did not go unnoticed. You were never an arrogant type, Hannah. Humility and gracefulness defined you. It still does," he added. "You always smiled but your smile was worn with genuine happiness that creased around your eyes and lighted the shine in your eyes so much more often. I believe you were quite pleased with the manner in which I proposed," he added as if an afterthought.

Hannah's face was aglow and childlike now. "Tell me," she said, "how did you do it? Pretend you are proposing to me, now, just like you did then. Ask me," she insisted.

Jared saw she was serious. His eyes held hers for what seemed countless moments, as she swayed slowly back and forth in the swing, smiling at him with anticipation. He rose and moved to kneel in front of her, as he had in 1798. He held her gaze and took her hands in his, and Hannah never knew when her breathing stopped. Everything else around them seemed silent or nonexistent. It was only the two of them, and she felt herself enter a surreal state as she realized he was going to do it, to reenact the proposal he had once given her more than 200 years before. Tears started to wet her eyes, as he repeated the words he remembered perfectly.

"As I remember, Hannah, I said to you, 'I am eternally and hopelessly in love with you. Would it sadden you even a little to become my wife?" Jared looked into her eyes a moment longer.

"I have no doubt I told you there could be no happier woman in the whole world," she told him, tears falling across her face.

"In fact, you did tell me that," he reminisced and smiled at her. Jared then stood and sat beside her this time. "After we were married, we both were ready for change, as neither of us was happy about the changes that were happening in Wales and throughout Europe. Although we were not among the peasantry and the slaved factory workers, and we weren't forced to live in the slums, we saw enough of it to make us sick. I had seen enough premature death and sickness from unsanitary living conditions with dysentery that it was taking a toll on us. There had been too much civil unrest in our lifetimes, locally and throughout Europe. Then, you became pregnant. That's when we made the decision to migrate to America. We acted quickly so that we would arrive before you entered your third trimester. You were four months pregnant when we left Wales. The journey lasted more than six weeks. We were able to escape the worst of the seasickness by using ginger and peppermint. Many people did not fare so well.

"At this moment, I can't imagine what that had been like, despite the boat ride to the Farallones that had only been for less than a day," she said. "Six weeks or more would have been unfathomable. I saw people get sick just on that ride, which was nothing comparable to crossing the Atlantic in that time period."

"The waves throw one's equilibrium off and anything in their stomach is tossed around causing unease. It's hard to hold down food for it to digest. The continual vomiting results in dehydration. In more modern times, conditions on transoceanic ships are improved with cleaner and more adequate water supply and better preparation. Modern medicine has medicinal treatments that are effective in preventing seasickness, but in that era of time, there were only herbs, and not everyone was informed so did not carry them. They were ill prepared and paid dearly for it, sometimes costing some their lives. Most of your sickness at sea was morning sickness. The journey had been fairly uneventful for us. There had been a couple of storms but we all pulled through. Most days were sunny and clear. We encountered a few blue whales and a lot of humpbacks and some gray whales, just as we did on the sail to the Farallones. There were also many dolphins that approached the ship and swam along beside it."

"The trip turned treacherous as we neared Boston. We were met with hurricane force winds just as we were nearing the port, three miles out. Visibility was impossible and the ship was out of control when we hit a large rock structure that damaged the keel and bow that caused water to fill from below deck. The storm had already filled the boat with water that the crew were unable to fill buckets fast enough to keep us afloat for long. By then, we were nearly to shore, and the ship sank as the storm started to subside. Some of the passengers perished, but the rock was large enough that others were able to cling to it and survive, as the winds died. The waves carried you and me to shore. I was a good swimmer and so were you, but you were not able to make it, and I dragged you to shore and pumped your chest until you coughed up the water. We barely made it.

She looked at him in horror. "The baby?"

"You carried the baby to full term," he answered.

"That's why I've always been afraid of being out on smaller boats, isn't it?" understanding now.

"Yes. The ship we crossed the Atlantic on was the size of a large yacht by today's standards, nothing in comparison to the cruise ships there are today. You have come a long way, Hannah, and you have never stopped persevering to be strong and embrace the inner power within you. Your true nature is to be adventurous and spontaneous. I see that returning now." His smile was warming. He loved her, and she saw that in the way he looked at her.

"What was our life like in America?" she asked, excitedly. "Where did we live?" she asked.

"We arrived in Boston and stayed there for a short time, long enough to recover from the trip and explore a while, and I was offered work in another practice, which I did for a couple of years. We both longed to get out of the city, though. It happened that I met a man with his family from Maine who were in

Boston visiting. He was also a physician. We spent some time getting acquainted with them and became friends. When they prepared to return, they invited us to go with them and stay with them until we were able to get settled. He invited me to work with him once there. We left Boston and migrated to Bar Harbor where we settled, and it remained our home the remainder of that lifetime."

"Were there Native Americans there?" What was it like?" she asked, full of questions, but not wanting to ask all she was curious about.

"There were the Algonquin. Everyone was peaceable and civilized. We made friends easily. Being right on the Atlantic, of course, there was shipping and fishing, but the land was agricultural, too. We both loved its charm. You developed an art of painting and was actually quite talented with it," he smiled.

"Really! How ironic, as I love taking pictures of different landscapes and nature's beauty. I suppose that has stayed with me," thoughtfully awed by the correlation. "What kind of painting did I do?" instantly curious.

"Mostly landscape. There were hills and the maritime, which was all quite picturesque, and in fact, many artists were attracted to the location, including scholars and writers. It was a place one could connect to nature and solitude. Occasionally, we enjoyed long walks and hiking through the hills. You made some trousers for yourself for that very purpose," he laughed thinking about. "It was not a time when one saw women wearing trousers very often," he reflected. "They were practical attire for hiking, however."

"I wish I could remember," she said quietly.

"You will. At the end of this life, all your soul's memories will return to you."

"We were happy there?"

"Yes, we enjoyed being away from large cities, and we raised a family. It was a good life, Hannah."

"Like you said, the time will come I will remember everything my soul has experienced. Until then…"

"Yes, until then," he answered.

He took her hand and she rose to meet him.

"Thank you, Jared. I know you didn't offer to tell me, but I don't want to know, just yet, if ever, who our children were, our families back in Wales. I would be too tempted to look them up, and that's just something I don't think I need to know. It explains you, us, and the closeness we share, and knowing there were other lives before that one. Maybe another time, but this is enough for me to process for now."

"I agree," he replied.

She turned and wandered back into the house and went straight to the bedroom. When she crawled into bed and pulled the cover over her shoulders, within seconds she was asleep. Jared lie on the bed next to her and folded his arm over her lovingly and protectively. "Sleep, Hannah," he whispered. "I'm here."

Chapter Twenty-Nine

Visit From the Mentor

After Hannah was asleep, Jared watched the waves rolling in with high tide reflected through his eyes, as they scanned the sea. The small debris, carcasses, and waste floated through the ocean's depths unceasingly swallowed under nature's force and were coughed up. He could see fish and mammals further out in the deep that swam and frolicked while others preyed. He could hear the sounds of pods that were miles from shore communicating with other members. The sea had become polluted over the centuries, much more so since the industrial age had begun.

Life in the sea bore similarities to life apart from it, the weak with little or no *realized* resources to protect themselves against powerful predators who care for no other life or the objectives and goals attached to them except its own. Every living thing has a similitude on the planet in which mortality is a reckoning on the mind, body, and soul. Peace is a gifted treasure.

Mortals have their choices, imagination, and what they believe. They have love, if they choose it, and they have hate, if they choose that, but it still comes down to choices and what they believe. The reality each person experiences is the manifestation of those choices and beliefs. The choices another makes continually summon the beliefs of another. All beings, mortal and immortal alike, continually must be confronted with what they believe. No mortal truly has the power over another that they *think* they have, lest it is loaned to them.

Jared pondered all this and knew he could not interfere with Hannah's choices. She had returned to earth to deepen her understanding of the power within to overcome and rise above mortal ignorance and forgetfulness, to learn more of what it takes to conquer mortal suffering and deception. He had been on many battlefields over thousands of years and learned much about loss, human suffering, and about strength and courage. Life experiences are the guiding compass that sculpts one's feelings and manner of thinking in terms of goals and desires. One solitary experience can reshape who we become, how much more, the sum of them all. How complex life is, yet truth is simple, and no matter what one believes, truth remains unchanged across time and eternity.

Jared had seen the interest in Hannah's eyes with the doctor. He is single though not unattached. He was in a relationship, he knew that, too. Jared knew who he was to her in the immortal life, so feeling threatened or insecure was not something he felt as an immortal. He also knew she needed companionship and someone to spend her life with. The timing in meeting that companion was important. Mortal love is not perfect, as love mortals share is flawed. Many of them have dichotomous love-hate relationships, wanting perfection yet unable to give it. Being immortal, he had learned to possess a higher, more perfect love.

With the mortal/immortal relationship, there were complications. Those kinds of relationships are not common, but he knew they existed. In all cases, the immortal must wait for the mortal to transition over before they can be together. It is not the immortal that chooses not to wait but the mortal, for they must satisfy their fleshly desires that the immortal cannot give them. They are easily distracted with life, cellphones, TV, work, being tired, pets needing attention, and being lost in thoughts or stressed. They struggle to be tuned in to the immortals around them.

The mortal/immortal relationship is a challenge to maintain for mortals on any level, since they typically do not see the immortals who surround them. With Hannah being young, it would be a long wait for her in earthly time. Jared could not and would not expect her to deny herself a normal relationship indefinitely. He would never ask that of her. He only asked that she wait until she reestablishes a redefined relationship with herself. Relationships and love on earth are vital to her earthly experience, to everyone's. He would be faced with the decision how he would conduct himself with her when that time came.

He loved watching her sleep, reminding him of so many other lifetimes he had shared a marriage bed with her as a mortal, himself. He loved watching the expressions on her face and listening to her thoughts.

She gave him pleasure in a way that most are incapable of enjoying or experiencing in the mortal world. He was inside her mind, and he could feel what she felt. He was completely in tuned with her.

There was a blue light that flashed beside him, radiating in all directions, and then another being stood beside him who was at least a foot taller than Jared at nearly 7-1/2 feet tall, with shoulder-length gray hair and black eyebrows, beard, and mustache. His eyes were grayish blue and his countenance youthful. He was dressed in tan trousers and a cream color tunic.

"Savrin, why have you come?"

Savrin smiled, "Jared", speaking his name in a matter of greeting, then paused before continuing.

"I know it's hard for you not to help her, but it is necessary that you don't shield her so much, Jared. You cannot and must not shield her from everything."

"It's taking all my strength not to," Jared refuted, gritting his teeth.

"I know, Savrin answered him empathetically, looking towards the sea, "which is why I am here."

Turning back to Jared, he continued, "Mortals must experience pain and suffering, or they don't grow and advance. You know this. I *know* you want her to grow." Savrin's voice was filled with compassion.

"I do! She has been through so much and has already advanced throughout all her life experiences. Yet, she insisted on returning to earth as a mortal again! I had hoped she would rest and take on other education. I admit, she is more resilient than I had expected," frowning with considerable thought to the matter.

Savrin nodded. "She's going to find her way, Jared. The more she experiences, the more she will learn! Remember, she *chose* this life with specific goals of what she would learn. You mustn't interfere, if she is to achieve her desired goals before she returns. Remember, this life has been her choice!"

Savrin observed Jared's thoughts and his willingness to refrain. He understood very well what he was struggling with and how difficult it could be. He himself had also been tested as Jared now is.

"Jared, you are so close to being a guide, yourself. This is the test you must endure, and it is the reason you've been granted your request to accompany her to this earthly life. This is your apprenticeship to prove how you will behave in critical situations with her, the one person you have the strongest bond with, stronger than any other, and as you advance, you will be given responsibility for more and more souls to guide and protect. This will be your most difficult test, Jared. I admonish you to remember what she is striving for and what *you* are striving for, that you don't stand in the way of her accomplishments."

"I have not forgotten," Jared assured him. You are right about this being the most difficult test. I can do this, Savrin. I know how important it is."

"I know you do, my friend. You realize you are approaching boundaries and very nearly crossed one when you incapacitated the two men. You had some assistance step in and intervene to keep you from crossing that boundary that caught them before they fell sixty feet to their deaths. I understand you acted on impulse, but Jared, we must rise above such impulse. We will work your reaction to the situation to their good rather than their detriment. What you did shall prove to be a life-changing experience for them, as it is intended to be. We do not have the authority to take life unless it is given to us. Our job is to intervene. Their hearts shall never be the same, nor shall they return to the manner of life they've lived. Good will come of it instead."

"As should be," Jared agreed.

"Be more mindful, Jared. I shall depart and leave you to your tasks. I wish you well."

Jared saw in his eyes that Savrin trusted him. "Thank you, Savrin," and placed his hand on Savrin's arm as a gesture of gratitude. Savrin had been Jared's mentor since returning from immortality. Jared valued his wisdom and all that he had learned from him. He dropped his hand back to his side, and Savrin was gone.

Chapter Thirty

In the Twinkling of An Eye

The following afternoon, while Hannah was in the middle of vacuuming and had the dishwasher and laundry going, the phone rang. At first, she wasn't sure that she had heard it, so she turned off the vacuum cleaner and heard it ring again and ran to answer it.

"Hello?" she answered curiously when she saw the call was from an unidentified caller.

"Ms. Barstow?"

"Yes," she answered.

"This is Detective Duffy. Ma'am, I was calling to let you know we completed our investigation into the attempted burglary at the liquor store last night, and I don't believe we will be needing any other *official* statements from you."

"I see." she remarked. "Are the men going to be alright?" she asked. Given what had happened, she was surprised they survived at all. She didn't think Jared was someone to be reckoned with if anyone tried to harm her.

He seemed to not be listening, then spoke again. "Mrs. Barstow, we brought in video forensic experts, who have all independently agreed that there was no tampering of the video surveillance tapes we recovered."

"Tampering? I don't understand," she lied.

"Let's just say the videos confirmed your statement, as well as that of the store employee's, who obviously didn't see any more than you did. Then there was the outside video surveillance that...suffice to say, we have no choice but to close the investigation." His voice was tense, tired, and filled with bemusement.

"Are you saying that the videos offered no explanation what happened to those men, how they ended up lying in the field clear across the parking lot?" she pressed cautiously.

"I wouldn't say that, ma'am, but as you said, there were only four people in the store, but there was another, um, well," she heard him clearing his throat and pausing, "whatever or whoever it was, let's just say, there was someone watching over you. You were not alone in the, how do I say, human sense of the word. On the other hand, it would appear there," he paused to choose his words, "there was something that broke the fall of both those men, because from what we witnessed on the video, they should have died from the fall they both were about to suffer."

"Are we talking about angels, Detective Duffy?" she asked with hesitation.

"Ma'am, I'm a firm believer in angels, always have been. I'm not ashamed to say so, but I'd never seen one captured on video until I watched those surveillance videos of the robbery. I can't believe I'm saying this, but if it *was* an angel, and I'm not saying it was, it was one big Arc Angel! It's the only thing that explains the force that threw those men 115 feet to the field. No one could survive the impact of a fall like that. It looked like they landed from an angle of at least 60 feet, just dropped midair. The shards of glass and damage to the doorframe confirm they were thrusted through the door at a high velocity, thrown, flown, or carried at least that high, he added, upward 60 feet and outward 115 feet. We've had a forensic reconstructionist busy most of the night and into the morning. The poor guy hasn't slept."

"So, there were no signs of explosives, like you first thought?"

"No ma'am. There wasn't. This case has everyone baffled, but you have been helpful, and I appreciate your cooperation. But off the record, did you see anything like what I just described to you? I can understand if you did and don't want to say, given the bizarre nature of it. Personally, I'd probably never whisper a word of seeing something like that to anyone for fear I'd spend the rest of my days behind locked doors, but I have to know, did you see those men whisked into midair and dropped?" he asked, like an astonished and curious child. He was not pressing her, only bewildered as any human being would be.

"Everything happened so fast. My eyes could not keep up, I'm afraid. I honestly don't know what more I could say, as it all seems like a blur now," she told him.

"Everything is right there on the video surveillance tapes we have, and it's conclusive there was in fact a supernatural force or being that…I apologize how insane this must sound to you. It's affected us all the same way here at the department."

"I believe, Mr. Duffy. It doesn't sound insane at all. It sounds like the world should believe more in angels, even if we don't see them. It is nothing short of a miracle," she admonished him.

"Perhaps you're right, Ms. Barstow. Perhaps so. Again, thanks for your cooperation. Hope you have a good day."

She thanked him and ended the call. When she looked up, Jared was inches away, looking down at her, his eyes swimming with adoration. He looked like he wanted to take her in his arms and kiss her, put a jeweled crown on her head, and whisk her away to one adventure after another, to the farthest star or the deepest depths of the ocean or to the most glorious heavens. She saw it all in the way he looked at her.

"You never had any reason to worry," he reminded her. "I wouldn't let anything happen to you. We are one and the same, Hannah. When I look at you, I see a second reflection of who I am. And I am your second reflection. We are the exact complements of each other. So, you needn't ever worry. I won't allow anything to happen to you," he promised.

"Nothing that will kill me, you mean," teasing him. I am barely recovered from my ankle sprain, the one you *didn't* step in to protect me."

He looked at her smiling, loving her wit. She punched his arm playfully, then as fast as she did it, she stopped, frozen, almost white as a ghost. "I feel you." She stared at her hand. "Jared, I *feel* you! Like flesh and blood feel you." Her mouth gaped open, and she stared up at him. He continued gazing into her eyes. His eyes sparkled while his smile never left his countenance. She raised her hand to touch his face, her fingers moved gently to touch his lips. She felt his flesh, not just pure energy as she had always felt before when they touched. She stared at his mouth, unable to move, touching their softness with the tips of her fingers. Like a magnetic field neither of them resisted, the distance closed between them. She tip-toed and leaned toward him, feeling his energy dancing more than she had ever felt it, and then, she was lost in his touch, as his lips brushed against her lips and then was lost in his kiss. She drank in the taste of him and felt drunken ecstasy. As he took her in his arms, she felt her feet leave the floor as if slipping out of a sleeve that just fell away effortlessly. She felt every part of her being leave the space she was in, felt herself slip from her mortal body as if all mortality was left behind. It was as if she were in a warm blanket that just fell away from her, as her soul seemed to separate from her body, starting from her feet upward. It seemed to her in that split instant she was entering another dimension. She had the sensation of being lifted beyond the realm of mortality, as the sensation moved up to her legs and then her trunk, slipping out of mortality and when the sensation slipped past her head, in the twinkling of an eye, there was nothingness.

Epilogue

Hannah felt her feet sink in the sand as the waves of the Andaman Sea rolled across her feet. Her cutoff cream khaki shorts came midway down her thighs with a loose-fitting purple blouse over an orange tank top. She carried her tennis shoes with her socks tucked inside them. Her sunglasses were frameless pink lens. Her silvery hair was tied back in a loose ponytail that fell to her waist. Phang Nga was the most beautiful place on earth she had ever seen with her own eyes. She had checked into a resort and spa, which was close to the beach where she had dined. Her journey in Thailand was only beginning, and she already felt like she had found a piece of paradise. She had no expectations. She only wanted to enjoy the surprises each day brought her and make room for spontaneity.

The last few weeks she had felt more clarity than she had felt in a long time. She had been packing, spending a lot of time reading, lighting whatever room she was spending her time in with candlelight. She had spent at least an hour a day meditating. She had been surrounded by such a spirit of peace that seemed to have made its home with her. She had gone to a masseuse once a week for three weeks who also massaged her ankle, which had completely healed, thankfully, she believed in part due to her meditations and mind-over-matter self-hypnoses. She had even gone jogging every day the last week she was in California with intentions of getting herself back in shape, starting with two miles, but the last two days she ran three with little effort and no setbacks with her ankle. Her diet had consisted of raw vegetables and fruits in order to do a cleanse and prepare herself for spiritual fasts while she was on her spiritual journey in Thailand.

She had been dreaming more than usual, too. The dreams had been so vivid, always seemed to be about other places and eras of time, where she would encounter people she *knew* only while she was in the dream. Once she would awaken from the dreams, she felt a lingering familiarity to the people in her dream and the places, the towns, and the structures, but that familiar feeling was quickly lost. She had felt intense love while she was having these dreams that lingered longer, like a slow-burn. Always, she didn't want to wake up from them. She had been giving thought to seeing a regression hypnotist when she returned to the States. She had the distinct feeling these dreams were related to other lifetimes. They had been occurring so frequently since Jesse and Ethan passed that she needed to learn why and what they meant. Sometimes they visited her, too, in her dreams. They were always whole and happy, yet she often forgot the details and was left with bits and pieces.

She believed in reincarnation, and something told her if she could be regressed, she may make sense of the dreams, perhaps learn why she was having them. Then she had experienced what she thought was a dream, but it had felt so real and otherworldly. She thought she had dreamt of being in the arms of a man she loved, someone who was not Jesse, someone not of this world. It had to have been a dream, but it felt so real. She couldn't remember ever going to sleep before it happened. Suddenly, it was if she were taken from her body, as if she had crossed over to the other side. It was in the middle of the day, and she had just gotten off the phone with the detective who was investigating an attempted burglary she had witnessed. He mentioned some very interesting evidence they had found on the store's security cameras. She had woken up on the couch later that evening thinking she had dreamt being whisked away with no memory of what happened afterwards. Had she merely fallen asleep after a fantasy or had she dreamt the entire thing? Something about it felt like an out-of-body experience. For now, she only knew she had no conscious memory of what happened.

The weather was so beautiful, the sea was aqua green with white sand, just simply paradise. There was not a large crowd on the beach, just a small crowd spread out. One could still have their space. As she walked along, she had the distinct feeling someone was following her, but each time she looked over her shoulder, there was no one. She had been sensing this for as long as she had been having the dreams. It felt like someone next to her, yet she was not afraid. There was an odd comfort in it.

She had driven to San Francisco two days before she flew out to visit Miranda and Alex again. It was actually Miranda who had suggested she see a regression hypnotherapist in the first place, insisting the dreams are related to past lives. Hannah agreed it was a good idea and had decided to go through with it. It made more sense to wait until she got back so she could keep going to the same therapist rather than try to see one while she is abroad. Hannah knew it was something she needed and wanted to get to the bottom of, and she had read favorable reports from people who had undergone regression therapy.

Sometimes she would hear a male voice speak in her mind, more in her soul, that she thought might be her Higher Power or maybe her spirit guide. The way it came to her always pierced her soul, a voice like whispers of thunder. Someone was watching over her and she knew that someone had always been with her and was with her now.

About the Author

Stacey Gatrost earned a B.A. in Psychology with minors in Philosophy and History from University of Louisville. Most of her career has been in healthcare and working with youth. *A Second Reflection* is her first novel. She is from Indiana and currently lives in Northern California.

www.ingramcontent.com/pod-product-compliance
Lightning Source LLC
Chambersburg PA
CBHW032253020726
47495CB00001B/89